PRAISE FOR
THE FOURTH RULE OF TEN

"Talk about a 'perfect Ten!' Savvy, sharp, and spiritual,
Tenzing Norbu is one of the most compelling
detectives I've encountered on the page."

—**Alison Gaylin**, Edgar-nominated author of
Hide Your Eyes, Heartless, and *You Kill Me*

"Gay Hendricks and Tinker Lindsay have created highly
engaging crime thrillers, packed not only with action,
but also with insights, making the series
a wonderful genre-buster."

—**David Michie**, author of *Why Mindfulness Is Better
than Chocolate, The Dalai Lama's Cat,* and *The Dalai
Lama's Cat and the Art of Purring*

THE
FOURTH RULE

OF

TEN

ALSO BY GAY HENDRICKS AND TINKER LINDSAY

The First Rule of Ten

The Second Rule of Ten

The Broken Rules of Ten

The Third Rule of Ten

All of the above are available at your local bookstore,
or may be ordered by visiting:

Hay House USA: www.hayhouse.com®
Hay House Australia: www.hayhouse.com.au
Hay House UK: www.hayhouse.co.uk
Hay House South Africa: www.hayhouse.co.za
Hay House India: www.hayhouse.co.in

THE
FOURTH RULE
OF
TEN

A TENZING NORBU MYSTERY

BOOK FOUR OF THE DHARMA
DETECTIVE SERIES

GAY HENDRICKS
AND
TINKER LINDSAY

VISIONS
HAY HOUSE, INC.
Carlsbad, California • New York City
London • Sydney • Johannesburg
Vancouver • Hong Kong • New Delhi

Published and distributed in the United States by: Hay House, Inc.: www.hayhouse.com® • *Published and distributed in Australia by:* Hay House Australia Pty. Ltd.: www.hayhouse.com.au • *Published and distributed in the United Kingdom by:* Hay House UK, Ltd.: www.hayhouse.co.uk • *Published and distributed in the Republic of South Africa by:* Hay House SA (Pty), Ltd.: www.hayhouse.co.za • *Distributed in Canada by:* Raincoast Books: www.raincoast.com • *Published in India by:* Hay House Publishers India: www.hayhouse.co.in

Cover design: Charles McStravick • *Interior design:* Pamela Homan

Library of Congress Cataloging-in-Publication Data

Hendricks, Gay.
    The fourth rule of ten : a Tenzing Norbu mystery / Gay Hendricks and Tinker Lindsay. -- 1st edition.
    pages ; cm. -- (Dharma detective series ; book 4)
    ISBN 978-1-4019-4594-7 (pbk.)
    I. Lindsay, Tinker. II. Title.
    PS3608.E5296F68 2015
    813'.6--dc23

2014023073

Tradepaper ISBN: 978-1-4019-4594-7

10 9 8 7 6 5 4 3 2 1
1st edition, January 2015

Printed in the United States of America

CHAPTER 1

Topanga Canyon, Calif.
July 5, Year of the Water Snake

A vast herd of faceless children. Thick. Boundless. They slog forward, their pace slow and strained, their arms outstretched as if striving to get somewhere that's perpetually out of reach. They are compelled by yearning, by faint hope mixed with despair.

Now I am in the midst of them, pushing through the morass of mixed and sticky emotions. I cast my eyes around, searching for a tool, a magic wand maybe, to wave over these struggling young souls that I might ease their effort and aid them in their journey.

Fear invades. Acrid and biting, it's sharp enough to pucker my mouth. What if I'm one of them? I'm in the middle of the herd, after all. My own footsteps are labored and sluggish, as if I'm wading through tar. My own heart is filled with a nameless longing. Am I, too, trapped in a futile journey?

No. This is not real.

I bend my knees and drop into a crouch. With a burst of muscle and hope, I propel myself up, away from the throng, and out of the oppressive grip of the dream.

My heart thumped against the struts of my rib cage. I turned my head to check the red digits of the clock beside my bed. Three forty-three A.M. and dead quiet except for a low rumble emitting from Tank. My cat, too, had been pulled from sleep. Now he sat upright next to my head, Sphinx-like, purring, gazing at me with wide-eyed interest.

I slid my palm from the dome of his skull to the soft fur that surrounded his neck like a downy muffler.

"It's okay, big guy. Just another weird dream."

Tank lowered his head and placed it between his paws. His eyelids dropped like blinds, snuffing out a pair of glowing green coals. Within seconds, he was sound asleep again. At 3:43 in the morning, this was a good skill to have. Unfortunately, only one of us had it.

I lay in the darkness as my pounding heart returned to a steady, slow beat. I consciously revisited the dimensions and images of the dream. There was something compelling about its emotional tone.

Allow.

I softened my awareness to feel into this particular flavor and found it buried in the borderland of belly and solar plexus: fear fueled by desperation.

Allow. Allow, Ten.

Inside the desperation two other distinct feelings huddled close, like fraternal twins fed by the same womb: the deep anguish of one being—trapped in a difficult journey leading nowhere good—and the powerlessness of another, unable to help.

I knew what the dream was about.

The clock had advanced an entire minute. Three forty-four A.M. Woo-hoo. I surveyed my brain-space to determine if there was any possibility that I might get back to sleep. The answer was an instantaneous negative. I slipped out of bed without disturbing the rhythm of Tank's easy snores.

The wood floor felt cool and smooth against the soles of my feet. I reached my arms high, then bent to lay my palms flat against the hardwood. As I straightened, I declared the morning officially underway. A new day, and my first opportunity to practice a new rule: let go of expectations, for expectations lead to suffering.

A sigh escaped. No matter what events July 5th might bring, anticipated or not, I was fairly certain of one thing: the day was bound to be less upsetting than the Fourth of July had been . . .

CHAPTER 2

The long line of cars snaked up and over the hill. Grumpiness emanated from the family-filled vehicles like toxic gas. The Fourth of July traffic was brutal. Where was everybody going, anyway? Why weren't they home cooking burgers?

My car crawled, too, all the way from Topanga to Bill and Martha Bohannon's home, just south of Hancock Park and a two-hour drive that should have taken less than half that. I finally parked outside their house—a simple, California craftsman with walls the color of moss—at 5:30. The smell of charred meat let me know Bill was already stationed at the outdoor grill. I was the first car there, so the bad traffic was probably citywide. That fact made me feel a lot better, which tells you what kind of mood I was in.

I climbed out of my Shelby Mustang. Streaming slants of sunlight framed the Bohannons' bungalow in burnished gold. I tipped my head back, closed my eyes, and then inhaled and exhaled three times, deeply. Children's laughter floated from Bill's backyard. I searched for and found gratitude—for the promise of frosty cold beer and friendship, and for the ability to reset my mood at any given time, if only I remembered to reach for that tool, the one that lets go of what was and accepts what is.

I have two favorite American holidays: the Fourth of July and Thanksgiving, probably because my parents celebrated neither. No fraught history to haunt current traditions. For the past decade I'd spent both at Bill and Martha's house. My ex-partner from the LAPD Robbery/Homicide division might be married to a woman of German descent, but Martha's commitment to celebration was decidedly un-Teutonic—sometimes I think she chose their house primarily because of the annual fireworks display visible from their backyard.

An American flag flapped merrily from its pole by their front stoop, and red-white-and-blue ribbons were tied in bows on the wide branches of their front lawn's pride and joy, a stately magnolia tree. Some bows were tied more neatly than others, signaling that the twins must finally be old enough to participate in decorating.

Life was good. I had just successfully closed three missing person cases—to be accurate, two missing adolescent persons, and one runaway hairless Chihuahua who turned out to be stolen—but all three came from blue-blooded stock, with the kind of pedigrees that meant I was paid well. I hadn't dipped into my Julius Rosen emergencies-only fund for months, and had even taken on a part-time—very part-time—personal assistant. Most impressive, at least to me, I had made it for more than a year without getting entangled in any romantic relationships—a record.

Tank seemed to approve. I was a steadier, happier roommate without a girlfriend.

For a brief moment, I allowed myself to wonder if my ex, Julie, might be inside, but I brushed off the thought. It floated away, the faint trace of longing I still harbored for her almost as insubstantial as a feather.

Besides, Martha would have told me if her sister was coming.

My smile widened in anticipation of fabulous food and drink, a slew of grimy kisses from a pair of twin redheads, the warm love of best friends, and fireworks: like Martha's red-white-and-blue bows in the branches, my expectations for today were elevated, jaunty, and filled with promise.

As I reached into the back of the Mustang for the six-pack of Chimay White, a whispered warning slithered into my reverie: *Take care, Tenzing. Remember what the Buddha taught: expectation is the enemy of serenity and a root cause of suffering.* I recognized the voice's source—Lama Yeshe, one of my two best childhood friends. Yeshe and Lobsang had anchored me throughout the troublesome early years spent in my father's Buddhist monastery in Dharamshala, India. My father had served first as monastic disciplinarian and then as head abbot, but whatever his role, he was none too pleased with his rebellious son.

Time has a way of changing everything. Now my father had passed, Yeshe and Lobsang were themselves abbots, and I was living thousands of miles away in the City of Angels. But the Buddha's pearls of wisdom followed me across the ocean. It turns out they have value whenever and wherever you live.

Let go of expectations. Our Tibetan teachers at Dorje Yidam had urged us to practice this simple yet powerful step at every opportunity. According to legend, a monk once asked the Buddha (the *bhikkhu's* voice, in my imagination, plaintive): "But how can I actually live as you suggest, without expectations?" The Buddha had answered with a question of his own: "How can you actually live if you *have* expectations?"

Just in case, I dialed back the anticipation of Maude and Lola peppering me with kisses. They were just about three years old, and it had been a few months since we'd spent any extended time together. In toddler years, that's a long time, and I didn't know how they might now express affection toward Uncle Ten.

Before I could knock, Martha flung open the front door, her smile wide. I stepped into her hug, but not before noticing weary crumples of gray skin under her eyes. I chalked it up to an over-40 mother with twin preschoolers.

She accepted my six-pack with a quick nod of thanks before calling over her shoulder, "Girls! Uncle Ten's here!"

I squatted just in time, as Maude and Lola careened into me and wrapped their small, dense bodies around mine. I hefted the girls, wiggling and squealing, through the foyer and living room and on out the open French doors to the backyard.

"Beer, please!" I shouted back to Martha, laughing.

Bill, as I had guessed, presided over the grill, dressed in full suburban finery. A towering red chef's toque was perched atop his head and he was sporting a blue apron with the embroidered words *Best Dad in the World*. A bit over the top, but I was inclined to agree. As midlife parents who'd been rewarded after years of IVF with the appearance of twins, Bill and Martha had showered their girls with the freely flowing love and joy reserved for unexpected gifts.

I set the girls down and looked them over. Lola was wearing black leggings, a pink T-shirt, and sparkly shoes. Her red hair was plaited into some sort of complex, inverse braid. She clutched a small stuffed monkey.

"I like your monkey," I said. "What's his name?" Lola studied her toy for a full minute.

"Monkey," she finally said. Lola tended to be long on contemplation but short on words.

Maude was dancing from foot to foot, her hair a nimbus of red wires, as electric as her personality. She wore a miniature version of a sports uniform, the bright-blue shorts long and baggy, the matching top emblazoned with the words *Property of the L.A. Dodgers*. Bill, a diehard Dodgers fan, had passed his passion along to at least one of his girls.

"Nice uniform," I said.

"This isn't a uniform, Uncle Ten," Maude scolded. "This is my teamer outfit!"

"Ahh," I said. Maude grabbed at my hand.

"Did you bring a treat?" she said, bright with hope.

"Not today," I admitted, mentally kicking myself. Maude's face fell. Her eyes glittered with welling tears, and her lower lip trembled. A beer magically appeared in my hand as Martha stepped in, her mother-radar sensing imminent disaster. She knelt and cupped Maude's reddening face in her hands.

"Maude, sweetheart, we just talked about this, remember? How sometimes when Uncle Ten comes over he brings you girls a little something, and sometimes he doesn't? How

THE FOURTH RULE OF TEN

you love him either way, just like he loves you no matter what?"

"I know," Maude wailed, tears now streaming down her cheeks. "But in my mind, he bringed me something!"

Expectations. The Buddha in me nodded and smiled with compassion.

"Get your butt over here, Ten!" Bill called, as Martha held Maude against her chest until the flash-storm passed.

I crossed the yard as Bill deftly flipped a burger. He stepped back from the grill and joined me for our ritual, awkward man-hug.

"Don't worry," Bill said. "I make Maude cry hourly. It rarely lasts more than two minutes. Check it out."

Sure enough, both girls scampered off giggling.

"So, here you are," Bill continued. "Glad to see you're still alive and well."

"You're the one who keeps canceling. What was it last week? The mayor needing to meet with you?"

"Right," he said. "Me, plus his personal army of network news reporters. God forbid he shows up when there aren't any cameras rolling." Bitterness spiked his voice. He rubbed his head, realized he was wearing the chef's hat, and yanked it off, irritated. He stuffed it into the front pocket of his apron.

I studied my friend with concern. His frame, always lanky, looked even thinner than usual. Martha's eyes may have been ringed with gray, but all Bill's gray had migrated to his hair. The last month alone had added a large swatch of silvery strands, turning his dark-blond hair almost platinum. As a police administrator, Bill earned a lot more than he had during our days as lowly homicide detectives, but the job came with a serious stressor: daily political wrestling matches between the city administration and police headquarters.

I pointed to his hair. "Very distinguished. Almost foxy."

"Just call me George Clooney," he said. He called across the lawn to Martha. "What do you think, honey? Am I sexy,

- 7 -

or is it time to break out that bottle of hair dye for men?" Martha was either out of earshot or chose to ignore Bill. As she disappeared into the house, I watched Bill's smile fade. I stepped in.

"Or you could get a job that doesn't bore the living crap out of you."

"Ouch." Bill clutched at his heart. "You really know what buttons to push, don't you?"

"Says the man who taught me how to push them."

That earned a laugh, and for a moment Bill looked young again. I wanted to probe a little deeper, but Martha and the girls reappeared with several more guests in tow, mostly divorced detectives. I tipped my bottle at Sully O'Sullivan and his partner Mack, still with Robbery/Homicide and joined, as usual, at the hip. Marty Schumacher, another veteran detective, trailed behind them, his cheeks ruddy and veined from a few too many happy hours. He spotted me and beelined over.

"Norbu! How the hell is civvy life treating you?"

"Not too bad," I said.

"You gettin' any these days? Or are you, you know, still going without?" Marty was obsessed with the notion of monastic celibacy and convinced I must be a staunch practitioner of sexual abstinence. For once, he was right, but no way was I giving him any satisfaction in that quarter.

"None of your business," I said, but he had glimpsed the cooler of beer and sped off. Conversation versus alcohol? No contest.

I scanned the swelling crowd. A small spore of dread had somehow planted itself in my gut, in between beers and greetings, and I searched for a cause. The origin didn't take long to locate. Of the jovial faces surrounding me, only one, the host's, was unsmiling. But his was the one I most cared about.

CHAPTER 3

The first round of food was decimated. The sky was growing dark. A few distant booms let us know fireworks were starting to erupt across the city.

"Boomie-lights time! Boomie-lights time!" Maude shrieked. Bill slipped next to me.

"Can you grab another bag of ice from the kitchen, Ten? In the freezer."

"Of course." I was glad to do it. I had tired of having the same conversation about two dozen times: "Work's fine. No, I don't miss the paperwork. Yes, I still carry a gun. No, nobody in my life right now . . ."

I did a spot check-in of my mood before pulling the freezer drawer open. I felt a little sad, but I wasn't sure why. Perhaps it had to do with the distance I sensed between Bill and Martha. Their adoration for the girls was still palpable, but the normally warm temperature they generated as a couple was considerably cooler today.

A loud knock at the front door interrupted my introspection. I crossed into the foyer to welcome the tardy arrival. Before I opened the door my detective reflexes kicked in, and I glanced through the small barred window at the top to observe.

Two women, neither of whom I knew. They definitely came from the same gene pool, though one was a good 20 years older than the other. Mother and daughter, if I had to guess. The younger woman rapped sharply a second time. I opened the door.

She was tall, maybe 40, with broad shoulders and a wild mane of brown hair streaked with gray. Her snug jeans and men's button-down shirt, knotted around a small waist, complemented a strong, lithe body, fit as well as feminine. The overall impression was striking. I glanced at her left hand. No telltale wedding band.

The woman next to her stared at the ground. Her floor-length, gray cotton tunic loosely covered a stockier figure, more cinder block than hourglass. One sleeve fell to below the wrist, but the other, the right sleeve, exposed most of her arm, not unlike the monk's robes of my tradition. Odd—as if the outfit itself were a hybrid of customs and beliefs. A white silk headscarf encased her head and hair, its folds framing the same high cheekbones; prominent nose; and clear, wide-set brown eyes. Her beauty was faded, and somewhat marred by the stubborn set of her jaw and a pair of deep, downturned creases bordering her mouth. Her big-knuckled hands were chapped. No wedding band either, but the fourth finger of her left hand sported a narrow, indented strip of paler skin, hinting at a recently removed ring, if not husband.

My nod included them both. "Hello," I said. The younger woman appraised me with steady eyes.

"I hope I am in right place." An accent. Eastern European?

"I'm sure you are. You here for the party?"

The stockier woman barked a bitter laugh. Her companion shot her a look. "Mama. Shush!" she said.

So I was right. Mother and daughter.

"This is Bill Bohannon's house, yes?" the younger woman now asked.

"It is," I said. "Bill's out in the backyard. There's a barbecue going on right now. Would you like to come in?"

She rejected the invitation with a sharp jerk of the chin. She was tall enough to look down on me. I registered again the strong angles of her face, the defined planes, and the piercing gaze. With her streaked mane and flaring nostrils, she resembled a restless thoroughbred. I'm not a lover of horses, and so far I wasn't taking to her, either.

"Please bring him to me here," she announced and crossed her arms, as if giving commands and having them obeyed was normal. Was she military of some kind?

"Okay," I said slowly. My intuition was sending up flares right and left. Something wasn't right here. "Whom shall I—"

She cut me off. "I am Mila," she snapped. "Mila Radovic."

"Tenzing Norbu," I said, offering my hand. She stared at it before responding with a short shake. Her grip was muscular, her palm dry. I turned toward the other woman, but her glare repelled any further niceties.

Mila rattled off a string of words in a language I didn't understand. The mother shook her head, stolid as stone. "No, name not important," she stated, her own accent thick and guttural.

This was shaping up to be a fairly unpleasant interaction, and I was ready to take a break. Still, my steps were slow as I retraced my path through the house and into the backyard. The noise of the gathering had amplified in direct proportion to the rising percentage of alcohol entering various bloodstreams. Adding to the racket was the *tock-tock, tock-tock* of four detectives playing drunken doubles Ping-Pong. Bill had returned to the grill and was swabbing barbecue sauce on a couple of chickens, cut into quarters.

Maude, Lola, and two other kids had somehow roped Sully and Mack into overseeing a prolonged game that required tossing bean bags into a pair of plastic bowls.

I moved to Bill's side. The noise of the revelers seemed to fade. My heart felt heavy in my chest, though specifically why I couldn't say. Sometimes I wish my system wasn't wired like a Geiger counter, able to sense radioactive emotions invisible to the naked eye.

"Hey, Bill. You've got visitors."

"Hold on," he said. He maneuvered sizzling chicken breasts off the grill and onto a carving board. Sully and Mack fell upon them with carving knives. The aroma of caramelized barbecue sauce on chicken skin smelled intoxicating. When meat starts to smell that good to me, I know an altercation is looming.

Everything is about to change.

As I prepared to tell Bill more, Martha materialized. She glanced between us, eyes laser-sharp and emotional antennae quivering. "What's up?" she asked me.

"Two women are at the front door," I said. "They're asking for Bill. They're not from around here. Shall I invite them in?"

Bill's body jerked, as if electrified. "No!"

A tight look swept over Martha's face, which rendered it unreadable, only her eyes expressing uncertainty. She turned to Bill.

"I'll take care of this," Bill said. He patted Martha's shoulder and immediately took off. Now Martha's entire body stiffened. I followed Bill across the backyard and through the living room, with Martha right behind me.

Bill stopped abruptly, just short of the front doorway. Mila Radovic let out a sharp, anguished cry. She lunged inside and threw her arms around my frozen friend, not unlike how Maude and Lola had embraced me a few hours earlier, when the world was simpler. Bill tolerated the embrace, slack-jawed, arms dangling at his sides.

His head swung helplessly back and forth between Mila and Martha, who had stepped around me.

Mila released her clutch and moved back a foot or two. She stared at Bill's loose arms. She raised her right arm like a whip and cracked him across the face with an open palm. It was a mesmerizing moment—between them and nobody else. Then a satisfied cackle from "Mama," still standing outside, broke the spell. It seemed at least she had gotten what she came for.

But what was that, exactly?

Mila's mother let fly a round of foreign words, delivered to her daughter with intensity. She gestured at Martha. Mila moved as if to grip her mother's shoulders, but the woman stepped back, eyes flashing.

Mila turned, directing her words to Martha. "I am Mila Radovic. This is Irena Radovic. She is my mother." Then she wheeled toward Bill, willing him to complete the introductions. Sweat glistened on his forehead and cheeks. He swiped at his brow.

"Yeah. Uh. This, this is my wife, Martha. Martha Bohannon."

Bill's face contorted, as if doused with a dire mixture of fear and confusion. I was rattled. He and I had encountered many dangerous situations through the years, some of them life threatening, but I'd never seen him this jammed up.

Mila faced Martha, her tone softer. "Please. Forgive for the intrusion. I come only because I am desperate."

Martha's reluctance to engage did visible battle with her natural kindheartedness. She offered a weak, pained smile. "Of course. What is it? What's wrong?"

Mila shot a second pleading look at Bill, willing him to say something, but he stood mute, as if caught in a hypnotist's trance. She turned back to Martha, her voice firmer. "Our son is missing."

Martha's smile wavered. "I'm sorry? Your . . . whose son?"

My stomach tightened. Bill stared at the floor and his cheeks flushed scarlet.

Now Mila, too, looked down. Her mother rolled her eyes. "What I say?" she said to Mila, and moved to take her arm. "Useless. We go."

Bill shook off his stupor. He reached toward Martha. "Martha. Mila and I were . . ." He coughed. "We . . . we had a . . . We have a son."

Martha shook her head. She stumbled into the living room, her gait a little unsteady, and sat on the couch. The cushions whooshed, as if they, too, had just received a punch in the stomach. I swiftly crossed the room to sit next to her. I placed a steadying hand on her back. Martha looked around wildly, as if hoping to find a different reality somewhere, anywhere. Finally she located Bill's eyes.

"This can't be . . . . Are you serious?"

Bill nodded.

"How old is this . . . is he?"

Mila's eyes flashed. "*He* has a name! His name is Sasha!"

Martha's eyes flared with an answering bolt of aggression, aimed first at Mila, and then redirected at her husband. "How. Old?" she repeated, biting off each word.

Bill's voice was low. "Sasha is . . ." He appeared to be mentally adding up the years. "Nineteen?" he asked Mila. She nodded. "Nineteen," he said.

"Nineteen," Martha whispered, defeated by the number. "Nineteen years old." Her breath was shallow. I found myself taking several deep inhales, as if by doing so I could provide her with much-needed oxygen. The corded muscles in her neck resembled tightly twisted ropes.

Bill said, "I'm sorry."

Martha gasped a sob-laugh and shook her head. "You're *sorry?*"

Mila made a curt, dismissive movement with her hand. "Please. Sasha is gone. Missing." She directed her words to Bill. "You are the father. We think he is here, in Los Angeles somewhere. I need help finding him. No time for family drama."

Martha's spine straightened. "Excuse me? Family *drama?!* We were doing just fine until about fifteen minutes ago!"

I knew that wasn't true—they weren't doing just fine. But she'd just received an unexpected gut-kick and would believe what she needed to.

Bill held up a hand. "Stop it, both of you. Martha, you need to let her speak." I heard it in his voice: the Good Cop persona was taking over from the Errant Husband. "Mila, tell me what happened. Exactly."

Irena had moved to the corner of the room. She closed her eyes and began to move her lips, as if in prayer.

Martha slumped, defeated. She clutched at my left arm, finding my wrist and gripping it tightly.

"Sasha is very smart. Full of passion," Mila said. "Also, very stubborn." Mila glanced at Bill. "Like father," she added, and I felt Martha flinch at the intimacy this observation implied. "He studies to be a journalist," she said with pride creeping into her voice, "so he can change world. And . . . but . . . not a good world, where we are. Terrible people. Gangsters."

THE FOURTH RULE OF TEN

"Where is that?" I asked.

"Bosnia," she snapped, as if it were obvious.

And the blurry, piecemeal images sharpened into a picture. Bill had served briefly in Bosnia as a rent-a-cop for a private military contractor early on in his career as a policeman. The six-month tour had fattened his pocketbook at a time when he was hoping to settle down with Martha and needed the extra income. He had mentioned his participation in the bloody conflict to me only once or twice—he didn't like to talk about it. Me? I knew little about that war, or its aftermath; I'd been young, and the struggle took place in the early nineties, around the time of my mother's suicide. My mind had been preoccupied with other battles.

"Where we live, everything bad is controlled by these men," Mila continued. "The drugs, the weapons, and also the sex, young girls. Terrible. Buying and selling like, like they are nothing more than toys for playing. Sasha decides to investigate them. He starts writing about these things on a computer, he write on his . . . how you say? Log . . . ?"

"Blog," I said. Martha pulled away, as if my providing the word for Mila was a betrayal of some sort. I regretted my impulse to speak.

"Yes," Mila said. "Blog, on the Internet. Now I am scared. I am thinking these bad men take Sasha."

A tomb-like silence filled the room as random flashes of light and deep, distant booms provided a bizarre background— a mimicked bomb raid, and an apt soundtrack to the drama unfolding inside. Irena now stared out at the light show, as if mesmerized. Martha started to cry, quietly. Mila ignored them both; she was locked in on Bill.

Bill stroked his mustache. I'd seen him do it a thousand times while thinking through strategies.

"Okay," he said finally. "Go wait outside, Mila."

Mila's nod was tight. She and Irena left.

"Ten," Bill said. "Can you keep them occupied while Martha and I talk?"

I was already halfway to the front door. We were a team, Bill and I, and dividing and conquering was second nature to me at the start of any investigation.

As I shut the door behind me, the soft click of the latch had the sad finality of a coffin lid closing over what had been, so very recently, a vibrant living thing.

CHAPTER 4

I caught up with Mila and Irena just as they reached their car, a white Ford Taurus, clean and cheap looking. I checked for, and found, evidence that it was a rental—a small sticker with a bar code on the rear window. The narrow rectangular dimensions told me they'd chosen Avis. Hertz bar codes were fatter, and Enterprise's longer—just a couple of the many random factoids useful only to cops and P.I.s.

Mila reached for the handle.

"Mila, wait. Please, don't leave yet."

Mila shrugged, but stayed where she was. Irena muttered something to Mila, climbed inside, and closed the car door. Again, Irena closed her eyes.

"Is your mother all right?" I said to Mila.

Mila's face tightened. "Ignore her," she said. "My mother thinks I am wrong to come here. She prefers to rely on her god for help."

Now that I had Mila's attention, I wasn't sure what to do or say. I was childishly irritated at her, at both of them, for interrupting the party; for hurting Martha and exposing Bill; for dashing my expectations of fireworks, friendship, and a celebration of freedom. From now on, every Fourth of July would be painted in darker hues. But looking at her more closely, my anger leaked away. Her stiff shoulders and tightened lips could not mask her pain, hard as she tried to keep the hurt hidden. It took courage to come here, a brand of courage I wasn't sure I'd ever possess.

I touched my chest. "I can't imagine what you must be feeling."

It seemed as if the armor softened slightly.

"I used to be Bill's partner on the force," I continued. "Now I'm a private detective, and I often look for missing people in Los Angeles. Maybe I can help you find your son."

Her eyes searched mine intently—it was like being frisked from the inside. I waited.

"All right," she said.

"You say Sasha was a journalist of some sort? Can you tell me anything more?"

"Sasha writes for a paper, but after a few months he quit. He says there is no room for truth there, at his job. Instead, he makes interviews on a blog he starting, interviews with girls. How they come to the city for a better life, they think. But is a trick. Sometimes they are taken. Sometimes their fathers, their mothers, too, are selling them for having sex. Thirteen, fourteen years old. One is only twelve!" Mila shuddered. "In war, is bad enough, but this is just for making money!"

"Was Sasha trying to expose these men?"

"He says no. Not at first. At first, just wanting to help these girls. But he keeps looking, following the trail, like a dog. He finds something, a lead, he says. Something big. He starts to get threats. Then one day his blog just . . ." Mila swiped her right hand sideways. "Gone! Disappears! I say to him, 'Enough, it is dangerous,' but he ignores me. I am so angry at him!" She shook her head. "But also, so proud. I want to slap him and, and, at the same time a part of me wants him to keep going." Mila found my eyes. "How is this possible? Do you know what I am saying?"

"Yes," I said. "I do. I'm sure it's pretty common to feel mixed emotions around people we care for. I certainly do. But I'm curious, how did Sasha first get involved with trafficking?"

Mila's eyes flicked away, first moving to the car, then to a point over my left shoulder.

She's about to lie.

Rather than lie, though, she evaded. "Sasha wants to be a hero all his life—even as a boy he makes trouble for, how you say, the bulls? The bad ones, the ones who go after the weak."

"Bullies?"

"Yes. Bullies. Where we live there are many such men. During the war they kill everything, after the war they take everything, and now they run everything."

"Why not move away?"

She met my eyes. "Do you, what is it, fly, no, flee from things you know are bad? Do you run from bullies? Or do you face them, try to help?"

In truth, I've done both. Mila watched and waited.

"Both," I finally said. "But I like myself better when I face them."

"So do I," she said. "And so does Sasha."

The front door slammed. Bill crossed the front lawn in four strides.

"Sorry. My wife and I have a lot to talk about. Obviously." He waved his hand, as if brushing off a pesky fly. "Tell me about Sasha."

BOOM! The night sky thundered and a bouquet of color bloomed overhead. I stepped away from Mila and Bill. A second flash illuminated Irena, who was rigid in the front seat. She faced forward, eyes closed, lips moving, not deigning to give any of us—not even the sky—a glance. The wrapped white folds of Irena's headscarf gave the illusion of a bandage, sealing off hidden wounds so they could heal.

Sprays of luminous red, white, and blue arced overhead and sizzled out. In the distance, an answering display exploded into fountains of sparkle and sound, probably originating from the Hollywood Bowl. Colored mandalas tattooed the inky night.

I was flooded with weariness and the urge to be home. The festivities were over for me.

BOOM!

Mila and Bill were speaking earnestly now, head bent close to head. She touched his arm, and he covered her hand with his own. If this were a domestic surveillance job, if I had been hired by Martha to investigate Bill as an errant spouse, I would have to tell her that going by the body language, her husband and this other woman were, indeed, intimately involved.

The observation broke my heart.

A fresh barrage of fireworks resounded through the warm evening. Cheers and applause rang from the backyards up and down the street, and I heard children scream with delight, or dread, or maybe both.

I decided to check on Martha before I drove away. I owed her that. I opened the front door and silently crossed the foyer to the living room. She had moved to the rocking chair, and I was pummeled by the vivid memory of a younger, glowing Martha sitting in this same chair, her babies propped like footballs, one under each arm, as she nursed them. I shook the image off.

Two cop-wives knelt beside Martha now, as she dully pushed the rocking chair back and forth, back and forth. Her cheeks were parchment pale. Lola was curled up tight on her mother's lap, sucking on her two middle fingers—something she hadn't done for a year. Maude stood close by, silent, her body stiff.

I couldn't face any more emotionally charged interactions. I backed out of the room.

Outside, I skirted Bill and Mila, still talking, and hurried up the street to my car.

I sat in the front seat in silence, ignoring the dancing sky. I'd known exactly one couple in my entire life, one husband and wife who seemed to really love each other.

One.

I couldn't bear it.

I started the car. This was one of those times I conclusively chose to flee, rather than face more trouble.

CHAPTER 5

I dressed silently in the dark, pulling on my oldest, softest sweats. Tank was a still, dark mound at the foot of the bed.

I should have stayed, talked to Martha last night.

I again checked the red digits glowing on my bedside table. Three fifty A.M. It was going to be one of those days, when time took its own time.

The dream still had a tight grip on my heart and my breath was shallow. *All those children, struggling to be free.*

I padded across the dark living room and stepped behind the tall folding screen that designated my meditation area.

The small, stone statue of the Buddha was barely visible and motionless on my crowded makeshift altar. Hanging above it, my *thangka* depicting the Wheel of Life was only a suggestive blur of wisdom in the dark.

Impulsively, I executed three fluid prostrations before the still figure and hanging silk. I pulled a round embroidered cushion from against the wall, sat, and closed my eyes.

I invited the Buddha, the Dharma, and the Sangha to support me, taking refuge in the forces that shared my commitment to truth. I called on my former teachers to protect my spiritual health and to keep Bill's newfound son Sasha safe. And I asked my benefactors, all of them, to please help my friends Bill and Martha.

After meditating for close to an hour, I executed a double set of yoga asana postures, ate a toasted corn muffin with a generous smear of almond butter, and downed two mugs of French-roasted Sumatra. Propelled by caffeine, I ploughed through a mountain of domestic chores, scouring kitchen counters, wet- and dry-mopping my hardwood floor, dusting my bookshelves. Anything to distract me from fretting about Bill and Martha.

Why hadn't he called?

I was starting to seriously contemplate washing my windows when exhaustion walloped me like a fist to the head.

The advantage to starting your day before dawn? Things get accomplished.

The disadvantage? By 10 A.M. you're cooked.

I was three steps from bed when my cell phone vibrated in my pocket. I pulled it out.

I stared at the familiar number, as innocent as a grenade.

Maybe he and Martha have kissed and made up. Maybe it was all a bad dream.

I answered.

"Hey, Bill. How's it going?"

He groaned. "I'm up to my eyeballs in a shitstorm of my own making, thanks, but I don't want to talk about that right now. I need to come over."

"Of course. You want to come now?"

"Yeah. Actually, I might need to bunk at your house for a day or two."

My insides went still. So much for them making up.

"Martha says she 'needs some space.'" Bill's voice took on an edge I couldn't at first identify. "Translation? 'Park your sorry ass someplace else tonight.'"

Defiant. He sounded defiant.

"Okay, sure. You're welcome to stay for as long as you need. You know that."

"Thanks. I could probably use a nap before I go in to the office. I didn't get much sleep last night."

You and me both.

I made a fresh pot of coffee and took a steaming mug onto the deck to wait. Tank was below, stalking a small lizard lying in a patch of sunlight near the scrub oak. Tank pounced, but the lizard darted away and he came up empty-pawed. Unfazed, my cat claimed the square of sunlight for himself, settling on his right side. He looked like a trussed calf, his outstretched legs meeting at the ankles. His green eyes gleamed with pleasure as he soaked in the warmth. Maybe that was the plan all along.

A crunch of tires on gravel signaled Bill's arrival. He must have been close by when he called. I met him at the kitchen door. He looked haggard, with the bloodshot eyes and slumped shoulders of a beaten man. But his mouth was staked with stubborn lines, as if rebellion was poised to push through the exhaustion.

"Don't bother telling me I look like shit," he said. "I already know."

I pointed toward the carafe on the counter. "It's fresh."

In ten years of friendship, I'd never seen Bill turn down coffee, but he shook his head and sat across from me with a grunt. He wouldn't meet my eyes, also a first.

I probed the gap between us carefully.

"You in the mood for some conversation," I said, "or do you want to get some rest first?"

"Fuck if I know what I want," he said. "Ah, the hell with it." He got up and poured himself a cup of coffee, and my universe righted itself. "Might as well get this over with." He sat and squared his shoulders. "Fire away, detective."

My brain was a whirlpool of confusion and doubt. I started with the first question to escape to the surface. "How long have you known about Sasha?"

His answer was prompt. "Twenty-two days"—he checked his watch to do the math—"minus three hours. I found out I had another kid exactly three weeks ago yesterday. I'd just gotten back from lunch. My phone rang, and it was Mila, out of the fucking blue. She was worried, she said. Her son, she said, *our* son Sasha was getting threats." He shook his head, remembering.

"You must have been . . . stunned."

"I almost blacked out. I'll never forget that call, not as long as I live. I was sitting at my desk, thinking I had one kind of life, and suddenly the phone rings and I'm in a parallel universe."

"But you hadn't actually seen Mila before she showed up yesterday? Recently, I mean?"

"Seen. Talked to. Nothing. Not since I left Bosnia."

"Bill, I have to ask. Are you sure Sasha is yours? Could Mila be lying to you?"

"I wondered the same thing," he said, "but she sent me a picture. He looks just like me. And he was conceived exactly when we were together." He spread his hands. "Look, I'm not trying to justify what I did, but . . . but, I was lonely as hell, scared out of my wits, smack in the middle of a war zone, and she was—well, you've seen her, so you know what she's like, how she is. And Martha and I, we weren't even married yet, barely engaged, not that that's an excuse, but . . . Ten, I'd never felt anything like that in my life. I was suckerpunched. It was crazy, like being hijacked by a tornado."

Coup de foudre, I thought. The thunderbolt of love.

"Then she dumped me, and it was over, just as quick." Bill stared into his mug, as if it held secrets of its own. "I'd be lying if I said I never thought about her again. I've thought about her a lot. She was the road not taken, the me I never became."

The twist of grief in my chest caught me by surprise.

Julie.

The last time I'd seen her, she was driving away from my home here in Topanga, from a relationship with me, because I couldn't give her what she wanted: intimacy, honesty, trust.

Exactly what I now wanted from a relationship.

The road not taken.

"But you didn't stay in touch with Mila?"

His exhale was heavy with regret. "I tried. Back then, I mean. More than once. Like she says, I'm stubborn. But she never responded. Anyway, then I came home to Martha and tried to make myself forget it ever happened. The breakup was bad, you know?"

"How bad?"

"Really bad." Bill closed his eyes for a moment, remembering. "I was pretty much responsible for the torture and death of Mila's brother."

"Oof."

"I mean, I didn't know it was her brother, obviously."

I just nodded.

"I was stationed at a checkpoint between zones. We'd stopped these seven guys, Bosnian Muslims, just inside the border of the Serb Republic. Routine, but it turned out they were heavily armed and had illegally crossed the zone of separation, so we did what we'd been told to do—disarmed them and transferred them to the Serb police."

Bill finished off his coffee. I refilled his mug.

"Thanks. Yeah, so, they were escorted into the local station, but the bastards transferred them the next day to another station thirty miles south, you know, away from prying eyes. After that, nothing, until a report came back that all seven had died. Of natural causes, the Serbs said."

"Natural causes?"

"I guess they considered hours of severe torture *natural*. The International Red Cross screamed foul, of course, but according to the Serbs, these men were stone zealots, the kind that these days fly airplanes into buildings. The Serbs insisted the Muslims had murdered a bunch of unarmed Bosnian Christians a few days earlier. Good riddance, right?"

I said nothing.

"Except one of the Muslims was Mila's brother. Fucking terrible luck, you know? And according to Mila, her brother said the Bosnian Christians were actually Croatians, armed and aggressive, and it was self-defense. It was all one big holy mess by then, so who knows? Meanwhile, Mila's father—he was some sort of Muslim intellectual—had disappeared, though at the time Mila was sure he'd been sent to one of the prison camps."

I thought his words over.

"Mila doesn't strike me as an extremist type."

"She isn't. Wasn't. Her brothers were a different story, though."

"Brothers? She's got more of them?"

Bill nodded. "Two more, I think, though who knows if they're even alive? Then there's Mila's mother. You saw her, she's another piece of work. Always marched to her own drum. Irena's first husband, along with all his family, was Croatian, a whole other kind of Christian."

"Mila's still a Muslim?"

"I think so. She's always been more about peace and tolerance than anything else, or at least she was when I knew her. Bosnian Muslims in general were moderate—no burkas and veils, at least not back then. She was halfway through medical school when the Serbs got seduced by that madman and fucked everything up."

"Medical school?"

"Yeah. She was way more into healing than harming. She hated war, any war, but especially that one. She was vocal about it, too. That made her unpopular with all three sides of the conflict, and both branches of her family."

Do you run from bullies? Or do you face them, try to help?

He said, "The tragedy is, for centuries that whole area, Bosnia in particular, was the poster child for religious tolerance. Catholic Croats, Muslims, Orthodox Serbs—all of them married each other, practiced their own beliefs, accepted each other's differences, you name it. Then Milošević made his power grab, and before you could blink you had mass slaughter, neighbors killing neighbors, brothers and sisters turning on each other. Politics and religion, run amuck. Mila's family wasn't the exception, it was the rule. After six months I fled, beyond grateful for the separation of church and state here in the good old U.S. of A."

"I can relate," I said. "Don't forget, I grew up in an exiled Tibetan community surrounded by hostile Hindus."

In truth, I didn't even have to leave the walls of Dorje Yidam to experience the cutthroat side of belief. At my monastery, even senior lamas wrangled constantly over the pettiest of issues. Everything had the capacity to devolve into a power play. Who gets to choose the topic for our nightly dharma talk? Who gets to lead the procession when His Holiness comes for a visit? Who collects the most *dana* at the Saga Dawa festival? Egos battled for power and prestige on a daily basis, on and off the meditation cushions. And this, in a community dedicated to the practice of loving-kindness.

I've since learned that it's the same in the Pentagon, the Vatican, the politburo, and every other organization created and run by the most aggressive members of the species. The bullies, in other words. I've often wondered if the world would work better if women ran it instead.

"Ten," Bill said, "Mila and I . . . we need your help. But I've got to ask. How does all this affect you and me?"

Uh-oh. So now he and Mila were a "we." I wondered if Martha knew.

"I'm not sure," I said. "I mean I can't really fault you for having an affair with Mila back then. There was a war going on, you were away from home, you did what you did. I get that."

"Yeah, well, there's plenty to find fault with, believe me. I could have—"

"Bill, stop," I said. "How many times have you told me that you can't go back and change the past?"

His voice was low. "Part of me still can't believe I slept with her. I broke every rule."

"I hear you," I said. "Got a few of those in my own past, as you know. But what I don't get is why you didn't tell Martha, right away, I mean. You let this affair fester in the back of your head for close to twenty years, man!" I felt myself getting a little heated in the face.

"You've never been married," he said. "You don't understand how it works. And who said anything about festering? It was over!"

"I may not be married, but I know what happens if you keep secrets like that caged up inside you. Believe me, they always come back to bite you, one way or another. I've got the scars to prove it."

"I didn't want to destroy the trust we had between us. Is that a crime?"

My mouth twisted. I exhaled, puffing my lips to loosen the irritation. "You ran a con on yourself, partner," I said. "I mean, sure, you damaged that trust when you had the affair with Mila. But you totally trashed it by not telling Martha when you got home. And then you married Martha, gave her your trust, knowing you weren't worth trusting."

"What I *knew* was the affair would hurt her. I didn't want her to feel bad."

"Sorry. More bullshit. You didn't want *you* to feel bad. You didn't want *you* to have to deal with her reaction."

He squirmed but he didn't disagree. "Whatever. The guy who had that affair's a stranger to me now. That guy? He figured if he just pretended the whole thing didn't happen, it would go away. And you know what? For a while, it did."

"Yeah, well, how's that working for you now?"

His eyes narrowed. "What the hell's going on with you, Ten? I feel bad I hurt my wife, okay? I fucked up. What else do you want from me?"

My belly muscles clenched tight in defense. What else *did* I want? I tried to parse the sour mixture in my gut: resentment, helplessness, hurt. And then I realized. *Valerie. Ma mère.* Once again, I was displacing hurt and aiming anger at an innocent party for wounds caused by one of my parents. My mother's constant affairs—her denial, withholding, and secrecy—took a huge toll on my childhood.

What childhood? You never even got to have one. Never got to feel safe because of her carelessness.

And now my best friend was doing the same thing to Martha, not to mention Maude and Lola.

Bill studied my face, waiting for me to say something.

"Okay, well, this might be bringing up some old stuff," I said.

He waited.

"I'm still mad at my mother for some things, okay? And I'm taking it out on you. All she did with her life was have affairs and lie about them."

"Hey, it's not like I'm up to my ass in affairs."

"I'm not saying you are."

"Then what's the problem?"

What *was* the problem? I could feel something else, something hard and hot burning in my gut, but as soon as I got close, it darted away, like Tank's lizard.

I felt into the space. *Allow.* The release of energy was telling. Hurt and anger bubbled up.

What an asshole.

"How could you keep this from me?" I said, my voice tight and high. "We're partners! How many times have I confided in you about my love life, all my mistakes, my messes? You know everything about me, and, and now suddenly here's this big *thing* you never even told me about. What else are you hiding?"

"Jesus," Bill said, "you sound just like Martha. You know what? I need this like a fucking hole in the head." He shoved upright and his weight tipped the kitchen table, knocking over his mug. A brown river of lukewarm coffee snaked across the wooden top and dripped onto my just-mopped floor.

"Ah, shit," he said, "I'm sorry." His face reddened. "I'm sorry. I'm sorry for my entire fucking existence, okay?!"

Who was the asshole, now? *He came to you for relief, not more grief.*

I moved to Bill's side and took him by the shoulders.

"I'm the one who should apologize," I said. "I'm not being much of a friend."

He twisted from my grip, his face wan. "Let me stretch out on your deck for a little while. I can't think straight."

I followed him onto the deck, dragged the chaise lounge over to a shady spot on the far side, and left to find a pillow. By the time I got back, Bill was already snoring, Tank curled at his feet, keeping careful watch.

CHAPTER 6

I was way too riled up to take the rest I so desperately needed.

I changed into swimming trunks, running shoes, and a T-shirt; grabbed a beach towel; fed the four-legged family member; and soon was slaloming the Shelby down Topanga Canyon to the coast. Once I hit the PCH, I aimed north for Zuma. I used the remaining 20 minutes of driving to alternate deep breathing with visualizing an empty parking space, just one please, and just for me. As I pulled into the jammed lot, a slightly rusted open-air Wrangler, teal blue, crammed with lean-muscled young men and bristling with boogie boards, reversed out of a slot. I pounced. After appeasing the uniformed parking attendant god with the peak season offering of $10, I crossed shimmering asphalt to the curved expanse of south-facing beach.

The midday sun fell on the Pacific, shattering into small shards of light. I stepped onto a flat scimitar of sand littered with fragrant bodies, some fully sprawled on towels, others poking tentative limbs out from under striped umbrellas. A headless baby wailed, trapped within the too-tight onesie his or her mother was trying to tug over his or her body. Farther up the beach a group of teenagers—taut, flawless, and four to a side—leapt and punched a seamed white ball over a net as they traded grunts and cheers.

I plotted my course. Zuma is a two-mile curve end to end, an ideal running distance. I started with a leisurely jog. As I traversed the damp, packed sand that lies close, but not too close, to the water, I gradually accelerated my pace, dodging boogie-boarders and castle-building tots when necessary.

To my right, a series of light-blue lifeguard stations, like sentinels on wooden stilts, marked my route.

I left any thought of Bosnia, or Bill, far, far behind. Which was the whole point.

By the time I reached the far end of the crescent, I had warmed up nicely. I wheeled around and proceeded to execute a series of 50-yard wind sprints all the way back to the first lifeguard station. I stripped to my swimming trunks. As I waded into the waves, my skin seemed to shrink-wrap around my bones, and I estimated the water temperature to be just north of 60 degrees. For 15 minutes I churned through the chilly water, trying to stay out in front of my coagulating blood cells. Back on shore, I labored through 40 push-ups and 40 lunges as best I could, given the soft surface.

I returned to the Mustang for a beach towel and finally claimed my own personal patch of sand for a well-earned rest before heading home. I closed my eyes. Sun-sculpted flames painted the inside of my lids red-orange. My muscles soaked in warmth. Merciful sleep beckoned with multiple outstretched arms, like the goddess Kali.

My cell phone rang.

Shit.

I rolled onto my stomach and squinted at the screen. The area code was 213, no one I knew.

"Hello?"

"Yo, G-Force here. This my bro Ten?"

My brain flipped through its database of names and came up blank. Still, I was sure I'd heard this voice before.

"I'm sorry, who did you say this was?"

"'Who did you say this was?'" he mimicked with a high voice. Then, "Told you. G-Force."

"Okay. Well. Do I know you?"

"Ought to," he said. "You busted my mofo ass enough."

I sat up, recognition dawning. "Godfrey. Godfrey Chambers."

Loud laughter crackled over my phone. He said, "Heh-heh-heh. Who I was, but not who I am."

"Ah."

"G-Force, now. Dropped the old handle up at Pelican; name was holding me back. Two gangstas come at you—one name Godfrey and the other G-Force—who you gonna respect?"

"Point taken," I said. I've faced my own challenges with the name Tenzing Norbu, especially at the Police Academy. Add Lama to the front of it and you might as well be wearing a neon sign saying "Bust My Balls." "What's up?"

"So, I been down from Pelican Bay close to a year now. Doing good, too. Sober, piss tests clean, seeing my PO every month, even got a straight job if you can believe that shit."

"Good for you," I said, and meant it. Any stint of rehabilitation, no matter how brief, was cause for congratulations. I shook beach grit out of my towel, shoved my feet into my shoes, and headed for the car. I paused, midstep.

"How in the world did you find me?"

"Caught your new act on TV a while back. Damn, Ten, you really smoke them two dudes? I didn't know you had it in you! Anyway, saw you was retired from the po-lice, took it from there."

"Okay, and . . . ?"

"Yeah, so, I got some money comin' to me from my uncle, see, but the insurance company's holdin' it tighter than a church lady clutch her purse."

"How much money are we talking about, Godf—G-Force?"

"Thirty-three grand."

I didn't believe him. Why would Godfrey Chambers even be bothering about $33,000? He read my silence correctly.

"You thinkin' ain't much, not for G-Force, ain't you?"

"Yes. That's exactly what I was thinking."

"It's a shitload to me these days."

"I find that hard to believe. You must have put some away when you were slinging dope. Fifty wasn't even a good week's take for you back then."

"I know, man, but that was then. My number two guy flat cleaned me out while I was pumpin' iron. He off in Costa Fuckin' Rica now, spending my millions."

"That's too bad," I said.

"'Preciate that."

I climbed into my car and a silver Mercedes-Benz immediately pulled alongside and hovered, like a hungry shark.

"So, what you gettin' paid these days, Ten?"

"Five grand a day, three-day minimum."

He whistled. "Who's the playa now? You doin' okay! Too rich for my sorry ass, for damn sure."

"I'm not complaining."

The driver of the Mercedes honked his horn.

"Hang on. I'm putting you on speaker now." I placed the phone on my lap, backed out of the space, and pulled away. The Benz slid in right behind me, and the driver gave me the finger. I wondered what gods he prayed to and hoped they believed in dispensing karma.

The phone sat silent. *Maybe G-Force won't ask.*

I sure as hell wasn't going to offer.

"So what do you say, Ten? Help a brother out?"

I made a petulant face at the phone. But something stopped me from an automatic *no*. On the one hand, if I was going to do pro bono work, an ex-con wasn't my first choice. On the other hand, if he was, in fact, staying clean and sober, he deserved a helping hand. Jean, my favorite waitress at Langer's and a member of the recovery tribe, was big on the importance of being of service to struggling addicts. She'd never forgive me for booting G-Force to the curb.

"Okay."

"Whoa. You sayin' yes?"

"Yes."

"'Preciate that," he repeated. Someone in his life, maybe his AA sponsor if he had one, was teaching G-Force healthier habits, such as expressing gratitude.

"What would you like me to do with the insurance company?"

"Whatever it is private detectives do, man. Get me my money. Shake 'em down!"

Somewhere out there in the ether I pictured an anonymous agent red-flagging this conversation: Tenzing Norbu. July 5th. Requested by ex-con, Crips member, and known dealer of drugs to "shake 'em down." In my few short years as a private detective I'd already rattled several different branches of law enforcement—city, county, state, and federal. I was a wiretapping dream come true.

"Isn't this a job for a lawyer?"

"Me an' lawyers don' get along. They take more than they do, feel me? Ten, I need that thirty-three K to finance my new operation. I got an investor who'll match my scratch once I get hold of my money. Then G-Force back in business."

More red flags, these ones mine. The G-Force I knew had been employed exclusively in the dope trade since he was in the sixth grade. "Exactly what kind of business are we talking about, G?" My voice was tight with disapproval.

He erupted with laughter. "Heh-heh. Listen to the man. Talkin' about a gym, bro! I'm goin' into the personal trainin' business. I even got a tagline I went and got registered! Check it out: The G-Force Workout: Pump Iron Like You in Pelican Bay!"

Well . . . yeah! Grammar aside, I could definitely see the approach catching on with gang wannabes stretching from Compton to Beverly Hills. They all dream of doing time, or at least of having done it; it's the height of gangster chic. Of course for those unlucky or unskilled enough to actually end up incarcerated, the romance wears off quickly, but culturally G-Force might be onto something.

"I coulda financed my gym the first month I was out if I'd gotten back in the game, but I took myself a vow: I ain't never doin' that shit again. Never."

"So what are you doing?"

"Don' laugh. I been workin' at a car wash."

I laughed, but under my breath. Before we sent him up to Pelican, G had a private fleet of black Escalades.

"So you've been washing cars for a year?"

"Naw, I mostly dry 'em. Machine do the washin'."

"Minimum wage?"

"Yeah, but they's money in tips. You do a good job, man slip you a five if he's feelin' generous, a dollar if he ain't. Shit adds up. On a good day I take home a Benjamin, sometimes more. Enough to eat on. But it ain't gonna open no gym."

G-Force was not only rehabilitating himself—he was trying to make the shift from employee to entrepreneur, only legally this time. To start fresh. Be his own boss.

Just like me.

"Anyway, this ain't charity, Ten. I know you too rich for me, but this a real opportunity for you, too."

"How's that?"

"May be straight, but I'm still the G-Force. Got information to trade, y'feel me? I still got homies connected to just about every decent-sized crew in town. You get me my uncle's money, and I give you a year of high-class informant shit ab-so-lutely free!"

In his previous incarnation, Godfrey Chambers, or G-Force, or whatever he wanted to call himself, was an unusually reliable criminal informant for Bill and me, even as a low-level courier. He'd never steered us wrong on a piece of intelligence and helped us bust up a couple of crews before acquiring an insatiable taste for the deadly product he was helping get off the streets. Soon, his habit trumped every other concern. He clammed up, disappeared, and eventually resurfaced as a mid- to high-level dealer with his own crew and a bad drug habit that led to seriously sloppy mistakes. Next stop, Pelican Bay.

I considered his offer to inform again briefly—who knows, he might be even more useful now. A few years in state prison can up a man's street credibility big time.

Good sense prevailed.

"Not a good idea, G-Force. The day I find myself needing that kind of information and you find yourself providing it is the day we're both not where we should be."

He grunted, though I couldn't tell if that meant he agreed.

"Look, I can give you a day or two tops on this, okay? Free of charge. That should be sufficient. If I don't get anywhere, I'll hook you up with my friend Clancy—he's just getting started and charges a lot less."

"Okay. But I don't like owing."

"Think of it as payback for your help in the past."

I was almost home by now, and my stomach tightened at the thought of Bill, asleep on my deck, surrounded by his own world of trouble.

"Okay, man," G-Force said. "I can't seem to get no traction with these people. I'm thinkin' it has to do with the particular color of my skin, but what do I know?"

"Text me the details, and I'll see what I can do." I waited for it, counting inside, smiling . . . *three . . . four . . .*

"'Preciate that."

CHAPTER 7

The note was stuck under the coffee carafe, and vintage Bill:

Off to a meeting with the Usual Assholes.
Thanks for not kicking my butt more than necessary.
I'll call you once I've figured out what the fuck I'm doing and where the fuck I'm sleeping tonight.
B

I was betting he'd be back at home this evening—maybe not in his own bed, but at least somewhere on the premises. Looking after a couple of amped-up redheads by herself all day would hopefully put Martha in a forgiving mood.

Tank wandered out from under the kitchen table, his demeanor casual, as in, "Oh, you're home? When did you get back?"

I wasn't fooled. The tip of his tail was swishing up a storm and his whiskers lay flat against his face.

"Sorry. I'm on it, buddy."

As I emptied a can of beef-and-chicken into his bowl, Tank's nose repeatedly bumped against my ankle, encouraging me not to lose my train of thought. I set the dish on the floor.

"Lunch is served."

I toasted myself two pieces of sourdough rye and constructed a layered sandwich of sliced avocado, Big Beef tomato, and Persian cucumber. In a flash of inspiration, I used some leftover cream cheese and dill spread as a kind of mortar, to keep the cucumber slices from shooting out both sides with every bite, like organic shrapnel. I washed lunch down with the last of the coffee, and then I washed myself down in the shower. I dressed for the workday in my official summer uniform: jeans, black T-shirt, and sandals.

One last task. I returned to the bathroom and ran a brush over my damp hair. Uh-oh. Rubbing at the steamy mirror, I created a small, streaked circle of visibility to double-check, and confirmed. My hair was starting to do that "hedge" thing, the one that led directly to the "felt-tipped pen" thing if I didn't watch out. Time to give my lady with the clippers a call.

The purple shadows under my eyes reminded me that I'd been up for hours, but before my brain started in on why, I again set the whole Bohannon drama aside. There was nothing I could, or should, do until Bill knew his own mind, and who knew when that would be? Anyway, pro bono or not, a job was calling.

I checked my iPhone. G-Force had texted me a name—Roland Conway, Jr.—plus the name of an insurance broker-age company, Conway Associates Insurance, Inc. I'd never heard of either of them, which meant precisely nothing.

I crossed the living room to my desk, which was angled oddly in order to face the front windows. This was highly feng shui according to my first ex-girlfriend, Charlotte, aka She-Who-Hates-Cats. Or was it Mike who made me do it? I forgot, but either way I'd come to love the off-kilter arrangement. I fired up my computer. My office was now officially open, my work underway.

I goosed my research assistant, Mr. Google, into action. He quickly located a website, and with two more clicks offered up a thumbnail picture of Roland Conway, Jr., Senior Adjuster, Life Insurance Claims Department, at the Westlake Village office. He looked to be about 40 years old and had been an employee of Conway Associates Insurance, Inc. (CAII) for 16 years. I used my mouse to enlarge his image. Sandy-blond hair fell in wisps over a high, domed forehead. The eyes were pale blue, somewhat watery. The wide smile, displaying teeth as straight and whitewashed as fence pickets, almost compensated for a weak chin. The Buddha says the human mind automatically responds to external stimuli in one of three ways: attraction, aversion, or neutrality. I tend to lean toward aversion, if I'm honest, and true to form, I disliked Conway on sight. Or maybe I was just triggered by the American flag pinned to his lapel. In my experience, such public exhibits of patriotism more often than not camouflage a private distrust of almost everything else.

I returned to the main site and called the office number displayed.

"Conway Associates. How may I help you?" a female voice chirped.

"I'd like to speak to Roland Conway, please."

"Senior or Junior?"

"Junior."

"Whom shall I say is calling?"

How refreshing. Someone at CAII actually insisted on correct grammar.

"Tenzing Norbu."

"May I ask to what this call refers, Mr. Norbu?"

Unheard of. No dangling participles, and not a single stumble over my name. The language stickler in me, inherited from my Tibetan Buddhist father—monks can debate a single phrase of the Buddha's for months—and nurtured over the years by my own singular passion for clarity of speech cheered, even as the constantly corrected child in me balked.

"I'm a private investigator. I have been hired to investigate a claim. I'd prefer to leave it at that."

"May I put you on hold for a moment?"

I counted long, slow breaths, and had completed a third exhale when a deep voice, incongruous if paired with the weak chin and pale eyes, came on the line.

"This is Roland Conway."

"Thanks for taking my call, Mr. Conway. I'll come right to the point. A customer of yours retained me to look into a problem he's having getting a claim paid."

"All right. What is the claimant's name?"

"Godfrey Chambers," I said.

Mr. Conway made a sound somewhere between a sigh and a groan.

"Ah, yes," he said. "Godfrey Chambers. Well, then, I assume Mr. Chambers also told you that his uncle, Horace Latimore, named him a beneficiary, and that our company has refused to pay the benefit."

"Yes. That's what he said."

"And did Mr. Chambers, or Mr. G-Force as he likes to be called now, happen to mention that Horace Latimore is not, in fact, his uncle?"

Uh . . . no. Mr. G-Force had failed to mention that particular item. A small prickle of irritation crept up the back of my neck.

"That is a fairly important fact, wouldn't you agree, Mr. Norbu?"

"That depends," I said. *On who's trying to con me,* I thought. Even with my limited experience, I suspected an insurance company was at least as likely to be running a con as a recovering drug addict and criminal informant.

"Mr. Conway, I'm a bit late to the party," I said. "Can you fill me in? If Horace Latimore is not his uncle, how did G-Force get into the picture?"

"You'll have to ask him," Conway said. "All I can tell you is we've proven to our satisfaction that Godfrey Chambers is not Horace Latimore's nephew, and therefore does not qualify." He chuckled. "Not that it took much proof. Let's just say the evidence was pretty black and white."

Ten seconds later I had G-Force on the line.

"Anything you forgot to tell me about Uncle Horace?"

"Like what?"

"Like maybe he isn't your uncle? Like maybe he isn't African American?"

G-Force let out a howl. "You been listenin' to that stingy mofo Conway, ain't you? Lying sack o' shit!"

"I notice you didn't answer my question."

"Aw, man, I hate to hear that tone, like you don't believe me."

"G. Drop the wounded-victim act. I asked you a question."

"Fine. No, Horace ain't exactly my uncle, but it don't matter!"

"Why not?"

"'Cause my *name* in his will, that's why!"

Two hours in, and my serenity lay in shreds.

"G-Force, I assume you have a copy of this will."

"Lookin' at it right now!"

But, of course, he didn't have a fax machine or a scanner or any simple way to send it to me.

"Look," G-Force said, "I'll borrow a ride. I don't have to be at the car wash for a couple hours. Where you live?"

I didn't feel like entertaining G-Force in my canyon sanctuary, so we arranged to meet halfway, at a café I remembered as having great espresso just off the 101, in Sherman Oaks.

This time, I took my workhorse wheels. After losing my beloved Toyota to gunshot wounds, I'd recently replaced it with a metallic-gray, 2005 Dodge Neon. My new partner was small, zippy, and forgettable—just right for surveillance jobs. Most people relegated it to the category of cars that "all look alike." Not a lot of room to stretch out for extended periods of time, but good enough for my modest height and needs. I was hoping to add at least another 100,000 miles to its current 85,000, and assumed with time we'd become good friends.

A half hour later I was sipping an espresso in a corner table of the Crave Café when a beat-up Pacer the color of rust pulled up and parked on Ventura Boulevard, right in front. I almost ran outside: I've never seen a Pacer in the actual flesh, or should I say actual tin?

A black man unwound from the car, all six feet plus of him. It was G-Force, but I blinked at the changes. He had packed on probably 25 pounds since I last saw him, all of it muscle. Instead of a tangle of dreadlocks, his shaved scalp gleamed like polished wood, bracketed by smallish cupped ears, seashells that lay close and tight to his skull. His T-shirt and nylon gym pants were a far cry from the supple leather and thick gold chains of his former life of crime. But the angular cheekbones; graceful brows arching over dark, intelligent eyes; and generous mouth were the same, as was the small cleft pressed in his chin, like an afterthought. G-Force had been, and still was, a very handsome man.

He loped inside, clutching a manila envelope under his left arm. His eyes were wary as he took in the brick walls and hardwood floor; the menu items hand-scrawled in chalk behind the counter; and the plates of grilled chicken panini, arugula salads, and strawberry crepes. I waved, and he was at my table in three long strides.

"Want anything? You have to order at the counter," I said.

He shook his head. "Naw, man, place makes me jumpy."

I registered the customers occupying the scattered tables: trim soccer moms in yoga outfits with streaked blonde hair; hipsters with Van Dyke beards tapping out dialogue on laptop screens; businessmen in designer jeans and sport coats, no ties. Every Achilles has his own heel—maybe for G-Force, it was yuppies.

"Not your kind of clientele?"

He surveyed the room like a stand-up comedian assessing a new audience. "Nothin' wrong with them, exactly. Just can't figure out what category to put 'em in now."

I waited, curious.

"Used to be they johns. S'posed to steal shit from, sell dope to, boost they cars. But now?" G-Force shrugged. "I ain't slinging or boosting or any of that crap anymore. Don't know what category they in. Understand?"

"I think so. Your way of seeing people is changing."

"Yeah. Got me flat mystified half the time. Only category I got left is, people that might need to get they car washed."

"Well, in L.A., that's everybody," I said. "So wherever you are now, you're in the right place."

G-Force lowered his head and eyed me, his arched brows pulled close. I wondered if I'd gone too far. Then, his face split into a dazzling smile.

"Heh, heh, heh," he hooted. "Man, you speak the truth! Car wash my ticket to the bigs, heh, heh!" He flipped his chair around with one hand, as if it weighed nothing, and straddled it like a pony. He rested his forearms across the top. Whatever that did to his biceps, it caused me to flex my own, and vow to double my push-ups routine. The Buddha calls this "comparing mind." Never works out well for one's self-esteem.

I reached out my hand. "Insurance policy, please."

He slid an envelope across. I pulled the documents out—a copy of Horace's will, plus the policy. I leafed through both before rereading the material more slowly.

Both documents had the usual boilerplate legal garble, but the list of "Uncle" Horace's bequests was clear, as was the sum total of his actual estate: $128,000 in a savings account, $14,000 in a checking account, a half-interest in a coin laundry, and a 1998 Toyota Camry. Plus, one life insurance policy.

Only one sentence in the will dealt specifically with G-Force:

My nephews, James Lunzy and Angus Lunzy, and Godfrey Chambers, are beneficiaries of my $100,000 life insurance policy. I bequeath the funds to be divided equally among them.

The money in the savings account, the Camry, and the half-interest in the laundry went to someone named Christian Peet.

I glanced up at G-Force. "These two, James and Angus Lunzy, they're contesting your third of the one-hundred-thousand-dollar insurance policy?"

"Yeah."

"I don't understand. It's quite clear. Why would the insurance company be stonewalling you?"

"They sayin' Horace ain't my blood uncle so they don't have to pay."

"Did you tell them Horace was your blood uncle?"

He chewed on his lip. "Uh, no, not exactly."

"G-Force. Please. What is your relationship to Horace Latimore?"

G-Force looked around, as if checking for spies. He kept his voice low.

"Horace my Eskimo."

"I'm sorry. Did you say *Eskimo?*"

"Yeah. You know, he the one showed me the way."

"The way *where?*" I mindfully uncurled my fists, thus preventing me from leaping across the table and punching him.

"At first we just pen pals. You know, when I was at Pelican Bay," G-Force said and turned his chair around. He settled into it, warming to the subject. "But then Horace came to visit for real, and started taking me through them steps. Horace the man. Really saved my ass, you know? He even let me stay with him 'n' Christian when I first got out. Said he wished they could adopt me."

"So he let you live in his igloo?" I teased, but the look on G-Force's face humbled me, and I regretted my flippant words.

"Horace my sponsor, but he says, in his heart, G-Force his son, his own son." G-Force's voice grew thick. "Man so sick and all, but still he take me in. He's like my hero. Guess that's why he changed his will."

"And how did . . ." I asked, glancing at the line, "how did James and Angus Lunzy feel about that?"

"How you think? Shit, man, them two boys resent me for breathing. Horace didn't have no kids of his own. Horace was uh . . . was . . ." G-Force resorted to an effeminate flap of the wrist.

"Homosexual?"

"Yeah. Ain't no big thing, not to me. Anyway, so, but Angus and James? They always knew they could stop by the laundry and get a Benjamin from Uncle Horace. Horace love his sister, Wanda, more'n anybody else on earth—she Angus and James's mama—so when she passed, long time ago, he tried to take care of 'em." G-Force shook his head. "They take his money, but they treat him like shit."

"How so?"

"You know, callin' him a faggot, minute his back is turned. Make me wanna whup they ass. Only family they got, no reason to be like that. But Horace, that man a saint. Not their fault, he say. They the sick ones."

"He sounds pretty wise."

I reread the will, with fresh eyes.

"So Christian Peet was his partner?"

"Horace with Christian pretty much his whole life, drunk and sober. They the only people I know stayed together like that. Christian still run the laundry, probl'y be fluffin' and foldin' 'til he drop, too."

For a brief, painful moment, I thought of Bill and Martha, and their almost 20 years of . . .

Let it go.

I studied the key line in the will one more time.

And then I saw it:

My nephews, James Lunzy and Angus Lunzy and Godfrey Chambers are beneficiaries.

My punctuation-prone brain must have automatically inserted a comma earlier, between the "Angus Lunzy" and the "and Godfrey Chambers." I'd expected a comma, and so I'd slotted one in. But it wasn't there. A simple enough omission, but one that CAII was using to justify cutting G-Force out of the will. Somebody over there, some crook disguised as a Grammar Nazi, must have pounced on the interpretation that Horace was leaving $100,000 to three nephews before proving that Godfrey Chambers was not a blood relative, not by a long shot.

To me the intent was clear: Horace wanted to divide the insurance money between both nephews, plus Godfrey Chambers. Otherwise, why put his name in there at all?

The whole situation was absurd, and made no sense. CAII may have found a tiny loophole, based on a missing comma, but they had nothing to gain by cheating G-Force— the underwriter had to pay out regardless.

No, the only persons to gain from this were Angus and James Lunzy.

So that's where I'd start.

"What do the nephews do, G-Force? If you know."

"This and that. They mama leave them money when she die, too. Horace say they never been self-supporting and never will be as long as someone else there to pay."

The net gain to Angus and James was $16,666.00 each. Was that enough money to contest Horace's wishes? Sure it was. I'd seen people killed for a lot less. Once, when I was still a rookie on patrol, I'd arrived first at a scene to find a pair of dead bangers bleeding out on the floor of a Mexican restaurant. Double homicide and messy enough to make you swear off salsa forever. According to the bartender, they'd gotten into an argument about who was going to pick up the tab. Banger One apparently thought Banger Two had eaten more than his share of carne asada. When the homicide investigators emptied their pockets, they found rolls of $100 bills—a combined total of close to $10,000.

The unpaid bill came to $12.39. That was the first time I truly understood the insanity of the mind's attachment to being right.

In this case, though, the culprit at first glance was pure and simple greed. Didn't explain everything, but at least I had an initial clue.

"Can I keep these for now? I'll need to make copies for my file."

"'Course." G-Force stood up. "Think you can get me my money?"

"I'll try my best."

"'Preciate that." I'd forgotten how big G-Force's hands were. He held out a paw, and I allowed my knuckles to be crushed.

As we walked outside, I had to ask.

"G-Force?"

"Yeah."

"Why *Eskimo?*"

G-Force crossed his arms and leaned against the Pacer, smiling slightly. "It's like this. Brother walks into a bar, says to the bartender, 'No such thing as God.'

"'Why you say that?' says the bartender.

"'Last year,' man says, 'got sent to Alaska on a job. Three days in got caught in a blizzard, worst one in a hundr'd years. Buried to my neck in snow, no food, no idea where I was at. So I prayed to the man upstairs, prayed my butt off, said I'd never do wrong again if on'y He save my freezing ass. But He lef' me there to die.'

"Bartender just stares.

"'What?' brother says.

"Bartender says, 'You here, ain't you? You ain't dead.'

"'Yeah, well, ten seconds after I quit praying, here come an Eskimo. Give me food, take me to his igloo so I have somewhere to sleep.'

"Bartender shake his head. 'You even dumber than you look.'

"'What? I'm jus' sayin', God didn't save me. Eskimo did!'"

G-Force punched my arm lightly. "Heh-heh-heh. Horace told me that story first time he come to Pelican Bay to visit. That Horace, he something else."

As I breezed along the 101 North toward Conway Associates, I offered up my own petition to the Great Beyond:

please, let this ridiculously good Friday afternoon traffic hold until I get to Westlake Village. Then I passed a pleasant, jam-free half hour identifying and appreciating all the Eskimos in my world. Chief among them was Bill Bohannon.

CHAPTER 8

The long, narrow building, set behind a newly constructed industrial complex just off Agoura Road, was of pebbly stucco—squat, one-story, painted an uninspiring beige, and fronted by an equally long, narrow parking lot. Unlike its gleaming neighbors, this drab structure had been here for some time. In the distance, a sad little ridge of drought-scorched hills pretending to be mountains made for a depressing view. I parked my Neon at the far end of the lot. It was almost five o'clock, and I was exhausted. I swallowed a huge yawn as I scanned the immediate area for possible caffeine franchises. Not a one, not even a Starbucks. My plastic Starbucks gift card, a thank-you gift from a happy client, was burning a $100 hole, minus one Caffè Americano to go, in my back pocket.

Maybe on the way home.

Each individual business in the building was marked by a faded awning with stenciled numbers denoting the office address. I didn't see any surveillance cameras, high tech or otherwise. Maybe these were not the kinds of businesses that experienced break-ins. I rechecked my text from G-Force as I strolled closer, and soon located the insurance firm almost precisely in the middle of the row of modest enterprises. The numbered awning, once navy blue, had faded to a color closer to purple. The business, its double doors of frosted glass etched with the initials CAII, was flanked by a tax consulting agency and a run-down fertility clinic, both of which triggered in me instant pangs of anxiety.

I pushed against the doors and stepped inside. The temperature was a good 15 degrees cooler than the afternoon heat behind me. Despite its lofty title, Conway Associates Insurance, Inc. was underwhelming. The space was maybe 900 square feet, longer than it was wide, with a small reception area up front and a smaller conference room to my left. I counted two more frosted glass doors, closed, leading into what I assumed was a pair of private offices, one on the right side, in no-man's-land, and one at the back, facing the direction of the hills. I also noticed an emergency exit in the back—the old-fashioned kind complete with a metal panic bar.

One wall boasted several framed, fading endorsements from local clubs and businessmen's associations. No sign of a security system in place here, either. No infrared, ultrasonic, or microwave detectors. No photo-electronic beams. No nothing.

The overall impression was of an enterprise struggling to stay afloat.

A youthful, plump woman with thin wire-rimmed glasses and an erect back perched behind a curved Plexiglas desk, tapping a computer keyboard industriously. Her hair was light brown and twisted, rope-like, into a bumpy knot on the top of her head, Siddhartha-style. She presented me with a sweet smile.

"May I help you?"

I recognized her voice: Miss Grammar-pants.

"Yes, I'm here to see Mr. Conway?"

"Senior or—"

"Junior."

She tap-tapped again, and frowned at her computer.

"I'm sorry, did you have an appointment?"

I glanced behind her at the two doors, one to my right and one at the back. I had a fifty-fifty chance.

"Thanks, he knows what this is about," I said over my shoulder, and headed right, for door number one, the one in no-man's-land. Junior didn't get the mountain vista, I was betting.

As I entered, the man inside startled like a deer. He half-rose behind his desk while one frantic hand clicked and moved the mouse of a large desktop computer. The computer pinged, and then fell silent. Roland Conway, Jr.'s pale-blue eyes met mine. His were rinsed hot with something. Irritation, maybe?

No. Fear.

He stepped around his desk.

"I'm sorry. Who are you?" The deep voice belonged to someone much heftier than the man before me. One of Mother Nature's little tricks, to keep her entertained.

I put out my hand.

"Tenzing Norbu. We spoke earlier, Mr. Conway."

He ran his right-hand fingers through his hair, pushing back thin bangs. They resisted his efforts to tame them and flopped back onto his forehead.

"I'm sorry," he repeated. "I wasn't expecting any appointments this late."

I waved at the door vaguely. "A misunderstanding," I said. "No need to apologize."

His jaw muscles tightened. He wanted to say more, but good manners, like good grammar, are hard habits to overcome, something I was counting on. He gave my hand a damp squeeze and herded me into one of two small armchairs set against the wall to one side of his desk. I sat and looked around the Spartan room, no bigger than a monk's quarters. The walls were empty and painted an insipid green. The industrial carpet was gray and flecked with tiny blue-and-green accents, like confetti. Between the armchairs, a small, pie-shaped table held a single eight-by-ten silver-framed photograph of a beaming clan, of Conways I assumed, in all their multigenerational glory. Many rows of smiling, straightened teeth. Next to the photograph sat an orchid, also too perfect-looking to be real.

Roland Conway, Jr. took the other chair and angled his body firmly to block any view of his empty desk.

He doesn't want me near that computer.

"What can I do for you, Mr. Norbu?"

I held up the insurance documents. Best to get straight to the point.

"You can tell me why you are stiffing my client, G-Force."

His expression hardened. "I already told you . . ."

"Comma or no comma, you guys don't have a leg to stand on, and you know it as well as I do."

He licked his lips and swallowed. His Adam's apple rose and fell.

What is he so afraid of?

My gut rang like a bell. A clear answer, the kind I have come to trust as truth. I voiced the message out loud.

"Are you being forced into this decision by Horace Latimore's nephews, Roland? Are they blackmailing you?"

He stood.

"This meeting is over," he said. "And unless you or Mr. G-Force can afford what it will cost to legally contest our finding, so is his claim. Tell your client if he doesn't like my decision, he can sue me."

I arose from my chair, bowed slightly, and left his office without another word, an alternate plan already forming. First, I checked on Grammar-pants. She remained thoroughly engaged in her typing. I reached in my pocket for the Starbucks gift card. I bent it into an L-shape while moving, in silence, to the emergency exit. I leaned against the panic bar until the door cracked open slightly and slipped the bent card between the spring latch and the jamb. Hopefully, somewhere outside this building, a small green edge of plastic was sticking out like a tongue. I let the door return to a closed position, soundlessly. With any luck, the card would hold. With any luck, I hadn't just destroyed 95 dollars' worth of free coffee.

I stopped by the front desk on my way out. Miss Grammar-pants was now intently reading her computer screen as she scrolled.

I peeked.

Facebook posts. So I wasn't interrupting the rolling wheels of commerce.

"May I ask you a question?"

She turned to me, her mild features arranging themselves into a pleasant-enough smile.

"Is CAII family-owned?"

"Family-owned, family-operated," she said. "We've been in business for over sixty years. Mr. Conway, Sr.'s father started the company. After he died, Mr. Conway took over, and then Roland, Jr. joined *his* father, straight out of Cal Poly graduate school."

"Are you a Conway, too?"

"Almost." She held up her left hand. A small diamond winked at me. "I'm engaged to Roland the Third. He's just finishing up business school at Cal Poly."

"Just like Dad. Very impressive," I said.

"Oh, yes. It's a wonderful company to work for. We're known for our excellent personal service. Look!" She motioned to the wall of plaques proclaiming said superior service, both civic and otherwise.

"Very impressive," I repeated.

I smiled my thanks and left. CAII's website said the offices closed at six, so I didn't have long to wait. I hunkered in the cramped front seat of the Dodge, out of eye-view, and tried to keep from falling asleep. Soon, an older, rotund version of Roland Conway, Jr. left the premises. The father's remaining strands of hair, more platinum than sandy, had been reduced by time to a feathery horseshoe of fringe. Junior's future.

He claimed a dark-blue Audi sedan and took off. Roland, Jr. was next, ear pressed to his cell phone. He climbed into a dark-maroon version of the same Audi. I jotted down the plate numbers, just because. Finally, the female future-Conway locked up and left. She climbed into a lowly Honda Civic with a dented door. Maybe she'd get an Audi for a wedding present.

I moved the Neon to the far end of the lot, by the Dumpsters. I waited for another hour, meditating with one eye and one ear open, which meant not very successfully, and then I waited some more. The sky began to darken slightly, turning the distant hills into smudges of dark brown. Fluorescent office lights blinked off up and down the bland building. Worker bees left their hives, one by one.

My formative years in the monastery, marked by relentless routines, were challenging enough. I'd last ten minutes in a place like this.

Once the area had finally emptied of cars, I reached behind the seat for my go-to nylon sports bag of detective tools and fished out a pair of thin latex gloves; a small Maglite; and the poor man's slim jim, also known as a wire clothes hanger. I also grabbed my dark-blue hoodie, good for cool nights, or clandestine jobs.

My phone pinged. A text from Bill: HEADED BACK TO YOUR PLACE.

So I'd guessed wrong again. Still, his return meant I wouldn't have to face another round of feline tail-twitching and flattened ears. HOME BY 10, I typed. HELP YOURSELF TO WHATEVER. FEED TANK, PLEASE?

I pulled on the gloves and hoodie and moved to the back of the building. It abutted an empty expanse of weedy and unkempt land fenced by industrial chain link and claimed by a blaring construction company sign. I was looking at the next Westlake Village lot slated for development. A narrow concrete walkway paralleled the stucco structure, and I jogged along its length until I reached the approximate middle. I aimed my flashlight at a few exit doors and found what I was searching for: a small piece of green plastic beckoned like a little flag, inviting me to enter. Score one for me.

I messed with the wire hanger until I had fashioned a narrow, triple-strength hook at one end. Pressing the protruding flap of card securely against the jamb, so it wouldn't move or fall, I slipped the curved end of the hanger inside and jimmied it until I managed to catch the hook around the panic bar.

I had one chance to make this work.

I lowered to one knee and tugged downwards, keeping the pressure steady while leaning away from the door. Just as my mind was declaring how ridiculously lame this idea was, the door gave slightly, enough for me to use my fingers to widen the gap and then reach through to leverage the panic bar and pull the door open.

Seconds later, I was inside. My heart was racing. Even though I had checked for motion detectors earlier, my ears half-expected the harsh blare of an alarm.

The dark space waited and watched, silent.

I crossed to Roland, Jr.'s office. It, too, was locked, but this lock was child's play, and I quickly gained entry with the help of a paperclip borrowed from the desk of Miss Grammar-pants, and my trusty Starbucks card.

I crossed to the computer and used my flashlight to find the power source. I switched it on, and the computer hummed to life.

Let's see what you've got hiding in here.

The screen lit up with some generic space-themed background, and I waited for the parade of icons—access files into Roland's private world—to start marching across the screen.

And waited.

And waited.

After a minute, I realized that what I saw was all he had: a single icon denoting his hard drive, and a second image I ignored for the moment. His computer desktop was as empty of clutter as his real one. I clicked to open the hard drive, but it was password protected. I didn't know nearly enough about the man to start guessing, and my computer-hacking knowledge was just as limited.

I focused on the second icon, which was purple and cream and shaped oddly, like an . . .

What on earth . . . ?

A faint sound outside chilled my blood. I powered down the computer, switched off my Maglite, and snuck back to the door. Peering around the doorjamb, I saw a dark figure leaning against the front entrance, his flashlight dancing from wall to wall. He tapped the flashlight against the frosted glass, then cupped his hands around his eyes to look inside.

I held my breath. *May I be safe and protected . . .*

He moved on. A security guard, making his rounds. I stayed where I was until any immediate danger of discovery had passed. But I didn't dare investigate further. Something had made the man suspicious. He'd be back this way soon.

I relocked Roland's office door, slipped out the back exit, and was in the Neon and aimed toward home within minutes.

An onion.

For some unknown reason, Roland Conway, Jr. had a small, purplish onion icon on his computer desktop. I had no idea what it symbolized, but I had the next best thing: Mike Koenigs, cyber-genius extraordinaire. He was my source for all matters digital, and given his nocturnal habits, he was just about to start his day.

"Onion? Sure, I know what it is." Mike's voice rose from the cup holder, where my phone was nestled.

I sped along the 101 at 75 miles an hour listening to my phone while gripping a Starbucks egg salad sandwich with one hand and the steering wheel with the other, just another typical SoCal multitasking driver. A few years ago, I would have pulled me over in a heartbeat.

"Anything else on his desktop, boss?"

"No. Just that and his hard drive, which was password protected."

"And what did you say the guy does?"

"Insurance adjuster. Works with life insurance claims. Why?"

"Because the man is flat-out paranoid. There's only one other person I know who is that careful about keeping his digital footprints invisible, and you're talking to him."

A glop of egg salad dropped somewhere out of sight. Served me right.

"Explain, please?"

"Dude uses Tor."

"I'm sorry . . . ?"

"The Onion Router. T-O-R. Get it? Spells Tor. I'm surprised you haven't heard of it, especially now that you're so buddy-buddy with that FBI agent."

"First of all, Gus and I haven't spoken in months—she's way too busy with her promotion and her new girlfriend. And second of all, this is me, remember? I'm still getting the hang of my iPhone. Which is why I have you, my friend. So I repeat, explain, please? I have about twenty more minutes of driving ahead of me."

I heard the distinctive pop of an aluminum top, followed by a slurping sound, followed by a sigh of pleasure. Mike was fueling up with his first Red Bull of the day.

"So, Tor started as a Navy project. Some smart dudes at the Naval Research Lab developed it as a way of protecting top-secret government communications. Ironic, right, because now Tor's the only way Joe Citizen can protect himself from that same government."

"But what *is* it?"

"It's an anonymous routing tool. You know, so no one can analyze your traffic, get inside your virtual pants, so to speak."

"How does it work?"

"Like any other browser, except unlike Firefox or Safari, say, this one doesn't leave an obvious trail. So, most searches? They move in a straight line, from point A to point B, and leave a clear route back to a wealth of data for whoever wants it. Tor directs your requests onto, like, twisty impossible-to-follow paths. Virtual tunnels and anonymous circuit-hops and random encryption keys and erasable footprints. There's no way anyone can trace your communications back to you, okay? The ultimate protection against Internet surveillance, in all its nefarious forms. It's genius."

"And you use Tor?"

"You bet. Me, plus, let's see, the military, journalists, whistle-blowers, anarchists, human rights activists, corporate wonks, cops—lots of cops, especially underground ones."

"And criminals?"

"Oh sure. Many, many criminals. Everybody's got skeletons to hide."

Roland, Jr. jumping up from his desk. His hot eyes and damp handshake. Everybody's got skeletons to hide.

I turned into my driveway, tires crunching against the gravel. Bill's old Volvo sedan was parked to one side of the garage.

"Thanks, Mike. This has been a huge help."

"No problem, boss. Next time I come by, I'll set you up with Tor if you like. Shoulda thought of it earlier—God knows what kind of file the NSA's got on you."

The kitchen light was on. Through the window, a weary Bill slumped at the table. He lifted a bottle to his mouth, and I could almost taste the cold snap of hops. I headed inside.

"Hey," I said. I leaned down to stroke Tank as he wove figure eights between my ankles.

Bill half-hoisted the distinctive, chunky amber bottle belonging to one of my prize Redhook Pilsners. He grunted, as if toasting defeat. Two more empties stood guard, witnesses to his glum mood.

I quickly grabbed one of the two remaining Pilsners from the fridge and joined him.

"Martha still mad?"

"Good guess, Sherlock."

I let the sarcasm pass, choosing instead to enjoy my first swallow of crisp honey and malt. A second long pull, and I was ready to try again.

"How about Mila? Any word from her?"

"Nothing yet." Bill tipped his bottle sideways and watched as a final droplet of beer gathered and swelled on the glass-necked rim, as if preparing to make a jump for it.

At the last possible moment, he stopped the spill with the tip of a finger.

"Ahhh, sooo," Bill said, and wiped his finger on his pant leg.

"That's supposed to be my line."

"Not today, O Mysterious Man of the East. I've already had three Redhooks. My turn to dispense some Zen wisdom."

I decided not to remind Bill, for the millionth time, that my Tibetan Buddhist roots, shared with the Dalai Lama, were from the Gelug—or Yellow Hat—tradition. For Bill, everything spiritual west of Long Beach was Zen.

I took another sip of beer and said nothing.

"I've been thinking about this whole marital communication thing, wondering if I ever actually understood the basics."

"I hope you aren't going to ask *me* what they are."

His chuckle was hollow. "Didn't used to be anything like it is now, you know? Way I was raised, you never showed your feelings, never let on what was really happening inside."

I waited. I knew there was more.

"You know, because if you did, nine times out of ten, you'd get the crap beat out of you."

I reflected on my own past experience, which was mixed to say the least. I'd learned early on not to reveal anything of significance to my father. He wouldn't beat me, but for sure he'd mock, ridicule, or punish me in some other way. My mother was a different story. Personal confessions didn't anger her, but rather tended to unleash dual tsunamis—of guilt on her part and shame on mine. I wasn't sure which reaction made me crazier, but I did know the echoes of these past patterns continued to resonate, warping expectations of all my present relationships.

Bill crossed to the refrigerator and retrieved the last beer. Tank lifted his head from his cat bed. His emerald eyes blinked twice at me, as if to say, "Look out for your pal over there. He's had three already."

"I was pretty fucking good at toughing things out," Bill said, sitting again. "Traffic. Patrol. Security gig at that hellhole called Bosnia—don't even get me started on that. Then life in the L-A-P-fucking-D, where most days I see stuff I don't want to think about, much less talk about after work. So I don't do either. But Martha, she does. She wants to know how I'm feeling, every fucking minute. I don't know how to talk to her about my feelings, Ten. I don't even know how to talk about them to myself. Jesus, I'm so screwed up."

I knew from past experience that at three beers, Bill had already sailed an unhealthy distance down the river of memory, toward the Sea of Infinite Regret. Pretty soon we'd both be adrift in the Meaninglessness of Life Itself and while we're at it, Just What the Hell Was God Thinking When He Made It So People You Love Die?

I gently removed the bottle from his hand. His eyelids started to droop, and I was plotting how to get him onto the sofa when his cell phone buzzed. Bill snapped awake like the well-trained cop he was, and snatched up his phone to read the screen.

His face lit up, and he dropped several decades before my eyes.

"It's Mila!" He answered. "Yes!" Listened for a few moments. "Thank God," he said. Then, "Right, I'll work on it and call you back."

Bill slid his phone into his pocket, his eyes flashing. "Okay, here's the deal."

A blip of joy registered as the familiar words transported me to our early days in Robbery/Homicide, when Bill, fully engaged in a case, would present his latest findings to the team. *"Okay, here's the deal."* I was momentarily happy that the Bill I used to know and admire was back. But I dreaded the cause.

"Sasha finally got in touch with his mother," Bill said. "He's not dead and he didn't get kidnapped. He told Mila not to worry, he's safe. He's gone underground, says he's onto some traffickers."

"That doesn't sound safe."

"Yeah, I know. The kid's got game." Bill's pride was unmistakable. I hadn't realized you could experience paternal pride when you'd only invested 20 minutes or so in being a father, but there's a lot about being a father I didn't know. Like, everything.

An unattractive little voice in my head, the one not wearing the red robe and Yellow Hat, piped up: *Yes, well, maybe the kid's got game, or maybe he's just as dumb as a bucket of bolts.* I kept the snarkiness to myself. All I needed was to be jealous of my ex-partner's newly discovered son, on top of everything else. As it was, I was going to have to chant for days to clear out the growing pile of mental deficiencies I was generating around this current mess.

"I'm glad Sasha's okay. Is he on his way home?"

"Not exactly. Mila told him to come back but he refused." A small smile played across Bill's face. "Looks like I gotta go to Bosnia. Want to come with?"

I covered my face with my hands. Maybe if I couldn't see Bill, he'd go away.

"Kidding," he said, "I gotta do this on my own."

Now, perversely, I felt insulted. Wasn't I the missing persons expert these days? I opened my palms like flaps and found his eyes with my own. "I remember a wise detective named Bill Bohannon telling me once to beware of those three-beer 'gotta do' somethings."

"I hear you," he said.

"Yes, but are you actually listening? Bosnia, Bill? Seriously? I can think of so many reasons why that's a bad idea."

"I know," Bill said, but his eyes had taken on a gleam I recognized.

"Sasha doesn't need to be rescued, he as much as said so," I bleated. Stress was causing the pitch of my voice to rise, but I ploughed ahead. "He's not a kid. He's nineteen. Remember nineteen? Remember how convinced you were that you knew best? You do this, and you're guaranteed to mess up your father-son relationship before you've actually even met. And what about Martha? What's she going to say if you just take off?"

"And if I don't go? What if I never hear from Mila or Sasha again? Ten, I need to know who my son is."

My own skeletons stirred, trailing heavy feelings like chains: of powerlessness, of the constant push and pull between parents. I'd never been anything more than a pawn in a lifelong, ugly chess match, a game they were bent on playing out to the bitter end.

It's hopeless. You'll never fix it.

"Thanks a lot."

I must have murmured the thought out loud.

I snapped out of the memory-trance. "Sorry, that wasn't meant for you. Old wounds again. I spent my childhood caught between two parents. Now you're caught between two families."

"No, I'm sorry. I hate dragging you into all of this."

"Forget it. Stuff comes up." I shrugged. "Doesn't mean I don't still think you're making the wrong decision."

He rubbed the knuckles of his right hand with his left, as if itching to throw a punch. "It feels like a test, you know?"

"Of what?"

"I'm not sure."

"Pretty tough to pass it, then."

"I know." Bill checked his watch and stood. "Shit, look at the time. Gotta go."

Another *gotta*. His steam was up. I had one maneuver left.

"Sure you want to drive with three beers in you?"

"Really?" he said. "That old ploy?" And he was out the door, his steps light.

I was beyond exhausted yet too stirred up to sleep. This was becoming a habit. I moved outside to the deck. Tank leapt onto my lap. I read somewhere once that owning a cat lowers your blood pressure. I alternated between ruffling and smoothing the fur on Tank's back as he purred, half-dozing. I waited for the medicine to take.

What if I was wrong? What if I was meant to go to Bosnia with Bill? I just couldn't think straight.

"Here's what I do know, Tank," I said. "Going where you don't want to go to do something you don't want to do is a perfect recipe for resentment."

I could feel the front edge of a headache descending like the angled blade of a guillotine. I dug my fingers into the tight muscles at the base of my skull and kneaded. The blade receded a little.

Maybe I didn't want to face the hurt look on Martha's face when she discovered my betrayal.

The moon was up, illuminating the scrub oak and manzanita with a night-light of blue. The glowing sphere was just past full, as if someone had taken a paring knife to one side. A soft breeze drifted across the dark canyon and brushed my cheeks, its breath cool and slightly salty.

Or maybe it was simple: I just didn't want to leave my place of refuge for a broken land, still torn and bleeding from a recent war. Weariness crept up my back and settled in my shoulders. I had been awake for over 18 hours. I hoisted Tank in my arms and carried him inside for his tuna water nightcap.

Bill would do what he had to. So would I. I'd get back to my own work, to G-Force and his money, in the morning.

Everybody has skeletons.

Bill's had put on flesh and walked back into his life. Roland's might be harder to locate in the present, but I was certain the key to unearthing them lay somewhere in the past.

CHAPTER 9

"Mr. Norbu? Mr. Norbu! You need to wake up now."

I groaned. I'd overslept, by at least two hours.

"I cleared up your desk. I fed your cat. And also I made you coffee. Here."

A skinny arm shoved a fragrant mug under my nose. I elbowed upright, making sure the duvet continued to cover the necessaries.

"Thank you, Kim." I took the mug. "I'll be right out, okay?"

Once upon a time, I had declared to Bill that if I ever got busy enough to need a personal assistant, I would check myself back into the monastery. Might as well have sent a direct message to the gods in charge: as of two months ago I had found myself hiring Kim for Mondays, Wednesdays, and Saturdays—ten hours total.

This was apparently one of those hours.

I dressed quickly, skipping the shower, and soon was inspecting a desk pristine enough to rival Roland's. Kim hovered over it like an anxious mother.

An angular twentysomething, my new assistant would have fit right in at one of Mike Koenig's underground electronic music events—spiky black hair, scrawny limbs, and bits and pieces of metal piercings protruding from both ears, her lower lip, her right eyebrow, and probably other places I didn't want to give much thought to. She'd answered my ad in the classified section of the *Topanga Messenger,* and I liked that she was local and affordable.

Other than being a potential lightning hazard, Kim was working out well. She could clear up bewildering tempests of disorganization with ease, she was happy to make a trip to Whole Foods whenever necessary, and she was very handy with computers. Not Mike-handy, but a major step up from Tenzing-handy. Tank approved of her, and she approved of Tank. She was also relentlessly cheerful, which I appreciated most of the time.

I marveled at my now-spotless desk. "Kim, you're a genius."

"Thank you, Mr. Norbu. What's next?"

Kim rarely wasted words, or time, another plus.

"Please, call me Ten."

I jotted down a quick shopping list: cat food, coffee, organic chunky peanut butter, chopped raw liver bits from the butcher section, and another six-pack of Redhook—all my little household's essential staples. I watched her chug away in her boxy Scion with a surge of relief. I really needed her help. I really resented the intrusion. The shorthand version of my relationship-challenged life.

I carted a second mug of coffee to my desk. After a swift visit to Google, which did not offer up any suitable resident's telephone number, I instigated a phone number search with that most elementary of tools, AT&T Direct. Sherlock would be so proud. I could always go to one of my paid services if this didn't work. The nice recorded voice on the phone immediately provided me with the numbers for two Roland Conways, one in Studio City, one in Mission Hills. Time for a quick "pretext" call. I decided to use my office fax line, the one that was blocked. No need to let anyone on the other end know who was calling.

I looked at the two phone numbers. Fifty-fifty, again. I chose Mission Hills.

"Hello?"

The voice was warm, but maybe a touch elderly.

"Hi, I'm not sure if this is the right number or not, but I found this wallet. At a Starbucks? The license says it belongs to a Roland Conway?"

"Oh," the woman said. "Oh dear, he must have stopped there on his way to golf. You're very kind. How did you get this number?"

"Directory assistance." That, at least, was true. "Listen, I'm happy to return it to him. I'm still in the neighborhood. I'll just need you to verify the date of birth, you know, just in case?"

"Of course. Eleven-nine-forty-three."

Shoot. Wrong Roland.

"I'm so sorry, this Roland Conway is about twenty-five years younger than that."

"Oh! You must mean Rolly, our son," she said. "February 29th, 1968. Leap-year baby."

"That's the one," I said while jotting the date down. "Do you have Rolly's cell phone number?"

"Just a minute. I know I have it written down some-where, oh! Here it is." She recited the number and thanked me again, profusely. I felt a momentary twinge of guilt until I remembered Roland's priggish mouth and pale, guilty eyes.

With a legal name and date of birth, and by first enter-ing the required prviate investigator's license number, I had enough of a scent to sic the hounds of Merlin, TRACERS, and LexisNexis onto Roland's trail. I added a national back-ground data search for good measure. If he had so much as an overdue book, I would soon know about it.

I crossed the living room and stepped behind the folding screen for time on the cushion. Last year, after abandoning any spiritual practice for months, I'd made a pledge to Yeshe and Lobsang to reestablish a twice-daily routine of inner exploration. Oddly, but inevitably, the time I expended sit-ting somehow translated into getting more done during the rest of my day.

While my computer minions were at work, I sat for a full 30 minutes counting breaths, allowing feelings to rise, swirl, and recede, and again calling upon my personal protectors to bring clarity to my friend Bill and ease to his wife.

I forgot to ask for easeful success in my own current endeavor. I soon was scrolling through the various reports on my screen with dismay. Roland's record was as pure as the Buddha's intentions: no bad debts; no traffic violations; no civil, state, or federal convictions; no drug habit; no divorce; no registered guns; no nothing.

So what was he hiding?

What would a man need an untraceable search engine for?

Oh.

I returned to the screen, took a deep in-and-out breath, and logged onto the State of California's sex offenders website. A few years back, I would have had to leave my house and pay an actual visit to a police station or two, but now, thanks to the latest iteration of Megan's Law, I could search for his name online. With my mental fingers crossed, I signed the disclaimer that said I wouldn't use this information to harass anyone, entered Roland's last and first name, and "Los Angeles" where it asked for county.

And found myself looking at a picture of Roland Conway, Jr., younger and more innocent-looking, but unmistakably the same man.

My first thought was, *How very sad.*

My second? *You creepy bastard.*

The birth date was the same, as was the height, but he'd added at least 20 pounds in the weight department since they'd last asked. His offense was 311.11a, possession of obscene matter depicting a minor. There was no indication of any conviction, which was strange. He must have been able to afford superior lawyers and somehow gotten off with a misdemeanor slap of the wrist and a fine—they probably had the whole thing expunged, which was why nothing had turned up in my earlier searches. But any sex offenses involving minors, including possession of kiddy porn, are as hard to remove as permanent ink. Unless Roland Conway, Jr. had a direct line to the governor, he would stay on this list for the rest of his life.

And if he were ever caught indulging in his dirty habit again, he'd go straight to jail.

I had found Roland's skeleton, with one short computer search. How hard could it have been for the Lunzy boys to do the same?

I knew what came next, but decided to take a very hot shower first. I felt polluted by Conway's behavior, and needed badly to scald the toxins from my pores.

Kim entered the kitchen, nylon bags bulging, just as I was heading out to the car. I'd already called Roland on his cell. He was meeting me in his office within the hour.

"I am back. And you are leaving," Kim said.

"Thanks for doing the filing and shopping. Great work, as always. See you in two days."

"But I have twenty-five minutes left." Kim started to chew at her lower lip, and the metal stud click-clicked against her teeth, like a code signifying distress.

She really was an odd person.

"Well, why don't you go ahead and put away the food, if you like. And give Tank some of the liver bits. He'll love you for life."

"Yes, Mr. Norbu."

"Ten. Please. You're making me feel so old."

But Kim was already busy unloading.

Roland's handclasp was even damper than before, and his eyes wouldn't meet mine. The reception area had been empty of fiancées—Saturdays and Sundays the office was closed—and I had made sure both the front doors were securely locked before confronting him in his private lair.

I wanted more than anything to wipe Roland's sweat from my palm, and his compulsion from my consciousness.

"I know what they have on you, Rolly," I said. "I know what you want to keep your family from finding out. I checked the sex offenders site."

He opened his mouth. Closed it again. His entire torso slumped, as if weighed down by a blanket of lead. He still wouldn't meet my eyes.

I waited.

"It happened while I was at business school," he finally said. "I just, I was working so hard. I never had time to relax. A friend turned me onto these," he swallowed, "these certain kinds of movies."

My phone buzzed in my pocket. *Not now.*

"I didn't know they were under age. I swear to God!"

"And that made it okay."

"No," he said. "No, it didn't."

"And what about now? What's your excuse now?"

"What do you want? What are you going to do?" he asked.

"Look, I'm not a judge. And I'm not a jury. I'm just a private investigator trying to get what's fair for my client. So what I'm going to do is sit in this chair and wait, and what you are going to do is make out a check for thirty-three thousand dollars to Godfrey Chambers. Then you are going to make absolutely sure that check is covered by sufficient funds."

Roland moved to his desk, sat, reached to turn on his computer, and then thought better of it. He pulled a checkbook from a side drawer and filled out a check by hand.

"I don't know how I'm going to explain this," he muttered.

"Maybe you can start by telling the truth," I said. "To yourself, first and foremost. I can promise you, from personal experience, that way lies the only hope you'll have of ever finding freedom."

He passed me the check, his hand trembling.

I paused at the door.

"And just so you know, I have a good friend who works for the FBI. From now on, you, Rolly, are officially on her radar. I suggest you cease breaking the law."

I left him studying the flecked carpet, as if counting the ways he'd messed up his life.

CHAPTER 10

I gave G-Force a call from the parking lot. The background din of car-washing machinery announced I had caught him at work. Saturday was auto-upkeep day for many.

"Yo, Ten! Right in the middle of things here. Whatcha need?"

"I have a check for you, G."

"Come again?"

"Your money from Horace. I got it."

"No way. Unh unh," he said. "You pullin' my leg."

"I have it right in front of me. I assume you can deposit a check for thirty-three thousand made out to Godfrey Chambers without getting arrested, yes?"

"Aw, man. Don't know even what to . . . to . . ." His voice thickened. "Shit, man, you getting me all choked up."

I was touched. I'll admit it. "So, should I bring it to you?"

"Here? Naw. Crap neighborhood. I get off work around three. How 'bout we meet at that coffee place again, the one with the sissy-ass food. Hell, I'll even buy."

"I thought you hated yuppies."

"Yeah, but now you got me my money, I'm practically one myself, you feel me?"

"I do. I do feel you, G-Force."

"You actually did it. Sheee-it," he said, and hung up.

I coasted south toward West Hollywood on a cushion of good feeling. This was work at its best: see the problem, fix the problem, avoid the misery.

Saturdays were my personal upkeep days as well. Next stop, Yvonne's. I hoped she had her shears sharpened.

I parked in the alley lot behind the salon. Yvonne used to work out of Topanga, but she moved to West Hollywood to attract a higher grade of clientele, mainly men and women who wanted more than just a trim, or, in my case, a buzz. But wherever Yvonne went, I would follow. Anyone can mow a lawn of hair like mine, but no one else's scalp massages came anywhere close.

My phone buzzed again, insisting I pay attention. Martha had sent me a text: CALL ME.

My buoyant mood evaporated.

At first, my return call was answered with dead silence.

"Martha? Are you there? It's Ten."

Finally, a whisper. "Bill's gone. And it's all my fault."

Tears sprung to my eyes. Shocking to me. Unbidden. I inhaled deeply, and lowered my shoulders on the equally long exhale.

"Martha, listen. There is no such thing. Nothing is ever just one person's fault. These situations are like a dance, and this one is far from over."

"You're wrong," she said. "It's over. He's left me and I don't know what to do."

"Is anyone there with you?"

"No. Yes. I mean, no, but Julie's coming later; her plane lands in a couple of hours."

Julie.

"What about the girls?"

"Television. They've been watching for hours."

"Martha, I have a few things to do, but I will come to see you later this afternoon, as soon as I can, okay?"

"Thank you." Her voice cracked. "I didn't know who else to call." She hung up, and my headache finally landed a vengeful punch of pain on the right temple.

Yvonne was waiting at her post in all her full-bodied, hoop-earringed, brunette glory, and I fell into the salon chair with a groan.

"That bad, eh?"

"Sorry," I said. "It's not me. It's my friend. He's messing up, big time. Know any good therapists?"

"Funny you should ask." Yvonne winked at me in the mirror, then swung my chair toward an attractive-enough, thirtysomething woman sitting to my right, dressed in a black velour tracksuit. Her hair bristled with enough foil to signal a fleet of UFOs. *Matronly,* I thought, dismissing her.

"Ten, meet Stephanie. Stephanie, meet Ten. He needs a therapist. For his," Yvonne air-quoted the word, "you know, 'friend.'"

Stephanie, to her credit, didn't miss a beat. "Tell your friend you know a brilliant and fascinating therapist with almost-awesome highlights." Her eyes, like Tank's, were an exceptional shade of green. Also like Tank, she used them to both look at me and *see* me.

Okay. Not so matronly.

A young Asian boy, maybe three years old, ran up to my chair. He was clutching a wooden truck. "VROOM! VROOM!" he yelled while driving it up and down my right arm. I looked around the salon for his mother, but came up empty.

"Hey, you. Where'd you come from?"

"He's mine," Stephanie offered, amused.

"Mine! Mine!" the boy echoed, giggling. He rolled his car across my chest and down the other arm.

"Sorry, usually he'll have nothing to do with strangers. Connor, come here, sweetie. Don't bother the nice man."

Connor's lower lip pushed out, but he lifted his car from its human track and moved to his mother. A shadow brushed across Stephanie's face. "My son's Cambodian," she said. "I think you remind him of home."

A friend once called me vaguely Asian. I guess Cambodian also qualifies.

Yvonne wheeled me around to face the mirror again.

"Enough chitchat. Same as usual?"

"Same as usual."

In the past, you could tell by the length of my hair which parent had me in their custody. At my father's monastery, I sported a barren cue ball, like all the other novice monks. Back in Paris with my American ex-patriot mother, I would endure a month or so of embarrassing fuzz until my hair had grown out to a tolerable inch or so. But Valerie was a recovering hippie and refused to let me cut it at all. Any additional hair beyond that inch meant black bristles going off in all directions, like a clothes brush assembled by committee. Unless, that is, I resorted to gelling it into submission—then I was a perfect candidate for The Human Magic Marker.

These days, I maintained the ideal inch-long buzz cut. The monthly commitment to hair preservation was a pain, but on the positive side, the process usually took only 15 minutes, and Yvonne spent the other 15 kneading the knots from my overworked skull.

"Let's go."

I followed Yvonne's confident sway to the sinks, where she shampooed my head into a foamy cap, rinsed, conditioned, and then started in with an extended scalp-rub. I almost groaned out loud, her strong fingers felt so good.

"Be nice to Stephanie," she said, when she had me nice and drugged. "She's had a hard life. Was even working the streets for a while, if you can believe that. Single mom. Lives for that boy she adopted. And from everything I hear, a helluva shrink. Someday she's going to make someone a very happy man."

"Thanks for the nudge, Yvonne, but I'm not looking."
Especially for another wounded bird.

"Fine. I'm just sayin'." She toweled my head dry with maybe a bit more intensity than was called for and marched me back to the empty chair. She draped a fresh towel around my neck, plugged in her clippers, and got to work.

Stephanie's eyes met mine in the mirror. The clear green of her gaze was intense, but relaxed. *Okay. Not so wounded.*

"So, you're a therapist?"

"I am. A clinical psychologist, to be precise. I specialize in abuse victims. PTSD stuff."

"Hmm."

"Adolescents, mostly."

The skin on my forearms puckered, as if pricked, into little bumps of recognition. The Sufi tradition holds that whenever your soul has need of a new teacher, the teacher will come, as if drawn to the flame of that need. Just another way of saying there's no such thing as coincidence.

"So you work with young girls?"

She checked on Connor's whereabouts. He was vroom-vrooming his wooden car up and down the far wall.

"Mostly. Victims of early sexual trauma. Also violence. Early childhood abuse, for the most part." Her eyes darkened. "Although lately I've been hired by the city to counsel more and more youngsters who are casualties of human trafficking."

The pricking sensation turned into full-on chills.

"Where, here?"

Her smile was grim. "I'm afraid so."

"I'm surprised."

"Join the crowd. People like to think human trafficking only exists overseas—in places like Russia or, or . . ."

"Bosnia?"

"Bosnia. Exactly. But it's a multibillion-dollar industry, and its reach is worldwide. California's one of the top destination states in North America, and Los Angeles is now considered a major hub. These days, even the local gangs are getting involved, with some of them intersecting transnationally. I could go on and on."

"Okay, Ten. You're good to go," Yvonne said.

The teacher had arrived. But I had run out of time.

Yvonne whisked the towel from my shoulders and dusted off my neck with a chubby pink brush. I rubbed the top of my head. The consistency was that of cropped sod. Perfect.

I fished two twenties and a business card out of my wallet. I handed the money to Yvonne and the card to Stephanie.

"Stephanie, may I call you later?" I glimpsed Yvonne's satisfied smirk, and quickly added, "I'm dealing with a situation that involves human trafficking. I'd love to talk shop with you."

"Of course." Stephanie handed me a card of her own. "And I promise that next time I won't look like a science experiment gone very, very wrong."

I laughed. I liked her. She reminded me a little of Julie. I glanced at her card.

"Your office is in Santa Monica? I'm not too far from there. Topanga Canyon."

"I hear Topanga's beautiful. I've never actually been up there," she said. "Maybe someday."

I decided to ignore the hint, if that's what it was. The new me. A year ago, I would have upped the flirtation, just in case I needed an ego-lift later in the day. As I headed out the back door, little Connor ran to block my exit.

"Mine!" he shouted, grabbing my knees. "Mine! Papa! Mine!"

I peeled him off of my legs and fled.

I had just enough time to order a yuppie-certified meal of chai latte and a grilled flatbread sandwich before G-Force strolled inside. He caught me reaching for my wallet.

"I got this," G-Force said, and counted off 20 singles from a folded wad of tip money.

We sat at "our" table. I passed G-Force his check. He studied it closely. Finally, a high beam of delight illuminated his handsome face.

"Shee-it, Ten. No wonder you so pricey." He tucked the check away with care. "Sure there ain't nothing I can do?"

"Actually, I did think of something," I said. "G-Force, I heard some information today that surprised me a little. Do you know anything about gangs getting into human trafficking, local gangs, I mean?"

G-Force went very still. He lowered his voice, leaning close.

"I been hearin' some about that shit, yeah. More and more lately. It's the comin' thing, you feel me? Brothers call it *running meat*. I ain't thought too much about it though; idea makes me sick."

He stopped talking as a slim waiter in skinny black jeans, a pumpkin-colored T-shirt, and plaid Converse high-tops delivered my meal. It was a beautiful thing to behold: creamy, melted buffalo mozzarella, tinted green with pesto and layered between fresh tomato slices, dripped from both sides of thick grilled slices of sourdough. There was even a dish of extra pesto, as well as some sort of roasted tomato spread, and in case the slab of sandwich didn't satisfy, a side salad of baby greens.

I looked across at G-Force. He was eyeing my oozing sandwich with something akin to horror. I ignored him.

"What exactly have you heard?" I took a huge bite. Using my thumb and forefinger, I severed the string of mozzarella stretching like a thin hammock between the bread and my mouth.

"It's big business, man. You got your Asian gangs doin' it, you got the Mexicans and the Salvadorans doin' it, and now a bunch of new playas comin' in from those places used to be Communist. Everybody want a piece."

Interesting. Just what Stephanie was saying. I slathered on extra pesto and kept eating as my mind filed away the confirmation from a second source.

"Gangstas, they all about di-versa-fication these days," G-Force mused.

The waiter came by with a pitcher of water and refilled our glasses. He checked my plate, but I still had more than half a sandwich to go, which I guarded with both hands. G-Force waited until he had moved out of earshot again.

"Cartels tryin' to branch out, see. They scared shitless the politicians gonna make dope legal. Just a matter of time, ask me, before a man can stroll down to the corner store, buy his weed and blow. That happen, how the poor brother in the hood goin' make a buck? Dope trade drying right up soon, everybody knows it. Everybody looking for other options."

"And you're suggesting *people* might be the new commodity." *Running meat.* A chill snaked up my spine.

"Ain't saying it right, but it's happening."

"What about your old crews? Are any of them in on this?"

G-Force grimaced.

"Okay. Well. Wish I could say ain't got nothing to do with Bloods or Crips, but like I said, I been hearing things. Not so much about making dudes work in fields and motels and shit—but running hos on the side, yeah, they doing more and more o' that. From what I hear, some of the local Bloods even called a truce with each other. They working together, sharing territory and shit."

He took a sip of ice water. His eyes narrowed with thought.

"Like I said, whole idea give me the creeps, but now that I think on it, it's the ab-so-lute perfect business for brothers to be in!"

"How do you figure that?"

"Think about it, Ten. If you dealing dope, you gotta always be growing more. Harvesting, hauling it around, paying your crews. Other brothers picking leaves and trimming weed."

"So?"

"So if you're dealing hos, you don't need to do all that shit! Supply's endless! You work it right, you can even sell the same one over and over a bunch of times."

"Treating human beings like inventory."

"Yeah."

"There used to be another word for that, G."

"Yeah?"

"Slavery."

G-Force blinked at me.

"Shee-it. That the truth, brother," he said. "That the goddamn gospel truth."

CHAPTER 11

Traffic in L.A. is a giant force field, like gravity or the tides—never exactly the same, always something to be reckoned with, and the subject of millions of conversations a day. Depending on my mood, and how freely the vehicles are moving, my driving experience in Los Angeles can range from a joyous sheet-metal ballet to a steady repetition of patient breathing.

Expose me to no flow at all, no forward motion of any kind, as had been the case on the 101 for the past ten minutes, and I devolve to a place of equally immovable rage. I sit and steep with resentment at the perceived unjustness, the direct evidence that some angry god is meting out punishment for a random unskilled action from a past life. I ask you, what about that is fair?

I leaned on my horn, as three decades of Buddhist commitment to impersonal nonattachment flew right out the window. Everything about this logjam was personal, and aimed at me.

I sat back and relaxed my jaw muscles, which were by now fully clamped. I could be stuck here for hours. I called Martha.

"Bohannon residence."

My heart cartwheeled.

"Julie! Hi. It's, it's me. Ten," I said.

Silence.

My entire body contracted. "So, umm, I told Martha I would come over, but the traffic is suddenly horrendous. It might be a couple of hours, if it's a SIG alert, you know, if they've shut down a lane. Sig Sigmon's the guy who invented a device in the fifties for letting radio stations know . . . shit, never mind, I'm babbling. I'm going to be late. Is that still okay?"

"I'll put her on," Julie said. Nothing else.

What were you expecting, a parade?

"Ten?"

Her voice still sounded weak, but I definitely detected more Martha in there. Julie must be working her magic.

"How are you doing, Martha? Do you still want me to come over?"

"No, sorry, I'm going to bed. Tomorrow, okay? If it's not too much trouble?"

"Of course." I was shocked at her timidity.

"Don't worry, Julie won't be here. She's taking the girls to Griffith Park for the day."

No, but, but . . . I wanted to say, but didn't. "I understand. I'll stop by in the morning. And Martha?"

"Yes?"

Up ahead, the solid block of cars shifted from a frozen to a flowing state, for absolutely no discernible reason.

"Whatever you're feeling right now? It will change, that I can promise."

I hung up, my attention pulled like a dowsing rod to the fresh, bittersweet pressure newly lodged in my chest. Bill was gone, and Martha was hurting, but neither was the cause.

Julie was back, and my heart had suddenly remembered how to hope.

My car and I flew home. Tank was waiting at the kitchen door. He stalked, stiff-legged, to his empty bowl.

"I shouldn't do this," I said, removing the container of liver bits from the refrigerator. Usually he only gets liver every few days. A pair of sharp cat paws scaled my leg as I chopped the raw meat into bite-size pieces. "Ouch! Stop!" I moved him aside with one foot. "Guess who's back in L.A.?"

Tank rolled onto his back and aimed all four legs skyward, his feline salute of approval.

"That's right. Julie." I set the bowl on the floor and Tank flipped upright and raced to his dish before I could change my mind. "Eat up. I'm going to meditate. We both need to build our inner strength for whatever's coming next, buddy."

I stepped around the screen and offered a small bow of acknowledgment to my personal shrine. The battered suitcase, now topped with two planks of redwood, was repurposed into a meditation altar, covered by the discarded maroon robe from my earlier incarnation as a novice Tibetan lama. Though the small statue of the Buddha still occupied the center, my collection of offerings had multiplied over time and now included two photographs I had brought back from India following my father's death. I'd discovered the picture of my mother while clearing out my father's things. Valerie was maybe 19. She smiled into the camera, her gaze direct, unclouded as yet by alcohol or pills. Light-brown hair fell in waves to her waist, and her tall figure was graceful, as if designed for the sari draping her slender curves. But it was the light around her that entranced the camera's lens. She glowed as if illuminated from within; she was transcendently beautiful. No wonder my father had fallen so hard.

The other photograph was of Appa and me, more than a decade later. His outstretched arms looped a white silk *khata* around my ten-year-old neck, the reward for completing my ordination as a novice monk. My head was bowed, my father's expression stern. If I squinted my eyes, he almost looked proud.

I scanned the rest of my mementos. The red-tailed hawk feather from my first hike in Topanga Park, a shell from Zuma. A tiny jade carving of the Goddess Tara, also from my father's things, now sat in serene silence next to the mangled bullet that had grazed my right temple and changed my life. I enjoyed the irony of the juxtaposed symbols.

A kind, grizzled face caught my eye. I picked up the program from John D's memorial service two months ago and studied his features, smiling in the photo printed on the back. My heart caught as I remembered his final 24 hours of life. I'd spent most of them at his side, holding his papery, mottled hands in mine as I matched the reedy ebb and flow of his breath. John D was my first paying client and would probably always be my favorite. During one of our long, epic talks about life and death, he'd "allowed as how" he wouldn't mind having someone like me by his side when his time came. I never forgot.

As a young monk, I'd sat with more than one dying elder, but the moment of John D's passing was uniquely his. And mine. Uniquely ours. His breathing became so shallow his chest barely moved, and I knew death was close. I hummed passages from the *Bardo Thodol*, gentle reminders to my friend to let go of any remaining attachment to his singular bodily form, and to dissolve consciously into the eternal oneness of space.

I'd closed my eyes, and felt into his breathing with my senses, until I could barely discern any breath at all. I repeated the sutras more and more softly, as I was taught, until the sounds were more vibration than vocalization. Then this: radiant light, illuminating my inner field of vision, and a heart-based surge of joy. Waves of bittersweet bliss merged with parallel waves that seemed to come from John D's still form. The joy amplified—he was loving me, I was loving him, and a flowing, growing synergy connected and coursed between us.

A barely audible *Ahhhhhhh* escaped from John D's throat, a long, slow out-breath. The in-breath never arrived. Only a hallowed silence, marked by my own pained smile of recognition. For John D's final utterance was no death rattle, but rather a sigh of pleasure, the same exact sound he'd always made after lowering into his beloved Barcalounger at the end of a long day.

I set the program back on my shrine. I no longer wanted to meditate. I wanted to talk to Yeshe and Lobsang. To connect with two living, breathing hearts, in real time. I needed my friends.

I crossed the living room to my desk, fired up the computer, and opened Skype. A tiny Yeshe-image beamed from my screen, no bigger than the postage stamps I'd used for all those years when I'd communicated with my friends by letter. The Internet had made such things obsolete, but sometimes I still missed the sense of calm that came when I put pen to paper.

I connected, and typed into the message bar: *You there?*

Seconds later, a reply popped up: *Yes. I'll go get Lobsang.*

Soon their two wavering faces filled the desktop, grinning from a monastery office thousands of miles away. Yeshe sipped from a teacup. Lobsang toasted me with his, and 8,000 miles couldn't hide the twinkle of mischief.

"*Tashi delek!* We're just now enjoying that tea you love so much," Lobsang said. "Our sister monastery sent us a special offering from their yaks!"

Yak butter tea was the staple beverage of Tibetan monasteries, and still considered a treat in India. As a young lama, I'd barely tolerated the pungent brew, at times the only hot drink to be had on cold Dharamshala mornings. The greasy swill was a far, far cry from the rich, sweet *chocolat chaud* of Parisian cafés, warm nectar I inhaled like a deprived bee whenever I was returned to my mother.

Lobsang slurped a large mouthful and followed with a contented belch. "Care to join?"

"Very funny," I said, smiling.

"*Tashi delek,* Tenzing!" As usual, Yeshe's voice was louder than necessary. He didn't trust the new technology. His face moved closer, tipped to one side. "You look tired!"

"I am." They waited, happy to allow the silent connection between us to simply be. "I miss you," I said.

Yeshe touched his forehead, his smile shy.

"It is always a happy day when we see our dharma-brother's face," Lobsang said, "but especially today."

Something in Lobsang's voice suggested their morning had not been entirely untroubled either. "Is there unrest in the *Sangha?*"

"No more than the usual," Lobsang said, "but sometimes these young monks can be infuriating. Much more infuriating than we were at their age."

"I'm sure."

"This morning, they handed us a petition," Yeshe broke in. "A petition! Can you imagine? They say they need new equipment! You remember how, when we were boys, we worked with worn-down little pencil stubs? Now all the novices want to read the scriptures on iPads."

"Huh," I said. "I seem to remember the Buddha saying something about change being inevitable, Mr. and Mr. Skype. Better watch out. Next thing you know, you'll be on Facebook."

My friends exchanged an embarrassed glance.

"Don't tell me."

"The Dorje Yidam page goes *live* next week," Yeshe admitted. "Twitter, too."

"Apparently we need to build our platform, whatever that is, if we want to generate enough donations to finance the new roof." Lobsang frowned.

"Not to mention all those new iPads," I said, and Lobsang's scowl deepened. I laughed at his familiar expression of outrage. I'm pretty sure he was born with it.

The conversation had taken a very different direction than I'd imagined, to great effect: I'd forgotten why I felt the need to talk to them in the first place. But like a reverse blessing, the realization of the absence of pain brought the pain right back, and the Bohannons' struggles, Julie's return, even Roland's unearthed skeleton of shame triggered a fresh flood of unease. I shuddered, as if aftershocks from long-ago fault lines had shifted under my feet. Yeshe and Lobsang had been the only stabilizing factors during the hardest, most vulnerable years of my life.

They still were.

"Let me tell you what's been going on," I said. I sketched out the Bill situation and his ill-founded decision to go to

Bosnia. I added in the human trafficking angle, and touched on Martha's pain, and my own fears around the situation.

"Also, uh, Julie's in town. You remember Julie, Martha's sister? Anyway, she's here to, you know, to help Martha. Her sister."

"Ahh," Yeshe said, "and so we reach the core. Your heart is attached and therefore expectant, and with that comes unease."

"What core?" I said. "There's no core. I'm pretty much over her."

They said nothing.

"It's been more than two years," I added, irritated for some reason. "Anyway, a lot's been going on. And so, yes, I'm tired, but not the kind of tired sitting with my eyes closed will cure."

Yeshe bowed his head, deep in thought. He raised his eyes to meet mine. "You once told us that you live near a park, a place where you can be in nature, yes?"

"Good memory. Yes, Topanga State Park." I hadn't been there in a few years.

"I think you would benefit from getting your feet off city streets."

Lobsang's face broke into a grin, as if cheered by his own thought. "*Hon, hon*—yes, yes! Take a hike! Isn't that how Americans say it?"

They had zeroed in on something, for sure. Suddenly, I couldn't wait to get outside. "Thank you." I touched my forehead. "*Chagpo nang,* take care, my brothers. As always, you bring clarity to my muddled state."

"*Chagpo nang.*"

Fifteen minutes later my feet were pressing against Topanga Park's crumbled earth, baked by the summer sun, yet somehow fragrant with life. The sun was low in the sky, and a golden wash painted the woods with an air of warm mystery. Rather than running, I had driven the short distance to the park and left my car at the Trippet Ranch lot.

I stepped onto Musch Trail, and into a swarm of memories as thick as mosquitoes. At first, I tried to outpace the pesky thoughts. Walking briskly, I wound in and out of the sun and shade, my path dappled with subtle shifts of light. Two miles in, I hit Eagle Junction and hiked up the looping trail toward Eagle Rock. I longed to soothe my eyes with the sweeping panoramic view looming over the canyon.

I stood, panting, at the high outcrop of boulders, the park bathed in a golden sheen below me, when a thought swooped, hawk-like, into my consciousness: I had stopped coming here because I associated this place with Barbara Maxey, the catalyst for my first case as a private investigator. My first failure of a case, I should say.

I scanned the landscape below, orienting myself, and finally found the narrow streambed that led to the campsite, the one where Barbara had spent the last moments of her mortal existence. I hiked back down the trail and searched my way through trees and underbrush until I was standing by the little brook where she had slept, peacefully I hoped, until her past overtook her. I leaned against a tree she, too, might have leaned against, near the spot where her sleeping bag was discovered, her strangled body still half-zipped inside.

Finally, I was ready to meditate. I lowered to a sitting position, my back against the peeling bark of a eucalyptus tree. I closed my eyes, each breath slower and deeper than the one before, and went on a second search, this one inside.

What was this guilt about? Why hadn't I been able to put it aside? Light played over my eyelids as answers began to float up: I had failed her, failed to see her essence, to understand who she really was and what she really wanted. We had shared only a brief moment in time, but I could not wade past my expectations and judgments and actually connect with her, heart-to-heart. Instead I had remained trapped inside my head and oblivious to her needs. A day later, she was dead.

THE FOURTH RULE OF TEN

If I had connected with her—really seen her—would it have altered her destiny? Would she still be alive?

I breathed deeply, down, down, through the squirmy sensation of guilt and into its hot, tight core. The sensation began to shimmer and change with my breathing. A memory floated up, something my latest ex, Heather, had told me she'd learned during her psych rotation, while training to be a pathologist: guilt has only one positive use, as motivation for change. Only when remorse for past actions leads to constructive deeds in the present can balance be reestablished, or, as the Buddha might say, karma restored.

But what exactly was the positive action I might take? What would demonstrate I'd learned something from Barbara's case? I let the question dance in my head, light as a dust mote.

Nothing.

I started to chase the mote—tried to capture it in my fist. And then Yeshe's warm, quiet voice gave me the answer, the same one he'd given since we were both children: *The answer will come in time. Let go.*

So I did. I let go of my thoughts and let the awareness return to my bodily sensations. A faint feeling of guilt was still there, but like shattered glass, it had broken up into smaller components. Fear, anger, and a kernel of something else I couldn't quite put a name to. Something hot and hard and less easy to dissolve.

Shame. I felt ashamed.

Memories flickered, almost like a slide show, situations where my father had shamed me, especially about my feelings toward girls, well, toward one girl in particular. Pema, my first love. Her face glowed in my memory, standing in a pool of light by the monastery kitchen. Her face was radiant with an inner glow, just like . . .

. . . my mother's luminous features replaced Pema's.

I had never understood my father's seemingly automatic need to humiliate me. Now I did. The shame, the humiliation, was his! My very existence had brought disgrace on him, and was a constant reminder of his own wrongdoing. I had a sudden urge to laugh, sitting alone in the woods. Appa's shame around me wasn't even my business! It had nothing to do with me, and everything to do with him.

My problem was that I had taken it personally. Easy to see why—it was beamed at me from the earliest moments of my existence. But there was no need for me to keep taking it personally anymore. As I sat, eyes closed, I tossed the small, hot kernel back across time and space to my father. That was his problem, not mine.

Inside, an ancient twisted place un-kinked itself.

Every time I assumed an old wound was healed, it managed to reappear in my path. Was I doomed to always walk in circles?

A new thought percolated. *Maybe it's not the same wound, but a higher version of hurt, which requires a higher version of healing. Maybe it's not a circle, but a spiral.*

I opened my eyes and stood, placed my hands in the prayer posture, and bowed toward Barbara Maxey's final resting place. *I promise to listen for the next right action, the one that will bring meaning to your death.*

Darkness had descended, a comforting cloak. Time to go home. I felt refreshed and recharged, as if I'd dropped yet another burden I hadn't known I was hauling. I offered a second, telepathic bow of gratitude to Yeshe and Lobsang, back in the monastery. *Thank you.* Once again, my dharma-brothers had been right: I had needed to take a hike.

As I strolled toward my car, a cruising park ranger paused to lower his car window. "Any stragglers back there? Park's about to close."

"Nope. No stragglers. Just a couple of ghosts," I said.

He nodded. "Plenty of those here. Don't feed 'em they won't bother you."

Good advice.

CHAPTER 12

The insistent buzz dragged me from a dreamless sleep. I grabbed my vibrating phone from the side table. Bill, calling from Bosnia, at three in the morning. Not a comforting combination.

"Mmff."

"Sorry to wake you up, Ten, but I need your help with something." Bill's voice was loud, clear, and accompanied by a roaring sound, as if he were stationed inside a wind tunnel.

"Where are you?"

"Bathroom. Specifically, the men's room in the basement of the central *policija* station here in Sarajevo. Not to worry—I'm not under arrest. I checked in with the locals as soon as I landed."

"Good. I was worried about you."

"No need. So listen, I, uh, I picked up some intelligence from the cops here. That's where you come in."

Picked up was Bill-speak for reading something he picked up off of a random desk when no one was looking. I'd learned the art of half-truths from a master.

"Whatever you need," I said. I was almost awake. I padded to the kitchen, filled the kettle with water, and set it on the stove to boil.

"Can you do some surveillance on a building for me? Soon? As in, now?"

I grabbed a pen and Post-it pad from my junk drawer. "Where?"

"Out by Van Nuys Airport." He rattled off an address and I scribbled it down.

"What am I looking for?"

"Sasha," he said.

"Wait, he's here? In L.A.?"

"Maybe. At least, I don't think he's in Bosnia anymore. The last anybody here knew, he was on a bus, heading for the airport. And the other end of this alleged deal he's investigating is in Los Angeles, plus, maybe, Seattle, I think? Whatever. The local cops seem to be all over it on this end. They're trying to be helpful, or at least pretending to be. They even gave me a little office to use."

"In the bathroom?"

He laughed. "Yeah, well the *policija* here are . . . well, let's just say they've got many loyalties, not all of them mutually compatible. I'm pretty sure the whole building is wired up the wazoo, including my temporary office."

"Right. Bugs."

"Bugs. Probably for as long as there's been bugging. I mean, hell, the Russians alone listened in on anyone and everyone they could, neighborly or not, back when this was all still one big happy Yugoslavia. I doubt if anybody was inclined to take out the wiring, even after Russia stopped being Russia."

The kettle was whistling. I scooped loose leaves into a one-mug infuser and poured boiling water over the mixture of half-jasmine, half-green tea. The tart fragrance hit my nostrils like perfume.

"So anyway, long story short, here in the basement crapper they have a hot air hand-dryer that roars like a 747," Bill said. "I'm using it as an artful disguise."

"How do you know they didn't bug the hand-dryer?"

"Smart ass. So, can you pay a visit to that address for me?"

"I can." The caffeine hadn't hit my bloodstream yet, but the prospect of a predawn excursion had already worked magic on my adrenals. Nothing short of a tranquilizer dart would get me back to sleep. "Do you have a picture of Sasha you could e-mail me?"

"Don't need it. He looks just like me, only with dark hair." His voice caught a little on the words *just like me.*

I pictured Bill—tall, lanky, firm chin—added thick brown hair and subtracted a mustache. "Other than his one call to Mila, has anybody heard from him?"

"Not that I know of. I haven't been able to get hold of Mila today. She's not answering her cell phone."

"So, how do you even know he's back here?"

"I don't. I told you. But it's the best shot I have at the moment. The guys upstairs seem to think Sasha's somehow gained access to the same information they have on these bastards. The bad guys weren't the only ones following Sasha's blog. But this address is all, and I mean *all*, I could get my hands on. I need eyeballs and boots on the ground."

The whole thing sounded a bit desperate, but I kept that opinion to myself.

"When are you coming back, Bill?"

"Not sure. I want to check out my end here a little more first. You can reach me on my cell if anything comes up. I'm set up for calls, and the reception's better than home. You're coming in clear as a bell. Crazy, right?"

"You're talking to a man who just got his first smart-phone a couple of years ago. It's all crazy to me. I'll be in touch."

I changed into black jeans, a black T-shirt, a black baseball cap, and black Nikes. I added a black windbreaker. I unlocked the gun safe in my closet and retrieved my newish 11-ounce Smith & Wesson Airlite, black matte finish, but a rosewood grip. What can I say? I'm a sucker for wooden handles. The compact revolver looked more like a popgun, but the seven rounds of .22 Magnum bullets it could hold told a differ-ent story entirely. My Wilson Combat would always be my first choice for hazardous duty, but this little guy was better suited for small jobs of an unknown nature.

What was I forgetting?

Right. Tank. I scooped dried cat-kibble into his bowl. Unless absolutely necessary, he wouldn't budge until 6 A.M.

or eat until 7, but knowing how these things work, I took precautions in case the exception happened.

I closed the door silently behind me. Tank clocked in at close to 18 hours of snooze-time almost every day. Resting was one of his spiritual superpowers, and I tried, as much as possible, to avoid disturbing his practice with my own comings and goings.

Traffic was sparse, and 25 minutes later I was taking the Sherman Way exit off the 405. I spotted my goal seconds before the brisk, sunny female voice on my phone's GPS told me my destination was ahead, on my left.

This was apparently my week for long, low industrial buildings. As I drew closer, I noted this one was the color of wet cement. The area, with its close proximity to an airport, must be a freight destination—I'd passed several similar warehouses as I approached. The side facing me appeared to house at least half a dozen businesses. Loading bays with roll-up doors divided the one-story structure, all of them dark, deserted, and sealed up tight. No lights inside. No trucks or cars outside. If something was happening, it was happening on the other flank of the building.

I checked for higher ground to use as an observation point. There wasn't any.

My Neon executed a neat, tight 180 and I retreated several blocks before cutting over to approach the building again from a different angle. As I edged closer, the little hairs on the back of my neck suddenly stood up.

Someone's watching me.

An LAPD car slid out of the dark alley I'd just passed and pulled directly behind me. I checked my rearview mirror. Two uniformed officers in the front seat. Back seat, empty. The passenger-cop reached out an arm, and the sharp, single *woot* of the siren made me jump, even though I knew it was coming. The officer at the wheel gestured me to the side of the road. I pulled over and sat still, hands in plain sight on the steering wheel.

So far, not so good.

Nothing happened for 30 seconds or so, and I used the time to slow my breathing. I assumed they were running my plates. Finally, the driver's side door opened and expelled a burly cop straight out of central casting, as Bill liked to say. Mustache? Check. Steely eyes? Check. Beer and donut-belly making a slow creeping escape over his belt? Check, check, check. He hitched his pants, unsnapped his holster, and approached my window with the slow swagger that says *I got all the time in the world, asshole.* "License and registration, sir."

I handed them over, along with my business card, which included my private investigator license number. His breath was more of a slow wheeze. He studied everything, double-checking that the names, and I, matched. At least he was LAPD. I tried, but couldn't recall meeting a single cop from the Van Nuys division. No names to drop. I'd have to rely on my innate Tibetan charm.

He lowered his meaty face to window level.

"Private detective, huh? You working a case?"

"Yes," I said.

"What kind?"

Technically, this was none of his business, but I was pulled over on a deserted street in his jurisdiction in the middle of the night. Not the ideal time to remind him of that fact.

"Missing person," I said. "Runaway kid."

He handed me back my papers.

"I'll let you know if I see any."

Was he joking? I met his eyes. They were hard as flint.

"Okay. Thank you, Officer." This seemed to mollify him a little.

"So what makes you think the kid's back here?"

I waved in the general direction of Van Nuys Airport and manufactured a semi-lie. "His father gave me a tip he might be squatting somewhere near the airport."

He shook his head. "Like I said, haven't seen anybody."

I murmured another "thanks" and pulled away in my little Neon, feeling a bit like a runaway kid myself.

My exit route took me straight past the back of the building. Bingo. Three vehicles were parked in front of one of the bays. Narrow windows blazed with fluorescent light from inside.

And two upstanding members of the Van Nuys LAPD were still trailing me, a block or two behind.

Time to call off my surveillance project for the time being. I connected with Sherman Way again and headed back toward the freeway. The police car peeled off, and I lost sight of it.

The freeway ramp rose to my right. At the last minute, I drove past it, motivated partially by stubbornness, and partially by a sudden, acute need for human fuel.

Sadly, at this hour, Taco Bell was my only choice, but at least it had its own private lot. I parked and walked inside to study the menu, a symphony of bad choices. Finally, I settled on a low-fat bean burrito (fresco style) and a Diet Pepsi to go—the memory of that Van Nuys officer's bulging fast-food belly was still a little too "fresco" on my own mind to go wild. While I waited for my paper bag of food, I pondered his odd response when I'd said I was working a missing persons case. Most officers' first reaction would be to ask for more information: "Boy or girl?" or "What's the kid's name?" or "When was he reported missing?" This guy didn't seem interested in anything beyond moving me along.

And why didn't the second guy get out of the patrol car and move to the passenger side of my car, also standard procedure for that situation? What kind of uniform lets his partner carry out a middle-of-the-night stop solo, with no visible backup? There was no reason to stay in the car, unless you didn't want to show your face.

I climbed back in the Neon, unwrapped my burrito, and took a bite of beans, onions, red sauce, and *pico de gallo*. Not too bad. I poked my straw into the plastic cup lid and washed the burrito down with a long pull of slightly metallic carbonated liquid. At moments like this, Dorje Yidam felt like a world—and several lifetimes—away.

I chewed and swallowed bite two, this one not nearly as satisfying, for whatever reason. I couldn't decide if my suspicions were useful intuitions or just middle-of-the-night paranoia. I'd been awakened partway through a sleep cycle and sent on a crazy, potentially dangerous errand. The combination of fatigue and adrenaline could be manufacturing fear-vibrations where there was nothing to fear. Wouldn't be the first time my body chemistry induced expectations of danger as my mind turned a routine cop-stop into a criminal conspiracy.

As novice lamas, we were urged to be mindful at all times, to concentrate on choosing right thoughts and right actions. The right action for most people was to return home, get some rest, and make a new plan. The wrong action? Circle back under the freeway, park my car on a dimly lit side street, and attempt a stealth approach on foot. Wrong, and unwise.

But I was no longer a lama, I was a P.I.—and I had already come all this way.

I found a perfect spot, not far from where I'd been pulled over. A mere seven-block walk through a series of alleys would eventually spit me out close to the building. I checked my revolver cylinder, confirmed seven rounds, and tucked the Airlite into the right pocket of my windbreaker. I pulled the baseball cap low over my forehead. As I made my way into the gloom of the first alley, a chilly breeze brushed against my back. I always forget how cool Southern California pre-dawns are, even in midsummer.

I paused at every block to look for my Van Nuys friends, but they must have finished their shift, and so I continued the slow creep from alley to alley, hugging the shadows, until I reached my goal. There were still lights on inside and three cars parked out front: two black luxury SUVs and a BMW sedan with tricked-out wheels.

I squinted to make out the sign on the door:

Agvan Supply, Inc.
"We Supply the Very Best"

If this was indeed a human trafficking operation, some-body had an ironic sense of humor. And if somebody had an ironic sense of humor and was in the human trafficking business, that person was very dangerous.

Agvan. Something about that name was familiar, beyond the obvious "We need something original that starts with an A" marketing ploy. I set the thought aside for now.

I scanned the length of the side street, up and down. Still no activity, but the sky was growing lighter. Soon, early bird commuters and airport travelers would be hitting the road.

Once again, I balanced the wise versus the unwise. Wise? Get backup of some sort. Unwise . . . ?

I drew closer. There wasn't any side access that I could see, only the wide, ridged, metal roll-up doors, firmly unrolled, and the front entrance with the sign on it. From what I could tell of the roof, it was flat, with only a single large, round ventilation fan occupying its surface.

The roof, then.

At least this was a one-story building. I skirted the shadows on the opposite side of the street, darting across at the last possible minute. At the far end of the building, a Dumpster unit was conveniently pushed up against the wall. I eyeballed its height and realized the Dumpster, plus me, wouldn't be tall enough to reach the actual rooftop. Then I spotted a blue recycling bin.

Okay, now I was getting into really, really *bad idea* territory.

I wrestled the bin up onto the Dumpster and positioned the Dumpster so the pair of thick rear wheels was jammed against the warehouse wall. A chant of protection from my early training leapt into my brain: *Palden Lhamo, protectress who performs all pacifying deeds, pacify my illnesses, hindrances, and ghosts.*

I shimmied onto the Dumpster and after a few awkward attempts successfully hauled myself onto the top of the bin. I slowly stood upright, my feet wide apart. For one terrifying moment the bin seemed to buckle and tip beneath my legs. I shifted my weight, as if I were surfing, and the bin miraculously steadied, hindrances pacified for now.

I vowed to call upon Palden Lhamo more often.

From there, it was a fairly easy jump-and-pull onto the roof. It was also the point at which I left behind the official sanctions of my private detective license and became either an ex-monk with unwise habits or a flat-out delinquent. If my Van Nuys buddies happened to find me, I had no doubt which one they'd pick.

I was curious, though. Curiosity—genuinely seeking to explore and understand the unknown—is in constant danger of suppression by the forces of dogma, fundamentalism, and force. Therefore, genuine inquiry must be encouraged. Or so my justifying mind insisted, as I started my illicit creep along the rough surface of the roof.

I headed straight for the ventilation unit, which offered the best options for snooping. About 20 feet away, I was hit with a pungent blast from the fan. My salivary glands instantly erupted into song, but it took a few minutes for my brain to catch up. Curry! Real, home-cooked, Indian curry accosted my nostrils. I zipped back across time and space to Jogibara Road, a narrow thoroughfare in Upper Dharamshala, lined on both sides with an amazing array of restaurants. Our monastery diet was uniformly and deliberately bland, so the occasional outing into town meant a gourmet feast for our noses and, on the rare instances when we had money, our bellies. Then, rupees clutched in our fists, Yeshe, Lobsang, and I would head for the Malabar and order the spiciest *biryani* on the menu.

I sniffed the air. Was I smelling actual Indian food, or just Indian spices? My nostrils sent back the report: real food, recently cooked, and from the intensity of the gusts pouring out of the fan, in large amounts. Next question—were they feeding a truckload of people or just cooking a truckload of food?

I squatted close to the fan to peer inside. I saw only spinning metal and darkness. The assembly was solid as a rock. I had met my dead end.

I backtracked to the end of the building. This time, I lowered myself until I could hang by my arms and drop onto the actual Dumpster lid, avoiding the treacherous blue bin. My gut told me any protection from hindrances had just about run out.

I stood next to the Dumpster, thinking. Fatigue crept up my shoulders and into my neck.

Probably a good idea to head home . . .

The impulse came out of nowhere, hijacking good sense and sending me sprinting like a prankster to the BMW sedan. I gave the trunk a hard shove, and ran like mad across the street and into the shadows of the alley. Car lights flashed and the horn emitted a series of rhythmic blares. I patted down my windbreaker and paused at my left-hand pocket. *Ha!* I still had the small binoculars I'd used to track down that ridiculous stolen hairless Chihuahua. At least that case was good for something. I lifted them and focused onto the front of the building.

The door of the office opened. A thickly built man stepped outside, aimed his keys at the BMW, and with one click silenced the alarm. A second man materialized behind him, slighter in build, but otherwise very similar in appearance. His left arm was bent, and the fingers of his left hand wriggled and plucked the area just below his ribs incessantly, as if strumming an invisible sitar.

The first man waved the other back inside. He made a cautious tour of his car, expanded his inspection to the rest of the lot, and then walked with a slight sway in my direction, all the way to the curb. I stayed perfectly still in the inky darkness, binoculars glued. He double-checked both ends of the street, affording me a close, clean view of his face. He had narrow eyes and a square block of a head topped with a bristly crew cut and set on an equally square, truncated neck. His black jacket was of soft, expensive leather; his watch was big and gold; and his jeans were several salary levels above Levi's. He looked to be in his fifties.

He moved like a muscle-bound wrestler back toward the open door of the office. I spotted a desk inside and a dark-skinned woman, perhaps Hispanic, parked behind it, and little else. As he reached the door, he glanced up. I followed with my binoculars, and only then found the tiny surveillance video camera, just above the lintel.

Busted.

The door closed behind him. A smart man would go straight to the security monitor next, to double-check, see what he could see. I had to assume this guy wasn't lacking in intelligence. I dashed back through the alleys and jumped into my car. I was out of practice speed-sprinting, and my breathing was ragged. I fired up the Dodge and aimed for the freeway entrance. This time, I took the on-ramp, and I was lucky I didn't launch into space. I opened the driver's side window. Wind buffeted my face. I opened my jaws wide and bellowed, letting the airstream carry off a metric buttload of nervous energy. Twenty minutes later I was home.

Tank's food was untouched, and he didn't so much as twitch a whisker when I entered the bedroom. I unloaded the Airlite, returned the bullets to their box, and locked both revolver and ammunition in the closet safe. Four hours had passed since I'd started on this wild hunt for Sasha.

What a complete waste of time.

Well, not completely complete. I did have a name, *Agvan Supply.*

I made a proper pot of coffee, and got to work.

Agvan Supply had a website—rudimentary, but functioning.

They claimed to be distributors of fine gourmet foods, specializing in hard-to-find edibles. Color photographs of three such items dressed up the front page of their website: a sheep cheese from Bosnia, mangoes from India, and *medjool* dates from Algeria.

I remembered Julie telling me about these foodie websites. She, like other chefs, used them on occasion to purchase delicacies: once, an Israeli saffron for her bouillabaisse, and another time, for a private event, a pale-white mushroom found only in Japan.

I highly doubted Agvan Supply had chefs like Julie in mind as customers, but I resolved to keep my mind open for now.

The photographs of fresh produce were professionally done, and beautiful. That said, Bosnian sheep cheese and Algerian dates didn't do it for me. A heaping basket of mangoes, on the other hand, lit up my taste buds, prompting yet another wave of childhood nostalgia.

In India, two events were greeted with almost equal celebration—the refreshing drops of the first monsoon rain, cool and life restoring, and the arrival of the first ripe mangoes, healing in an entirely different way. The former provided instant relief from the relentless, oppressive heat of May and early June. Children ran through the streets to greet the rain, romping and leaping, their mothers too happy to remonstrate. Businessmen spilled out of office high-rises to stand in the pouring rain, their suits and ties growing soaked.

But mango season? That brought joy to the soul. Word would spread, magically, invisibly: *Mangoes! The mangoes are back!* Within an hour throngs would be crowding the bazaar to pounce upon the biggest and best the fruit stalls had to offer.

We were not allowed mangoes in the monastery. My father, as disciplinarian, forbade them. He considered them too sinfully delicious, certain to inflame our passions and make us wobble in our devotion to the austere pursuit of spiritual perfection. But I had a secret weapon—my mother. On two separate occasions, she paid a surprise visit to Dorje Yidam, and they happened to coincide with mango season. I've always suspected the mangoes, not me, were the real draw.

Before I was even born, Valerie—as she insisted I call her—had soured on my father, as well as his particular brand of austerity. She moved to Paris to raise me and take up another spiritual pursuit: the ultimate glass of chilled chardonnay. By the time I was walking, she was already adhering to a fairly strict religious regimen: approximately one glass of wine an hour from the moment she arose, late in the morning, to the moment she drifted out of consciousness, around 11 at night. She ultimately stabilized her spiritual practice, or should I say her practice of imbibing spirits, to a steady two bottles a day. While I seldom saw her falling-down drunk, I never really saw her sober, either.

Maybe we could have been close. I don't know. The alcohol was always there, between our hearts, like a wall of thick felt.

Valerie almost never talked about my father, but one day, in a wine-mellowed mood, she managed one confession: "Your father and I always had one foot in the bedroom, and one foot in the ring." I was only six, too young to understand exactly what she meant, but I hoarded and stored that nugget of information like a precious jewel. Decades later, during the "She-who-hates-cats" year, I found myself recalling my mother's description while repeating its pattern. Choosing to leave that contentious relationship with Charlotte proved surprisingly hard, but essential to my mental and emotional health.

Anyway, one March day, my mother arrived at the monastery doors in a flurry of silk and perfume and insisted on taking me on a driving tour of the villages surrounding Upper McLeod Ganj. I think I was around ten. Valerie didn't drink that visit, perhaps because of the heat, or perhaps because she couldn't find the right kind of alcohol anywhere close. But alcoholism is like a flea on a feral dog: it will not be deprived, and if scratched, merely jumps to another host. Normally noncommittal when it came to food—"Why

bother?" seemed to be drunk Valerie's attitude, "a full stomach only lessens the buzz"—on that day, dry Valerie latched
onto food to treat her disease. She ploughed through dish
after dish of hot curry, spicy enough to make her eyes water,
shoveling bites into her mouth with puffy torn-off pieces of
naan, to no avail. And then she found the cure, the pièce
de résistance. Mangoes, the king of fruits. I'm not saying
the withdrawal was pleasant for her—I remember her face
as painted with pain, as if her world had suddenly turned
vengeful on her. But even a discontent as prickly as hers was
soothed by the juicy flesh.

"Ahh," she'd said, standing by the fruit stall. The fruit
monger had prepared a prize Alphonso for her, slicing and
scoring each portion into squares before turning the skin
inside out so the little blocks of fruit opened and spread into
inviting, bite-size rows. He'd beamed as she scraped the sweet
flesh off with her perfect teeth, the juice dripping down her
perfect chin.

"Tenzing, you have to try this."

I remember watching, with pleasure and relief, how all
traces of misery had momentarily disappeared from her face.
Then I, too, tasted the orange, juicy flesh, and I, too, experienced guilt-laced pleasure.

"Good! Good!" the fruit monger had said to my mother.
"Make your boy smart! Make him handsome!" And I understood something in that shared moment of illicit gratifi-
cation. Valerie had as many rebellious feelings against my
father as I did. We weren't just wallowing in the sensory
sweetness. We were co-conspirators, using forbidden fruit as
a weapon against my father's oppression. The pain made the
pleasure that much more intense.

One foot in the bedroom, one in the ring.

Tank leapt into my lap.

"Good timing, big guy." I took several deep breaths,
detaching myself from the memory. Like a kite, its depar-
ture trailed twisted, melancholy streamers of sorrow. More
tangled evidence of the crazy, unconscious patterns that had

marked my relationship with my parents, complicated every relationship since, and probably doomed my time with Julie.

Let them go.

I focused back on the Agvan Supply website, one hand absently stroking Tank's back. I clicked around the site and found more descriptions of exotic products, such as Turkish halvah and Iranian pistachios.

On the "About Us" page was a single paragraph of text, no pictures:

Agvan Supply, Inc., formerly Tresinmerc, was founded by Yugoslavian brothers Milo and Jovan Stasic in 1945, and has remained a family business ever since. Following Jovan Stasic's recent passing, the company's ownership and operations have come under the direction of Mr. Stasic's nephews, Zarko Stasic and Stojan Stasic. The business name has changed, but the company is and always will be dedicated to providing the same high-quality service our customers have come to expect. Mr. Zarko Stasic says, "My father and uncle dedicated their lives to supplying quality product from around the world. We aim to continue that tradition. Agvan Supply's specialty is difficult-to-find foodstuffs; the rarer the item, the harder we will work to bring it to you."

A blocky, leather-jacketed body traipsed through my mind—a "Zarko" to be sure.

I printed this page.

"What do you think, Tank? Was that the man himself? Could it be that easy?"

If it was Zarko Stasic, he was working odd hours for a CEO. Unless, of course, some of the delicacies he was supplying were items that didn't travel well in the light of day.

I moved on to the "Purchase" page.

"We accept bitcoins," the payment form declared.

"Never heard of them," I said.

But when I squinted at the link to purchase these items with bitcoins, whatever they were, an odd feeling stirred in my belly, the one that straddles fear and excitement. The address was a long string of lowercase letters, numbers, and symbols, but that wasn't what caught my eye.

The final code in the link was: .onion/.

CHAPTER 13

I texted Mike: CALL ME WHEN YOU WAKE UP. I THINK IT'S TIME FOR TOR.

I texted Bill: NO JOY IN VAN NUYS. NO SIGN OF SASHA. CALL ME.

Then my head filled with fog.

I was due at Martha's later this morning.

Must take nap.

In seconds I had crawled under my duvet and slipped into that sweet space between waking and sleeping, the place where muscles loosen and the mind melts. Downward I headed, down, down when a niggling thought snared me. Something was wrong on that website. What was it?

The answer swam into focus: "Fresh Crop Just Arrived!" Words posted directly above the photograph of the heaped basket of Alphonso mangoes. Only Alphonso season in India was months past. Any mangoes left in the fields would be drowning under the monsoon torrents.

Finally, I slept.

Three hours later, midmorning summer sun baked my bedroom. I was sweating under the duvet. Tank's nose was close beside my ear as he emitted soft meows, doing his seductive best to wake me up. He didn't consider the dry food a proper breakfast—he never had. A proper breakfast came out of a can, and as amazing as Tank was, he still hadn't worked out how to open one for himself.

"Give me a minute."

Tank hopped to the floor and lowered onto his haunches, shooting me a death stare while I stretched out the kinks from my dawn Dumpster-clamber. Apparently, five minutes of stretching was enough. Tank stalked into the kitchen, tail high.

"Okay, okay."

I popped the lid on a favorite, Beef Feast, and served it to his royal highness. Tank's avid gulping was anything but regal. I waited until the contents of his bowl had been gutted, and his scratchy tongue and right paw started to address any residual beef that dared stick to his whiskers.

"Tank?"

He cocked his head, green eyes narrowing.

"Do you think I'll see her today?"

Tank blinked twice. I took that as a yes, and my stomach knotted accordingly.

My cell phone buzzed. Bill.

"Ten?" No roar in the background this time.

"That's me. Where are you?"

"In my hotel room."

"What hotel?"

He paused.

"Bill? In case Sasha turns up?"

He told me, and I scribbled the name on a Post-it. "Holiday Inn."

I crossed to my desk. In my state of exhaustion, I'd neglected to turn off my computer this morning. "You have your laptop there?"

"Yeah."

"Check out this website." I gave him the Agvan web address and waited.

"Got it."

"Now check out what it says just above the picture of the mangoes."

"Uh, it doesn't say anything above the picture of the mangoes. You mean above the dates?"

"No. Mangoes." I was staring right at it on my computer. Strange that Bill wasn't seeing the same thing.

I refreshed the page and sure enough, "Fresh Crop Just Arrived" now hovered above a picture of Middle Eastern dates.

"Okay, it moved. The thing is, earlier this morning the 'Fresh Crop' line was above the picture of the Indian mangoes. And that got me suspicious. It's not mango season in India."

Bill's cop-brain evaluated the slim slice of evidence. "And you're thinking maybe it's some sort of signal about what kind of human cargo is available? Right on the website?"

"Yes."

"Yeah, but it could also mean they're actually selling mangoes from someplace else and calling them Indian mangoes. That's a crime, but not a very big one."

"What do you think?"

"Definitely worth exploring," he said. "I'm not exactly sure how, though."

"I'll think up something," I said. "How are things going on your end?"

"I'll have to tell you later."

Did he think his hotel was also bugged?

I came in from an angle: "No hair dryer nearby?"

His voice acquired a sharper edge.

"It's late," he said. "I need sleep."

"At least tell me what's going on with you and Martha."

"Not now. Maybe you should investigate that yourself. Let's connect tomorrow, or I guess tonight, in your case."

"Have you heard from Mila?"

"Tomorrow!" he said.

He hung up before I could respond.

"This sucks," I told Tank. Despite the midday heat, I felt a chill. In my unsettled state, Bill was starting to sound not only like a cheating husband, but a criminal. I fled to my Shelby and fired her up.

A half hour later, I rang Martha's doorbell. Normally, I would walk right in, but these were not normal times. The small knot in my middle had expanded to the size of a tennis ball, and was composed of equal parts worry and anticipation.

Julie opened the door.

The expression that took control of my face had all the subtlety of a rhesus monkey's toothy grin, and I think we were both a little taken aback by it.

I tried to dial the corners down, but my goofy mouth wouldn't comply. I was just so happy to see her.

Maude and Lola crashed our reunion. They wrapped their arms around Julie's legs and clung from either side.

"Auntie Julie is here," Maude broadcast in my direction. Her face was solemn.

"I can see that," I said.

"She's taking us to the park, because we're sad. We're going to ride the train, and, and eat pocka-loo-loos."

"Pocka . . . ?"

"Popsicles," Julie said, her voice low. "At least, I hope so."

Lola, who had been quietly sucking on her fingers, removed them to add her own piece of news. "Daddy's on a trip," she announced, and replugged.

"Girls, go ask your mom to put sunscreen on you, okay?" Julie said, and they trudged back inside.

We met eyes.

"Hey, Ten," she said.

"Hey."

The delicious aroma of curry assailed my nostrils for the second time in 24 hours.

"You've been cooking?"

"For Martha," Julie said. "Mulligatawny soup."

"Ah, yes, distant cousin to the elusive rainbow pocka-loo-loo," I said, and was rewarded with a smile. A somewhat clumsy silence between us grew, and I shifted my weight, suddenly tongue-tied. Julie tended to have that effect on me. "So, this feels . . ." I scrambled for the right words.

"Awkward?"

"I was going to say, weird. But also, completely . . ." *Completely right.*

Martha appeared behind Julie, and the words died in my throat. Martha's actual body mass seemed to have diminished; she was swimming inside her bathrobe. Dark exhaustion ringed her eyes. She handed Julie a pink plastic bottle of sunblock.

"Can you do this? I can't seem to deal," she said. Her voice was dull. She crossed her arms, as if to protect her heart from overexposure. Maude's fearful look darted between the three adults, searching for a safe haven, and Lola reattached herself to Julie's leg.

Julie's worried eyes met mine for a brief stab of connection before answering her sister. "No worries, Martha. Girls? Let's go. We'll be back before dinner."

"Call me," Julie whispered as she passed me. "I'm worried."

Their exit left behind a hollow, abandoned silence.

Martha led me into the kitchen. The fragrant pot of stew simmered on the stove, and I realized how long ago I'd eaten my low-calorie burrito.

"Can I get you anything?" she said, the question automatic, and devoid of actual intent.

"I'm fine."

We sat across from each other. Martha's eyes reddened, glossy with tears.

"Damn it." Her hands tightened into fists. "God damn it to hell."

Martha never swore. I couldn't tolerate her pain a moment longer. I pushed upright, my chair scraping the floor as I moved around the table and opened my arms.

"Martha."

She stared at my outstretched limbs, as if measuring them.

"Martha, come here."

She stood abruptly and stepped into my invitation. My shoulder was soon hot with tears.

"That's better," I said. "That's better." I fished a handkerchief out of my right jeans pocket and handed it to her. She held it to her nose and gave two prolonged honks.

"Must be time for afternoon chants," I said.

"What?"

"Tibetan long horns are calling."

Her smile was watery, but at least she managed one.

I poured us both glasses of water, and we reclaimed our places at the table. Finally, I asked, "Have you talked to Bill?"

"Briefly," she said. "He called last night." Her tone was both hurt, and hard. "He'd just landed. He has *things to do* over there. Isn't sure when he's coming back."

"That's pretty much what he told me."

Her eyes raked my face, her expression hungry. "What exactly did he say to you? Did he talk about me at all? What did he tell you, exactly?"

I summarized the conversation, and she stared at my moving mouth, as if by reading my lips she might change the actual words.

"So I told him I'd be in touch," I concluded.

Martha shrugged. Fresh tears leaked from the corners of her eyes. "Meet the new Bill." She dashed them aside. "I liked the old one better."

I was inclined to agree, although doing so felt disloyal. But then, so did disagreeing, like choosing sides on a battle-field where I'd never belonged in the first place.

"Julie says I shouldn't make any decisions. Not when I'm like . . . like this. What do you think?"

"I think Julie is very wise," I said.

Martha lurched forward and grabbed my hands. Hers were icy cold. The words spilled. "Ten, I know Bill. He's a good man. He's just, he's acting crazy right now. But I know him! He doesn't want to be *that guy.* My God, he's always hated *that guy,* the husband who has a fucking midlife crisis and takes off, ups and starts a whole new family, like it was nothing!"

I kept quiet. My marriage experience hovers at right about zero, my record with long-term commitments several degrees below noteworthy.

Martha's eyes bored into mine. Her dilated irises were like dinner plates. It occurred to me that the shock of this event had slightly unhinged her. "I'm not ready to give up yet. But I've got to know that he wants what I want. And what I want is for this to be his family. I want him to show me, no, to *prove* to me, that we're number one, we come first."

My mind gaped as I stuttered the utterly ridiculous, "Well, let's hope so."

Martha's clutch tightened. "No! I need more than hope from you, Ten. I need you to go over there. Talk some sense into my husband. He'll listen to you! I know he will! I want you to bring my Bill back."

I wondered if Martha could hear the brakes squealing in my brain. "That's not a good idea."

"I knew you'd say that, Ten. But is that the partner talking? The friend of Bill's?" She squeezed so hard my knuckles ground against each other, bone on bone. "What about me? What about being *my* friend?"

I pulled my hands free, as a spark of anger flicked and took hold behind my concern. Since when did Martha poke with a guilt stick?

Bill wasn't the only one around here who'd changed.

She progressed from poking to twisting. "I've never asked you for anything, and I won't ever ask for anything again. Please, do this one thing for me, Ten."

"Martha . . ."

"Even Julie thinks it's a good idea." The final, painful turn.

The kitchen walls closed in around me. I couldn't seem to get enough air.

Don't do it. Don't agree.

Even Julie thinks it's a good idea.

"Okay," I said. "I'll go."

Martha sprang to her feet and ran to me. She cupped my cheeks and planted a kiss on my forehead.

"Thank you, Ten. Thank you. I know that Bill will thank you, too, one day."

My phone beeped, signaling a text, and I leapt on the sound as if it were a death row reprieve.

"I have to get going," I said. I submitted to a hug, ran outside, and again jumped behind the wheel of my Shelby. I zigzagged up and across three side streets to Melrose and veered left, cutting in front of an open-air Hollywood tour bus. "Whoa there, cowboy!" boomed a tour guide's electronically amplified voice, as a dozen wide-eyed tourists gawked at the crazy dude in the bright-yellow Mustang.

I accelerated up Gower toward the freeway, speeding like a drag racer, until a still, small voice of sanity piped up from the back of my brain.

Slow the fuck down.

I pulled over next to a towering church, just south of Franklin. "Come unto me, all ye that travail and are heavy-laden, and I will refresh you," announced a large sign.

I was so heavy-laden I couldn't breathe.

My lungs weren't functioning fully enough to allow me to count breaths. I moved on to plan B: I placed my hands on my thighs, closed my eyes, and lightly traced each finger with my inner eye while sensing their light pressure against my quadriceps muscles.

Thumb. Forefinger. Middle finger. Ring finger. Pinkie. Thumb. Forefinger. Middle finger. Ring finger. Pinkie.

After five rounds, I was able to switch attention to my breathing. With each in-breath, I directed warm acceptance to the taut, cantaloupe-sized tumor of resentment in my stomach, hoping to loosen, if not release it.

Nothing doing. If anything, the sensation hardened. My hands clenched into fists, just as Martha's had moments earlier. I was about to give up, when a familiar voice stepped in with reinforcements.

When have you felt this before, Tenzing?

Yeshe's voice was kind, as always. I brought my attention, led by my breath, back to the knot.

Ahhh.

Please, Tenzing, please, mon chéri? *Please go to the store, the park, the boulangerie, your bedroom, please, just go somewhere else for a little while. Please give Valerie a hug, pour Valerie a glass, tell Valerie you love her, you love her more than you love anyone else in the whole world. More than you love your father.*

Now come here, so Valerie can kiss you.

Every day it was the same thing. Guilt and reward. Demand, followed by affection.

The lumpy mass relaxed, imperceptibly. A memory drifted through. My mother, trying to get me to spend time with her latest lover, the one she wound up marrying. Didier. A drunk, like her, in acute denial of the fact, also like her.

Please, Ten. Just go this once, for me? He's going to be your new father.

The visit to the Louvre was a disaster. Didier picked me up from school, big, bumbling, a road map of vices outlined in spidery red veins that crisscrossed his bulbous nose. In an earlier incarnation, he'd taught university classes in child development, until this proved inconvenient to his drinking needs. But he continued to look at me as if I were more specimen than human.

As we trudged in silence through the echoing caverns of art, my 11-year-old brain realized two things. One, Didier hated spending time with me as much as I did with him, and two, he was equally powerless when confronted with my mother's wheedling requests.

I was sent early to my father's monastery that summer, soon after our sullen outing. Didier himself would leave Valerie six months later. And back I would come, the lucky winner, the child who got to witness his mother's death, and experience one final mantel of guilt landing on my shoulders and tightening, as if permanently latched.

The same summer Bill and Mila conceived their ill-conceived son.

When have you felt this before?

Slap, slap, slap. My memory dealt out situations like playing cards, one after another. All the times I'd overridden my intuition, let myself be conned by a woman into doing something I didn't want to do. And *whoopee,* what a payoff— a kiss on the forehead or cheek, first from my mother, and later, from whomever the girlfriend du jour happened to be. Maybe not much of a reward, but enough to apply a tiny drop of lubricant to that spot, deep inside the machinery, where the guilt was grinding away. The trouble is, a drop's never enough to smooth the gears. That's how guilt works.

My phone beeped again, reminding me I'd never checked the actual text.

WILL STOP BY TO INSTALL THE ONION ROUTER (TOR) AT SIX P.M.
MIKE.

For a second, my mind flailed, until the case came back to me: Sasha, Agvan Supplies, and the website, complete with mystery currency and impossible fruit.

OK, SEE YOU THERE.

I left the church, and its promise of ease, and pulled onto the 101 North, conflict pummeling my brain. Part of me wanted to go straight back to Martha's and yell "I'm not going. You have no right to ask," an impulse promptly muscled aside by, "You can't do that, Ten—a deal's a deal." The fracas grew even more complicated: Was the agreement I'd made with Martha even valid if I consented while in the trance of an old pattern called "overriding myself to please a woman"?

The dull throb of an emerging headache formed, back where my neck muscles joined my head.

Not again.

I rolled my shoulders up and back, trying to shrug off the kinks. I'd be home soon.

My tires crunched on the gravel leading to my house, as yet another possibility waved for attention from below the surface arguments, the part that was bored with work, that longed, like Bill, for some real action. There exists a rogue inside me, a rebel. He'd set off the car alarm this morning. He wanted to *do* something beyond chasing down someone's pedigreed Chihuahua. "Say what you like," this rebel now whispered, "but if the universe, in the form of Bill and Martha Bohannon, is offering Bosnia, who are you to argue?"

But was his whisper "Cosmic Insight," or "Bullshit Justification"?

This was useless, and I was growing more and more confused.

Decisions don't come easily to me. They never have. My tutor at Dorje Yidam, Lama Sonam, would be the first to admit that I tested his patience like no other novice. My problem seems to be one of hyper-perception—for every reason to swing in one direction, my brain will always, instantly, suggest an equally strong reason to swing back the other way. One day Lama Sonam, probably out of desperation, blurted out, "Lama Tenzing! The mind is not reliable! But the heart? The heart knows not how to cause harm. Let the heart decide."

"How?" I remember asking.

And he'd introduced me to my first-ever conversation with my heart.

Now I went straight out to the deck, and sat facing the canyon. The sky was overcast, the ocean just a distant promise.

I closed my eyes, and felt into my heart area. I entertained both decisions, making each one separately, and fully.

I am not going to Bosnia. I will stay where I am.

Interesting. My heart fluttered for a second, then clamped shut.

As I sat and kept breathing, the scared and confused faces of a pair of little girls, Lola and Maude, floated before me. If Bill left Martha, would they be consigned to a disconnected fate like my own, shuttled from household to household, never knowing where they really belonged?

I am going to Bosnia. I will find Bill there, and see if I can be of service to this situation.

My heart swung wide, like windows opening onto a spacious vista.

The first decision brought up fear and contraction. The second brought up a sense of clarity and expansion, and not just for Bill, or Martha, or even myself. For Lola and Maude.

The entire process took three minutes.

Tank leapt onto my lap.

"Looks like I'm going to Sarajevo," I said.

CHAPTER 14

I got to work. My first call was to my odd but efficient assistant.

"Hello."

"Kim, I'm glad you answered. It's Ten. Something's come up. Can you stop by?"

"Oh. Oh. Today is Sunday, Mr. Norbu. I work for you on Mondays."

Only I would hire someone more regulated than a Buddhist monastery. "Please, Kim? It's important."

Next call, Stephanie. She, too, answered after one ring.

"Stephanie. Tenzing Norbu. I met you yesterday morning at Yvonne's, remember?"

"You're kidding, right? My son hasn't been that infatuated since he saw Spiderman cruising the sidewalk in front of the Nokia."

"Very funny. Listen, I'm going out of town, but I wanted to run a few questions by you before I take off."

"Sure. When?"

"Umm. Today?"

"Wow. Okay, well, Connor's napping, but he'll be up any minute. I've promised him surfboard time at the South Beach Park on Barnard Way. Why don't you meet me there in an hour or so?"

I concocted an egg scramble with sautéed onions, mushrooms, and peppers, and piled the creation onto two slices of toasted sourdough, layered with Haas avocado I'd smushed with a fork right onto the bread. It took fifteen minutes to prepare, and five to inhale. Mindful, I was not.

I made a fresh pot of coffee, and was opening a can of God-knows-what for Tank when Kim plus metal accoutrements manifested at my kitchen window, like a hardware ghost in a helmet. She clutched a small backpack. Kim travels by bicycle whenever possible, which makes early detection difficult.

I motioned her inside. She went straight for Tank, who rubbed up against her ankle.

This was going to work out just fine.

"Thanks for coming. I've got some big favors to ask. First, can you book me on a flight to Sarajevo, a red-eye tonight if possible? And can you also get me a room at the Holiday Inn?" I handed her the name, scribbled on the Post-it.

Kim stared at me. "Tonight? That is unlikely."

"Try, please. Use the Rosen card." So much for not dipping into my Julius Rosen emergency savings fund. Still, I knew my ex-client would have approved of this mission. He may have been a crook, but he was also a big believer in the institution of marriage.

"You said favors, Mr. Norbu," Kim's voice broke in. "Plural. What else?"

"How about not calling me Mr. Norbu, for starters?"

"Oh. Oh," she said. A long pause ensued.

"Kim?"

"I was trying to think of how to address you."

"How about Ten? Or if you prefer, Tenzing."

"How would that designate the difference in social status between us?"

"The . . . I'm sorry?"

"You are the employer and I am the employee. You are of a higher status and should be addressed as a superior."

Clearly Kim was still determining how social relationships worked on planet Earth, or at least on planet Ten. A tiny sense of connection flared; I often found myself trying to figure out such things as well.

"There is no difference in status, Kim. We're equals. I make a list and you execute the list. You give me some of your time and I give you some of my money. We're in it together, just playing different roles."

She said, "With respect, sir, past employers have seemed pleased when I addressed them formally." She ruminated briefly. "How about *Chief?* Or *Boss?*"

There was no such thing as a routine conversation with Kim. They were either three words long, or an endless, crazy zoom into the unpredictable.

"Uh, no, those don't quite do it for me, either," I said. Time to admit defeat. "I have a better idea. How about if you go ahead and call me Mr. Norbu, and I just stop minding it?"

Kim blinked.

"It's probably time for me to accept that I'm an adult," I added. A memory flickered, something Bill had told me right before I left the force. We were eating Chinese, arguing over a new department regulation. Bill pointed a chopstick at me. "There's a saying, smartass—if you're not a rebel when you're twenty you don't have any heart, but if you haven't joined the establishment by the time you're thirty you don't have any brains. You, my friend, *are* the establishment now. Quit acting like Che fucking Guevara."

Kim's voice interrupted. "I would like to clarify. Are you saying that you would change your behavior on my behalf? So that I would experience less discomfort?"

I hadn't thought of it quite that way, but I could see how Kim got there. "Yes, I guess I am."

"You are a very unusual person."

"Thank you," I said. "Coming from you, that's a compliment."

Did her mouth actually twitch? "I believe you are joking. Is that correct?"

"Yes."

"Good. I felt an urge to laugh, although I would also be laughing at myself."

"The one sure sign of sanity."

"What else?"

"Sorry?"

"You referred to *some* favors. That would indicate several. More than two," she explained, her voice patient.

Right. I tried not to look at my watch. Now I knew why Kim usually chose brevity. Having an actual conversation was an endurance exercise, on both our parts.

"I've noticed how much Tank enjoys your company, Kim. I would love for you to care for him while I'm gone."

Her features froze, as her eyes locked in on mine. Now what?

"I'd pay you extra, of course."

Nothing.

"Kim? Are you okay?"

"I don't know what to do right now," she said.

"Okay. Um. So, is that a no?"

Kim dropped her backpack on the floor and burst into tears.

Now two of us didn't know what to do. In my head I heard the long-ago voice of Lama Sonam: "When confused by others, breathe. Find the compassion within you." I took a deep breath and tried to hold Kim in a space of loving-kindness while she blubbered.

Moments later, the weather cleared, and she rewarded me with a wide and unexpected smile. "I'm through crying. Would you like an explanation, Mr. Norbu?" Back to her usual brisk cheer.

"Uh."

She straightened, as if reporting for roll call. The words marched out, the pace precise and nonstop. "I have a problem they call autism spectrum disorder, in my case acute although high functioning—it is not yet known if autism spectrum disorder is due to abnormalities of the brain or the exigencies of familial and cultural conditioning—some pharmaceuticals show promise for alleviating ASD but as yet there is no standard treatment and I am not at present on psychiatric medications."

"Wow. Okay."

She ploughed on, her staccato-like delivery abrupt. "The hallmark of this diagnosis is awkwardness in social situations and failure to notice the unsettling effect my behavior is having on people I'm talking to. I am working with a new therapist who is teaching me a new way to handle awkward social situations such as stop and ask from time to time if the person I'm talking to would like to hear more detail. Would you like to hear more detail, Mr. Norbu?"

She watched my eyes carefully.

"Yes." *Do not look at watch. Do not look at watch.* "Please, tell me more."

She nodded. "When the awkward feeling comes over me I am learning to do two new things. First I say something true—so true that nobody can argue with it. That is why I said 'I don't know what to do.'"

Okay, that made sense. I'd recently added that very tool to my own toolkit, or a version of it. My third rule of behavior: tell the truth. To which I now silently added, "Or at least say something true enough that nobody is able to argue about it."

"And the second thing?"

"After I tell the truth, I stop and feel what happens to my body. People with Asperger's have a problem with feelings. What you said about Tank made me feel sad. A good sad, but sad. Therefore I cried. Did it upset you when I cried, Mr. Norbu?"

"I would say I felt more confused than upset."

"Yes. Friends and family members of people with autism spectrum disorder often report confusion in dealing with them."

"No problem, Kim. I spend half my waking hours confused, and that's on a good day."

She blinked several times, as one hand reached for the metal stud piercing her eyebrow. She twisted the stud, as if adjusting the volume. "You were making another joke, weren't you, Mr. Norbu?"

"Good catch," I said. She twisted the stud harder. "Yes," I added hurriedly.

"Would you like an explanation of why I felt sad?"

Breathe. "Definitely."

"I had a big brother once. He said nice things to me like that." She waited.

"Ah, well, thanks for explaining. So, uh, where's your brother now?"

She flung her arm out, as in, *somewhere in the great unknown.* "Gone. Would you like to hear more detail?"

My entire life was passing before my eyes. "No, thank you. Maybe some other time."

She stood, her body expectant.

"Kim?"

"Yes, Mr. Norbu."

"Airplane ticket?"

I escaped for the playground with a sense of having once again been granted a reprieve. It crossed my mind I might need to add a few nonverbal, uncommunicative men to my life, for the sake of time, if not sanity.

Kim called while I was still en route to the park. She'd booked me on the earliest flight available, leaving around 10 A.M. tomorrow morning, with two plane changes. I was facing prolonged intimacy with my fellow man, but sleep masks were invented for just such emergencies. She also agreed to take care of Tank, for as long as I was gone. She would be far more reliable with his feeding times than I had been this past week, if nothing else.

I spotted Connor balancing his sturdy legs on a bright-orange, bouncy, toddler-sized surfboard. One fist was airborne, like a Roman emperor declaiming to the crowds. The other clutched the hand of a new, improved version of Stephanie, her long, equally bouncy curls glossy and sun-kissed.

Connor caught sight of me and crowed, "Mine! Papa!"

Stephanie laughed. "His words. Promise."

"Mine! Mine!" Connor was consistent, I gave him that.

Stephanie moved him off the toy surfboard and over to the large wooden boat that made up the bulk of the park. He scampered up the ramp, and we sat to one side on a low wall, watching him.

"Cute kid."

"He's my life," Stephanie said. She glanced at me, before swinging her gaze back to her son. "So. Except for my eagle eyes, I'm all yours."

I pulled out my notebook and pen. "What do you know about overseas traffickers who may have relocated in Van Nuys?"

Stephanie considered the question before shaking her head. "Not much. A lot of my clients are domestic, like I said at Yvonne's. Either lured here from somewhere else in the States, or simply homegrown. Why?"

"I may have stumbled onto an international trafficking operation based a few blocks from Van Nuys Airport."

"Oh, well, I wouldn't be surprised. Even the airlines are starting to get in on the act. A couple of years ago some angel disguised as a flight attendant brought down a small child trafficking operation almost single-handedly. She'd noticed something off about a woman traveling from Central America with two young children. A little boy and girl, neither of them much older than Connor." Stephanie waved at Connor, and blew him a kiss.

"The boy was visibly scared, and the girl was sobbing inconsolably, but their mother completely ignored them both, couldn't be bothered. Maybe just a lousy mother, right? But when the flight attendant asked for the little girl's name, you know, so she could offer her some juice, the older woman didn't seem to know what it was. As luck would have it, our friend had just taken a workshop on human trafficking. Once they landed, she reported the passengers to a hotline and notified the authorities." Stephanie's eyes were fixed on the kids climbing and squealing up and down the wooden ship. "That one tip exposed a child trafficking ring in Boston, and led to the rescue of over eighty children who'd been brought illegally from Central America to the United States. One woman, paying attention."

Another Eskimo. "What an amazing story."

Stephanie wiped at her cheeks, which were damp with tears. "Sorry. This stuff really gets to me. Anyway, Homeland Security started calling flight attendants the first line of defense in human trafficking."

"I get it. Boots in the air," I said.

She smiled at me. "Boots in the air. I like that. And now there are wristbands with the hotline number, and both a bulletin and a brochure listing red flags to look for, and ways to determine if there's something wrong."

I was scribbling everything down, just in case. "I'm curious. What are they? The red flags?"

"Oh, you know. Some of it's pretty obvious, when you think about it. The adult they're with doesn't act like a normal parent—is either overly shielding, or under-responsive. The kid appears drugged, or fearful of talking or making eye contact, or suspicious of anyone in authority, or all of the above. Maybe the children are shabby and malnourished, or show signs of physical abuse, while their 'parents' appear fat and happy. Like that."

Stephanie's voice grew harder. "Not so different from any trafficking victims, actually. Tenzing, do you know that over twelve million adults and children are enslaved around the world? And less than two percent of them are rescued." Her voice lowered to a whisper. "So few. They're the lucky ones."

Yvonne's words about Stephanie rang in my ears: *She's had a hard life. Was even working the streets for a while, if you can believe that.*

Stephanie stood, brushing sand off the seat of her jeans. "Well. My son needs a snack, and I need to stop working on a beautiful Sunday afternoon."

I stood as well. "I can't thank you enough," I said. "One last question?"

Stephanie's voice rose. "Connor? Time to go!" She turned to me. "It'll take about five minutes and at least two more shouts to get my son off of that pirate ship. Ask away."

"If . . ." I struggled with the phrasing, "if I should happen to encounter a victim of human trafficking in my line of work, what do I say? How should I act?"

Stephanie's face softened. "Just . . . be respectful. Here's the thing. Whatever people might think, sexual slaves, any disenfranchised people, for that matter, don't choose their lives. Their lives choose them."

Stephanie cupped her mouth. "Connor! Three minutes!"

She turned back to me. "When a person starts from a place of scarcity and pain, when there's no psychological or emotional foundation upon which to stand," Stephanie's eyes again filled. "When, as a child, you've never been seen, or, or valued? You're a sitting duck. A tragedy waiting to happen. Pimps? Traffickers? They're just filling a preexisting vacuum. And the bond that forms between the two is almost unbreakable, because even abusive, inconsistent attention is better than no attention at all. When someone finally seems to notice you? You'll do anything for them. Anything." She held up two fists, and started to unpeel fingers as she counted. "Connor? I'm counting to ten! ONE, TWO . . . So sure, you can pull them off the street, but unless you treat that gaping, underlying hole of need, they'll run back to their pimp daddies as soon as they can. THREE, FOUR . . . The only way to break the cycle is to build a new foundation, and that takes time. Time, love, and genuine respect. FIVE, SIX, SEVEN, EIGHT, NINE, NINE and a HALF . . ."

Connor arrived, panting and giggling, and Stephanie scooped him up into her arms. She smiled at me over his dark hair. "I like to say my job is pretty simple: to love and respect my clients until they learn to love and respect themselves."

Connor stretched his arms toward me. I leaned in and gave him an awkward hug.

"Connor, you are one lucky kid," I said into his ear.

"Lucky!" he shouted, grinning.

Mike was waiting for me at home. The takeout pizzas I'd picked up from our local pizzeria were still nice and hot. Mike had three slices of pepperoni and sausage, plus a Red Bull, for breakfast, and I had three slices of cheese and mushrooms, plus a Redhook, for dinner. Then we got to work.

It took all of ten minutes to install The Onion Router. "Welcome, you are now connected to the Tor network," the site announced in cheerful purple writing. Now I had my own desktop Vidalia browser, complete with a lavender-and-cream onion icon.

"So what next?" I said.

"Next is, I did a little asking around, and I got hold of some black-market Tor sites that might help you with your research. They're on your desktop, filed under 'lox and bagels.' Onions. Lox and bagels, get it?"

"Got it."

Mike grew serious. "Some of these URLs are fairly gnarly. NSFW, if you know what I mean."

I didn't. I waited Mike out.

"Not Suitable for Work. Jeez, Ten, plan to join the twenty-first century anytime soon?"

"Did you check them out?"

"Nope. Can't go there."

"You? I thought you could go anywhere on the Internet."

"Let me rephrase, boss. It's not that I can't. I won't. I know how this kinky stuff can hook you, get under your skin, so to speak. Buying and selling weed online is one thing, but sexual shit? No thank you."

I remembered my scalding hot shower. I knew exactly what he meant. "How much do you think the Internet plays into the sex trafficking industry?"

"Shit, Ten, I couldn't say. But I know it's big business, and getting bigger all the time. Used to be you bought a sleazy ad at the back of the *LA Weekly*. These days, though, more and more's done on the sly, and on the Internet. Sexting, luring, nothing's off limits. And for every social site that bans certain personals, four more pop up on the dark web."

My nerve endings responded with an onset of tingling. "The dark web?"

"Yeah. That's what they call black-market URLs, and routers like Tor. The biggest is Silk Road. It's a massively successful virtual marketplace for drugs, run by some guy who goes by the username of Dread Pirate Roberts. But the dark web is literally crawling with these sites."

"Dread Pirate Roberts? Seriously?"

Mike stared at me. "Don't tell me. You've never seen *The Princess Bride.*"

"Umm."

"Dude, that may be the single saddest thing I've ever heard."

I ignored him. "So why don't governments shut these illegal sites down?"

"Because first they have to find them. No trails to follow, remember? Plus, even the money exchange is virtually untraceable now. That's where bitcoins come in."

I couldn't hold back a groan. My brain was swelling inside my skull, as if anticipating a fresh flood of geek-speak. "Mike, any chance you can explain bitcoins in twenty-five words or less?"

"Interesting challenge. Let's see: predetermined number of virtual, untraceable units based on mathematical formulas; value universally agreed-upon; mined by geeks; stored in anonymous wallets; survival dependent upon kindness of strangers." He mentally counted. "Twenty-seven words. Boom."

"Impressive." I thought about his description. "So you're saying the monetary value of a bitcoin is in fact based on nothing more than an agreement that it has a monetary value?"

"Hey, it's not as though our entire economy doesn't work that way. When was the last time you paid a visit to Fort Knox? Barter systems, man. I'm telling you, that's where the future's at."

It was getting late, and I still had to pack. I sent Mike home with leftover pizza and a promise that I would call him from Sarajevo if necessary. Mike's parting words were half advice, half warning.

"Here's the thing, Ten. The codes may be unbreakable, but in the end, real human beings are involved. And human nature remains fallible as fuck. We can't help ourselves, right? We just love to push the envelope, until eventually we make that one critical mistake."

"The voice of experience," I said, recalling Mike's own illicit past, and the pains I took to help him regain his footing.

"You should know."

CHAPTER 15

The morning was a mad scramble, what with last-minute instructions for Kim, a misplaced raincoat, and two chargers that hadn't charged their machines because I'd never plugged them in. I finally called Martha from LAX, Terminal Three. I'd made it to my gate with only 20 minutes to spare, this, after waking up in Topanga Canyon before dawn. I was facing 19 hours of travel, if all went well, including a touchdown in Newark, New Jersey, a change of planes in Munich, and an arrival sometime tomorrow—or was it the day after tomorrow?—in Sarajevo. For this sacrifice of time, serenity, and knee joints, I was out several thousand dollars. My openhearted conviction around the decision to follow Bill was suffering serious contractions of regret.

As I listened to her phone ringing, I concluded Martha Bohannon owed me, big time.

Eventually, a small-voiced someone answered with a tentative "Hi?"

Fifty-fifty.

"Lola?"

"Lola's going potty. I'm Maude. Who is this?"

"It's Uncle Ten."

"Oh." A whisper. "I thought you were going to be Daddy."

"Can I talk to your mom, please?"

"Can't. I said Lola's going potty."

"How about your Auntie Julie?"

"Can't. She's at the airport."

"She is? So am I!" My heart rate accelerated, and I found myself scanning the passengers around me. As if.

"Guess what, Uncle Ten? Auntie Julie's picking up Homer, because she's staying for longer, and Homer misses her."

"Homer?"

"Auntie Julie loves Homer. She says we will, too. Buh-bye."

"Wait! Don't hang up. Maude?"

Silence.

So Julie was still with that guy, the sommelier. What kind of lame-ass sober sommelier goes by the name of Homer?

I called right back, but was foisted onto voice mail.

"Martha, it's Ten. I'm on my way to Bosnia. Tell Julie . . ." I swallowed. "Never mind. I'll be in touch."

We took off just after ten. I was traveling light: a small backpack, and a single roller-bag hastily filled with the bare necessities, minus my Wilson Combat and Microtech H.A.L.O. knife. Obviously. A thickish wallet of cash would have to serve as my munitions. Handing out money to fixers and such had worked pretty well in the past, but in this new world of bitcoinage, who knew?

I switched off my phone and tried not to think too much about the hours and hours ahead, aloft in a series of huge tin cans packed with live cargo, Julie and her Homer canoodling somewhere far behind and below me. I had an aisle seat, and the passenger to my left, a blessedly skinny hipster with black horn-rimmed glasses and a small yin/yang tattoo on his forearm, immediately plugged into his iPod and fell asleep.

Once in the air, I picked at my breakfast, a rubbery cheese omelet and an ice-cold bran muffin, washing both down with a weak cup of tea. I retrieved my Kindle from my backpack and waded through a number of books and articles I'd downloaded about the Bosnian War. I never like to arrive at a new place in a state of ignorance.

The information was repetitive, and disturbing— no wonder Bill didn't want to discuss his time in Bosnia. After five plus hours, I'd exposed myself to as many tales of genocidal brutality and global denial as one sensitive soul could tolerate, and I set my research aside with a deep sense of relief.

I closed my eyes, intending to meditate, but my mind was quickly invaded with the haunting images of gang rape and torture, of random sniper deaths and full-scale tribal purging, of villages torn apart by warring families and former friends. When and how did these horrors start? And how could the rest of the world turn such a blind eye, allowing the atrocities to continue, not just for months, but years?

A sour knot of judgment formed in my throat, making it difficult to swallow. While no one community was without blame, the Serbians did seem to bear the greatest responsibility for the conflict. True, their initial resistance to peaceful resolution was encouraged by one power-hungry leader, and their later push for dominance was fanned into bloodthirsty flames by another. (First Karadžić, then Milošević insisted that the Serbian people were the most disenfranchised, and therefore had the most to lose—and gain.) But the slaughter of friends and neighbors was the conscious choice of thousands. How could that happen? What was the root cause?

I inhaled deeply, first through my mouth to address the tight twist of throat anger. Exhaled. Inhaled again, this time through the nostrils, directing the breath deep into my braced solar plexus. My belly softened.

Let go, Ten. Allow.

Bits of yesterday's conversation with Stephanie floated up: *Whatever people might think, sexual slaves, any disenfranchised people for that matter, don't choose their lives. Their lives choose them.*

Any disenfranchised people.

When you've never been seen or valued? You're a sitting duck. A tragedy waiting to happen. Pimps? Traffickers? They're just filling a preexisting vacuum.

As are megalomaniac dictators.

I considered a new thought: a neglected people can be as vulnerable as a neglected child. Both are vulnerable to bullies. Like the mind itself, both are easily manipulated by the planting of false expectations.

Tito's death. That created the vacuum. That made room for the horrors that followed.

I followed that idea. From everything I'd just read, Tito ruled Yugoslavia with a totalitarian hand, even as he called himself a good father.

Like my own.

Tito's form of dictatorship, while benign, was absolute, and kept most of his people in an immature, unformed state of dependence.

Like me.

When Tito died, a vacuum of authority was created, and like immature nephews squabbling over a deceased uncle's bequest, different factions immediately began to jockey for power. Bosnia's distinct social and religious communities, lightly stitched into one multicultural quilt, began to unravel as the tribes pulled away. Serbians, especially, grabbed for the most pieces, instead of figuring out a new way to share equally. Add to the mix a substantial influx of deadly weapons and unbridled bullies, and mass genocide was sure to follow.

Their lives choose them.

Was the infliction of suffering, small or large, always the byproduct of a starving heart? Were its victims destined to repeat the pattern unless and until their own hearts were healed?

If I was born Serbian, would my own hand grasp the sniper's gun, my own finger pull the trigger?

Yes.

My heart ached, the sensation sharp and unrelenting. Wherever I tossed my mind, it landed on a story of pain. I knew this state, though I hadn't visited here for some time. I was in danger of entering into a dark, sticky tunnel, hard to escape from once inside.

I turned to the only place I knew to go for comfort, a pure realm filled with compassion for all, and rejection of none. Including me. *Om mani padme hum. Om mani padme hum.*

We circled Newark for over an hour, and I again had to dash to my next flight.

Once I was buckled into the Lufthansa red-eye from Newark to Berlin, elbow-to-elbow with fellow travelers, I suffered through a slightly stale tuna wrap, trying to ignore the unnatural green color of the actual wrapping. I consciously avoided searching the rows for possible child traffickers. Anyway, weren't we flying in the wrong direction for that?

For some reason the movie channels weren't working, and a young female flight attendant wheeled through steerage with an unexpected peace offering, probably pilfered from the wealthier realms. I waved off the temptations of a personal ice cream sundae and chocolate chip cookies; no need to expose others to the sight of an ex-monk doing aisle laps to burn off his sugar-rush.

Instead, I retrieved my own special form of dessert—a small blue-green capsule with a lyrical name, manufactured especially for people like me. That is to say, people who have trouble sleeping on an airplane because they feel personally responsible for holding said plane aloft. The operative belief running through my head—*if I clench my muscles tight enough and fill my mind with enough obsessive thoughts, the plane won't fall out of the sky*—made the act of slumber impossible. But the pill worked its wonders, and drowsiness soon seeped into my cells. I sent off a final acknowledgment to the pharmaceutical geniuses who'd concocted a capsule that would enable sleep without causing a mind-numbing hangover.

"Sir, we're about to land in Munich. You need to raise your seatback." The flight attendant was shaking my shoulder.

I lifted my eye-mask. Her smile dazzled me. Was she this pretty last night . . . ?

I knew what was going on. Julie had her Homer, and I needed to even things out.

My Munich stopover was a little under two hours. I found a generic German bakeshop, and ordered an espresso and a slice of apple strudel.

How could Julie still be with that idiot?

The espresso was neither hot enough nor strong enough. I sat at a small, sticky table and ate stale strudel alone. I'd so hoped for a layover in Paris, but apparently Parisians are not very interested in visiting Sarajevo.

I make the slow walk from customs to the passenger arrival zone at Charles de Gaulle, small for my age, my head freshly shaved. I am starving. I hope I never have to go back to that place again.

Will she be here this time?

There she is.

Maman! Maman!

She takes me right to our favorite airport café for my home-coming treat, like always. She orders a pot of chocolat chaud and not un, but deux croissants, s'il vous plaît: one plain, and one almond. They arrive warm, straight from the oven, their flaky layers crisp and buttery. She fills my cup with hot chocolate and then sits back to watch.

I dip a crisp corner into my drink. The flaky pastry sucks up dark, velvet liquid, turning the golden layers dark brown. When the soaked part is exactly the same height as my thumb, I remove the dripping croissant. I bite. The combination of softened almond pastry and warm, sweet chocolate sends my deprived taste buds into a delirious dance of joy.

She smiles at me, happy that I am happy.

"Welcome home, Tenzing."

I push away from the table, my strudel half-eaten, but not before offering an impromptu mantra of gratitude for that gift from my mother. No matter what twisted gyrations her brand of mothering caused me, that homecoming gift of hot chocolate and croissants would always be her legacy.

Maybe not a firm foundation, but better than nothing.

CHAPTER 16

Kim had booked a taxi for me ahead of time. After breezing through customs—"Business or pleasure?" "Here to visit a friend." "How long are you staying?" "Not too long. A few days." "Enjoy our beautiful city."—I made my way to Terminal B, where Sarajevo Taxi had an exclusive hold on anyone wanting to enter their "beautiful city" by cab. I checked my phone, but though a couple of bars registered, I couldn't seem to receive messages or make calls. Bill would have to give me his secret code, once he got over his shock at seeing me.

I sat outside the terminal waiting for my car to show up, riffling through a Sarajevo travel guide for English-speaking tourists. The little book proudly informed me that the metropolis I was about to visit had come in 43rd in a survey called "100 Best Cities in the World." I pictured the department of tourism slogan: Come to Sarajevo—There Are at Least 66 Worse Places You Can Visit!

Maybe my mood was soured by jet lag.

The cab that pulled up was a green Mercedes, an older model coated in dust. It was topped with a perky yellow sign marked in black: Sarajevo Taxi 108.

Every Tibetan Buddhist *threngwa*, or prayer rosary, including my own, is made up of 108 beads. In one of our most beloved sermons, the Laṅkāvatāra Sūtra, the Buddha is asked 108 questions, and his answer definitively described the 108 delusions of the mind. At our temples, 108 steps lead up to the prayer hall entrances, and according to my favorite tutor, Lama Sonam, the human heart is capable of experiencing 108 feelings.

Sarajevo Taxi 108 was auspicious, a wink, if not a bow, from my benefactors, and my temperament lightened.

My chauffeur could have been a cab driver anywhere in the Western Hemisphere. Medium height, medium build, generic jeans and nylon jacket, slight paunch, and three-day stubble on his cheeks. His shaved head couldn't hide the V-shaped receding hairline, and his 40-year-old frame had been weathered by too many cigarettes and not enough fresh air. Still, he was amiable enough as he stubbed out a filtered butt and stuck out a hand.

"I am Petar," he said. "Petar Kovacevic. Welcome to our beautiful city." His smile revealed a gap between his front teeth big enough to drive a truck through.

"Tenzing Norbu."

"You come for working?"

"Visiting a friend."

"Ah. You stay for long?"

I was experiencing déjà vu. "Just a few days, thanks."

"I give you my number. You want see this beautiful city, you call me. Also Dubrovnik. My brother live there. I drive you one day. Beautiful beaches."

He started his meter and squealed out of the airport, merging onto a major thoroughfare without checking left or right. My seatmate on the last flight of the trip, a retired journalist and seasoned traveler, had warned that Sarajevo Taxi drivers were insane, and the fares were overpriced and non-negotiable for the seven-mile drive into town. He explained in detail how to take a taxi to the nearby tram station in Ilidža and then ride the tram into town, but I couldn't be bothered.

My billfold was now fat with the local currency, Bosnia-Herzegovina convertible marks, or known by the natives, according to my guide, as KMs. Eight American $100 bills translated into a variety of paper money ranging from 20 to 200 mark notes, each one a different pastel color and displaying a different stern-looking luminary from a different party, all with surnames ending in *ic*.

Apparently there were a lot of principalities to keep happy in postwar Bosnia-Herzegovina.

"What this name you said? Tanzing Norbu?" Petar asked.

"*Ten*-zing," I said. "My father was Tibetan."

"Ahh. Here, you would then be Tenzing Norbuvic, I am thinking. Always, we take our name from the father. Sometimes his name, sometimes his work. Like me. Kovacevic. Long ago, we work with the iron. We are kovac, how you say, smit?"

"Smiths? Like blacksmiths?"

"Yes! Kovacevic. Son of the smith. In English, Smithson! You see how it works?" He craned his head completely around to look at me, and I nodded, surreptitiously checking that my seat belt was fastened. "Long time ago, father's name is everything. It tells other tribe who you are, where you live. Whose sheep you can steal. Who you can marry." He turned back, and fished a half-smoked cigarette out of an overflowing ashtray. "Now, everyone just use Facebook." His eyes met mine in the rearview mirror. "What your father do?"

"He was a Buddhist monk."

Petar grunted, temporarily silenced by this. He lowered his window and lit up, sucking in a lungful of smoke before dangling his left arm outside, thoughtfully.

L.A. traffic karma must have somehow attached itself to my heels. All the brake lights ahead of us broke out in red, and an array of vehicles, old and new, many of them studded with Sarajevo Taxi signs, started to stack up end to end. A black-and-white, with *Policija* stenciled on its side, screamed past us, lights flashing.

"Pah!" Petar said. "Probably late for his woman."

"You don't approve of your police force?"

"What force? Is more like police *mess*. Everything for politics, nothing for the people. At the top, they take the money and turn the head. At bottom, they just take the money." Again, he twisted to meet my eyes. At least we were barely moving. "Ever since we have peace, too many presidents, no one in charge. Is like this with everything! Make committee for reforming police, write report, talk, talk, talk, draft law, and then Croats say no, not fair to Croats, and Serbs say no, too fair for Bosnians, and Slovenes say no, because everyone else say no. Nothing happen! They try to fix police for twenty years now, but nothing change. Only more confusion!"

I thought about the two cops in Van Nuys, and my suspicions. "It's a little like that everywhere in law enforcement," I said. "The right hand never seems to know what the left hand is doing."

"But here? Here we have one hundred hands."

He was very well informed, for a taxi driver.

A bright-blue tram that was attached to an overhead energy source by some sort of triangular leash zipped past us on its designated track. Our progress slowed to the pace of a drugged tortoise. I sighed, but Petar seemed to perk up at the potential for more uninterrupted time to talk. He waved his cigarette toward a series of rough-edged pockmarks, deep divots repaired with a kind of hardened, pink resin filling. Like blemishes, they spotted the road to our left.

"Sarajevo roses," Petar said. "From mortar shells."

I noticed several more. "Wow. Look at them all."

"You see on walls, too. We leave them to remember." Petar's voice grew indignant. "Every hour, every day, the shelling and the sniping. We have nowhere to go, nothing to eat. We cannot work. And other Bosnians, from outside the siege, they cannot use airport for helping us. Your UN say so!"

I had the feeling he'd spoken these words many times before.

"Many people die trying to cross tarmac with guns and food. And so we make tunnel, wheel in the food underground. I remember one time, old man and his granddaughter riding on wheeling cart holding sack of potatoes, big box of chewing gum for making bubbles, and bullets." He shook his head. "But I tell you this, if we not stop the Serbians, no one stop them!"

"It must have been terrible for you."

He grunted, temporarily placated. "You want, I show you tunnel, too. For four years, we hiding, living underground. Like rats. We are rat people."

He lapsed into silence. I closed my eyes for a moment, wishing him peace and freedom from these old wounds. Then I concentrated more on observation, and less on conversation.

Our final descent revealed a surprisingly lush, hilly terrain dissected with twisting roads. A river wound through the valley like a silver ribbon, with smaller streams branching off. The city itself had staked its claim in a hilly valley surrounded by Himalaya-like alps. Any area of flat appeared heavily industrialized, with sparser development spreading outward and upward into the hills, like a reverse flow of lava. From above, I could clearly see how civilization, here as everywhere, had marred nature with manmade evidence of ever-expanding human need.

We crawled past miles of overgrown fields bordered by small groves of trees interspersed with ugly, graffiti-splotched walls and run-down industrial plants: a typical airport-adjacent landscape.

The sky was a deep blue, but dark thunderclouds were collecting on the horizon, as if convening for a storm convention. The traffic, however, decided to clear, and we picked up speed. As we entered the outskirts of Sarajevo itself, I realized here, too, my expectations had painted reality with inaccurate brushstrokes.

In my mind, Sarajevo was still a bombed-out shell of a city. In reality, it was more like a woman who had undergone a series of cosmetic reconstructions, from a somewhat clumsy surgeon, perhaps, but with relative success. You could see the scars here and there, but the overall effect was far from unattractive.

The wide thoroughfare leading into the city proper was tree-lined and sported grassy sidewalk avenues and ubiquitous tram tracks.

"Bosnia Street," Petar commented. "Further up, we call it *Snajper,* sorry, 'Sniper Alley.' Back then, you walk, you die. You ride bicycle, you die. Children, womans, they don't care. Bang!"

The numerous high-rise buildings overlooking the street explained why. Snipers had any number of perfect aerial sites for their deadly hobby. I noted several Soviet-era apartment houses, badly damaged, I assumed, during the siege, but for the most part reconstructed. Unfortunately, they retained their earlier squat, unappealing form, every floor crowded with rows of windows, the multiple stories stacked like grimy egg crates.

Up ahead, the cityscape revealed more blocky apartment complexes, but also gleaming new skyscrapers, old-style brick buildings, numerous elegant spires, and the occasional globular mosque. One startling building, of blue glass, spiraled upward, as if a giant hand had wound its frame into a twist for fun. On both sides, sprawling hillsides were almost completely covered with optimistic, white stucco homes under slanted, terra-cotta-colored roofs.

Petar pulled to a stop.

"Your hotel," he said.

I tried not to wince at the hideous multistoried structure, the color of rancid yellow topped with an unmentionable shade of brown. Sarajevo's Holiday Inn, the only functioning hotel left partially standing during the Bosnian War, had also been renovated, and inexplicably returned to its former state of garish glory.

What were they thinking?

As if reading my mind, Petar provided me with an explanation so weird, it had to be true.

"Used to be famous circus here. Big, big tent, yellow and brown."

Another tram trundled past.

"Twenty-two KMs," Petar now stated, pointing a nicotine-stained thumb at his meter for confirmation. "Sorry. Bad traffic."

I handed over a 50-mark bill—pastel pink, "Jovan Dučić"—and asked for a 20 back—light tan, "Filip Višnjić." An eight-dollar tip seemed about right, given his wealth of knowledge.

Petar seemed astonished, and flashed me a gap-toothed grin. He passed over a Sarajevo Taxi card, stained with coffee, his number hand-scrawled on the back.

"So, you call, you need driver, yes?"

"I will."

"Okay, Ten-zing Monkevic. I see you soon then."

The air smelled slightly of electricity, and the mid-afternoon sky suddenly darkened, as if the sun decided to quit early. As Petar hastily unloaded my roller-bag from the trunk, I thought of Agvan Supply's website. I had a final question.

"Petar, can you talk to me about the name Zarko Stasic?"

He frowned. "Zarko is Serb name. Why you ask?"

I tucked that piece of information away. "No reason. What about Stasic? What does a Stasic do?"

His initial answer was tentative. "*Stas* mean strong, I think, or, no, more like important." He thought longer, and nodded, his voice definite. "Important. Long ago, first father rich. Very good at stealing sheep."

CHAPTER 17

The skies opened, and I was pelted with a Bosnian summer downpour worthy of the title "monsoon." A sharp gust of wind blew the rain sideways. I wheeled my bag straight past the doorman and pulled up, dripping, inside a huge atrium that comprised most of the hotel's lobby. The pattern on the carpet made me queasy. A central glass elevator rose up through a bizarre series of circular floors. Continuing with the circus theme, the interior bar regaled its customers with strips of yellow and brown fabric overhead, still trying to duplicate a tent, I supposed.

I checked in, using the credit card attached to my Julius Rosen account, and was given a third-floor room. The female desk clerk was young, blonde, and bored. She yawned, checking her watch before handing me a keycard. I elected to wheel my own bag. I would ask about Bill's room number upstairs—for whatever reason, front desks were much more likely to give out that kind of information to registered guests over the phone. Maybe they felt protected by the anonymity of a voice exchange.

Two of the four elevators were broken.

Upstairs, the corridor was gloomy and dank, and smelled of chlorine and stale cigarette smoke. My room was more of the same—the curtains were faded and full of small holes, and hung lopsided, half-off their rods. Stained carpet, dangling drawer handles, and mysterious burn marks in the lampshades. The sheets, at least, looked clean, but the queen-size mattress sagged in the middle like the spine of an old workhorse. Rain beat against the glass as I tried, unsuccessfully, to crack open the window. A small half-filled pool lay below, as well as a thick lock and chain to keep out any guest foolish enough to attempt a swim.

I missed my cat.

I went into the bathroom to relieve myself and noticed three curly black hairs clinging to the bathtub drain. A homicide detective's forensic jackpot, but the only crime here was charging anyone to stay in this dump.

Back in the bedroom, the hotel telephone was dead.

"Okay. I'm done."

I wheeled my bag back down the dim corridor, and took the same elevator to the lobby.

In my fairly limited experience, desk clerks all over the world have two qualities that endear them to detectives: a wealth of inside information, and a chronic lack of funds. According to his nametag, Tomas Duvic was now on duty; he was lean and tall, blue-eyed with a bleached-blond buzz cut. Younger than me, maybe 25.

Our conversation was quick and to the point.

"Could you call Mr. Bohannon's room and let him know Mr. Norbu has arrived?"

He pecked at a keyboard. "I am sorry, Mr. Norbu, but Mr. Bohannon, he check out last night."

I wanted to weep with gratitude, but managed to stay calm. "Do you know where he went, Tomas?"

"No. I cannot say."

Every rookie cop quickly learns the big difference between "no" and "I cannot say." He was giving me something to work with.

"Please. This is very important to me." I accompanied my heartfelt plea with a heartwarming gift of a 50-mark note. The bill disappeared into his pocket, a little circus magic.

"Mr. Bohannon, he leave word that if anyone come looking for him, they can talk to Detective Josip Tomic at Sarajevo Centar Police Station."

I wrote the name in my notebook: Josip Tomic. Maybe not 35 dollars' worth of information, but at least I had a starting point. "Okay. Where's the police station?"

"Next to St. Joseph's Church, across from city center. Not far from here. About two kilometers."

"Good. Also, I'd like you to cancel my reservation, please, and refund my card." Another bill, this one a 20, evaporated into thin air.

"I am sorry you are leaving," Tomas said, his voice smooth. "You are not liking the hotel?"

"Let me put it this way," I said. "If it turns out Detective Josip Tomic decides to keep me in a cell overnight, I'll consider it an upgrade."

Outside, a different doorman helped an elderly passenger into another Sarajevo Taxi, just beyond the jutting entrance, which was painted a different, also sickly shade of yellow. I waited, as rain dripped off both sides of the overhang.

The doorman came back up the walkway and smiled at me. His nametag identified him as Faruk Rosevic. Son of a florist, maybe?

"Excuse me, do you speak English?"

"Leetle bit," he said, holding his index finger a half-inch from his thumb. Some language is universal. As are some shortcuts. I palmed another magic bill from my wallet.

"Were you on duty last night?"

"No, Jurg is night bellman."

"Can you call him?"

He frowned. "Maybe not. He will be sleeping."

Another 50-mark barrier. I used my superpowers to make the bill disappear from my hand and reappear in his. He pulled a flip-top cell phone from his coat pocket.

"Here's what I need to know, Faruk. A tall American man left here last night. His name is Bill Bohannon."

He bobbed his head. "Yes. I remember him. *Policija.* From California."

"I need to find out where he went."

Faruk returned his cell phone to his pocket. "No need for Jurg. I know where he go."

I whipped out a final 50 and raised my eyebrows. Faruk's face, already mournful, took on the look of a heartbroken hound.

"Only one?" he said, his tone bewildered.

He and his countrymen might be newcomers to capitalism, but they seemed to be catching on fast. I was running low on 50s, and had no intention of moving up the pay ladder. I toughened my expression, and firmed my shoulders.

He understood perfectly.

"He went to different hotel." Now he rubbed finger and thumb together. "Very expensive."

"How do you know that?"

"Jurg tell me, after finish work."

"Why would he tell you a thing like that?"

"We talk about guests all the time. Is our only pleasure. This job is hard and lonely; we cannot even watch shows on television, like maids do. You like football?"

Not being able to watch TV while you work—that's really scraping by.

Faruk pointed to the bill in my hand. "Please I have one more? For my friend Jurg?"

He was walking a thin tightrope between capitalist and con artist, but I added a 20. The money might not find its way to Jurg, but that fell into the gigantic category called Not My Business. He seemed satisfied with his take, and wrote *Hotel Europe* in the margin of my tour book.

He began the process of finding and flagging a cab, but I had spotted one idling in the shadows of an alley just past the hotel, as if on a break. I followed a hunch. Sure enough, when I got close, the driver of Sarajevo Taxi 108 jumped out of his dusty green Mercedes.

"Monkevic! You don't like our Holiday Hotel?"

Into the trunk went my rolling suitcase and I slid into the backseat feeling as overjoyed as if I'd reunited with an old friend.

"Hotel Europe," I said.

Petar whistled. "Very fancy," he said. "You bring suit and tie with you, Monkevic?"

Our new destination was a 15-minute crawl along slick streets crowded with vehicles. I could have probably walked faster, but my description of the Holiday Inn made Petar laugh so hard the fare was worth it.

"You like this one much better," he said. "Right next to Baščaršija, marketplace in Stari Grad, Old Town. Very beautiful. I take you around, you like. Walking, I not charge, okay? Catholic Church. Orthodox Church. Synagogue for Jew, mosque for Muslim. Everything but Buddha temple for you, Monkevic. Maybe you stay, build one! Make father proud!"

By the time Petar disgorged me in front of the elegant entrance, the rain had slacked off to a slight drizzle. International flags flapped overhead. The exterior of the hotel was promising, part brick and stucco, part steel and glass, a tasteful blend of old and new. This doorman's eyes lingered on my minimalist baggage and casual dress, but he swung open the door anyway.

Quelle différence, as Valerie would say. The lobby was also a hybrid. Modern pillars, lights, and flooring were warmed up in the corners by antique armchairs and an Oriental rug. The bar-restaurant to my right was a gleaming mixture of glass chandeliers; more antique chairs; and clean, architectural lines. A sprightly piece of classical music played in the background.

The wide smile from a female desk clerk working behind an angled front desk the color of dark slate faded slightly when I confessed I didn't have a reservation.

"The hotel is extremely busy right now. I doubt we have a room available. Please give me a moment to look." Her pronunciation was slightly British, and impeccable.

"Before you do that, can I confirm that my business colleague, Bill Bohannon, arrived here safely?"

She tapped the keyboard with curved, manicured nails. "Yes, he checked in yesterday."

"Great," I said.

She squinted at the screen. "You are in luck. We have a cancellation on a deluxe single. Austro-Hungarian, all the moderns are booked I'm afraid. It's on the same floor as Mr. Bohannon."

I pulled out my credit card.

"How many nights, sir?"

"Two, I think. May I ask the cost?"

"Of course. One hundred seventy-eight euros, including surcharges."

Steep, but not as steep as I'd feared.

"Per night," she added. My face gave me away. "Breakfast is included," she added, "and we have a fully equipped well-ness center."

The Holiday Inn was less than half the cost. Bill had vaulted several levels above his Detective III pay grade. Outside, the rain had returned and was falling in sheets. I pictured three curly hairs crawling out of a tub drain, like insect legs.

"I'll take it," I said.

She gave me a lovely, old-fashioned key for a fourth-floor room. I saved a few KMs by bell-hopping myself there. The room was warm and immaculate, with fresh flowers by the flat-screen television and a bowl of fruit on a gleaming mahogany table, flanked by two more of the now-familiar antique, upholstered armchairs. Outside the rain-streaked window lay the cobbled streets of Stari Grad, dominated by a dramatic copper-tipped minaret. I finally felt as if I were in a different era and country.

I unpacked, which took all of five minutes. The bath-room was spotless, the huge tub deep enough to dive into. Maybe later. I stripped off my damp clothing and made do with a quick shower, using the handheld sprayer and very hot water to wash the airplane off. Clean pair of jeans, clean black T-shirt, and done. It was almost five o'clock in the afternoon, Bosnian time, and I still hadn't laid eyes on Bill.

Munching on an apple, I ordered up a pot of Viennese coffee, which arrived in five minutes, delivered on a tray by an elderly waiter. I inspected the tray—cup, napkin, red rose, small pot of sturdy roast, and a bowl of whipped cream. The scent made me whimper. I poured, spooned in fluffy cream, and stirred until the coffee was a uniform light chocolate-brown. One sip of the intensely rich brew and I declared my hotel investment a wise one.

The Buddha cautions us about such attachments, but the Buddha never tried to stay in the Sarajevo Holiday Inn.

One more cup, and I felt ready. I dialed the hotel operator.

"Can you please connect me with Mr. Bohannon's room?"

"Certainly. Oh, I'm sorry, sir. He has requested that any calls be diverted to the front desk. Can I take a message?"

"Can you give me his room number?"

"No."

No wiggle room there.

"But if you leave your message here," she added smoothly, "I'll make sure he gets it."

"Thank you, I may just do that," I said, and hung up. The truth was I didn't know how Bill would respond to my presence here. Who knows? He might even take off.

My eye fell on the tray of coffee. I called room service again.

"This is Bill Bohannon. On the fourth floor? I'd like to order a fresh pot of coffee for my room, please. As soon as possible." I hung up.

I imagined the chain of events that followed. Room service calls front desk. Front desk sees Bill has put a hold on calls. Front desk gives room service Bill's room number.

I stationed myself near the service elevator. After seven minutes, the same elderly waiter appeared wheeling a tray of coffee similar to mine, but with two cups, a bigger pot of coffee, and a bigger bowl of whipped cream.

He wheeled silently down the hall. He stopped in front of a door, lifted his fist to knock, and then paused, distressed. A "Do Not Disturb" sign dangled from the doorknob.

My man appeared paralyzed by this service dilemma. He double-checked his invoice, tucked inside a small leather folder. Squaring his shoulders, he knocked lightly.

In a moment the door opened and I heard Bill's distinctive rumble, somewhat gruff.

C'mon, Bill, it's coffee.

The cart wheeled inside.

After a moment, the waiter left, and I was looking at the same "Do Not Disturb" sign. I had come too far and was too exhausted to obey. I rapped sharply.

Bill yanked the door open, wrapped inside a plush hotel robe. He looked annoyed. Also different. Younger.

"*Tashi delek,*" I said, my voice bright. "That's Tibetan for *surprise!!!*"

Bill's eyes bulged. "What the hell are you doing here?"

"What the hell happened to your mustache?" I answered. His upper lip was pink and exposed, the bushy silver caterpillar gone.

Bill's head snapped around. And I finally understood. Mila Radovic sat cross-legged on a king-size bed, naked but for a shawl held across her front. She adjusted the shawl, wrapping it loosely around her, and strode over.

"What is this?" she said, her voice scimitar-sharp.

We were caught for a moment in time, players in a corny melodrama called *The Husband, the Detective, and the Half-Naked Bosnian Amazon.* Also, the *Elderly Waiter,* who apparently had neglected to get Bill's signature. He stood in the doorway behind me, leather folder in hand, eyes darting between Bill and me as he tried to pretend there wasn't also a wildly attractive half-naked woman in the room, one slipped shawl away from showing everything.

Bill scribbled on the invoice and pushed the waiter back into the hallway, closing the door behind him. The hotel personnel would feast on this for months. Who needs television?

I finally remembered to breathe as Mila disappeared into the bathroom and marched back out cinching a second hotel bathrobe tight. She stalked to the bed and again sat cross-legged, leaning her back against a leather headboard. Some small, unflustered part of my brain registered that this room was in fact a suite, and decorated in a completely different, post-modern style, all glass tops and bamboo wall coverings, with boxy chairs upholstered in thick beige corduroy.

Bill continued to glare.

"Martha asked me to come," I said. "I didn't feel good about it, and I still don't, but here I am." I was trying out Kim's technique of telling the inarguable truth. If it worked for people with autism, maybe it would work for me and my cheating ex-partner. I decided to save my more complicated feelings about Bill's betrayal of Lola and Maude for a later discussion.

Mila turned to Bill, angry. "You say your wife understands!"

"I did not! I said she was an understanding woman," he sputtered, as Mila jumped off the bed, grabbed a pile of clothes from a chair, and marched back into the bathroom. "There's a difference!"

The bathroom door slammed.

Bill groaned.

I pointed to the cart. "The coffee's excellent here, Bill."

"Shut up, Ten."

I helped myself to another cup. No need to let it go to waste.

"Where are you staying?"

I told him. Down the hall.

"Great. Fuck. Okay, just, just go to your room. I'll come talk to you in a little while."

I returned to my deluxe single, slightly deflated. I'd taken this trip fueled by impulse, and little else. What was I supposed to do next? I was exhausted. The carpet shifted under my feet as I succumbed to a strange sinking sensation, as if I were standing in quicksand, with nothing at hand to bail me out. I still couldn't even call Martha, unless I wanted to spend probably another $100 of my own money using the hotel phone. And even if I did reach her, what would I say? "I found your husband shacked up with Mila in a five-hundred-dollar hotel room. Shall I kill him, or remove him by force?"

Her answer would scorch my eardrums.

Bill showed up a few minutes later dressed in designer jeans and a trendy, striped button-down shirt. He looked ten years younger, despite the miserable expression. He'd brought the coffee with him, which was a small plus.

He plopped into an armchair. "Did you have to do this?" he asked.

"I'm here, so yes, apparently I had to do it."

"Don't get metaphysical on me, ass-hat. Just because Martha asks you to do something, you don't automatically have to obey. You could have said *no*."

"Well, I didn't." I was in no mood to explain the complicated squeeze-box of emotions that had forced a "yes" out of me.

"Do you have any idea how hard this is for me, having you just show up here like this?"

I said nothing, and the self-serving words from his trickster mind landed between us. They lay in a heap, like coyote scat.

"How's Martha?" he muttered, embarrassed at last.

"Why don't you call her and find out for yourself? You might consider asking about Maude and Lola, while you're at it."

He threw up his arms. "I will, I will!" He slumped even further. "Shit. Are they doing okay?"

"What does *okay* even mean? The girls are understandably upset. As for Martha, I think she's over the stage where she wants to strangle you. I mean, she said she wanted you to come home, although now? Who knows? And pardon me for asking, but do you have any plans to do that?"

He shook his head. "Sasha arrives back in Sarajevo tonight. I get to meet my son for the first time, Ten. No way am I missing that."

"And Mila?"

His head dropped. "No idea," he said. "All I know is I want her, more than I've ever wanted anything."

"Well, looks like you got her."

"Not quite," he answered. "Close. Until you showed up."

"Ahh." A small kernel of hope stirred in my chest. We met eyes.

"And you know what they say . . ." Bill's mouth gave a small twitch.

I did know, because Bill always made sure I did, whenever I screwed up a case.

"'Close only counts in horseshoes,'" we recited together, and shared our first quasi-comfortable moment. The hope grew.

"Shit," Bill said. "I'm having some kind of midlife crisis, aren't I?"

"Well, let's look at the evidence: You've run off to a foreign country. You've lost weight, shaved your mustache, and bought new clothes. And oh, yes—you're staying in a five-star hotel with a beautiful woman and no immediate plans to return home to your wife and two children, who are all totally saddened and disturbed by your disappearance. You tell me, Detective."

"Crap," Bill said.

"So what do I tell her?"

"Who?"

"Your *wife*."

Bill's face reddened, and he pounced on self-righteous anger, the universal weapon against shame. "Tell Martha I'm an asshole! That's what all of you think. Tell her you don't like the way I'm living my life. I'm sure that'll be a great comfort to her."

I'd run out of replies. Suddenly all I could think about was a nap.

"I'm exhausted, Bill. I hate the way we're communicating. I miss my friend, the one I knew I could trust." More of Kim's truth-telling technique: three observations in a row he couldn't argue with. The effect was startling.

Bill started to cry. I'd only seen this once before, at the birth of his twins. Then, the tears had flowed freely. This was more like a one-man wrestling match.

I sat quietly, trying to make space for whatever happened next.

Bill struggled and gasped, knuckling at his eyes, swearing under his breath, until he'd tamed the outburst. "I feel as if this is my chance to change my life, Ten," he said, "ah, fuck," and his voice cracked again. "Like I missed my chance twenty years ago. I don't want to miss it again."

I felt the heat rise in my own cheeks. "Your life isn't so bad. Some people would call it great."

He nodded, but his eyes disagreed. "Maybe it's an age thing. I'm coming up on fifty. I feel like I'm dying inside."

It was official: Bill had lost his mind. The old Bill would have taken a bullet rather than say something like "I'm dying inside." And there was worse to follow.

"Martha and I haven't had sex in over a year."

My belly cringed from this piece of news. Bill and Martha's sex life was a mutually agreed-upon off-limits topic, throughout the time we were partners, and ever since.

"I don't know what to say. You guys have always seemed rock solid. My ideal match."

"Used to be, but after the twins were born things started to change. And then they just kept on changing. She was with them twenty-four seven. She had to be. And wanted to be, she said. But after six months, she said she couldn't do it all by herself, take care of the girls, worry about me. And after a couple of years, she said she was going to crack if I didn't help more. I changed jobs for her, quit the gym, started to give the girls breakfast, come home in time to feed them dinner and put them to bed, but nothing was enough. Ten, I talked to you about all this, more than once. You didn't want to hear. And now you don't want to remember."

He wasn't wrong. When their reality didn't match my expectations, I'd chosen to ignore it.

I waved my arm around the room. "So all this is just a reaction, a form of punishment?" Bill's face tightened.

"You think that's what this is about? That I'm here to get back at Martha?"

"Easy, Bill. I'm not saying that's all. But look at your body right now. Listen to the tone of your voice. It's worth considering."

He stared at his clenched fists. "Anybody but you suggests something like that, I'd clock him."

A sharp knock on the door caused both of us to jump. I opened it. Mila stood waiting, dressed in her uniform of jeans and a men's button-down shirt knotted at the waist.

"Time to go," she said to Bill. "Are you coming?" Her tone was all business, but her lower lip trembled slightly, and her eyes were red. She'd been crying, too.

Bill stood. "Of course. Of course I'm coming."

A minuscule curve of the lips gathered force until a wide, bright smile occupied Mila's entire face, the first I'd seen from her. Joy lifted her high cheekbones and illuminated her dark-brown eyes. I felt something stir in my own chest. A smile like that could cause a man to make some very brave or very stupid life choices.

Bill moved to her side.

"Where are you going?" I asked.

"Train station," Bill said.

"Want company?" I asked. "You know, just in case?"

Mila's and Bill's expressions were matched portraits of resistance. I got the message.

CHAPTER 18

I stretched out on top of the big, soft comforter and tried to nap, but sleep wasn't happening. I pushed upright and shoved some pillows behind my back.

Meditation wasn't happening either.

I pulled out my tourist guide to Sarajevo and located my hotel and the train station.

A nice, brisk walk was just the thing to cure my insomnia.

My phone suddenly, inexplicably, decided to work, and a series of beeps and buzzes let me know I had lots of messages and texts.

Eight, to be precise, and all from Martha. The final text summed up her concerns nicely: WHERE THE HELL ARE YOU? CALL ME!!!

I calculated the time difference. Four P.M. here meant 8 A.M. there. Nobody calls a person that early. It's uncivilized.

I adapted my route to the train station to include the ancient, bustling marketplace, and was glad I did. The area was closed off to cars, and I shared damp cobblestone streets with a fascinating mix of people and architecture. The fastest way to get the feel of a new place is to take a nice long stroll and observe the expressions of your fellow pedestrians. Doesn't work in Los Angeles, of course—nobody walks—but the wide, busy walkways of Stari Grad were perfect for taking the pulse of the local populace. I expected to find "earnest, stressed, and careworn." Instead, I found everything: young, old, eager, exhausted, weighed down by shopping bags, and holding out beggar's cups. Two old men in berets moved life-size chess pieces around a giant board. A child and her grandmother scattered breadcrumbs inside a flapping swirl of hungry pigeons, next to an antiquated wooden fountain sporting a round cap of green copper. Couples pushing baby carriages, and men, as well as women, in business attire. I noted two or three women in headscarves, and one in a somber black burka, a pair of elegant shoes peeking out from under the hem. None of the women were dressed like Mila's mother Irena, though, with that odd combination of headscarf and monk-like tunic.

And everywhere I looked, magnificent places of worship from every conceivable tradition: chapels; temples; here a looming Gothic cathedral of white stone, with twin bell towers and a statue of a human God pointing to His heart; there a gracious mosque with an ornate urn-shaped fountain and a facade decorated in glorious blues and reds.

I'd always wanted to go to Jerusalem. Stari Grad felt like its Balkan twin.

I checked my map and left Old Town, following the river for about a mile. At one point my route took me across Latin Bridge, where Archduke Franz Ferdinand's assassination sparked the First World War. I touched the stone, feeling into the arched spans of history, expecting the dark weight of shame. I sensed, instead, a kind of faded resignation.

The Sarajevo train station was a looming curve of glass and brick that overlooked a wide courtyard that was divided into huge decorative squares of pavement. A man bent over the rim of a large, circular fountain, drinking from one of several stone fish-heads spouting water into its center. My throat was dry, but I took a pass.

The spacious, sleek station offered another homage to thirst, this one a gigantic mural of a dehydrated cartoon train sucking Coca-Cola out of a straw. I settled for a bottle of water from one of the kiosks lining the perimeter of the main floor. There were maybe 50 or so people milling about, but no sign of Bill or Mila.

I located the arrivals board, and saw that a train from Dubrovnik had just pulled in. There were no other imminent arrivals. Hopefully, Sasha hadn't come at an earlier time. I noted the number and rode an escalator down to the tracks. A train sat about a hundred meters ahead of me. I ducked behind a pillar and studied the clump of people gathered by the track. It wasn't hard to spot Mila and Bill—they stood half a head taller than anyone else in the throng. They were peering at the steady stream of disembarking passengers, by now slowed to a trickle.

Something caught my eye. A man, leaning against another pillar scarcely ten feet in front of me. He held his phone aloft, and I was close enough to see Mila and Bill's tiny heads captured on his screen. I grabbed my own phone and clicked. I only caught the back of his head. A greasy black ponytail hung down his back like a limp rope. He was wiry in build, and three or four inches shorter than me, which meant he was short.

I scrunched my head into my shoulders, lowered my eyes, and walked swiftly toward Bill and Mila, hoping to catch a closer glimpse as I moved past the other guy. A quick glance told me he was in his late twenties, or maybe older. Hard to tell. His sharp features were already grooved with deep-cut lines. Twelve feet beyond, I bent over, pretending to tie my shoelace, and noted the gun-like bulge in his right pocket.

I was planning a reverse cruise for closer study, when Mila's voice rang out.

"Sasha!"

Farther up ahead, a tall young man stepped into Mila's fierce hug, while Bill rocked awkwardly on his heels beside them. Jet lag must have taken over, because I found myself glancing behind to see if my sharp-faced spy was capturing the meeting with his phone. I broke a cardinal rule of surveillance.

I made eye contact.

Shit.

He jerked his phone aside, shot me a look of undiluted aggression, and bolted, heading for the escalators. Instinct took over. I tore after him.

My flying tackle brought us both down with a hard thud. He wriggled out from under me, and I grabbed a handful of greasy ponytail. He howled with pain, pulling away from me hard, and I felt like I had a mad dog on a leash. Shouts broke out around us. He twisted his head and tried to bite my wrist.

"Cut it out!" I yelled. His other hand went for the gun pocket, but I pinned his wrist to his side. A security guard ran up, pulling his gun. I had my guy in a viselike grip and was trying to wrest the phone out of his hand as he wriggled and squirmed. The situation was spinning out of control. I didn't want to let him go, but I also didn't want to explain to the local security why I had one of Sarajevo's fine citizens in a chokehold. Flashing my California private detective license wasn't likely to help.

Extreme times call for extreme versions of the truth. I pointed and bellowed, "HELP! THE PHONE!" Who was I to argue if the security guard mistakenly thought the man had stolen my cell phone? I tightened my throttlehold and the guard wrested the phone from his fist. I let go. "Thank you!" I panted, holding out my hand. He gave it over, triumphant. "*Dobro!* Good!" he said.

The "thief" began spouting off at the guard, and I took off running. The up escalator was broken, but I sprinted the motionless steps, two at a time. Bill was waiting at the top, Sasha and Mila behind him.

"What the fuck are you up to now, Ten? Are you trying to get us all arrested?"

Mila's eyes flashed with fury, while Sasha settled for mildly belligerent. For the first time, I noticed that he had a companion, a slender waif hiding behind him, with haunted eyes.

Terrible eyes.

I felt sure those eyes had witnessed awful things.

"Outside. Hurry!" I pushed past them and quickly walked across the expansive waiting room. I exited the doors that led to the main street, as opposed to the open courtyard. I slowed to a less obvious pace, and worked my way along several blocks until I came to a major intersection. Only then did I stop and look behind me. Bill arrived first, then Mila. Sasha and the girl were a few yards behind them. She clutched Sasha's upper arm with both hands.

I pulled them into a huddle. "Sorry. A guy was photographing you. I got his phone, but it was getting a little tricky back there."

Sasha's body came to full alert. He spoke for the first time. "We haven't been introduced. I'm Sasha, Sasha Radovic, and this is Belma." His English was excellent. At the sound of her name, Belma ducked behind Sasha.

"Let's get out of here." I flagged down a cab, Sarajevo Taxi 377. I opened the front passenger door and flashed a nice blue bill.

"Hotel Europe." My circular motion included the others. "Can you take all of us?"

"*Da.*"

I climbed into the front. The other four squeezed into the back. Fifteen minutes later we were safely back inside Bill's suite, and I could lower my shoulders.

Belma stared at the elegant sitting room. She whispered a few words.

Sasha smiled. "She says she must be dreaming."

I felt glad. Those haunted eyes deserved to see something besides suffering.

Bill reached for the phone.

"No," Sasha said. "Give it to me." I made a gut decision, and handed the phone to Sasha. He moved to the sofa to sit, Belma glued to his side. He started to scroll through the photographs. Across the room, Bill retreated into sullen silence.

"Not good."

"What is it?" Bill said. We both moved close to take a look.

"Look at this." Sasha flicked through a series of photos. Bill and Mila greeting Sasha at the train, Mila hugging Sasha, Sasha frowning at Bill, several shots of Belma clutching Sasha's arm. The final photograph grabbed my attention for a different reason. Not only had the man obviously made me as a fellow spy instantly, the angle of the image he captured of me, bending over to tie my shoelaces, visibly proved I both was, and seemed to somehow suddenly own, a monumental ass.

Bill lightly punched my arm. "You're a menace," he said, "but I'm glad you followed us. Even though I told you not to." A hint of amusement. Bill and I had a long history of me leaping headlong into actions he'd specifically warned me against. Some traditions have sticking power.

"Sasha, can you check recent calls and see if you spot anything?" I asked.

Sasha started to tap and scroll. Belma tucked her legs under her on the sofa. She nestled her slight body into Sasha, as if seeking shelter from a dangerous world.

"How old is she?" I asked.

"Uh, thirteen," Sasha said, distracted.

Thirteen years old.

Mila was on her own phone by the bedroom area, arguing with someone in a low, angry voice. As far as I could tell, Mila's emotions ranged from annoyed to really annoyed.

"Almost all the calls go to either Dubrovnik, over on the coast, or to Kosovo," Sasha said.

At the word "Dubrovnik," the girl hissed, her body shrinking into itself. Sasha murmured to her, his voice low. She relaxed a little.

"Belma's from Kosovo," he said. "It's a major supplier for human trafficking. Dubrovnik's the port most traffickers use from there. Belma arrived two weeks ago. That's how long it takes to desensitize the girls."

"Desensitize?" I wasn't sure I wanted to know the answer.

"Make them compliant," Sasha explained, his voice tight. "It's like brainwashing, only with their bodies. That's where we found her, in Dubrovnik, about to be shipped across to Italy."

"*Italy?*" Every answer led to more disbelief on my part.

Sasha shrugged. "Yeah, well, who's to say where she would have ended up eventually?"

"How was she taken?"

"She wasn't. She was sold, along with her two younger sisters." He darted a look his mother's way, but Mila was still on the phone, listening now, her brow furrowed. "To a couple of guys with ties to an international syndicate."

Two younger sisters, and she was 13. I couldn't wrap my mind around any of this. "But who sold them?"

Sasha's voice was matter-of-fact. "Her mother."

The air deadened, flattening the room. *Those eyes.*

I had to ask. "Does she know?"

Sasha shook his head. "No, and I hope she never will. She's clinging to a pretty thin lifeline as it is."

"How do they make the transfer without the girls knowing they got sold?" Bill asked. His eyes flicked over to Belma. "Can she understand . . . ?"

"Don't worry. She doesn't speak any English," Sasha said. "I'm not an idiot."

Bill opened his mouth. Closed it again.

"They grabbed the girls off the street on the way into town." Sasha directed his words at me. "The mother sent the three of them to the market to buy food. Belma's one of eight sisters."

Mila ended her call and joined us.

"Who was that?" Sasha said.

"Your grandmother," Mila answered. "She ask me to bring you and the girl to meet her imam. She says he knows how to fix all this. I say no. She screamed at me. Always the same with her and me."

Sasha glanced down at Belma. She had fallen into a light sleep. He gently extricated his body from hers. He found an extra blanket in the closet, draped it over her body, and motioned us to the bedroom area, across the room.

Mila lowered her voice. "How this girl becomes your charge?" I heard concern. I also heard, "Son, have you lost your mind?"

Sasha turned to me once again. He seemed to be avoiding both parents. "When I was a little boy I often brought home strays. Dogs. Cats. Once a wounded crow. They caused my mother endless trouble. She thinks I've graduated to human strays. Like it's a progressive disease or something."

Bill jumped in to defend Mila. "It's a reasonable assumption, Sasha."

Mila touched Bill's shoulder. "It's okay."

Sasha shot Mila a look. "No, it's not. It's none of his business."

Bill's second chance at life was looking pretty thorny right now. I thought of Maude's disappointed wail, just the other day, based on unrealistic expectations: *But in my mind, he bringed me something!* In Bill's mind, Sasha wanted a father.

I changed the subject. "So Sasha, how did you get from California to here, exactly?"

Sasha looked at me, as if seeing me for the first time.

"I'm sorry. And who are you, *exactly?*"

Mila jumped in. "He is detective, from Los Angeles. I ask him to help find you, when you disappear and we think you are there."

Bill held off adding the obvious, his and my connection. I think Sasha had him a little cowed.

Sasha looked me over, the same piercing gaze as Mila's. I stood easily, breathing. Finally, he nodded.

"I've been working on a piece called 'Extraction.' That's the term traffickers use for picking up the kids they've bought. Last week I followed these two kids, both boys, to Los Angeles."

"To Van Nuys Airport?"

"Where? Van Nuys? No, LAX. Some traffickers flew the little boys over with a woman, a nurse I think. I got video of her using these tiny syringes to give them injections; they slept the whole way."

Right. This jibed with what Stephanie had told me. I shuddered, as I realized the implication of what Sasha was saying.

"What happened when they got to LAX?"

He gave a weary shrug. "I lost them, outside the airport. Then I spent three futile days trying to track them down. I had a couple of possible addresses, but that city of yours, the freeways . . ." He trailed off, as if still in a state of disbelief. I understood. When I moved to Los Angeles, at Sasha's age exactly, I was overwhelmed by the scale and high-speed intensity of the roadways. It took two years of practice on surface streets before I got up the nerve to attempt a freeway.

"And then?" Bill prodded.

"I have a friend working with me on the story. She called while I was still driving around somewhere south of Los Angeles like a crazy person."

"Wait a minute," I asked. "Driving around in what? You're too young to rent a car."

Sasha's eyes turned shifty. "I might have used a fake ID."

"And where you get money for this?" Mila hissed. "Flying everywhere, renting cars!"

Sasha again ignored her. "Anyway, my friend asked me to come back, meet her in Dubrovnik. She'd followed Belma and her sisters to the port and wanted to do something radical."

Mila's eyes narrowed. "What friend?"

Sasha hesitated. Seemed to make a decision. "Her name is Audrey. Audrey Thatcher, Mother. I want you to meet her. In fact . . ." He glanced at his phone. "Audrey's arriving any minute. I already texted her to come straight here."

Mila's eyes became suspicious slits. "Where is this Audrey from?"

"Cambridge. In England."

"England? My God, Sasha!" She lapsed into a rapid stream of throaty Bosnian.

"Not now," Sasha said. "We'll talk about it later."

My eyes cut over to Bill, who was responding to this latest drama by acting completely paralyzed. He'd blithely parachuted into unknown territory. Now he was the third player in a two-person tug-of-war that had been going on for almost 20 years. He didn't know which end of the rope to pull on.

"None of that matters. There's something I want all of you to see," Sasha said. "I shot this on the train today." He touched the screen on his phone and a video of Belma began to play. He paused it. "I asked her to tell me something about her life. She speaks a dialect that I have trouble following sometimes, but I'll translate as best I can."

Belma's voice was as devastating as her eyes, a childish lilt burdened with fatigue and despair.

"She says she has always been hungry, that when she goes to sleep, no, sorry, that she tries to hurry to go to sleep each night so she can escape her hunger. The only time she can remember being full was after the men pulled her and her sisters into the van. The men had sacks of hamburgers. She and her sisters ate so many they passed out. She says she loves very much her two younger sisters." On the screen, Belma began to cry.

Sasha paused it. "Eight girls in the family. Her mother probably decided to sell off some of the younger ones. The gangsters gave the girls doped-up hamburgers to knock them out for the journey."

"How did she get separated from the other two?" Bill asked.

Sasha met my eyes. "It was my fault. Audrey and I decided to perform an extraction of our own."

"Jesus!" Bill said.

Sasha shot him a get-out-of-my-face look. "What do you care?"

Bill backpedaled. "Sorry, I just. It sounds a bit impulsive, rash, that's all."

Sasha's eyes swung between Mila and Bill. "Maybe *rash* runs in the family."

I intervened again. "So what happened?"

"Audrey tracked them to a little hotel with one of those ground-floor restaurants. The traffickers were having dinner downstairs. Putting away a lot of vodka, you know? They'd locked the girls in a second-floor apartment, a private one, over the restaurant. Audrey kept an eye on them and I went up the outside fire escape. I popped a window with a crowbar.

"I expected them to rush to my arms, but they were terrified of me, so I had to climb inside. Finally I got Belma calmed down enough to explain what we were doing, but the little ones refused to go down the fire escape. So I took Belma's hand, she linked up with the two younger ones, and we headed for the stairs. I just prayed that the gangsters would be too drunk to notice."

This was where the mission got harebrained. Bill and I met eyes. Madness.

"We were halfway down when Audrey saw us, and freaked out. One of the guys had left the table, and was headed right for us."

"Jesus," Bill said again.

"He ran for us. I got in a solid kick and squeezed past with Belma, but he was able to grab the two younger girls. Audrey was all over him, scratching and kicking, but he shoved her off. Then we heard the other guy yelling, so I just threw Belma over my shoulder and took off."

"Wow," I said.

"I was worried sick until Audrey called a few minutes later to say she was okay, she'd gotten away. She stayed on in Dubrovnik last night to enter everything, you know, update the information. I came here to meet you. End of story."

"Quite a story," I said. "Even for a journalist."

"You took a lot of risks." Bill kept his voice mild.

Mila muttered something, a criticism in any language.

"Yeah, well, I'm sick to death of writing about this stuff, pushing words around instead of actually doing something to change the situation." He glared at Bill and me. "Forget it. You couldn't possibly understand."

CHAPTER 19

Audrey was a surprise. For one thing, she was closer in age to me than to Sasha. Her shoulder-length, light-brown hair was cut for both elegance and easy upkeep. The rest of her was all woman, from the strong planes of her face to the small waist and the rich contours of her hips. Through no fault of her own, she looked a lot like a younger Mila.

Was father-son karma coming around once again? I wondered how it would play out this time.

She and her expensive leather duffel had arrived moments before, and she'd hugged Sasha long and hard. Extricating herself, she took in the rest of us, clustered in the bedroom area. No fear—just curiosity. Sasha put his finger to his lips and pointed to the sleeping Belma. Audrey smiled and nodded. He led her over to us, like a prize.

"Audrey, this is my mother, Mila Radovic."

Mila's handshake was perfunctory. "I am pleased to meet you, Audrey." The flat tone of her voice suggested otherwise.

Audrey ignored the chill. "Sasha has told me so much about you. I look forward to getting to know you better." Her clipped British accent was BBC proper. That, along with her tailored clothes and Omega Seamaster watch, spelled education and the moneyed class.

"And this is my . . . this is the man who fathered me, Bill Bohannon, and his friend, Ten Norbu."

So Sasha wasn't so uninformed, after all.

Audrey's clear eyes lingered on each of us. "Pleased to meet you," she said, shaking our hands.

"Okay, then." Sasha seemed relieved to get the introductions over with. "Well?" He spread his hands. "What do we do now?"

"I'm sorry, sweetheart," Audrey said, "but I need a moment to catch up. I mean, a month ago, I didn't know you even existed. Now? All this? It's a little surreal. Kind of wonderful, but weird, too."

She was right; I, too, was starting to feel spacey. Like a character in a time warp.

Mila's brisk voice broke the spell. "All right. We know situation is unusual. We need fix mess."

A thought prodded: Was Mila just highly practical? Or was she one of those Fun Cops who blew the whistle when people started feeling too good around her? Time would tell, but I had my suspicions.

A follow-up question muscled its way forward, irritating, but probably accurate: Was I assuming things about Mila to justify my need for Bill to be a good boy and come home?

My eyes strayed to Bill. He was pulling on his upper lip, where his mustache used to be. His jaw was set.

Foolish me. Bill was not going to be a good boy, not for me, not for Martha. He'd gotten hold of something here, like a dog with a bone, and he wasn't going to let go until he had wrangled some kind of justice out of it.

I wasn't talking about Mila. I was talking about Belma.

And I knew this, because I felt the same way.

Let go of expectations.

So I did. I let go of knowing what should happen next. Lama Sonam's calm voice reached out to me, from long ago: "Don't try to drive the bus from the backseat, Tenzing. Don't attempt to control what you cannot." Something released in my belly, that tight vise of obligations to Martha and expectations of Bill. I wasn't clear just who was driving, but I was very sure it wasn't me. I took a breath, and freed the bus to go where it needed to.

A scream pierced the room. Belma had bolted upright and was panting, her head twitching from side to side, her sight turned inward, on nightmare images. Audrey moved to her side and hugged her close. She stroked her hair, arms, and back, as if gentling a wild colt. Mila stared intently as Audrey soothed the girl.

Something in Mila softened as well, and I felt moved to put my arm around her shoulders.

Mila reared back, eyes again flashing, before she read my intent: I meant her no harm. She closed her eyes. All was still, except for the sound of Belma's rough breath, slowly returning to normal. I looked around at this random, and yes, surreal collection of people, a makeshift family united by concern for the girl on the couch. The sad irony was that this gathering would not exist except for one of the cruelest ideas human beings had ever come up with: buying and selling each other for harm and for foul.

Belma had climbed out of the dark place. She said something to Audrey in Bosnian. Audrey's answer was gentle enough to transform the guttural language into a kind of lullaby. Sasha stood quietly by, a comforting presence.

Audrey translated. "She asked why everybody was staring at her. I told her she was having a nightmare and we were loving her so she wouldn't feel scared anymore."

My job is pretty simple: to love and respect my clients until they learn to love and respect themselves.

I found myself on yet another memory spiral back through time, to a novice class at Dorje Yidam on "puzzle sayings," the Tibetan version of Zen koans. Lama Jamyang would call out a puzzle saying, and we were expected to grapple with the ambiguity in our minds until he called out another one. We'd usually get through a dozen per class. I'd always looked forward to the exercise; it gave me a good mental stretch.

One day our ancient teacher called out a puzzle saying that made us all erupt in laughter: If we're all here to help others, what are the others here for?

Watching Audrey love Belma out of her nightmare was an unambiguous, living reminder of what we were all here for.

CHAPTER 20

A vast herd of faceless children. Thick. Boundless. They slog forward, their pace slow and strained, their arms outstretched as if striving to get somewhere that's perpetually out of reach. They are compelled by yearning, by faint hope mixed with despair. At the back of the herd lag two terrified, vulnerable little boys, the easiest of prey.

I push through to the front. There is light ahead. I will lead them toward it.

A faint call to prayer stirred me to life. Dawn kissed the green-spired minaret outside my hotel window. In minutes, my shoe soles were traversing the rough cobbles of the Stari Grad, with its Ottoman-era sweeps and curves. Seven solid hours of sleep lay behind me. I was determined to spend the next few exploring, before the others woke up, and the next round of hard decision-making began.

Last night had not ended well. We'd all agreed that reuniting Belma with her two sisters was a priority, but deciding how to do so created a fresh round of bickering and jockeying for control, even with one of us no longer interested in taking the wheel.

"One thing I want to make clear," Sasha had said at one point, glaring at Bill and me, "this is my problem to fix. If I want any help, I'll ask for it."

The logistics were nightmarish, the potential for failure huge. Dubrovnik was hours away, and the sisters might have already been shipped off to who knows where.

I'd left the others making lists of pros and cons, and returned to my room. Naturally, Martha called the moment I walked in the door.

"Ten! Finally!"

I wasn't in the mood.

"Will you excuse me for a moment, Martha?"

I walked down the hotel corridor and knocked on Bill's door. He opened it, eyebrows raised.

"Can you come out here for a moment?"

"What for?"

"Just do it."

He stepped outside. I raised the phone to my ear. "Martha, I've got Bill here. Time to talk to each other. I'm officially resigning as middleman."

I handed the phone, and my room key, to Bill. "Bring it back when you're done. I'm going to bed."

I must have been dead asleep by the time he was finished talking, because my phone and key were on the coffee table in the morning, and I hadn't heard a sound.

Vendors were starting to unlock shops and set up their wares. I left the cobbled streets and silent clock towers of Stari Grad and headed east. Soon I was laboring up a narrow road, steep enough to live comfortably in San Francisco, until I reached my goal. A sharply sloped, well-tended lawn bristled with hundreds of pointed memorials. Narrow rectangular pillars carved out of white stone were planted in rows in the emerald grass like spears of grief. All bore the birth and death dates of Muslim boys, some too young to marry or drive a car, but not too young to die in the Bosnian War.

I wandered between markers, and paused, heart heavy, to sit at a small, central gazebo. Below, the city preened, glowing and, yes, beautiful in the morning light.

I sensed I was not alone. I turned. To my right, near a small copse of trees, a woman sat cross-legged by one of the graves. A thick curtain of brown hair, streaked with gray, hid her face.

But not from me.

"Mila?"

She raised her eyes. I braced for the scowl, but received a half-smile. "Are you following me?"

"No. Just needed a walk."

I moved to her side and bent to read the name carved into the white stone: Yuri Radovic. "Your brother?"

She smoothed the grass with one palm.

"Bill was thinking I am blaming him for Yuri's death. I do not. Human nature is to blame."

I sat beside her.

"I know I come across as hard woman. Cynical. But I think seeing truth the only way to survive."

I said nothing.

"I call my mother last night, to tell her Sasha is okay. You know what she say? 'No thanks to you.' And then she tells me all the ways I am failure as daughter, as mother. Back to her old ways. My mother, she finds answers in her imam, her new way of believing. But it only makes her more stiff. More angry."

Mila traced the carved letters with one finger. "She was not always like this. But life makes her tired, wears her down, you know?"

"The war?"

"*Da,* of course, but before that, too. Her first husband, he is—how you say it? Light of living? She loves him very much."

"The light of her life?"

"Yes—light of her life. He died of heart attack only three years after they get married. My mother is eighteen when married, but her husband is much older. Catholic Serb. War hero. He and his younger brother very successful, they have all the government contracts in the sixties. Exporting machinery. Importing goods for Tito. Then my mother's husband dies and everything, gone! Twenty-one and widow with two babies—my half-brothers." Mila made a face. "I'm sorry, I talk and talk. It is this place. Brings up so many memories."

"No, it's interesting. So when did you come along?"

"Irena, she moves back here, to Sarajevo. She is lucky, because many widows back then, no one wants them. But my father meets her at a lecture and that is it. My mother is the light of *his* life. They marry in 1970. Then she has me, and my baby brother, Yuri. Finally she is happy again. Because now she has Yuri. Things start to be okay. I finish school, study to become a doctor . . ." Her voice trailed off.

"What did your father do? For work, I mean."

Mila's eyes softened. "He is, sorry, was a professor, of religious studies. He loved his work very much. Always teaching forgiving, accepting different gods. This is why the Serbs send him to Omarska, I think."

Omarska death camp. I had seen the pictures of its skeletal captives in one of my books.

A bird landed in the soft soil next to us. Pecked up a few morsels of something, and flew off again.

"I'm sorry," I said. "Did your father survive?"

"No and yes. His spirit, it dies, but he came back after the war is over. His body dies last year. He is killed last year." Her laugh was harsh. "My father survives Omarska. Then he is killed at home. Shot in the head." She looked at me. "Murdered."

"Oh, Mila." I was too unsettled to say anything more. How much tragedy can one family experience?

But Mila had moved on. "You have any brothers or sisters, Tenzing?"

Usually I hedged at this question, but I had no defenses up. "A half-brother. Nawang." I hadn't thought about Nawang in years—it felt strange to say his name out loud.

"My mother has four children, but she only loves one. When he died, and then husband disappears, she gives up. Stops eating. Talking. Even washing. So you see," Mila turned to me, "I cannot stay with Bill, then. I have to take care of my baby, and my mother!"

"What about the other two, your other brothers?"

"Half-brothers." Her face grew grim. "Their father is Serb. What do you think?"

She stood up, brushing grass from the seat of her jeans. I followed suit. We stood side by side, gazing at the peaceful terra-cotta roofs and flowering gardens below.

"What about now? Do you ever see them? Your half-brothers?"

She stared at the view, as if memorizing every house. "You remember when I talk about bullies? The first time we meet?"

"I do."

She turned to me. "I am talking about them, Zarko and Stojan."

My blood ran ice-cold and I shivered, although the morning was already hot. I kept my voice casual. "Mila, can I ask you something? Irena's first husband: What was his name?"

Her mouth twisted around the answer. "Stasic. Milo Stasic."

Both our phones buzzed at once. Bill was calling me at the same time as Sasha was calling his mother.

"Where are you? Sasha's come up with a plan," Bill said. He was letting his son take the wheel. I hoped that was wise.

Mila's terrified look said otherwise.

"So Audrey and I will go back to Dubrovnik with you, Ten, if that's okay," Sasha explained. "My mother will keep Belma with her."

I looked over at Bill, who was keeping very quiet. He shifted his weight, trying not to sound too resentful. "I'm to stay put here and figure out what to do with the three girls once you bring the sisters back. *If* you bring them back."

Sasha had been emphatic about leaving Bill out of this. I sympathized. I was no stranger to struggles between sons and fathers. Maybe it was a sign of immaturity, but I had a much easier time understanding things from Sasha's perspective than from Bill's.

"How do you plan on the three of us getting there?" I asked.

Everyone looked at Sasha. Sasha shrugged. "Not sure. Train, I guess. Though they may still be watching the station. Why?"

"I have an idea," I said.

Petar picked us up in his own car, a slightly dinged-up but serviceable Hyundai station wagon, burgundy, with a topcoat of grime. Perfect for surveillance, actually.

His gap-toothed grin flashed even wider when I handed over a carton of his favorite smokes.

"Thanks, Monkevic. But you still pay me for drive, yes?"

Sasha and Audrey climbed into the back, and I sat up front with Petar and his overflowing ashtray. I wanted to mine him for a little more information. I just hoped Sasha and Audrey would be tired enough to doze off. I didn't want them listening in.

We set off around two in the afternoon. My tourism book estimated the drive from Sarajevo to Dubrovnik at four hours. Knowing Petar's skills, I subtracted an hour, which would get us there before sunset.

Soon we had left all traces of urban sprawl behind us and were climbing and descending a narrow mountain road marked by hair-raising views, scarily slender bridges, and tunnels gouged through unreceptive terrain. Petar chain-smoked as he adeptly hugged the thin strip of asphalt, occasionally laying on his horn to force an oncoming car to give way. I was very glad he was driving. Give me an L.A. freeway over one-lane mountain deathtraps any day.

Sasha and Audrey chatted quietly. I stared at the blur of scenery until finally the backseat was silent.

Petar cleared his throat. "That boy. He your friend you come to visit?"

"Not exactly."

He nodded, as if he already knew.

"Petar," I said, "we're not going to Dubrovnik to sunbathe on the beach."

THE FOURTH RULE OF TEN

He nodded again.

"Someone there needs our help. Two someones, in fact. You don't need to get involved, but I wanted you to know."

"What kind of trouble these people in?"

"Girls. Two young girls." I stepped across the line between like and trust. "Human trafficking kind of trouble."

His response surprised me. "Monkevic, what you do? You monk, like father?"

"No. Actually, I used to be a police officer, but I left the force three years ago. Now I'm a private detective."

He slapped his thigh. "Ha! I know this! We are brothers! Me, too, I used to be *policija*." He laughed at my look of surprise. "*Da!* Police, like you! Six years ago, I leave. Not enough money for raising my daughters." He corrected himself. "Not enough pay. Plenty, how you say it, money under table."

"Right."

"Driving taxi okay. But sometimes I miss excitement. I like when heart go *bang bang*, like bullet, you know?"

"I do know. So, you're okay with this, with what we're doing here?"

"How old these girls?"

"Eleven and twelve."

"Mine? Ten and twelve," he said. "Yes, Monkevic. I am okay with this. Today is good day."

Over the course of several roller-coaster turns and tunnels, he told me about his daughters, and I told him about my cat.

"You have woman?"

I thought about Julie. "Not really, not at the moment. I did have one once, but she left."

He grunted. "Good woman important, Monkevic."

I brought our conversation back to trafficking. I now had a link, however unlikely, between Milo Stasic's newly renamed Van Nuys company, Agvan Supply, and Sasha Radovic. But I didn't know where Bosnia fit in.

"Have you heard anything about using the Internet for illegal trafficking in this country? Not the regular Internet, but a hidden one? A dark web?"

"I not hear of this dark web."

"These guys do all their business online. Even use cyber currency for payment. Computer bytes, instead of dollars, or marks. Cyber-criminals."

"I not hear of this," he repeated. "But I believe. In our country, police system have many levels, many . . . compartment?"

"Departments."

"*Da.* Part of bullshit reform. One keeping borders safe, another for if you rob bank or shoot wife. One for politicians to keep job and"—Petar made a rude gesture—"screw the people. But new department is SIPA." He pronounced it see-pa. "For big investigation. SIPA very important. Many targets. Organized crime, terrorists. International activity. Also, this trafficking."

"Like the FBI and Homeland Security, combined."

"*Da.* But when they make SIPA, they make stupid mistake. They give SIPA trafficking, and give cyber-crime to other department."

"You're kidding."

"No. Now SIPA told to get traffickers, but not allowed to look on Internet. Like fisherman using net with huge tear in middle!"

Talk about a loophole, and a business opportunity for the cyber-criminally inclined.

Petar, upset, stubbed out one cigarette and lit another. "Now you see why I quit, Monkevic? At least when I drive taxi, every job I start, I know I can finish."

Thanks to a monster one-lane traffic jam, caused by an overturned truck full of Croatian goats headed for market, we entered the medieval town of Dubrovnik around 7 P.M., well past dusk. The city was set in a curved, rugged coastline like a gem in a jagged tiara. The Adriatic Sea was ink black, but in the morning it would be the purest shade of aquamarine.

Petar found us a cheap hotel near the harbor area known as Gruz. "Holiday Hotel cousin," he joked, but the shabby exterior, at least, was easier on the eye.

Sasha and Audrey bent and stretched by the car, working out the kinks. I handed Sasha some cash. I'd replenished my supply from an ATM next to the marketplace fountain this morning.

"I have money," Sasha said stiffly.

More like Audrey has money, I thought. What I said was: "Relax. This is to pay for me, okay? Go on inside and make sure they have rooms available. I need to square things up with Petar." I'd actually paid him hours ago, but they didn't know that.

Audrey and Sasha disappeared inside. I turned to Petar.

"I need a gun," I said.

CHAPTER 21

My room was squeaky clean, and tiny. One small, firm bed; a wooden chair; and a bathroom the size of a broom closet. The Tibetan lama in me felt right at home. A special feature did give me pause—on top of the dresser was a rodent trap, along with instructions in three languages on how to set it. With harbors come rats. A small package of mini-marshmallows served as bait. I'd stayed in some pretty exotic places, but this was the first one that came with a mousetrap as an amenity.

I lay down fully clothed. Next thing I knew, my phone was buzzing insistently.

"I find gun," Petar said. "Meet me outside in one hour."

I'd slept hard. I checked the time: 8:30.

Rested, with teeth freshly brushed and hair damp from a hot shower, I left my little room with body and mind finally located in the same general region. Good thing, if I was about to become armed and dangerous.

Sasha and Audrey's room was next door. Sasha still had custody of the phone, and I asked to see it. I recognized the type from my police work with gangbangers. A throwaway; prepaid, disposable, and cheap.

"No tracking device, at least," I said.

"You're sure?" Sasha asked.

"Positive. Have you decided which number we should call?"

Sasha nodded. "Of the two that came up the most, only one is a Dubrovnik exchange."

"Good. Sasha, you're the closest thing we have to a native. How do you feel about making the call?"

He swallowed, glancing at Audrey. "Sure. But, you know, language may not be a problem. Most of these guys speak English as well as I do. But if you think it's better, I mean, what do you think, Audrey?"

Sasha was stalling, which told me he was too nervous to make the call, and too proud to admit it. I tried to address both issues.

"Good point," I said while reaching for the phone. "I'll call. We'll know right away if they speak English. If they don't, you take over."

I speed-dialed the top contender and activated the speaker. We listened to three rings.

"Yah."

Serbian, Croatian, Russian, take your pick.

"Hello. I have the telephone that belonged to a man at the Sarajevo train station yesterday. Do you understand me?"

Silence, then: "Yah. Yes."

"I need those two girls. How much?" If this operation was run on cyber-fuel, the middlemen didn't see a lot of actual cash in their pockets. Or so I hoped.

Sasha grabbed my wrist, his eyes wild. "What are you doing?" he mouthed.

I shook off his hand. "How much?"

"Twenty thousand. Euros."

Sasha and Mila gaped. I winked at them. "What's your name?" I said.

"What's yours?"

"George," I lied.

"Kurt," he lied back.

"Kurt, you've got a deal, but it will have to be in KMs. Where can we make the swap? I need a public place."

"Okay. Restaurant Dubravka, right by main entrance to Old Town."

"When?"

"Eleven-thirty. Sharp. The restaurant closes at midnight. Once I've checked the money okay, my partner will release girls."

"Where will they be?"

"Close by."

"How will I recognize you?"

"I find you. I know what you look like."

Shit. Weasel face must have sent the photos off right before the fracas. That meant they'd seen Sasha as well. We'd have to adjust accordingly.

I closed the phone. Sasha and Audrey exploded like a pair of weed-whackers.

"Are you insane?" Audrey said.

Sasha chimed in. "You're going to buy them back? What is wrong with you?"

"Calm down," I said. "Do you have twenty thousand dollars?"

"Of course not!"

"Neither do I. Not in my pocket, anyway. Nobody's going to be buying back anybody, okay?"

I quickly sketched out my plan. They had to agree, because it was the only plan in play.

"Get to work," I said. "I'll be back in an hour." Somehow, without knowing when exactly it had happened, I was in charge again. I liked the feeling a little too much.

I found Petar waiting outside, and he drove me several miles out of town, to the Croatian version of a seedy bar, which was, in fact, a seedy bar. He'd somehow unearthed a broke individual with a beat-up .38 revolver and a handful of ammo. We found the owner of the weapon slumped over a beer in a booth. I deduced he was a sailor, due to his leathery lizard skin and rolling gait. He shuttled us to the alley behind the bar for a test run. Petar helped him lift the lid of a Dumpster, its insides putrid. I aimed the gun at an empty lard can. Petar lowered the lid to muffle the noise. The sailor covered his ears. I squeezed the trigger. *Boom!* Petar lifted the cover and all three of us peered inside. A satisfyingly large hole had killed the can dead. Even better, my hand and arm were still intact.

"You want to try?" I asked Petar. My turn to man the Dumpster.

Boom!

We grinned at each other. Men and their guns.

I closed the deal with 200 marks and a round of unpronounceable Croatian lager.

I was now a full-scale felon in a foreign country. Since my arrival in Bosnia-Herzegovina I'd stolen one citizen's phone and bought an illegal firearm off another. I was a one-man crime wave.

I eyed Petar with affection. A one-man crime wave with an awesome accomplice.

He dropped me back at my monastery-away-from-home with an hour to spare.

"Thanks," I said, leaning into his car. "Now go see your brother. And if I happen to wind up behind bars, bail me out."

"Good luck, Monkevic," he answered, and disappeared into the night.

Fifteen minutes later, Sasha, Audrey, and I were ready. We proceeded on foot, away from the harbor, toward Dubrovnik's own exquisite Old Town. Even at this hour, the area thronged with people, most tourists, most in some state of intoxication. A trio of drunken men in red-and-white-checkered football jerseys stumbled by, singing a ragged chorus, barely upright.

We crossed the busy thoroughfare toward one of the arched gateways into the pedestrian-only Old Town area. The restaurant was to our right. I heard music from an outside patio, a couple of classical guitars. We were still a half hour early, early enough to check out the restaurant gift shop. Instead, I showed them the public parking lot nearby.

Belma had told Sasha the vehicle that kidnapped her was a dirty white van. We scanned the cars in the lot. No van, white or otherwise.

Petar and I had scoped out the area earlier, and concluded this was the only place that made sense for our boys
to park their van.

"Do you have my number programmed on your phone?"
Sasha flashed the display. Up on the screen and ready.

"So all you need to do is . . . ?" I asked.

"Stay out of sight," Audrey said, "and watch for a white
van. Once we see it, we call you."

"That's right. And what do you do after you call me?"

Sasha said, "I keep hidden, while getting as close as possible to the van."

"I walk into the lot, acting as if I'm looking for my car,"
Audrey said.

"Don't forget to hold out your hand as if you're holding
keys."

"Right. I move as near to the van as I can."

"And if either of you see the van start to pull away?"

"We know what to do." Sasha patted the bulging pockets
of his windbreaker.

I drew the .38 out of my pocket. "Just so you know, I
have this. If I have to use it, disappear. Get as far away from
me as you can, as fast as you can."

They nodded.

"So, you're both still okay with this?" I had been asking
this question a lot today.

"What about the girls?" Sasha asked.

"Right, of course. I'll bring the girls back to your room.
Just wait there until I show up."

"And if you don't show up?"

I didn't have an answer for that, so I didn't give one.

I pocketed my gun, shouldered my backpack, and
headed for the glow of the busy restaurant. Inside, a singer
was crooning about his lady being a tramp.

Surreal didn't even come close.

Open umbrellas protected the tables, from moonlight,
I guess. Behind the restaurant, towering white fortress walls
spotlit from below glowed with an unearthly light. Far below

the patio terrace, the sea ebbed and flowed. The tables were full of late-night diners, except for one. This small corner table was occupied by a solitary man who was facing outward. A glass of beer sat untouched in front of him. One finger tapped along with the music. I checked my watch. He must have just gotten here. I caught his eye and nodded. The man whose name wasn't Kurt nodded back. Shaved head. Heavy dark brows. Dead eyes.

Neither of us was inclined to shake hands, and neither said a word. I gently set my backpack on the ground next to him and unzipped. Not-Kurt lifted it to his lap. He peered inside, scowling at the loose pile of money, mostly small bills, that lay across the top.

My phone vibrated in my left-hand pocket, the one without the .38. The van had arrived.

Not-Kurt shot me a look and reached deeper into the bag, and my fondest hope came to fulfillment. The mousetrap snapped. Not-Kurt howled. He extracted his hand and stared in disbelief at the dangling trap.

Before he could shake off the shock, I pulled him upright and executed a standard police academy move, a grab-and-spin that pinned his arm behind his back. The mousetrap was still attached to his middle finger.

"I have a gun," I murmured in his ear, and shifted to grip his shoulder. His body felt odd, as stiff and thick as a board.

Singing loudly, and off-key, I staggered us both out to the street. No one around us paid the slightest attention. We were just another couple of vacationing tourists who'd had a few too many.

In case my companion thought I was bluffing, I pulled out my .38 and pressed the business end of the barrel into his side with my right hand, still guiding him with my left up the street and into the parking lot. I heard an engine fire up, but I couldn't see from where.

Where are you, white van?

I heard tires squealing, at a distance.

Was I too late?

I urged my man toward the back of the dark lot, now shifting to use his body as a shield. He remained stone silent.

A dirty white van, facing frontward, was wedged between two Mercedes-Benzes, about ten yards in front of me. A blinding pair of lights flashed, like a demon's eyes, and the van lunged forward.

Do it!

Glass shattered as Sasha and Audrey pelted the windshield and side windows with their pocketed rocks.

I dragged Not-Kurt directly in front of the van. When faced with a live barrier, nine times out of ten human instinct will cause the driver to slam on the brakes. The van lurched to a stop, kernels of glass crunching underneath its tires. The driver door opened and a body rolled out in a crouch and aimed a nasty-looking automatic right at us. Two facts registered: this man was a dead ringer for my old pal Detective Sully O'Sullivan, of the LAPD Sully and Mack team, and the automatic was a dead ringer for a Glock. I twisted Not-Kurt's arm to propel him forward. The situation was looking more and more deadly.

"Speak English?" I called out to the holder of the Glock.

He nodded.

"Good. How about, you just give me the girls and I give you your partner back?"

"Fuck you," he said, and fired a shot straight into his partner's sternum. The impact knocked us both backward, me on the bottom. Not-Kurt was yelling up a storm, clearly also Not-Dead. *Body armor,* I thought. *Shit.* The worst he was going to get out of this was a sore chest. I had a lot more to lose.

I glimpsed Sasha's white face peering from the shadows, like a ghost.

"Run!" I yelled.

Trapped underneath Not-Kurt, my right hand fished around for the .38, which I'd dropped when we fell. My fingers found the handle, and I tried to unpin my arms to get off a shot.

More brake squeals, these much closer.

Not-Sully lifted his Glock and aimed, this time at my head. Not-Kurt shifted to one side. I weighed my options and concluded I had none, when a bulky mass galloped in from the right and tackled my would-be killer. The force of the horizontal takedown caused both men to slide partially under the van, headfirst.

"Monkevic," I heard from underneath. "You alive?"

My energy surged, and I shoved and rolled out from under my adversary, pushing to my knees and aiming at the first promising target, Not-Sully's leg, which was kicking at Petar's leg. At least I hoped it was Petar's leg. It was hard to tell what belonged to whom. A corner of my vision registered Not-Kurt running hard for the shadows. Good riddance, coward.

I lowered my sight to just above a neon-orange Nike—no way would Petar be caught wearing a shoe that conspicuous or expensive—and shot its wearer, right in the ankle. Another howl.

I ran to the van and jerked open the side door so violently it almost came off its hinges. Two pairs of dark eyes watched from the farthest corner. The blank and utter silence of their stare was worse than any tears.

Audrey and Sasha ran up and jabbered to the huddled pair in Bosnian. Sasha said the name Belma several times, which finally did the trick. They crawled to the door. Sasha helped one girl down, and Audrey helped the other.

"Go! Go!" I said.

They pulled the girls close and hustled back toward the main boulevard, turning right toward the Old Town entrance.

Not-Kurt was long gone. I aimed at Not-Sully's other ankle, just in case, but he was moaning and not moving. Petar shimmied out from under the van, clutching the Glock like a trophy.

That's when we heard the sirens.

Petar and I met eyes. We wiped off both guns and tossed them into the van, as if we'd rehearsed the move beforehand.

"Get out of here," I said, and he melted into the shadows, just as the first wailing *policija* car arrived. I raised my hands in surrender, counted breaths, and waited for my fate to unfold.

Time spent in a Croatian jail cell offers a man a fine opportunity to contemplate the nature of many things. Sitting on the metal bench, squeezed between the red-and-white-checkered jerseys and sullen faces of three cellmates sweating off a very bad binge, I mostly contemplated the well-known fact that for alcoholics, one is too many, and one thousand is never enough. My buddies were so massively hungover that any sound caused a special kind of agony. I was content to stay silent, meditating on and off, and they were content to slump where they were placed, exuding foul fumes.

At some point a cart arrived on the other side of our cage. A guard thrust three tin pans of food through an opening. Two pieces of white bread each, and a pile of cold, gluey beans. I think. No side dish of whipped cream for this crowd. I wolfed mine down, and even eyed my companions' meals.

The Croatian cops had carted Not-Sully off to the hospital jail, and plunked me in a holding cell until they figured out what to do with me. I had no idea where anyone else was, or if anyone knew where I was. Apparently you don't get that free phone call in Croatia. In any case, they'd confiscated my wallet, cash, business cards, backpack, cell phone, plus my belt and shoestrings, in case I went suicidal, though it was more likely I'd keel over from my cellmates' toxic fumes than any self-inflicted harm.

After my glop and bread, I closed my eyes again, and after a few false starts, settled into an awareness of my body. I let the clanging and shouting around me be what it was, and dropped into a deep state of gratitude. The girls were out of that terrifying van. I was content.

Some time later, a jail official opened the cell door and pointed a silent finger at me, like an executioner. I was about to be either freed or hanged. He led me up the corridor, through two more heavy, double-locked doors, and out into the administration area, where a familiar figure slouched.

"I bail you out," Petar said, "just like you ask."

CHAPTER 22

I slept for most of the drive back to Sarajevo.

When Petar and I had stepped outside the police station, the sun was just up, and a slight breeze was blowing in off the sea. It tasted of salt and smelled of seaweed. I'd inhaled, and with the exhale, exhaustion descended like a dense blanket soaked in brine.

Petar had put the four others on a train back to Sarajevo first thing, the moment he'd determined by lining a pocket or two that Not-Sully had flipped on Not-Kurt, and both were now in custody. Once you're detained in Croatia, the police have 24 hours to either charge or release you. As for charging me, with no way to tie me to either gun, and helped by a little more "money under table," they'd chosen to let me go. Petar had given them a heads-up regarding the mousetrap inn, and other potential leads, and promised to escort me out of Dubrovnik immediately.

With heavy-lidded eyes, I watched the magnificent, monument-studded settlement recede behind us. Dubrovnik was spectacular, but I wondered if the tourists understood that deep within its turquoise-bayed beauty a different tale was told; even the clearest-looking water can hide a flourishing infestation of bacteria.

When I opened my eyes four hours later, I thought I was having a recurring nightmare. We were back outside the ugliest facade in Sarajevo.

"Really, Petar?"

"I wait here," he said. "Your old partner not so happy to meet me, I think."

Bill was sitting at a table in the circus-tent bar, my roller-bag at his feet. He didn't look that thrilled to see me, but I chalked it up to jealousy. Only one of us had gotten to play the hero in front of Bill's son.

"You're staying here again?"

He grunted.

I looked around. "Where are the others?"

"I called that number you gave me. That friend of yours, Stephanie? Nice lady. She connected me with some collective here that runs a shelter for victims like Belma. The shelter agreed to accept all three girls. Audrey's taking them there now."

I allowed the relief to sink in. A waitress set two cold beers in front of us, and for a moment it felt like old times.

"What about the others?"

"No idea. I'm out of the Sasha loop at the moment. But I'm meeting Mila later."

"And Martha?" I hadn't talked to Bill alone since I'd handed him my phone with his wife on the other end.

He set his half-empty bottle down. "No comment."

"I take it you're not flying home with me."

"No. Not yet."

"So what do I tell the girls?"

"Ten . . ." Bill shook his head. "Tell them I'll be home soon, okay?"

His voice still had the faintest trace of stubbornness, but I knew he was feeling remorse.

Bill glanced at me before looking away. "Thanks for coming, Ten. Thanks for helping. Thanks for keeping Sasha safe. And thank Petar for me, too." I knew how much these words cost him.

"I'd better get going," I said, standing. There was only one Lufthansa flight out of Sarajevo daily, and it wouldn't wait for an ex-monk or an ex-cop. I pulled Bill into an approximation of a hug.

"Be safe," I said. "Be well."

As Petar drove me to the airport, a chant from my past rose up from some forgotten corner inside. I called upon the Goddess Tara to watch over Belma and her two sisters, to protect them from fear, injury, and suffering. *Om tare tuttare ture svaha.* "To you, O Tara, embodiment of all the enlightened ones' actions, I bow—in happy or unhappy times—with body, speech, and mind." I invited into my heart Tara's immense compassion, and offered the humble hope that these young girls soon experience inner safety, inner peace. I wanted to send them every gift I could before they left my world forever and entered into their new one.

I gave Petar a couple of my business cards and a very big tip.

"You find me job in Hollywood, Monkevic! I come for sure!"

I slept through the first flight and most of the second Munich-to-New York leg. No pills necessary. Somewhere over the Atlantic Ocean, I jerked awake. I had been dreaming about Tara, the many-armed goddess. She sat upon a throne, one leg bent at the knee, the other straight. Her hair was jet-black, and her skin color cycled through many hues: white, green, bloodred, and finally an angry mustard yellow. Her waving limbs reached for me like a sea creature, first with love, but then with a kind of avid hunger.

Why am I thinking about Tara again?

Now a small feral cat, black with yellow-green eyes, darted across my memory field. I'd named her Lhamo, after a goddess as fierce as Tara was kind. I had rescued Lhamo during one especially long stay at Dorje Yidam. Or maybe the cat had rescued me. I was 12, and suffering the early banishment after my ill-fated visit to the Louvre with Didier.

I tried not to think about that fateful time in the monastery, when a stray cat felt like my only friend. That brief glimpse into the dark mysteries of tantric practices. The shock of my body's first urges.

I especially tried not to think about the brilliant Lama Nawang, who took me under his wing—Yeshe would say bullied me—and who might or might not be my half-brother. Like a fiery comet, Nawang had scorched a brief trail across my life, introducing me to esoteric and forbidden spiritual practices, inviting me to break every rule, deny every vow I'd taken. He'd disappeared from the monastery, and my life, as suddenly as he'd entered it, leaving me to shoulder all the consequences.

I'd never dared ask my father if Lama Nawang was telling the truth about our connection, not even on Appa's deathbed. I didn't want to know.

So why, Tenzing? Why Tara? Why Nawang?

Why now?

Miles aloft, in the rarified atmosphere above the earth's surface, I let go of conceptual ideas. My mind loosened its hold on analysis, on expectation. The space filled with nothingness.

I let go of nothing.

Agvan. Agvan Dorzhiev.

Thought returned, and with it, the solution to one small mystery, why I thought I knew the name Agvan, of Agvan Supply. We'd studied the life of Agvan Dorzhiev in our History of Buddhism class, that same terrible year, 1993. The year of Lama Nawang. Of my mother's death. Of an atrocity called the Bosnian War. The year Sasha was conceived.

The year I discovered the world of Sherlock Holmes and vowed to change my life.

I scoured my memory and dredged up what I could about Dorzhiev.

He was a Mongol, I remembered that, born in the 1800s. He grew very close to the 13th Dalai Lama, the one before His Holiness, close enough to bathe him, to serve as his debating partner and spiritual advisor. From what I could recall, Agvan had trained as a monk in Tibet and was initiated into the powerful, ancient art of Tantric Buddhism. But mainly he was interesting because of his connection to Russia.

More started coming back to me about this strange man. He would shuttle back and forth between the Russian courts and the monasteries of Tibet, trying to ally the two, exposing Russian royalty to Buddhist teachings, and the Buddhists to Russian ways. At one point, he even believed the White Tsar might be a reincarnation of White Tara, though later he dropped that idea.

We studied his life as a cautionary tale, a reminder to keep spiritual matters separate from political maneuvering, at least where our most sacred, confidential practices were concerned.

Agvan Dorzhiev. Agvan Supply. The pieces didn't fit together, no matter how I turned them.

It had to be a coincidence.

But I spent the rest of that flight, and all of the next, clouded by unease as I shifted and moved the events of the past week around—Agvan Supply, with its mysterious deliveries; Sasha Radovic, and his sudden shift from journalist to activist; the reappearance of Mila into Bill's life; and her strange mother Irena's first husband, Jovan Stasic. Yugoslavian industrialist, descendant of a stealer of sheep.

I couldn't make sense of any of it, and so I dozed, restless and dreamless, until I landed in Los Angeles, after crossing ten time zones in three different airplanes, and spending 18 and a half hours disobeying gravity. I'd made two of these insane four-day time-defying trips over the past three years. The wreckage to the body was immense.

It was almost midnight, and I was longing for a home-cooked meal and the dense, furry welcome of a certain Persian Blue.

I called Martha from inside the airport shuttle to long-term parking. The gods spared me: I got her voice mail.

"Sorry it's so late, Martha. I just got back. Call me in the morning, and I'll fill you in as best I can."

It was after one when the Dodge and I crunched up the gravel road to my house. The lights were blazing inside and out. Kim waited in the kitchen, packed and ready to go home.

"Thank you," I began, when a mass of silver-blue fur shot across the living-room floor. I scooped Tank into my arms.

"I missed you, Tank," I said.

"I am worried," Kim said. "Tank did not eat his dinner."

Tank struggled from my arms and stalked a few feet away. Now that he knew I was okay, he needed to regain his position of superiority.

"He looks fine," I said. In fact, Tank's belly was even bulging a bit, and swung lower to the ground than usual. I paid Kim with a check, and watched her drive away, grateful beyond words for her help, but still with that deep sense of relief. I'd been with too many people, for too many days in a row.

I rolled my bag into the bedroom. I would deal with its well-traveled contents later. I stepped into my bathroom to rinse my face.

"Whoa. Tank, buddy!"

At first, I thought he'd left me a passive-aggressive message, directly from his bowels. Then I registered the details, and realized that the parts added up to a suspiciously ratlike whole.

Tank slalomed between my ankles, purring and proud. No wonder he looked fat. He'd eaten the better part of a rodent sometime today before depositing the discards on my bathroom floor as a welcome-home present.

What could I do? Tank was a predator, prone, like all of us, to primitive impulse. He was just doing his job.

By the time I'd cleaned up his mess, I'd lost my appetite, but I forced down an omelet and toast. It was two in the morning, and I was wide-awake.

I moved to my computer, with the conscious plan to clean up my e-mails, but my conscious mind wasn't in charge. The home page of Agvan Supply's website had changed yet again. My breath caught: two photographs dominated the page. The first photo captured an idyllic meadow of sheep. The second was a close-up of a long wooden table, piled high with rough sacks of some kind of animal hide that were stuffed with a white, curd-like cheese. Wooden scoops, each a different color, jutted out of the sacks—green, red, yellow, like the Taras in my dream. A message bannered over both photos: BOSNIAN SHEEP CHEESE. JUST ARRIVED!

Time to go shopping. This time I knew enough to bring along my weapons, as well as my best binoculars—Barska Gladiator zooms I'd purchased new a few years back.

My little Dodge, thinking it was done for the day, coughed a couple of times in protest before reluctantly ferrying me back to the warehouse in Van Nuys. I parked a block away, out of immediate sight.

I trained the magnifying lenses on the office area, noting the same BMW sedan, along with two other cars of unremarkable make and model. I zoomed in on the front door and prepared to wait.

Just after 4 A.M., my patience paid off.

A pair of identical, unmarked, white delivery vans, these clean and almost brand new, pulled into Agvan Supply. The drivers backed the vans to the metal roll-up door and climbed out. The first driver was tall and bulky, and wore a black leather cap pulled low. The second was wiry and short, and could have been the long-lost brother of the Sarajevo train station spy. He even had the same greasy ponytail hanging down his back.

He banged on the metal door. Moments later it clattered open.

The man I assumed was Zarko Stasic ambled out. He clapped Ponytail on the back. Then both drivers opened the back doors of their vans and followed Zarko inside.

I stayed put.

The two drivers reappeared. They stationed themselves next to the opened van doors. A line of people filed out of the warehouse. The drivers helped them inside the vans. I counted twelve into one, ten into the other.

White. Male. No children, and no women. One old man wore a black beret and bore a striking physical resemblance to the old men playing chess in the Sarajevo marketplace.

I knew what I was seeing—a fresh supply of Bosnian sheep cheese being loaded up for market.

The drivers slammed shut the rear doors of the vans. Zarko again stepped outside, accompanied this time by a second man, also familiar. He could have been Zarko's slighter twin, but for the oddly bent arm. I was certain I was looking at Stojan Stasic, Zarko's younger brother. Like Zarko, Stojan kept watch, fingers nervously twitching and strumming, as the vans pulled onto the street and headed in my direction. I wasn't worried about the drivers—I was worried their bosses might spot me if I followed.

Go back in. Go on.

They did.

The streets were mostly empty, and I kept several blocks between us as I followed the vans onto the 101 North. We were heading in the direction of Ventura.

The traffic was sparse, mostly comprised of truckers driving the late shift in their 18-wheelers. The huge trucks provided a nice draft for me to ride and gave me plenty of cover. I was able to keep both vans in sight without hugging their tails.

They exited onto the 23, known as the Moorpark Freeway, and headed east toward Simi Valley. Three lanes in both directions, but no more trucks to hide behind. I fell back several car lengths.

Where were these guys headed?

After a long stretch, the road shrank, turning into what my GPS called Los Angeles Avenue. Up ahead lay State Route 118 to Simi Valley.

But for now, we were down to two lanes, one coming, one going. We passed through a few orange groves. I stayed well back, which gave me enough time to plot my next move when the vans suddenly braked sharply and exited onto a gravel road. They appeared to be headed for some farmland, maybe a mile away.

Following them onto that open gravel drive was not an option. I continued to the nearest turnaround, waited until both lanes were clear, and executed the turn, a move my Neon was made for. Back I drove, found another turnoff, and U-turned again. By the time I was on the gravel drive, the vans were long gone, but I knew they must be up there somewhere. I watched my speed. I didn't want to run up behind them unexpectedly.

About a mile in, the road split. To my left, a dirt lane climbed steeply upward to a copse of trees. The gravel road continued right, a flatter route. I opted left, for higher elevation and more cover. I bumped my way to the trees and pulled off to park. I opened the glove compartment. What to carry, besides the binoculars? I'd brought along both weapons. I opted for the Airlite reluctantly. My plan was to continue uphill by foot, take a sighting, and return to the car once I'd hopefully located the vans.

I scrambled 20 yards to the apex, and took marginal cover behind some brush. The sky had lightened some, and I soon located the vans, maybe a quarter-mile away, parked by a fallow field of ridged earth. Beyond lay more fields, these planted in neat rows, the crops bright green and low to the ground. I zoomed closer. Green, dotted with red.

Strawberries.

I moved my sights to the vans. The headlights were still on, but nighttime was dissipating quickly. The heavier-set man hurriedly unloaded his human cargo. I swept the glasses left, looking for the other driver. I couldn't locate him anywhere.

Not good.

My nose smelled him first. I stood up slowly and turned. Ponytail's stance was casual, but his nasty assault rifle was anything but. He reeked of cologne, some chemist's idea of lavender and musk.

"On knees," he said. "Hands behind back." Balkan accent. I'd been hearing them all week.

My Smith & Wesson screamed for attention from the right-hand pocket of my windbreaker, but my fingers were full of binoculars. How had he climbed 20 yards without my hearing him? I felt like a complete idiot.

"On knees! Now!"

I knelt.

"Why you here?"

I decided on the same ploy as the last time I got caught spying on Agvan Supply.

"I'm a private detective. I'm looking for a missing person." I took a gamble. "His name is Sasha Radovic. Do you know him?"

"No," he said. "Not on list." So this guy wasn't a close acquaintance of Stasic. He also wasn't very bright—he'd just given me more information than I'd asked for.

I took a bigger gamble. If I guessed wrong, I'd soon be worse off than Tank's rodent. I shifted my binoculars to my left hand and reached for my pocket with my right.

"STOP!" He stepped close, and I was staring down the barrel of a lethal killing machine, a Heckler & Koch HK416. Top of the line—Stasic wasn't fooling around when it came to arming his people.

Next time, I'd choose the Wilson.

"Take it easy," I said. "I was just going to show you my business card." I slipped my hand inside.

Ponytail may not have been brilliant, but he was remarkably cooperative. He even lowered his gun to reach out for the card.

I flung the binoculars at his head. He flinched instinctively and I followed up with a sharp punch to his forearm. The barrel jerked sideways, causing his deafening shot to miss wide. My eardrums exploded, but I launched into his chest and jammed my little Airlite under his chin. Good thing Ponytail had been picked to follow me—no way would this move have worked on the burlier guy.

"Okay. Your turn," I said. My voice sounded weird, through the ringing of my ears. "On the ground. Weapon first."

He placed his assault rifle on the dirt and knelt. My foot nudged it out of his reach. I picked up the assault rifle. Now I had a different dilemma: both hands full of weapons, and a sudden need to look through my binoculars again.

Back inside the pocket went the Airlite. I kept one eye on Ponytail and focused the other on the field. The second driver was peering our way. He wielded his own top-of-the-line burp gun. The passengers under his charge were milling around haphazardly. He motioned them still with his weapon.

I patted down Ponytail and found a burner phone in his pocket. I slipped it into my own.

"Let's go," I said.

I marched him down the incline. As we drew close to the field, I saw his partner's muzzle, pointing upwards.

I flicked the safety off the Heckler. I was about to experience my first Serbian standoff.

Ponytail rattled off a burst of gutturals to his mate.

"Speak English," I said.

"I told Bozo you looking for missing person, someone we don't have."

Bozo? It was too easy. I resisted comment.

Bozo lowered his weapon, but I kept mine trained until he was within earshot. "You don't want to get hurt," I called. "I don't either. Give me some information, and we can all go home."

After a moment, Bozo nodded. I, too, lowered my weapon, but kept it close. I halted with Ponytail about ten yards from the hostages and their captor. They looked anxious, but not overly so, considering the artillery involved.

"Where are you taking these people?"

"We stop in this place. A larger vehicle come to pick them up. Here soon."

Was he telling the truth, or employing the timeworn "backup's on its way" tactic?

I addressed my next question to the group of silent men.

"I'm not here to hurt you. Do any of you speak English?"

An elderly man, thin to the point of emaciation, raised his hand like a schoolchild.

"I'm taking these two men into custody." At this, Ponytail let out a sharp comment, probably a Bosnian curse, which I ignored. "Tell everyone you're safe now. Help is coming." My plan was to call 911, plus the local cops, and wait for more good guys to arrive.

But apparently, I had it backwards.

The elderly man spat a rapid stream of invective at me. At his words, the other men's voices merged into a swelling growl of complaint. A couple of them took a few steps forward, their expressions threatening.

"Go away," the old man said. "Leave us alone."

"Uh."

He motioned to the vans and their two captors.

"This job our only hope."

"I don't understand."

"We pay good money. Our families, they sell everything to send us here. Do not send back to Kosovo. We die there."

"Shut up," Ponytail snarled. I nudged him with the rifle butt, and he went quiet.

The old man's laugh was bitter. "You cannot frighten us, even with death. We have nothing—we count for nothing. We are dirt." Despair coated his every word, and centuries of poverty, of bitterness, informed his grim features.

"Maybe we die," he said, "but here, at least, first we can work."

"Where are they taking you?"

He drew himself up. "We work in restaurant. Pay good money."

I looked at Ponytail. He shrugged. Not his business.

"What kind of restaurants? Where?"

"All over," the old man said.

A thousand questions hammered at my brain, but the biggest one was whether or not to take the action that would insert them into an impersonal system, conspicuous for its cruel disregard of individual circumstances. These were not child victims, but grown men who had paid dearly to come. Once I brought in the cops, Immigration would be close on their heels. The do-gooder in me pulled hard in that direction. But was that really a choice for good? Maybe the compassionate act was to leave these men alone. Maybe I needed to respect their wishes, however misguided.

We are dirt.

I didn't know what to do.

An engine rumbled behind me. A large yellow school bus lumbered along the gravel road, the most innocuous backup imaginable, but backup, nonetheless.

What was I doing here, beyond trying to be a hero to a group of grown men with no interest in being saved? But leaving felt just as wrong.

I was about to do something very ill advised, and not for the first time.

I motioned the old man close. Still keeping the rifle trained on Ponytail with my left hand, I used my right to reach into my jeans, praying I still had a few spares. *Yes.* I shook the old man's hand, transferring the business card from my palm to his.

"I can help. Call if you change your mind," I said.

I aimed my next words at Ponytail's partner, Bozo. "I'm leaving now. Don't do anything stupid."

I herded Ponytail into the driver's side of his van and jumped into the passenger seat.

"Back to my car. Quick!"

He slammed the van into gear and made a slithering U-turn, then gunned us toward the trees. We flew past the school bus, and I glimpsed a handful of startled faces peering out the side windows. We reached the trees in minutes.

"Stop," I said.

I shoved the barrel of the Heckler under his nose. "Tell your boss he only gets one free pass. And this was it."

I climbed out. He wrenched the van around and sped away. I kept the Heckler steady and trained until long after he was out of range.

CHAPTER 23

Dawn had come and gone as I entered Los Angeles via Hollywood, on the 101 South. I decided not to exit at Topanga, but continue toward downtown. I pressed voice control on my cell and heard the double tone that signified my phone was poised to act: "Call Mike K., mobile." "Calling Mike K.," a mechanical female voice replied. I mentally crossed my fingers. Mike, a cyber-jockey and amateur techno DJ, lived a night-shift life, and 7 A.M. was right around bedtime.

"Yo."

"Oh, good. You're still awake."

"Barely."

"I need to see you. I have a few questions. Mind if I pay you a visit?"

"Long as you're not driving from Bosnia."

That reminded me. Things had gotten so crazy over the final 24 hours over there, I'd never found the right moment to tell Bill about the Stasic connection. I calculated the time, adding nine hours. Four P.M., worth a shot.

"Call Bill Bohannon, mobile."

Bill sounded harried.

"Hey, Ten. You home?"

"Yes."

"Heard from Martha?"

"Not yet. Bill, I forgot to tell you something. Something strange I found out from Mila. You remember that address you had me follow up on in Van Nuys? Agvan Supply? It turns out the owner may be one of Mila's half-brothers. Bill, I need to know how you got that address."

Silence.

"Bill?"

"The fever's broken, Ten."

"Sorry?"

"The fever's broken. Listen. Hear that?" He must have held up his phone. I heard ambient noise, the low hum of people talking, a female voice making some kind of announcement over a loudspeaker. "That's the sound of my flight about to board. The sound of my sanity returning. It's over. I'm heading home. Well, technically I'm headed home via Zurich via Belgrade, God help me, on some Serbian flying tank."

"Bill . . ."

"They want me out of their lives, Ten." Another announcement. "Okay, gotta go . . . I'll see you on the other side. Don't tell Martha, I want to surprise her. I just pray she'll unlock the front door."

Well, okay. I tested this new knowledge. One less thing to worry about. Which begged the question—why was I worrying about any of this anymore?

Because it wasn't over for me.

Mike's building was a modernistic stack of granite and glass, as elegant as it was practical. Mike called it a meta-living space. Before I punched in his code and pulled underground to park in a visiting guest slot, I had one more call to make. I leafed back through my notebook, praying I'd tucked it in here somewhere, and found the information on a rain-wrinkled business card.

After a few false tries, I managed to maneuver through the overseas codes.

"*Da!*"

"Petar? It's Ten."

"Who?"

"Monkevic."

"Monkevic! You find me job in movies already?"

"Sorry, I'm not that connected. But I'm hoping you are . . . Listen, back when you were a cop, did you spend any time at the Sarajevo Centar station? The one next to St. Joseph's church?"

"Of course. I work there for years."

I double-checked the name of the detective who had worked with Bill when Sasha went missing in my notes. "Did you happen to know a policeman called Tomic? Josip Tomic?"

"Yes. Many times. Josip is good man."

I felt a stab of hope. I explained what I needed. "The information may be in a file, or on a computer, under the name of Sasha Radovic, or maybe Milo or Jovan Stasic. Or even Agvan Supply. I don't know. What I do know is, that file may hold the key to this operation, and where they're keeping their victims over here."

"I will look," Petar said. "Not many *policija* safe to ask, but Tomic is good man."

I took the parking lot elevator to Mike's penthouse loft. Inside was as practical yet hip as out, with a gourmet marble cooking island and a gleaming bamboo floor. A picture window of glass offered a panoramic view of downtown, dominated by the glowing, platinum-winged structure known as the Walt Disney Concert Hall. Both Mike and his girlfriend, Tricia, were in plaid boxer shorts, Tricia's topped by a skinny tank top, and Mike's by a black T-shirt with a yellow peace sign silk-screened across the front. I tried not to react to Mike's pasty, stork-like legs.

The loft smelled faintly of marijuana, and was a futuristic mix of modern art, postmodern furniture, and post-postmodern computer and music equipment. Tricia gave me a vague smile, and wandered about for a minute or two before climbing into their platform bed in the corner and falling asleep.

"Glad you made it back in one piece, boss," Mike said. "I hear Bosnia's gnarly, man."

"Actually, it's beautiful," I said.

"Whatever. I'm glad you're here. I dug up some shit on your mango smugglers. Let's do some show-and-tell."

For the next hour, Mike rattled off information while pulling up various sites on his various computer screens, and I tried to keep up, using my notebook and pen.

"So yeah, after I eliminated Silk Road as Agvan's marketplace, I drilled down a little deeper."

"Silk Road?"

"The drug marketplace I told you about."

"Right. With the pirate."

"A-plus for remembering that. Anyway, Agvan uses another one. Also underground, also untraceable. This one came on the scene pretty recently. Name's an acronym: *N-D-R-S-N-T.*"

He showed me on the computer, and I wrote the letters down. NDRSNT.

"What's it stand for?"

"No idea. But it's got a mishmash of users and suppliers, as far as I can tell. So-called foodie sites like Agvan, fantasy gaming sites. A few I didn't want to touch, going by the pictures. But also, a few NGOs, you know, nonprofits. Schools for Tunisian children. Libraries for Tibetan refugees. Like that."

"Weird."

"Indeed. Even weirder is the fact that they all seem to be shifting from bitcoins to a different cyber currency."

"There are more than one?"

"Sure. Litecoin. Peercoin. All it takes is code, and people willing to give the currency value. These're called DNA-coins."

"As in human DNA?"

"You tell me. Anyway, that's as far as I've gotten." He shut down his computers. "So. What did you want to ask me?"

What *had* I wanted to ask Mike? I was so overwhelmed with his presentation I had to think a minute. "Oh. Right. Can you check up on a Serbian industrialist, Jovan Stasic, for me? See what he might have been up to in the 1960s?"

"Jovan Stasic. You got it. Once I've caught a few z's with my lady. Nighty-night, boss."

I was home by noon, my head a whirl of cyber-thoughts, but I still made sure to disarm and lock up the artillery, legally licensed and not. I fell asleep instantly, and woke up three hours later with a pair of green eyes staring at me fixedly. Tank had situated himself on the pillow next to my head, purring. He licked his cat lips, as if he'd just finished a snack.

"I don't want to know," I said.

Tank arched his back into a perfect, upside-down U and hopped off the bed.

My sleep cycles were all messed up. Without moving, I tested my own body with a head-to-toe stretch. I was the opposite of limber. Every nook and cranny was stiff and sore from too many hours buckled into an airplane seat. My wild dawn escapade came back to me in a rush. I must have left my good sense, along with my flexibility, somewhere over the Atlantic.

"I got lucky, Tank. Got away with something, for sure."

As if the very thought caused the universe to reprimand me, my doorbell buzzed—an insistent, irritating sound.

"Crap." When the front doorbell rings, it's never anyone I want to see—people I know well come in through the kitchen.

A second series of short buzzes, followed by brisk knocking. Someone was losing patience.

"All right!" I pulled on sweats, crossed the living room, and pressed my eye to the one-way DoorScope I'd installed last year, replacing a far more complex and paranoid security system.

Two officers. Not LAPD. Not L.A. Sheriff's Department. I ran to the kitchen and checked their patrol car. Ventura County.

Moorpark is in Ventura County.

Double-crap.

I inhaled and exhaled twice. Made my mouth smile. Opened the door. "Come in."

The older officer—black, midforties, and whip-thin—pointed to his younger, beefier partner with a buzz cut and the ruddy complexion and eyebrows of a redhead. "Deputy Johnson. I'm Deputy Sergeant Thomas Gaines."

"Tenzing Norbu," I said. "To what do I owe the honor?"

Johnson frowned. "'Scuse me?"

"He means why are we here," Gaines translated.

"Oh," Johnson said. My prejudices kicked in: clearly Deputy Johnson had a long and secure future with the Ventura Police Department.

"Coffee?"

Both men brightened.

I made a big pot of Sumatra, extra strong. Tank wandered in to check his food bowl. Empty. He gave me a long soulful look, stuck his tail in the air, and stalked out again.

I set down three steaming mugs, and pulled up a stool. The officers had already claimed the two chairs.

I decided not to talk. Some information arrived faster in a vacuum.

Gaines looked around.

"Nice place."

"Thanks."

"Been here long?"

"About seven years."

I sipped and waited.

Gaines broke first. He pulled out a plastic evidence bag holding a small white card. "You want to explain what your business card was doing in the pocket of a homicide victim in Moorpark?"

Everything went very still, the way I imagine it feels right before a nuclear bomb detonates.

I swallowed. "Who was the victim?"

Johnson bristled. "We're asking the question—"

"Who was the victim?"

Gaines again. "Don't know his name yet. Old. Maybe early seventies."

I set my mug down carefully. "When?"

"Shut the fuck up," Johnson growled.

"Johnson," Gaines warned. He checked his notes. "Mr. Norbu, where were you between the hours of eight and ten this morning?"

They must have killed the old man just a few hours after I'd left.

My fault. All my fault.

"Mr. Norbu?"

"I was with friends, at a loft in downtown Los Angeles. From six o'clock on. They'll verify."

I pulled Gaines's notebook over and jotted down Mike's number and address. He relaxed visibly.

"You're the guy that was on television last year. That private detective."

"Yes."

"Bet you see a lot of good shit. You know, husbands fucking their secretaries." This, from Johnson, naturally.

I was gripping my mug so hard my knuckles were white. I relaxed my fingers, one by one. "I do missing persons, mostly."

"But you used to be LAPD, right?" Gaines said.

"Right."

"Ever work any Mexican cartel cases?"

I held onto my poker face, but barely. Where was Gaines going with this? My connection to Mexican drug lord Chaco Morales and my part in his untimely death were supposed to be completely off the public's radar. Had somebody talked?

I played dumb. "Not really. Why?"

"Because this homicide? We think Sinaloa may be involved."

Now I was completely lost.

"Why?"

Gaines ticked off the reasons. "Execution-style slug to the back of the head. Body found facedown in a field. Simi

Valley's right next door? Crawling with runners connected
to Sinaloa. And the bullet came from an assault weapon,
ten grand if it cost a penny. Who else uses an HK416 to pop
a guy?"

"Excuse me," I said. I walked into my bedroom and
unlocked my gun safe. Walked back out to the kitchen.

"You mean like this one?" I laid the Heckler on the
kitchen table.

"Holy fuck," Gaines said. "You got some serious explaining to do."

I gave them an edited version of the truth, the "looking
for Sasha" version. I mentioned the vans and the school bus.
I even gave them a vague description of the warehouse near
Van Nuys Airport, but that was all they'd get for now. Gaines
seemed smart enough, but I didn't want Johnson anywhere
near Agvan Supply. Not yet. Not when I was getting close
to some answers. If Zarko Stasic took off, I would never find
him again.

Or learn if he had the two little boys who led Sasha to
Los Angeles and instigated everything else.

I wrapped up. "So once I'd disarmed the first driver, the
one who threatened me with this Heckler, I determined my
missing person wasn't on either van."

"And then you just let these guys go?" Gaines frowned.
"Didn't cross your mind to call the authorities?"

"Of course it crossed my mind. But the old man begged
me not to. And nobody was paying me to do anything but
find a kid. I made a judgment call."

Nobody said a word. The result of that call spoke for
itself.

Remorse choked my solar plexus. Even the partial truth
was hard to swallow.

"Anyway. I'm pretty sure this isn't Sinaloa. More likely
traffickers from Serbia or Croatia." I pushed the rifle toward
Gaines. "Take it. Maybe it will help with your investigation.
And call if you need anything else."

They both stood.

"Don't leave town," Gaines said.

Johnson had to add his own two bits. "Yeah. Got that, asshole?"

Gaines gave Johnson a look that would stop a charging elephant in its tracks. I didn't envy the man. Partner like that, you had to work twice as hard.

As soon as they were gone, I got straight to work.

Correction: as soon as they were gone and I'd fed my cat, I got straight to work.

CHAPTER 24

The Buddha likened the undisciplined mind to an oxcart loaded down with bad decisions. Suffering will follow such a mind, he taught, as inevitably as the wheels of the yoked cart follow its plodding oxen.

Right now, my mind was more like a runaway circus train, and the chimpanzees were loose. When my adrenaline was raging, Bill used to tell me the same thing I suspect the Buddha taught his followers: "Time to slow things down."

I ate two ripe bananas to placate the simian population and spent the next two hours stretching, lifting weights, and meditating, all on my outside deck. The exposure to afternoon sunlight helped reset my internal clock. The reminder to my body to breathe put the monkeys back in their cages, so I could think clearly.

I had started my meditation by taking refuge in the three jewels, the Buddha, the Dharma, and the Sangha—my teachers, their teachings, and my community of fellow travelers. And I realized three things. First, that the Buddha was right. I couldn't afford to let my primitive mind run the show. Secondly, while I was no longer personally or professionally responsible for the doings of Agvan Supply, a young girl's haunted eyes, two little boys, and an old man's brutal ending had shifted my motivation to the most powerful category of all: spiritual calling. Righting such wrongs *was* honoring the Dharma. Why else was I a private detective?

Which brought me to the Sangha, my community. As much as I loved going solo, I needed to ask my friends for help. It was time to call in the Eskimos.

I made up a short but powerful list of names while munching on a peanut butter and Nutella sandwich, washing the gluey bites down with swallows of cold milk. The brilliant Kim had restocked my refrigerator.

First call, Federal Agent Gus Gustafson, formerly ATF, but a few rungs further up the Department of Justice ladder after a big bust in Baja California, Mexico, last year. She and I had bonded over that case, as well as a mutual hatred of departmental stupidity.

"Ten Norbu! How the heck are you?"

Her voice was as I remembered: slightly husky, and full of humor.

"I'm well. How's the new job?"

"Lovin' it, thanks."

"And the new girlfriend?"

"What does a lesbian bring on her second date?"

"Uh . . ."

"A U-Haul. Get it?"

I wracked my brain for an appropriate response.

"We're living together, Ten! Officially cohabitating. Do keep up." Her laugh was full, straight from the belly. She sounded great. "Okay, enough of that. I'm sure you're not calling to check on my love life. What's this about?"

"Human trafficking. I may have stumbled onto something."

"Shit, Ten, you'd better not be nosing around our Crips investigation."

"What Crips investigation?"

Silence. Then: "You did not just hear that, okay? Seriously."

"I understand." I gave her the unedited version of my previous week of travels.

"You're a trouble-magnet, Ten. You know that?"

"Not on purpose."

"Right. It's all karma. Okay, well, first of all, those poor bastards from Kosovo, or wherever they came from? They weren't heading for any restaurant jobs, well paid or otherwise, I can at least tell you that. Their job site was right under their feet."

"What do you mean?"

"I mean the strawberry fields. Strawberries are routinely sprayed with methyl iodide, a seriously toxic fumigant. Now that everyone's caught on, it's much harder for the agribusinesses to find local pickers, including from Mexico. So they've started importing from overseas."

I was writing everything down. I never knew what would prove helpful.

"Either way, guys like your dead man, they never get out from under their debt. It's a racket, old-fashioned debt bondage in a new and different form. What's the owner's name again?"

"Stasic. Zarko Stasic."

"Doesn't ring a bell. But that doesn't mean anything. You know what it's like around here. The right hand . . ."

". . . doesn't know what the left is doing. Got it."

"I'll pass this information along. If anything helpful comes back, anything I'm authorized to pass along, I mean, I'll let you know."

Another call was coming in. Martha. Yesterday, I hadn't wanted to talk to her because Bill wasn't coming home. Now, I didn't want to talk to her because he was.

"Thanks, Gus."

"*De nada.* I'm really glad you called. Don't be a stranger, okay?"

"I won't."

"And Ten? Don't be a cowboy, either. These guys are not to be messed with."

After we disconnected, I reviewed my notes, and my eye landed on the first one:

CRIPS!

I'd unconsciously underlined Gus's accidental slip, twice. Because in my line of work, there are no accidents.

I added the name G-Force to my list, followed by a question mark. I walked out to the deck for a moment, to think. The summer air was still, the wood warm under my bare feet. I could stop right here. Right now. Leave the rest to fate.

I walked inside and called G-Force's number.

"G-Force Workout. Help you?"

I stared at the phone. "How on earth . . . ?"

"Heh-heh. Knew it was you. Just practicing for when it's real, dawg. What's up?"

I told G-Force what I needed.

His answer followed a long silence, as if he were weighing options. "I get this for you, we square?"

"Yes."

"Okay then. Later."

My final call was to Clancy Williams, reformed paparazzo, and backup surveillance guy whenever I needed an extra set of eyes. He was, as usual, thrilled to get the extra work. Freelancers are like addicts, they can never have enough.

I sicced him onto Agvan Supply, starting tonight. He took down the pertinent information, and had me describe the layout.

"What am I looking for?"

"Any traffic in or out, but especially delivery vans."

"Vans again, huh. Déjà vu." He was referring to a previous job involving Chaco Morales and his fleet of cleaning service vehicles.

"Can I help it if criminals use vans?"

"Bad juju. Just sayin'."

"If it helps, you should also be on the lookout for yellow school buses."

"Now you're talking."

I showered and forced myself to lie down. To my surprise, I slept for four solid hours. Then I changed into ninja apparel.

By 11, my Dodge and I were back on the 101 North. Same drive, different choice of weapon. A Jackass Rig shoulder holster occupied the passenger seat floor, stuffed full of four pounds of Wilson Combat Supergrade. The Airlite was good for concealment but seemed a bit puny suddenly, like arming yourself with a squirt gun. I'd taken Gus's words of warning to heart.

I also had a small but mighty roll of bills, all-American dollars for this job.

En route, I had a sudden urge to check up on Sasha. I still had his number on my cell.

"*Da?*"

"Sasha, it's Tenzing Norbu. Are you awake?"

"Oh. Hello." His voice sounded deflated.

"I just wanted to see how you were doing."

"Okay, I guess. Audrey's gone back to England for a few days. Maybe longer."

That must be the pain I was hearing.

"How's your mother?"

"Fine. She's all worried about my grandmother again, though. Hasn't heard from her. Can't reach her anywhere. You know Mom."

"I'm sure Irena's fine." My next sentence came out of nowhere, and landed before I could reel it in. "Sasha, did your research ever turn up anything about a place called Agvan Supply?"

I listened to his breathing, how it altered slightly. "No. Why?"

An alarm went off in my head. What was I doing? "No reason. Never mind. Just glad to know you're okay."

"Ten?"

"Yes?"

"Say hello to my father for me."

What on earth had prompted me to ask him that?

There are no accidents.

By the time I reached Moorpark, where the 23 narrowed into Los Angeles Avenue, it was after midnight. I started gas station hopping.

First I hit a Chevron. I filled up, using my ATM card, and went inside to trawl for information. The kid behind the cash register was a slight, nervous-looking Hispanic, barely out of puberty. Small, red pimples crawled across his forehead like a column of ants.

"I'm a detective," I said, and flashed him my P.I. license. He snapped to attention, which told me there was no need to also flash money. "Were you on duty last night as well?"

He nodded. "Yes, sir. Every night."

"Did you happen to notice a yellow school bus driving by?"

His blank look told me all I needed to know. I headed for the next station. A Shell. Different cashier, same drill. Same result.

But the third, a generic gas and mini-mart combination, produced a mini-jackpot, after I'd fed the female slot machine.

This cashier was ghost-pale, with hair like shredded wheat. She displayed no reaction at all when I showed her my P.I. license, but the mention of a school bus got an immediate response.

"Yep," she said. "Bus come here about 5 A.M. I remember, because he put in close to a hundred gallons of diesel." She pulled out a package of gum.

"Gum?" she asked.

"No thanks," I said.

She shrugged, and loaded in a stick, working her jaws around it.

"He's gassed up here before." Her eyes took on an avid gleam. "He in trouble?"

"Probably not. Anything else you can tell me?"

Chew. Chew. Chew. She studied her nails. Chew, chew.

I passed over a 20, and she opened the register, shuffled through some credit card receipts, and dealt me one.

"Give it back. I need it for my boss."

"No problem."

The name on the card's imprint was V. Stankic, the signature an undecipherable scrawl. I shuddered to think what Stankic's forbearers did.

"Can you describe him for me?"

"White guy, lotta chin."

"Long hair? Short hair? Age?"

"Real short hair. Black," she squinted, "like yours. Late-thirties. Five foot ten or eleven." She was good.

"Accent?"

"Only said a couple words, when he bought smokes. I never noticed an accent."

"Brand?" You never knew. Bill had tracked down a murderer once because he still smoked Lucky Strikes.

Chew, chew. My meter had run out. I parted with another 20.

"Marlboros," she said.

"One last question: Which way did the bus go, after it fueled up?"

She thought it over. "Came and went from thataway." She pointed north on Los Angeles Avenue, which would soon run straight past my gravel road.

I kept driving, and was soon officially in unknown territory, at the mercy of the hovering satellite gods of my GPS. Apparently, I would eventually reach the town of Fillmore. I headed toward civilization, until I found the next available gas station to ask another round of school bus questions.

Private detective work is often comprised of just such a series of inane shots in the dark.

This time, I hit pay dirt on the first try, another generic mart with a couple of rusting pumps outside.

"You're kidding, right?" this guy said. Bad Mohawk, worse teeth, and a snake tattoo that wrapped around his neck before slithering southward. Little pick-marks dotted his forearms: a meth head, sadly destined to stay right where he was, or worse, if he didn't clean up his act.

"Why do you think I'm kidding, Bennie?" I wasn't trying to name names—it was stitched on his shirt.

Bennie slouched from behind the counter and opened the door. He pointed up the road. A few hundred yards away, a blaze of security lights lit up a chain-link corral of yellow school buses, about two dozen of them.

"Maintenance yard for the district," Bennie said. "School buses coming and going all the time."

"Right." My stomach rumbled, loud enough for us both to hear. "Anywhere to eat nearby?"

"Fillmore IHOP's open. Or Micky Dee's."

I returned to my car to think. Something was bothering me, but it hadn't quite risen to the level of conscious thought. I needed a closer look at the maintenance yard and some caffeine.

I pulled alongside the yard. A stark, black-on-white sign read:

YARD HOURS 5 A.M.–5 P.M.
NO EARLY ARRIVALS PLEASE!

I checked the time: almost one in the morning.

I was too early, or too late.

I continued on into Fillmore and found the IHOP. The coffee was hot, the pancakes as big as river rafts. The worrying thought solidified, and broke into three concerns.

I paid a return visit to Bennie. "Couple more questions."

"Sure, man."

"It's July. Aren't schools closed?"

"Year-round system," he said. "Plus, summer camps use the buses. Sometimes on weekends, too."

"Okay. Second question. Do you always work this shift?"

"Nah, I mostly work days. I been double-shifting this week so the other dude could see his old lady in Orange County."

"So, when you said you saw buses coming and going all the time, you were referring to daytime, right?"

He scratched his arm. "Yeah. Daytime."

"What about last night? Or tonight, for that matter? Any school buses?"

He moved to his neck, scratching and picking. "Yeah! Both nights, a bus left the yard, around midnight. Last night, it came back maybe four hours later."

"Did you happen to see the driver?"

"Not really. White, I think. Crew cut."

"Has he ever fueled up here?"

"You're kidding, right?" he said again.

I pasted an expectant look on my face.

"They got their own diesel pumps! Right inside the yard!"

"Brilliant," I said, as if he were some kind of genius, and he beamed. Let him find his joy where he could.

Still, that was interesting. Why would a district-owned school bus stop to fuel at an obscure mini-pump up the road? It was beginning to look like a rogue driver was doing a little moonlighting on the side, transporting human contraband.

There was a certain evil genius to this. Who would ever think to pull over a school bus? It was hard to imagine a less threatening vehicle.

I was in the mood for action, not a couple of hours of old-fashioned, butt-numbing surveillance. A low buzz hummed in my bloodstream, like a hunting dog catching a scent. I told the dog to lie down, and pulled onto a side road parallel to the stable of buses. I focused my binoculars on the well-lit yard.

The joke in the squad room back in the day was there should only be one question on the detective exam: Can you sit on your ass for long periods of time without needing to pee?

I made it three hours before irrigating a small, defenseless bush. I checked on Clancy.

"Anything?"

"Nothing. Don't even see any cars in the lot here. How about you?"

"Nothing yet."

More sitting and watching, until my personal witching hour, 3:43 A.M., brought a school bus along with it. The engine gears ground as the bus downshifted. It halted, brakes squealing, at the front gate. The gate slid open, and the bus pulled into the yard. Moments later, the driver hurried back through the gate. He was middle-aged, a bit thin in the hair department, a bit thick in the torso, and carried a bicycle helmet under one arm. He unlocked a multigeared bike from the opposite end of the chain-link fence and clambered on.

I kept my lights off and rolled to the road. Moments later, he rode past, hunched over his handles, pedaling along the level bike lane at a pretty good clip. I switched on my headlights and pulled onto the road, accelerated past my target, then eased up enough to keep him in my rearview mirror.

We were approaching the thick of town, such as it was, and several more cars joined us. It wasn't too hard to jockey into a safe position while keeping him in sight.

He stuck his arm up like an L, turned right onto a side street, and right again. He pedaled more slowly into a scruffy-looking complex, a two-story U-shaped building wrapped around a small swimming pool. He dismounted, puffing from the exertion, lugged his bike up some metal stairs to the second floor, and wheeled it to an apartment door, midway along the outside corridor. After fumbling for a key and unlocking the door, he and his bike disappeared inside.

I parked across the street and settled in for another spell of surveillance.

This spell didn't last long. Fifteen minutes later he hurried out with his bike, dressed in navy pants and shirt, as well as a neon safety vest, like traffic monitors wear. I focused on his face. His eyes were sunken, and the harsh lines across his brow and framing his mouth carved his face into a mask of worry. His hair was wet, as if he'd just showered, and slicked back. The receding hairline aged him even more. I moved my estimate up from early- to midforties. The door slammed behind him. He was halfway down the metal rungs when it flew open again. Out flew a middle-aged woman in a bathrobe and a very bad case of bed-head. Somebody woke somebody up. They exchanged yells, and I checked for wedding rings. Husband and wife.

After a final shout, he hauled his bike to the ground floor, mounted, and whizzed out of the parking lot. Such is the grip of domestic drama that he pedaled right past me, our faces not six feet apart, without noticing a thing. He couldn't get away fast enough.

I decided to stay put. I was pretty sure he was on his way back to the bus yard, just in time for the 5 A.M. opening—almost as sure as I was that his wife would stay angry. Angry wives are a detective's dream. They'll tell you just about anything you want to know about their husbands, and usually for free.

But not at five in the morning. Talking to the missus would require more waiting.

Shortly before seven, the door opened. Angry Wife had changed into a light-blue maid's uniform. Like her husband, her worn face and thick body suggested years of hard work and unhealthy eating habits. I felt for her. Most of the cops I knew had the same issue, a direct result of long hours and fast food. She hurried down the stairs and disappeared into a door near the front office of the complex. Five minutes passed. She reappeared, pushing a cart of cleaning supplies. She maneuvered it to the rooms across the way.

Time to make my move.

I found her reenacting the fight with another uniformed maid, this one Hispanic, and exhausted by the look of it. The Hispanic maid patted Angry Wife on the shoulder before escaping with her own cart across the lot and disappearing into the supply room, as if finished for the day.

What was a cleaning maid doing ending her shift at this hour?

I purchased two cups of coffee from the vending machine and made my way to Angry Wife for a little chat.

As soon as she realized my intention, her pupils shrank, transmitting fear, but she didn't change posture except to square her shoulders. That was telling. Frightened animals, human or otherwise, are wired to respond in four ways: fight, flee, faint, or freeze. Angry Wife may have been worn out by life, and weighed down by worry, but she was a fighter.

Of course, if you're one of the newer, upgraded models of human, the ones who waved good-bye to their Neanderthal cousins with their puzzled grunts 50,000 years ago, you have an additional tool. Even as the ancient wiring urges you to fight or run or curl up in a ball or keel over, you have another choice. Talk. Things. Over.

"Good morning," I said.

"Good morning." Her eyes raked my body, as if checking for dynamite. "Can I help with something?" Her accent was heavy and very familiar.

"Excuse me for prying, but are you from Bosnia-Herzegovina?"

Her shoulders snapped back. "Why you ask this?"

"I just returned from a visit to Sarajevo." I sipped from my coffee. It was no gourmet brew, but better than nothing. I offered her the second cup. "I'm sorry, would you like this? I usually drink two cups, but . . ."

She stared at me for a long moment before taking the coffee warily. "I am Croatian. There is difference."

"I spent time in Dubrovnik as well. Amazing beaches." At this she smiled, and took a sip. I was in.

"I am a detective, a private detective. Do you know what that is?"

"Yes."

"I want you to know I'm not a policeman."

"I know what private detective is. I watch television. What do you want?"

"I'm investigating some illegal activities that may be going on in these apartments."

Her jaw hardened.

Interrogations are never about asking the perfect question, or catching the person in a lie. Bill taught me that. The answers lie in the silences, the open spaces. In this way, interrogating was similar to a practice I'd learned years before, at Dorje Yidam. They called it "right listening," but "spacious listening" was more accurate. The practice was not unlike my fourth rule, and simple, in theory: Just let go. Of opinions, judgments, evaluations, even expectations around what the other person is saying. Let go, and listen as if suspended in space. Let the word vibrations pass through you. Let go of being a monk or a private detective or a maid or a bus driver and extend beyond the differences, to the space from which all roles emerge. Simply put, just *be*.

Not as easy to do as it sounds, but well worth the effort. Or non-effort, I should say. The technique is powerful, because human nature, like any other, truly does abhor a vacuum.

I resisted filling the increasingly awkward gap in conversation and put the technique to the test. Ten seconds of spacious listening from my side, and Angry Wife proceeded to pour her personal woes into the charged silence. The words were heavily accented, but the gist was clear: "My husband drive bus, make me clean up sex hotel to pay rent. I not come to America for that." She covered her mouth with her hand, as if to prevent more confessions.

"*Sex hotel?* Is that what this place is?"

Her intensity was high, but her voice was low. "This side sex hotel," she said. "Other side apartments." Now she whispered. "Other side worse."

I couldn't hold on to spacious listening—condemnation stepped in, tainting the silence with my harsh judgment. She could tell. She rediscovered her resistance. "No more questions. I don't want trouble." She handed me the empty cup. "Thank you for coffee." She wheeled away without a backward look.

I circled the entire complex by foot, finally finding a name by the front office, which was closed for business.

The Oceanview Vista Motel.

No ocean, and no vistas or views, but I doubted the clientele cared.

I shouldn't have drunk the vending machine coffee. Pulling away from the motel complex, my mind jittered and jumped like a toad. I quickly checked the passenger seat floor. Jackass Rig holster and Wilson Combat were still there, safe and accounted for. My breath slowly calmed as I turned onto Los Angeles Avenue.

Only a few school buses remained in the yard. The rest were out ferrying young souls to their fields of play, oblivious to a world in which other children were forced to do the unspeakable.

CHAPTER 25

Martha's message was frantic.

"Please, please call me, Ten. I need to see you. I just, I don't know what's happening."

Hancock Park was on the way home. Time to behave like a grown man.

I found a Starbucks off the Highland Avenue exit and used my mangled but still valid gift card to purchase four coffees and an assortment of pastries.

The red-white-and-blue ribbons still hung in the branches of the magnolia tree, bedraggled and drooping, as if from exhaustion. Martha opened the door a crack, red-eyed, and another five pounds thinner. She was swimming in a pair of striped men's pajamas—Bill's, I assumed—and her breath smelled of wine.

"Drink this," I said, handing her one of the coffees. I listened for the twins, among other people, but the house was an echo chamber of hurt silence.

"Nobody's here," she said. "Julie took them all on a hike up Runyon Canyon."

"All the more for us," I said brightly, though her words pinched. I should have left things at that, but some masochistic imp got hold of my tongue. I handed Martha a scone. "So, Homer's with them?"

"Who told you about Homer?"

"Maude."

"Maude. Of course. Yes, he's with them, obviously."

"What's . . . what's he like?"

Martha waved at the air, distracted. "He's fine, I guess. The girls seem to like him a lot, even Lola."

My coffee tasted of acid, my croissant of chalk.

Don't ask.

"So, where's Homer sleeping?"

Martha finally focused on me. "In Julie's bed, if you must know. Are you here to discuss Homer, or can we please, please talk about my life? Which happens to be falling apart, in case you hadn't noticed."

Martha was slurring her words. She was either still drunk from the night before or she'd started early. My heart contracted, and then hot anger took over.

"Are you *drunk?*"

Martha started to cry. "I know. Mother of the year, right?"

And just like that, compassion doused the heat. I led her into the living room. Her body shrank, as if recalling the explosion there ten short days ago. I so wanted to tell her that Bill was on his way home, that he might land on her doorstep any minute, but I'd given him my word. So I just stood, an awkward witness to her pain.

This is why triangles aren't a good idea when it comes to intimate relationships. The geometric configuration too easily creates a vortex of confusion.

Buddha came to the rescue.

"Martha, the pain you are feeling right now? It will pass. It will change, I promise." Martha snuffled. I took her by the shoulders and pulled her into a hug. "What Bill does next is out of your control," I told the top of her head. "But what you do next isn't."

What she did next was lift her face and plant a long, sloppy kiss on me, right on the lips.

"Martha, umm, I didn't mean . . ." I disengaged as swiftly but humanely as possible.

"I'm sorry. I'm so sorry," she said, her cheeks inflamed. "Do you hate me?"

"Absolutely. I'm horrified to discover a woman I love and admire finds me attractive enough to kiss. I may not actually survive."

She smiled, but her eyes weren't convinced.

"Sit." I patted the sofa. She sat, and I took the chair.

"I'm going to say something, and I want you to listen closely. It may be difficult to hear, but it's time you knew the truth."

She closed her eyes, bracing for the worst.

"You are a catch. A smart, beautiful, sexy, warm, trustworthy, and irresistibly lovable catch. Any man lucky enough to have you would be a fool to let you go. And Bill may be acting like an idiot, but he's not a fool."

A quick sob caught in her throat, but she was taking it in. I could tell by the way her body responded, like a thirsty plant soaking up water. She opened her eyes.

"Thank you," she said.

I left her as she headed for a hot shower and clean clothes. Sounded like a good plan for me, as well.

But it was not to be. Kim had left me a text: I AM HERE. WHERE ARE YOU? YOU HAVE A GUEST.

Agh. G-Force. He'd called late last night to say he needed to see me right away. I'd invited him for breakfast at my house and proceeded to put the entire conversation into cold storage. Good thing it was Saturday, which meant Kim was there to let him in and jog my memory.

THIRTY MINUTES, I texted back.

G-Force was sitting in my kitchen, a bag of frozen peas pressed against his mouth. He lowered the peas, exposing a puffy upper lip, more like a flesh-colored duvet, really.

"What happened?"

"Thit. Thit happened," G-Force said, his voice badly muffled by the overhang. "All 'cauth o' you." He handed off the peas to Kim. "Now who be owing who?" He shot a hasty look at her. "Not you," he said, "talkin' to Ten here."

G-Force had obviously just completed Kim's crash course on clarity of speech and intention.

"You want a scone?" I waved my bag of Starbucks leftovers.

"Nah. I'm good. Can' eat thit w' thith lip."

I moved G-Force out to the deck, so Kim could do what she did inside, and in peace.

"Okay, G-Force. What's so important?"

G-Force attempted a whistle at the view. "Looka' that. That the othean, out there. Am I right?"

I refrained from discussing the view, and initiated my second round of spacious listening within 24 hours.

G-Force shot me a sideways look, the briefest of eye-flicks. He went back to studying the canyon vista. "You ever hear of a dude named Tory Wigginth?"

My chest tightened. Tory Wiggins was a key gangland presence, a Crip king we'd never managed to dethrone. I breathed past the automatic fight response his name prompted, relaxing again into a state of acceptance. "Yes."

"Real name Victory, but nobody call him that. Why he named Victory, he born the night Kirk Gibthon hit that home run."

"Mmm." It was hard to keep a straight face.

"Tory the man, few yearth back, major playa, you feel me? Weed, mothtly, and some hath. But he a ghetto thtar, no doubt."

Ghetto star, my brain corrected.

G-Force kept going, avoiding my eyes. "That carwath I been working at? Tory own it, a couple otherth, too. Tory the one give me the money for my gym. And latht night, he give me thith." G-Force pointed to his swollen lip, before lapsing into silence.

I entered the conversation, but my heart was open, so my voice was mild. "So you're saying your business partner is Tory Wiggins, *the* Tory Wiggins."

I needn't have bothered withholding judgment— G-Force provided enough for both of us. He jumped to his feet, almost knocking over the deck chair.

"Oh, thweet Jethuth—listen to the man! Where you learn to thling guilt around like that? You th'posed to be thome kind of Zen dude! You thoundin' like my mom!"

"I wasn't judging, G-Force. I was confirming your own words. Cops call it *corroborating a statement*."

G-Force collected himself. "Thorry, man. I wath 'thspecting you to jump my ath, you bein' ex-po-lithe and all." He sat back down. "Anyhow, I knew Tory way way back, when he wath Reverend Victory Wigginth, preaching out of Compton."

Tory Wiggins, a preacher? Now that, I didn't know. "Why'd he stop? When did he start dealing?"

"Not important. That neighborhood? Everybody get turned, thooner or later."

G-Force finally met my eye. "But Tory? He turn back. He quit the Cripth, got out, left all of it, a few yearth back. For real. We never knew why. But now, I do."

"Go on."

"Latht night, I athk Tory what he know about Cripth running meat. Before I can get out why I'm athking, he pop me one, right in the mouth."

"Sorry."

"Don't be. Five yearth ago, he'da ithed me. Heh-heh."

Tank strolled outside. He pinned his green eyes on G-Force.

"Thee-it. That your cat?"

I nodded. "Tank," I said.

"That cat got thoul. That cat badath, like Yoda."

Tank jumped onto my lap, having confirmed that G-Force gave off an acceptable enough vibration to warrant staying. G-Force picked up the thread. Happily, I had finally, fully adjusted to his lisp, and was able to translate accordingly.

"Anyway," G-Force went on, "Tory got no kid of his own. But he had a big sister, A'lelia. Fine woman, 'til she got shot. Some mofo Blood clipped her."

I actually remembered this case. About eight years ago, A'lelia Wiggins was walking with her young daughter in Watts when she caught a drive-by bullet meant for someone else. The tribal warfare that followed was brief, but bloody.

"Tory take in the little girl, Yolanda. But Yolanda never get her head right, after her moms gone and all. Four years back, she disappeared. But everyone know, she go with Bone. She in the game."

"The game?"

"That's what they call it. Bone a Crip, too, but not one of us. Part of the Rollin 60's crew. He showed up, promised Yolanda the world. But after that she have to prove herself, understand? Otherwise, he gone. That's how it works."

Reel in the vulnerable with treats before imprisoning them with threats.

"Tory track down Yolanda, just the one time, shacked up in some motel. He beg her to leave Bone, but Yolanda, she already deep in the life. She bottom bitch, you know, in charge of all the others in the stable."

Stable. Like they're animals.

I reined in my righteous indignation. I was ashamed to remember, but when I was still on the force, some of the guys used to call pulling in prostitutes the "garbage run." We'd expected trash, and so made sure we found it.

"How old is Yolanda? Today, I mean."

G-Force grimaced. "Seventeen. If she still alive."

So she started working the streets when she was 14. Another achingly young casualty of what was beginning to feel like a global war.

"Anyway, Tory give up dealing dope after that. Probably time anyway, weed market slowed way down, and he never into pushing other shit. But still, he stop. Now Tory all about putting money back into the hood, you feel me? S'why he loaned me half the scratch I need. But when I ask him about Crips pimping, it all come back, and Tory lose his shit."

"You took one for the team, G-Force."

"No big thing. Once he hit me, he settled down. He wanted to know all about you. That's why I needed to see you, Ten. Tory send me to ask you something."

I didn't know what was coming next, but I knew it was sure to further complicate my life.

"Tory want to hire you," G-Force said. "Pay you to find Yolanda and bring her home."

Oh, man.

I told G-Force I'd have to think about Tory's offer. He left with my promise to let him know, once I'd decided.

Technically, Tory Wiggins was still on the LAPD's "most wanted drug dealers" list, reformed or not. And who knows if he'd actually reformed? Criminals are con men. Conning is what they do.

On the other hand, people can and do change. If I didn't believe that, I'd have given up on humankind long ago, starting with myself.

Kim had left. I dug up Tank's favorite rubber-tipped brush and spent some time tending to his soft fur while my brain dealt with its own tangles.

We were both nice and calmed down by the time Stephanie called with a crisis and a heartfelt request of her own.

"Stephanie? I've been meaning to thank you for making those calls to the shelter in Sarajevo. I don't know how to thank you enough."

"Don't thank me. Thank Human Rights Watch. HRW put me together with the active safe houses over there. As for paying me back, not to worry. I have just the thing. My babysitter's got the flu, and I have an emergency call on a new client and a two-year-old with nowhere to go."

"Stephanie, I . . ."

"It's only for a couple hours, two and a half, tops. Promise. The client's coming to me, in Santa Monica. Connor's crazy about you—keeps talking about you. Ten, I wouldn't ask if it wasn't an emergency. I'm fifteen minutes away right now."

"But what do I do with him?" I'd watched the twins several times, but never for more than an hour, unless they were already asleep for the night. And as delightful as Maude and Lola are, those were some of the longest, most exhausting hours of my life.

"Not to worry. He comes with a fully equipped backpack. Vroom-vroom car, blankie, snacks, and a couple of Diegos."

I had no idea what a "Diego" was, but it sounded pharmaceutical.

I played my last card. "Uh, is Connor allergic to cats, by any chance?"

"You have a cat? Connor loves cats. Connor? Remember Mommy's friend Ten? He has a cat!"

"Tat!" I heard. "See Tat!"

Tank sealed the deal.

By the time I'd finished a mad scramble to put anything obviously dangerous out of a small boy's reach, including double-checking that my firearms were safely locked away, Stephanie and Connor were at my door.

"Hey, Connor," I said, out of breath. I knew enough to squat down. Little kids prefer eye-level communication, I recalled. I didn't want to scare Connor and accidentally set off one of the four F's.

"Tat!" Connor marched right past me and hunkered down himself to make deep, soulful eye contact with Tank.

"I'll be back, Connor," Stephanie called out, but Connor was lost in Persian Tat-land.

Tank's languid tail swished, a sure sign that he was having a good time. Connor reached for Tank's fur.

"Gentle," I said. "Like this." I took Connor's hand and helped him stroke the soft fur along Tank's spine. Tank ratcheted up the purrs.

"See? Nice cat."

"Nice tat," Connor said.

Tank took care of 15 minutes. For the next 40, I plied Connor with every edible snack and drinkable bottle and box in his backpack. "Diego," I discovered, was a DVD of a children's show starring a young Latino rescuer of animals, not a drug, at least not in so many words. I followed up the food-fest by propping Connor on the sofa with my *Diego*-loaded laptop and his blankie. One hour down. One to go. *No problemo.*

I was helping Connor and Diego save an endangered rhinoceros when Tory's delegation paid me a visit.

I knew it was trouble calling the minute I saw the car: a white Escalade with tricked-out wheels and smoked windows, a high-end gangster ride. The two black guys who climbed out wore black suits and black bow ties, very dapper.

They approached at an easy stroll and climbed the outside stairs to the deck. Something about them, their outfits maybe, or their somewhat exaggerated gait, rang a little false, but I couldn't take any chances.

"Stop right there," I called out through the kitchen window. I slid open a kitchen drawer and fisted a corkscrew. "I need to let you know I'm a private detective and I'm armed."

"¡Al rescaté!" I heard Diego cry from my laptop in the living room. "To the rescue!"

"Who are you?" I said to the front man, who had the bulkier build.

"We're the, uh, the delegation."

Right, the delegation. "Okay, what does the *delegation* do?"

"Right now? Invite you to meet somebody you probably want to meet anyway."

"Who's that?"

"Mr. Tory Wiggins."

Tory may have quit being a gangster, but he hadn't given up his gangster ways, not entirely. And he clearly didn't have a lot of patience.

"How did you guys find me?"

"Go, Diego, go!" Two voices, one shrill and piping, the other belonging to Connor.

"G-Force," the second guy said. "Tory tracked his phone. Tory likes to know how his business associates spend their time."

"¡Gracias!" Diego's piercing voice piped up. This time Connor hadn't joined in.

The first guy grimaced. "Your kid into that show, too? If I had my way, I'd gag Diego. Dora, too. But my daughter can't get enough."

"Oh, that's not my . . ."

But he was onto other things. "I'm going to reach in my pocket and pull out something Tory wants to give you. Don't go shooting me."

The best I could do was unscrew a cork at this point, but luckily he was none the wiser.

He extracted a shrink-wrapped block of cash. He set the money on the deck, just outside the kitchen door transom.

"Tory says you can keep it, or bring it back to him if you don't want it—either way's fine with him. He just wants to lay a little good faith on you. That's five thousand dollars there. Think of it as a down payment."

The living room was ominously quiet. I turned my head to quick-check the sofa.

It was empty.

"I'm sorry, but I can't . . ."

He and his buddy ambled back down the stairs and crossed the driveway to the Escalade. They bumped elbows, as if to congratulate each other on a job well done. The first guy called back, "I left Tory's information on top of the cash."

Where is Connor?

I was close to full-on panic, helped not at all by the distinctive whine of Stephanie's blue Prius whirring into the driveway. She pulled to a stop right behind the Escalade, like a dewdrop challenging an iceberg. The "delegation" eyed her, as if they'd never seen a woman driving a Prius before. They climbed into their four-wheel monolith, she reversed out of their way, and they lumbered off.

"Connor? Connor!" There were only four rooms to check, including the bathroom. I found Connor behind the living-room screen that blocked off my meditation area. He was vroom-vrooming his car along the edge of one wall, a confiscated carved wooden Buddha from my altar at the wheel, as inscrutable as always.

I scooped Connor up and was back in the kitchen just as Stephanie walked inside.

"I think your friends left you this." She traded the brick of cash for her son.

"Uh."

My cell phone pinged news of a text from my pocket. On stress-induced automatic pilot, I pulled it out to look.

BILL'S BACK. ON MY WAY OVER. THERE IN FIVE. I had to read the name twice to believe it. Julie.

Training to become a Tibetan Buddhist lama gives one many tools for life. A handle for this kind of situation wasn't one of them.

"You're obviously busy. Maybe we should go," Stephanie said, a slight edge to her voice.

"No, wait," I said. "The weirdest thing just happened. I'll explain all after I get Connor's stuff."

Her face softened. She kissed Connor's cheek. "Did you have fun?" she asked him.

"Tat! Diego!"

"Add a four-course snack and that pretty much sums it up," I said.

I ejected the DVD and returned Diego, vroom-vroom, blankie, and a sippy cup to Connor's backpack. I kept my carved Buddha.

I walked Stephanie and Connor outside, mentally working out how to explain the delegation with their block of cash. But I was spared by Connor's huge yawn.

"Oops. Time to get this little guy home for his nap. Thanks again, Ten. You were a lifesaver." Stephanie leaned in, Connor balanced on one hip, for a nice, long three-way hug.

Thus giving Julie, who picked that exact moment to arrive in Martha's minivan, an eyeful and a half.

Then it was my turn to stare. Julie opened the back of the minivan, and reappeared weighed down by the saddest-faced dog I'd ever seen. His muzzle appeared flattened, as if someone tried to iron out his wrinkles by mistake. White head, except for a circular tan patch over one eye, and a pair of upright ears, like cones. The downturned mouth was the polar opposite of a smile. I heard Tank hiss from behind and above me on the deck.

This wasn't a triangle, this was a hexagon from hell.

¡Rescaté me!

"Stephanie, this is Julie. Julie, Stephanie. Also, Connor."

"Papa!" Connor chose to announce for the first time today, patting my arm. Julie took in Connor's Asian features. Her eyes narrowed.

Stephanie handed Connor off to me like a football and walked over to Julie. She made a fist with her right hand.

Now what?

"And who's this handsome fellow?" Stephanie asked. She offered her curled knuckles to the dog for a sniff. Apparently, he was too overwhelmed to respond. I could relate.

"This is Homer," Julie said.

CHAPTER 26

"It's not what you think," I called over my shoulder to the kitchen. I'd persuaded Julie to put Homer on a leash, sent Stephanie and Connor away with a promise to call, and was on my hands and knees, about to check under the living-room sofa for my disgruntled cat.

Tank wasn't there either. I sighed. He'd show his face again when he was good and ready, and not before.

"What if I'm not thinking what you think I'm thinking?" Julie's voice replied.

I gave up trying to untangle the sentence and returned to the kitchen.

Julie had claimed the kitchen stool, a twinkle in her eye, and Homer hanging off both ends of her lap. I moved to stand by the window.

"I'm just relieved," she said. "I couldn't figure out why you weren't calling me back. Come to find out you thought Homer here was my one-and-only." She nuzzled the top of the dog's head. "No offense, Homer. You come close."

I studied the competition in more detail.

His solid body was short and squat. His pink muzzle appeared badly squashed, wide black nostrils aiming north, and his mouth curved downward, the opposite of smiling. The brown eye patch gave him a slightly rakish look, to balance out the scowl.

"What is Homer?"

"He's a rescue dog. I got him from a shelter, back in Chicago."

"No, I mean what kind of dog?"

Julie scratched behind an upright ear. Homer opened his mouth and his tongue lolled with pleasure. The change was startling—like sunshine breaking through dense cloud cover, carrying with it a promise of joy.

"He's an English Bulldog. When I got him last year, he was ten pounds thinner, but I soon took care of that." Under Julie's steady ear-ministrations, Homer had started to drool. "I got Homer for protection. You know, with me being a single woman again."

Homer looked more likely to hold the burglar's flashlight between his teeth than scare him off, but I held my tongue. I also stayed where I was, by the window overlooking the deck. Truth was, I'd been uncomfortable around dogs ever since a mangy Dorje Yidam stray removed a small chunk of my left calf when I was ten. According to Tibetan legends, the wild dogs that inevitably roamed the periphery of Buddhist monasteries were reincarnated monks who'd broken their vows in a past life. Mine was apparently a lapsed vegetarian, and I still had a scar on my leg the size of a 50-cent piece to prove it.

I focused on the other part of Julie's sentence, the "single woman" part.

Dog in her lap or not, Julie felt too far away. I moved to the kitchen counter and leaned against it, a little awkwardly. The uneven tempo of my pulse belied the casual tone of my voice.

"So what happened? With that guy, I mean. Your boyfriend?"

Julie set Homer on the floor. He flattened like a rug, his two back legs sticking out behind him, as if his hip joints were made of elastic. He laid his wrinkled head on his paws and went straight to sleep. Julie met my eyes.

"Alcoholism happened," she said.

"Ah."

"I went to a few of those meetings, you know."

"You're an alcoholic?"

"No. Because I was living with one. They like to say that insanity is doing the same thing over and over, expecting a different result."

"Expectations. I know a lot about that."

"I should have known better. He'd only been sober for nine months when he returned to his old job as a sommelier. He swore it would work, that he'd stick to just sniffing the wine. He said he could base his choices and descriptions on aroma alone. But he stopped going to his meetings. He was too busy, he said. Then sniffing became swishing and spitting. Swishing and spitting became swishing and swallowing, and pretty soon, he was off to the races. He lost me after about a year. He lost his job six months after that." Julie's eyes filled. "Such a waste, you know? He's a really good guy, just with a really bad drinking problem."

I refrained from commenting. My heart was too happy to be here with Julie, to have her in my kitchen again, to bother judging her ex.

"An alcoholic can't ever give another person the intimacy they crave, or the love they deserve. The alcohol, the ism itself, comes between them and everything else. For me, it was like trying to reach someone barricaded behind a wall."

My mother, her once beautiful features puffy with wine and drained of inner light, floated like a ghost across my heart.

"What about you, Ten? Any girlfriends?"

I thought about Heather, her own struggle with food as self-medication, and for the first time made the connection. "I had a remarkably parallel experience," I said. "Great woman. Unresolved addiction stuff. She's doing much better now, but it's been over between us for more than a year."

"And Stephanie? I'm guessing Connor isn't your love child, at least. Martha couldn't have kept that a secret for long."

"Stephanie's a professional friend. I was watching her son as a favor. She's been a big help with the Sasha situation."

Julie shook her head. "God. For a moment I'd put that madness out of my head. Bill and the Mila woman? I'm still in shock, you know?" She made a face. "I have to confess, when Bill showed up this afternoon, I skedaddled. I couldn't face the fireworks."

"I know what you mean."

"But Ten, whatever you said to Martha this morning, she was a different woman when I got home with the twins. She'd washed her hair, put on makeup, and was wearing a pair of jeans she hasn't worn in years. She was positively sassy! And don't think Bill didn't notice, either, when he arrived with his tail between his legs. So I'm not ruling anything out."

Tank brushed against my right ankle. I scooped him up, so he could observe Homer from the safe haven of my arms. "Tank, meet Homer," I said. "Homer's from Chicago. Okay. Let's see if you two can be friends."

I placed Tank on the ground and he immediately strolled over to the sleeping bulldog to inspect, whiskers and tail on high alert. For better or worse, Tank's curiosity has always trumped any primal fear-mechanisms. Homer raised his square head off of his paws, with some effort. He executed a sniff or two of his own.

The two animals apparently found each other worthy of co-existence because Homer collapsed again, zoning out, and Tank lay down beside him, after giving me an inscrutable look. Soon Tank, too, closed his eyes.

I was attacked by a sudden yawn. I moved away from the counter. "I'll tell you one thing about two-year-olds, they're more exhausting than working the graveyard shift. I need a nap."

Julie's lips curved into a smile. "A nap sounds good."

Was I misreading the glint in her gold-flecked eyes?

Maybe not. She slid off the stool, skirted the two sleeping animals, and in two steps stood right in front of me. She stretched, her arms toned from all those years of vegetable chopping. A light spray of freckles dotted her smooth skin.

A deep twisting sensation invaded my groin area, half-pleasure, half-pain. The tightness mounted to my chest, cutting off my breath. "Julie, it's been over a year."

"Me, too," she said. "Way too long."

My heart was trying to gallop straight through my rib cage. But I had to say my piece. "I've never forgotten what a wise, beautiful woman once said to me. At the time, I didn't understand, but now I think I do."

"What?" Julie's lips were almost close enough to kiss. "What do you understand?"

"That the sum of a relationship has to equal more than the two parts. A healthy, intimate relationship, I mean. And for that to happen, each part has to take responsibility for its own happiness. Otherwise, it's not worth doing."

Julie's breath brushed my cheek, like the flutter of wings. "Well, listen to you." She stepped even closer, and we moved together as one, until we were pressed against the kitchen counter. Her mouth shifted to my right ear. "So, guess what? I have this idea for a restaurant, Ten. My own restaurant, I should say. I want to call it Julie's Impromptu."

"Good name." I swallowed. The light scent of soap and jasmine on her skin was acting as an accelerant on my pheromones. "What kind of food will you serve?"

"Whatever I feel like making that day," she murmured. "My plan is, intimate setting. Twenty or so seats. Maybe a semicircular counter, with the equipment right in the middle. That way, everyone can see me do my thing."

I never knew a business concept could be so . . . so sexy.

"Impromptu," she almost whispered. "In other words, spontaneous."

"Spontaneous?" I interlaced the fingers of my right hand with hers.

"Spontaneous." She interlaced our left hands, and pulled my chest against her soft but firm breasts.

"Whatever strikes you at the moment?"

"Whatever strikes me." Her breath tickled my ear.

"So everyone has to let go of expectations?" I traded, moving my mouth to her other cheek. I kissed the fragile skin right beneath the lobe. "Sounds exciting. What about dessert?"

"Dessert's a surprise. Sorry, but you're just going to have to wait."

"Until . . . ?"

"Until I've decided what to serve."

And with that, she led me to bed.

We did sleep, eventually. But only after a delicious period of deep familiarity intermingled with fresh, new discoveries, and an early evening pause to feed and water the livestock, ourselves included. My phone beeped and buzzed, more than once, but I left it alone, and eventually whoever was trying to reach me did the same. The bedroom was dark by the time naptime had somehow morphed into bedtime. Our bodies nestled like twin spoons under the covers, an almost perfect fit.

"I missed you, Julie Forsythe," I said. "I've been missing you for ages. I don't think I realized how much until now."

"Me, too, love." Julie kissed my back, a sweet spot right between my shoulder blades. "Me, too."

CHAPTER 27

I parked on the street and climbed out of my Mustang to confirm that the low, level building of sand-colored brick, occupying a fraction of a block on West 106th Street, matched the address the "delegation" had left for me yesterday. I was way south of South Central, almost in Compton. Boxy single-family residences lined the quiet street. A few brave trees had taken root in tiny yards, here and there. Overhead, the tangle of telephone wires formed a crisscrossed canopy, strung between peeling utility poles.

I double-checked the number. I was in the right place.

To my left, the building ended in a small parking lot, adjacent to a smaller concrete playground. Children here had to make do with a single sandbox slightly bigger than a Kleenex box, plus two plastic picnic tables huddled close under tented blue canvas, the only source of shade. According to the sign, this portion of the building housed a Head Start program.

The rest of the structure plodded its way to the corner of 106th and Vermont. The windows were mesh grilles, all but one striped with metal bars. The middle window frame accommodated a very old air-conditioning unit, which was coughing and humming. A single white cross was tacked to the far edge of the flat roof, like an afterthought. I spotted another sign, this one enclosed in glass, on a strip of grass by the front sidewalk. The lettering was faded but legible: Grace Missionary Baptist Church.

Okay, maybe Tory Wiggins had given up the high life after all. Returned to his roots, so to speak. Maybe the "delegation" was in fact his "congregation."

I parked in the empty lot, my bright-yellow Mustang as conspicuous as a giraffe. I strolled up the sidewalk to the front entrance, a heavy metal double-door, like you'd find at an indoor gymnasium or pool. The packet of cash felt bulky and uncomfortable in my pocket.

A hulking man with ebony skin sat alone in the front pew of the plainest, oddest place of worship I'd ever visited, the decor more Home Depot than anything else. The ceiling tiles were pebbled, the ceiling itself very low. The flooring was dull-gray industrial carpeting. No sign of crosses or statues anywhere. Instead, what looked like a pilfered segment of wooden banister provided railing for the two makeshift steps leading up to a raised dais. A plywood lectern faced the room, a microphone clipped to the front lip.

"Mr. Wiggins?"

He stood and turned, a towering refrigerator of a man. "You must be Tenzing. Thanks for coming." The deep rumble of voice reached me by way of undulation, like a bowling ball traveling its wooden alley. "Come on up. Take a seat."

I moved up the center aisle, flanked by maybe 20 rows of pew. My feet scuffed the carpet. At the front, I slid across curved wood until I was maybe a foot away. Tory's neck was as thick as my thigh. His black hair was close-cropped, and well-salted with gray. His eyes were so dark they swallowed up the pupils, but they shone with intelligence. Only a fool would underestimate this man's physical or mental prowess.

"Is this your church?"

"Used to be." He shot me a look, as if daring me to make fun. "I like to come back here now and then. Helps calm me down."

"I like it," I said. "Simple. No nonsense."

He gave my forearm a light cuff. Well, light for Tory. To me, it felt like an anvil landing. He could have snapped the humerus bone in two like a twig, if he'd so chosen. G-Force was lucky he'd wound up with nothing more than a fat lip.

"I know some about you, Ten. G-Force told me a little, and I've done more digging on my own." Tory's words rolled from his mouth like polished marbles, each one distinct and refined. Either he'd worked hard to drop the ghetto slang, or he'd never embraced that way of talking to begin with.

I could well imagine a voice like his filling this space with a godly thunder.

"I know you like to solve problems for people," he continued. "I know you can run hot at times. I also know that you're chasing some bad men right now. The worst kind of men." He tipped his head, studying me. "But now that you're here, up close and personal, I sense something else."

More silence from me. I wasn't going to help with this instant psychoanalysis.

"You like to clean up your little piece of the world. You're after justice above all, even if it means bending the rules. Even if it's the kind of justice they don't necessarily dispense," Tory waved vaguely toward downtown, "over there at the courthouse." His smile seemed tired. "Tell me I'm wrong."

I couldn't. He wasn't wrong, not completely.

"Though maybe that's just you on a good day. On a bad day, who knows? If you're like me, on a bad day maybe you're a self-righteous prick."

I had to smile. Tory rewarded me with his own gold-toothed grin.

"Thought so," he said.

"Okay, Mr. Wiggins," I said. "Enough mapping out of my deficiencies. What are we doing here?" I pulled out the bundle of money. "Besides you trying to talk me into taking a job I don't want to take."

"Relax," Tory said. "How about we just take a couple of deep breaths first? Before we get into all that. Isn't breathing what you monks are supposed to be good at?"

Reformed drug dealer or not, Tory gave good advice, and I complied. I inhaled, testing the atmosphere. The air inside the empty church, while warm and slightly stale, was still flavored with the unmistakable purity and weight of a space that has received a steady diet of prayer and praise, directed to a higher power. Its spirit-infused density reminded me of the old prayer hall at Dorje Yidam. I inhaled and exhaled again. Around me, the empty, whispering pews seemed to settle as well, as if accepting an invitation to experience a deeper peace and silence.

"Tell me about Yolanda," I said.

Tory closed his eyes. His voice was like a low growl. "I don't know how that girl got such a claim on my heart, but she did. Child was shattered by her mother's death, and I felt responsible." He corrected himself. "I *was* responsible. Not directly, but still. I tried to help her, raise her like my own, but nothing worked. Yolanda was broken. A perfect target for a man like Bone." On his lap, his hands curled into fists. They looked like big hams. He glanced over. "That's what kills me, you know? I could always spot the broken ones, too, back in the day. When I was on the lookout for easy marks." He seemed to drift off for a moment. "He inked his name on her, you know. Over her heart. Branded that child, like she was his cow."

"I'm sorry," I said, "I truly am. But I don't think I can help. My investigation into trafficking has nothing to do with local gangs."

"I understand, I do." His voice grew urgent. "But I've been hearing some things. Things about Crips getting together. Pimps joining forces, not just with each other, but with big-time traffickers from other countries. Bad men. No, more than bad. Evil."

My antennae pricked. "What other countries?"

"Thailand. China. Russia. All over." Tory scrubbed at his head with his meaty palms. "I hate this shit! Can't wrap my head around the wrong of it, you know?"

"I feel the same way," I said.

"I know I made my own mistakes," he said. "I justified my actions because it was mostly weed. Told myself it was just business, that nobody ever took another's life under the influence of bud, no matter how high the grade. But I was still breaking the law. And Yolanda's mother, she was a victim of that lawless life, a life I helped perpetuate." Tory bowed his head for a moment, as if weighed down by remorse. "I accept that. But I can't accept what's going on now. The way we are enslaving our own flesh and blood, in the name of commerce." He turned, his eyes genuinely full of pain. "The way I see it, any girl—white, black, yellow, born here or somewhere else—if she's selling her body to line someone else's pocket, she's a slave. She's hurting. She's in pain. And even if she isn't mine, she's somebody's Yolanda."

He nudged the stack of money back across the pew. "Please, Tenzing. Please take the money."

I took it, if for no other reason than to ease the tidal waves of agony emanating from the big man.

"And if you need help, tell G-Force to give me a shout. I've still got muscle I can call on, people that owe me."

I snorted. "Your delegation?"

His look was amused. "So you spotted that trick. Those two guys? They're church deacons. And the Escalade's from another life. Still, it got you here, didn't it? Takes a hothead to know a hothead." He stood and offered his hand. "The offer stands. Call if you need anything."

"Okay," I said. "I will."

As I pushed open the heavy door to the outside world, Tory's parting words reached me, low and laced with regret.

"I just want to know she's okay," he said.

Slowly winding east along the residential boulevards so I could hook back onto the freeway, I opened my phone to call Julie. I wanted to make sure last night had happened. That she was real, that *we* were real. As I scrolled for her number, my phone vibrated in my palm.

She was calling me. I put her on speaker.

"Hey!" I said. "Are you still at the house?"

"I wish." Her voice sounded tinny, her stress evident. "I'm at Martha and Bill's. Can you come over? The shit may be about to seriously hit the fan."

"What's going on?"

"Mila and Sasha just landed at LAX. They're headed to the house. And they're asking for you."

"I'm on my way."

I realized I'd never checked my messages from last night, so I pulled over right before the Harbor Freeway on-ramp. First, my favorite ex-paparazzo, Clancy: "Yo, Ten, it's been like a graveyard over here. Nobody in or out for two full days. No people. No vehicles. Certainly no vans or school buses. Either I got the address wrong, or everybody's taking their summer vacation. I'm telling you, this is not a going concern. Let me know if you want me to stay put."

I called Clancy right back.

"Yo."

"It's me, Ten. Take a break, okay?"

"Sorry I couldn't help."

"No, this does help. Nothing happening may mean something else did."

The second message was from Mike, and landed like a lead ball in my belly: "Boss. When you get this, call me. Some serious, serious shit going down."

Mike rarely showed emotion, but his voice was stitched tight with something close to fear. I checked the time. He'd be dead asleep. I called anyway. His voice mail picked up. I disconnected and called again. He answered the third round of rings.

"Yeah. I'm here."

"Mike, Ten. Sorry, I . . ."

"No, s'good you called. Hang on."

I waited as face-washing, toilet-flushing noises happened.

"Okay. I'm officially functioning."

"What's going on?"

"I'm not really sure." These words rarely came out of Mike's mouth. "So, when was the last time you checked that Agvan site online?"

"Night before last. Why?"

"Because it's shut down."

"What do you mean? Like, undergoing repairs?"

"I mean gone. Vamoosed. Like the dark web went even darker. Not only that, the NDRSNT directory's coming up as an error page for the time being."

"How could this happen?"

"Could be a raid. That'll make sites go underground faster than a fuckin' prairie dog, to prevent the feds from planting malware that could expose buyers and sellers. Or maybe these guys just got spooked for some reason."

"But you think the FBI's involved?"

"Actually, I don't. I think somebody wants this business to disappear, jump off the radar screen for the moment."

"Agvan Supply?"

"Probably, or whoever owns them."

I put Clancy and Mike's messages side by side. There was only one conclusion—Zarko Stasic had also put two and two together, and was either shutting things down, or, more likely, regrouping so he could take his business elsewhere.

Why had I set off the car alarm, almost certainly landing myself on Agvan Supply's security camera feed? Why hadn't I told Deputy Sergeant Gaines exactly where to find the old man's killer? Why had I sent Zarko Stasic that macho message, via Ponytail, a taunt he'd answered with a much deadlier message of his own?

What had I expected him to do, invite me over for a duel?

Yes. I had expected Stasic to fight instead of flee. And my expectations had probably doomed those two little boys, not to mention countless others, to lives of degradation and terror.

"I'm sorry, boss," Mike now said. "I hope my hacking didn't somehow poke the sleeping bear."

So Mike, too, felt responsible.

"This is all on me, Mike. All on me. Listen, you've been a huge help, and I appreciate the heads-up," I said. "Let me know if anything changes."

I took the Gower exit off of the 101, headed south, and soon pulled up outside the Bohannon house. The curtains were drawn. Another cheap white rental car blocked the driveway. I unbuckled my seat belt. Closing my eyes, I rotated my shoulders backward and forward, loosening up my rotator cuffs. Next, I flexed and stretched my neck muscles, shifting my head side-to-side and front-to-back.

I rested one hand on my belly, inhaled until my lungs were beyond full, and let out two loud *HAHs* while feeling the deep contraction in my diaphragm. As a gust of fresh air clears away the smoke, the expulsion of carbon dioxide freed up space in my belly and purified my head of expectations.

I was ready to face whatever lay inside the house.

The white hood of the rental was still warm, and the engine was making a small, tick-ticking sound of disapproval. Mila and Sasha hadn't beaten me here by much.

Dread wrestled with acute curiosity. More than a small part of me wanted to find out—no, make that was *insanely curious* to find out—how this situation would finally play out.

Yeshe's voice chided from afar: "Tenzing, do not expect, or control. Offer yourself as a channel of ease. Bring loving-kindness, and the balm of compassion."

I'll try.

Everyone had assembled in the living room. Martha sat in the rocking chair. Her arms were crossed, but her eyes were more troubled than angry, and her chin had lost yesterday's rigid, stubborn set. Bill stood next to Martha, his hand resting on her shoulder, I was happy to see. Sasha and Mila also stood, their backs to the French doors that overlooked the yard, staring at the carpet. And Julie, my Julie, sat cross-legged on the floor, both hands buried in Homer's wrinkled neck.

Bill shot me a look. "Good. You made it," he said.

"Where are the girls?"

"Stashed upstairs for the time being," Martha said. "Thank God for Dora."

For once, I was in the loop.

"I'm sorry we come here without asking," Mila said. "But there is no time."

THE FOURTH RULE OF TEN

Sasha put his hand on Mila's arm. "No, let me." His eyes found Martha's. "Mrs. Bohannon, I apologize for intruding into your life this way."

Martha's eyes softened at his forthright words. It was hard not to like the kid. I checked on Bill and almost laughed. He'd gone from not knowing he had a son to being ashamed that he had a son to being proud of his son, all within a few weeks. Now he was staring at Sasha with something that bordered on awe.

Martha said, "Thank you. I'm sorry it happened this way as well." She stepped forward and shook Sasha's hand. He held onto it.

"There's something else." Sasha's smile was rueful. "All my life I wanted a sister. I used to beg my mother to get me one."

"Is true," Mila said.

"And now I learn that I have two, two actual sisters."

"Half-sisters," Mila said. Sasha shot her an affectionate look, and I realized that her tendency to nitpick might not be personal so much as her personality.

"I want more than anything to meet them. And I'm very afraid you won't allow this." Had Sasha, too, been taking communication lessons from Kim?

Martha went very still.

"I know my existence causes you pain." Sasha's voice was devoid of self-pity. "But I didn't choose the parents I was born to."

His point was well taken, if debatable, at least in my tradition. Some Buddhist teachings claim that after many lifetimes of retiring karma, certain sentient beings can consciously choose their parents for their next span of life lessons. Given my tussles with my father, I quite liked the idea, although like a lot of metaphysical theories, its accuracy was difficult to prove.

Either way, Sasha's observation did the trick.

Martha shook her head. "You know what's so weird about this? Maude and Lola have been bugging me since

- 259 -

they could talk about getting them a big brother. Lola even asked Santa Claus for one last Christmas. Remember, Bill?"

"I'd totally forgotten that," Bill said.

"I told Lola life doesn't exactly work that way, but now?" Martha covered Bill's hand with her own, "Who knows? Maybe it does."

For just a moment, we all smiled at this unexpected answer to a four-year-old's request.

Then Sasha cleared his throat, crossing his arms as if for protection, his anxiety suddenly palpable.

Our lighthearted reprieve was over. Martha sensed the change immediately, and her reaction was instant.

"What is it, Sasha? What's wrong?"

Sasha seemed frozen in place. Mila touched his back, as if to let him know she was right there.

Something compelled me to speak. "I think we'd better sit down for this," I said. Mila shot me a grateful look. Soon we had rearranged ourselves, forming a circle, as if by silent agreement. Homer's thick body draped across Julie's legs, like a piebald lap rug. We were an odd assembly of characters, to be sure. A blended family, although some were more reluctant than others to be in the mix. But the desire to alleviate Sasha's obvious agony, and to understand his mother's grim, unmistakable resolve, bound us as surely as blood.

Bill spoke first. "Mila? You want to start? Because I'm completely clueless."

"Better Sasha talk first," she said.

Sasha nodded. Seemed to gather himself. "I know my mother told you guys that I'd started an investigation into human trafficking a few months ago. But what she didn't tell you was why."

I remembered that side-flick of Mila's eyes, when I'd asked her just this question.

"I suspect," Mila now said. "But I did not know why for sure."

"The *why* has to do with my grandfather," Sasha said. "And my step-grandfather, I guess."

Irena's two husbands.

"I loved my grandfather. *Deda,* I called him. Deda was a good man, gentle and very kind. He was the fairest person I ever met, fair to a fault, I sometimes thought. I only knew him after he was released from Omarska, after his time in the prison camp. But even as a child, I could sense how that trauma clung to him, draining him of energy and light. He never talked about it. But the darkness was always there. Deda would listen to his classical records for hours, staring out the window in his study. But he never saw the trees, or the sun, not really."

"My father has no room for joy," Mila added. "Only for grief."

"Anyway, when I got back from my first semester in college, I persuaded my mother to buy Deda a laptop computer. My grandmother was never home, she'd gotten all wrapped up with this new religion. I thought if I showed Deda how to do research online, browse the Internet, he might reengage with the world again. He used to be a professor, you know, a brilliant scholar. Anyway, it seemed to work, at first. But then, he became obsessed with it. Secretive, too."

"He spends hours on the computer," Mila said. "Days."

"And then, one night, someone, a burglar we thought, broke into the house. I was away at school."

"I hear a shot," Mila confirmed. "I run to my father's office. He is dead, shot through back of head."

"Any sign of a struggle?" Bill spoke for the first time, all business.

"No," Sasha said. "But my grandfather wasn't the type to fight. Anyway, whoever it was, they stole his computer."

"Anything else?"

"His wedding ring. They never figured out who did it."

Mila's voice was steel. "I know. I know who killed my father. Is Zarko."

"We don't know that yet, Mama, not for sure," Sasha said.

Random images pixilated and formed into new ones. I felt lightheaded, as the pieces of this story spun and danced in my brain like fireflies.

"When I came home last summer, I decided to listen to one of Deda's records. I chose his favorite, Beethoven's 'Ode to Joy.'" Sasha shook his head. "Not that it brought him any."

The truth of his words sank in.

"So, anyway," Sasha continued, "when I pulled the record from the sleeve, a computer disc fell out with it. Deda must have hidden it there. He'd handwritten something on the disc with a marker, a bunch of initials, you know, that stood for something else."

My sense of dread grew. "An acronym," I said.

"Yeah."

"N-D-R-S-N-T," I said.

Sasha stared. "But, how could you possibly know that?"

"Zarko killed my father," Mila insisted, as if caught in her own loop. "Now I will kill Zarko."

The rest of us met this declaration of war with a kind of stunned silence.

Bill's voice broke the spell. "Ten."

I hadn't heard that degree of steel in his voice since the time I ran into gunfire without waiting for backup.

"You feel like telling me what in the name of God is going on here?"

At that, Julie set Homer down. "I don't know about anyone else, but I need a cup of hot tea." She left for the kitchen, with Sasha and Mila trailing behind her.

I stayed where I was, glued to the sofa, as Martha and Bill conferred, their voices low. Bill looked over at me, pulling at his upper lip. The kettle whistled, and Martha hurried out.

"How would you feel about moving these operations over to your house?" Bill said, sitting across from me. "Martha and Julie can stay here with the girls. I'm not sure they need to know any more about this."

I'd been thinking the same thing. We hadn't heard the worst of this tale, and I couldn't yet guess where it might lead.

"Let's meet up at my house in an hour," I said. "And Bill? Bring your gun."

CHAPTER 28

Tank seemed no worse for wear after his close encounter with a wrinkled canine. He'd licked his cat bowl clean, and promptly fallen asleep on the deck in an oval of late afternoon sun. A platter of artichoke hummus, lemon pita chips, satsuma tangerine segments, raw almonds, and cherry tomatoes would have to do for the humans. I'd set a cast-iron, round-bellied pot of green tea to steep on the kitchen counter, and four chipped but clean mugs, almost matching, awaited their payload of hot brew.

I'd had to smile as I busied myself around the kitchen. That look on Martha's face, when I marched into the kitchen and exchanged a good long kiss with Julie before I left! It might be my best gift to Martha yet—something new to obsess about, rather than the Bill and Mila show.

My last words to Julie, hurried but sincere? "I'll keep you posted. I promise."

Her last word to me, delivered in a whisper? "Dessert."

Before the other three arrived, I'd managed to gather up and even execute a hasty review of all my notes, downloads, and other items of research regarding Agvan Supply. I was fairly confident I could add to the coherent side of the ledger, as opposed to muddling things up even more.

I ushered everyone into the living room, and set the platter of food and the tray of tea on the low glass coffee table. I poured. Soon, we each held a steaming mug. The sharp tang of green leafy brew saturated the room.

This time, we'd formed a square: one perplexed Detective III (chair), one overeager ex-monk (chair), one angry Sarajevan (sofa), one naive journalist (chair).

GAY HENDRICKS AND TINKER LINDSAY

"Where were we?" Bill pulled out his notebook, a small black Moleskine with its own narrow elastic belt. He snapped it open and waited for someone to answer, pen poised.

"'Ode to Joy,'" I said. "Sasha, you'd just discovered the disc of your grandfather's downloaded computer file."

"Right." For the first time, Sasha spoke directly to Bill. "How much has Ten told you about my uncles?"

"Half-uncles," Mila snapped.

Bill tipped his chair on its two back legs and stared upward, as if searching the slat-and-beam ceiling for the facts. "Let's see. Back when I was stationed in Sarajevo, I knew your mother had two older brothers, sorry, half-brothers. As I recall, they may have fought with the Army of the Serbian Republic, right?"

Mila merely grunted.

"So I knew there was no love lost at the time. That's about it," Bill said. I cleared my throat. "Oh, right. Until Ten called me in Sarajevo to tell me about Agvan Supply, and its possible connection to the Stasic brothers."

Mila erupted, instantly furious. "You keep this from me!? Why!"

Bill put up a hand. "Mila, don't get in a twist, okay? I was about to board an airplane home. You'd just kicked me to the curb! 'Never call me again' were your exact last words." He shook his head. "Jesus, you've got a short fuse."

Not only had the "Mila fever" broken, I suspected Martha was looking better and better to Bill by the minute.

"According to my grandfather's research," Sasha continued, "Milo Stasic's company was called Tresinmerc. Why do you think Agvan is the same operation?"

"I don't think so, I know so." I had printed out the "About Us" company description, and I read it aloud to the others, concluding with: *"Our father and uncle dedicated their lives to supplying quality product from around the world. We aim to continue that tradition. Agvan Supply's specialty is difficult-to-find foodstuffs; the rarer the item, the harder we will work to bring it to you."*

Mila spat out a Bosnian invective, adding "Evil men!" in English.

Sasha's response was much more measured. "Yes, this makes sense. According to my grandfather's notes, Milo Stasic, Grandmother Irena's first husband, or rather, his company, Tresinmerc, was partly responsible for brokering a major trade agreement between the governments of India and Yugoslavia, in the early sixties. They exported industrial goods to India. Machinery, tools, sometimes even entire industrial plants and equipment.

"India paid Yugoslavia a fortune for these items. In return, Yugoslavia imported foodstuffs from them: fresh fruits, cashews. Also tea, coffee, tobacco, like that. Plus hard to find items, like shark oil and Bengal tigers." He shrugged. "The agreement was a bit lopsided. My grandfather had downloaded the actual treaty and added his own commentary in a separate document: 'Worse than robbery!' he'd said. And, 'The people always lose!' He wasn't a big fan of profit-based business practices, such as Tresinmerc's."

Long ago, first father rich. Very good at stealing sheep.

"Anyway, after Tito died, Tresinmerc went into a decline. Almost went bankrupt, more than once, including when Milo's brother Jovan died in the late 1980s. Then the Bosnian War happened, and soon after the Dayton Accords, Uncle Zarko and Uncle Stojan took over."

"And mangoes and cheese came to mean a different thing entirely," I said.

"What prompted your grandfather to look into Tresinmerc in the first place?" Bill asked. That was Bill, always drilling down to the core, asking the key question.

"I think it started because Grandmother Irena got so strange. According to his notes, she'd been disappearing for days, and spent hours and hours praying in their bedroom. It really bothered him that she started to wear a hijab, you know, a robe and headscarf again. When he challenged her about it, she spouted all this nonsense about a new world order and kept mentioning Tresinmerc. Praising her first husband, Milo Stasic, and their sons Zarko and Stojan."

Mila broke in. "With me, too, she does this! Tells me I have to go with her to meet new imam. Take Sasha to meet his uncles. That big change is coming. I tell her I will die before I do these things!"

I thought over this new information.

Sasha drained his mug of tea. "Anyway, after I found this disc, I picked up the investigation where my grandfather left off, and it led me pretty quickly to the human trafficking trade in Sarajevo. I started a blog, which hooked me up with other people trying to put a brake on the explosion of the sex slave industry in the Baltics." His voice softened. "That's how I met Audrey."

He drifted off for a moment. We waited.

"But a month in," he said, "Tresinmerc shut down its operations, and I couldn't figure out where they'd gone. Next thing you know, someone was messing with my own website and blog. My followers kept getting error messages when they tried to log on." His eyes glinted, and I saw Mila's fire in his look of determination. "You know what? They did me a favor! I'd gotten wind of those two little boys, and Audrey and I decided to take action against the monsters, instead of just writing about them."

"And then you lost the trail," I said, remembering.

"Right, I lost the trail, here in Los Angeles. The rest you know. I'd pretty much given up on ever finding my uncles, or those kids, until Ten called, asking me about Agvan Supply. It got me thinking."

"Sasha comes to me right after," Mila said, eyeing her son with pride. "And we come to you."

Bill was pulling at his upper lip furiously. Sasha watched as his father's cop-mind went to work, fascinated by the turning of the wheels despite some residual resistance to the holder of the brain.

Mila's brow was ploughed deeper than ever with furrows. She clenched and unclenched her hands, as if itching for a

THE FOURTH RULE OF TEN

fight. I could definitely see why she assumed one or both of her brothers had murdered her father. If he'd chosen to expose Tresinmerc's new line of business, he could not only bring the company down, but also land his stepsons in jail.

I still wasn't sure where Irena fit in, though. Or how the brothers had managed to move their operations so secretly and easily. There had to be an international connection— companies didn't just die in one country and reincarnate in another like that. And now, Agvan Supply was headed underground as well.

Bill had left his chair and was pacing the borders of my living room, hands shoved deep in his pockets.

He halted. "Are we agreed that catching these fuckers is the goal?"

"Yes," I said.

"*Da,*" said Mila.

"Plus finding those two little boys," I added. Sasha shot me a grateful look.

Bill nodded. He rocked back on his heels.

Here it comes.

"Okay, here's the deal," Bill said. "Number one: we need to get in contact with Zarko and his brother. Mila, do you have any way of calling them?"

Mila shook her head. "I have not talked to them since before my father is killed."

"Sasha?"

Sasha, too, shook his head.

"I might," I said. I held up Ponytail's throwaway phone, a piece of my one-man, ongoing investigation. "I'll bet the guy I took this from used it to call Zarko the minute he spotted me spying on them in Moorpark. He'd have needed to ask for instructions."

I flipped open the phone, powered it on, and checked recent calls against the date and time in question. Sure enough, on the Saturday, at 4:27 A.M., he'd made a call to the initial Z, at a 213 exchange.

"Mila, do you have your own cell phone here?" I asked.

"Yes," she said. "I have."

"Can you make calls in the states with it?"

"I can with mine," Sasha jumped in. "Audrey upgraded my data package before I left. So we could, you know, talk."

"That's good," Bill said. "We'll use yours."

Sasha nodded, but his eyes asked *Why?*

"If Zarko's on the run, he might not pick up a local call," I explained. "But he probably won't be able to resist a call with a Sarajevo exchange."

"Number two," Bill said. "If we're going to hook them, we need bait."

"I have bait," Sasha said. "I have this." He held up his grandfather's DVD.

Bill glowed with pride. "Brilliant," he said.

Sasha pulled out his phone as if to start punching in numbers there and then.

No.

"No," Bill and Mila said at the same time.

"It can't be you, Son," Bill said. "They know you to be their enemy. And it can't be me, or Ten either, for that matter. They'd never go for it."

"I will call." Mila's hot eyes gave a split-second view into a depth of hatred unfamiliar to me. "I know these men. I know how to deal with pure evil."

That word again. At Dorje Yidam, we were taught that good and evil weren't exclusive unto themselves, but rather two elements of the same whole, opposites forever linked, along with right and wrong, truth and ignorance, love and hatred. To embrace such contradictions was the first step in finding the middle way, in learning to walk the eightfold path, and the only hope for a life lived in balance.

"Ten," Bill said. "Let's take a little walk."

Bill and I moved onto the deck, but not before I'd grabbed two Belgian Chimay Whites from the fridge, and poured them with care into two wide-mouthed glass steins.

We hoisted the steins to observe the rich, foamy heads; took our first slow swigs; and even sighed in unison after swallowing, like synchronized swimmers.

Bill gazed across the canyon, but his focus was elsewhere. "So what do you think?"

"I think Mila's our only play," I said. "And a complete long shot."

"If I know her, she's going after them whatever we decide," Bill said. "Sasha, too." He shook his head. "I mean, *if* Zarko Stasic answers, and *if* he agrees to meet, both huge *ifs*, she's walking into a fucking dragon's lair, and we have no way to protect her. No way I'm letting that happen. Too dangerous."

I took a second perfect pull of a beer in perfect balance. Smooth and harsh. Bitter and sweet. I craned my head to look into the kitchen window. Mila stood by the sink, rinsing our tea mugs, her brow creased. Fierce, like the protectress Palden Lhamo.

You like to clean up your little piece of the world. You're after justice above all, even if it means bending the rules.

Mila dried her hands on the seat of her pants. She wore her usual uniform: jeans and a men's button-down shirt tied at the waist.

I turned back. "I have an idea," I said.

First I talked, and Bill listened. Then we leaned against the railing, running potential scenarios and outcomes past each other.

Just like old times.

We reached the same conclusion: everything went back to that warehouse in Van Nuys—the address in Sasha's missing persons file that Bill first discovered was the hub of a wheel that connected Sarajevo, Agvan Supply, NDRSNT, and us.

The sky was a bowl of faded blue, and as I watched, a thin slice of pale moon materialized, as if by magic, just above the tree line. Tank had followed us out, and pushed his way between my legs.

I turned to my friend and previous partner.

"You know this is totally nuts, right?"

"Yeah," Bill said. Then: "Isn't it great?"

CHAPTER 29

Mila entered Zarko's number into Sasha's phone and put the call on speaker.

I counted the rings: one, two, three, *he's not going to answer*, four . . .

"*Da?*"

Mila said, "Zarko? I am Mila. Mila Radovic."

The silence stretched, until it was so thin I thought the room itself would snap.

"I am surprised. You said you no want to speak to me again. Why you call now?"

"I need to see you."

"What for?"

"I have something you want."

During this next soundless gap the phone seemed to go dead.

"Zarko?"

"Why you speak in English?"

Mila picked up the phone, turning off the speaker and switching to Bosnian with impressive speed and smoothness. In her native tongue, her engine accelerated from zero to sixty in about ten seconds flat, until she was battering Zarko with a long burst of vocal bullets.

Sasha offered a whispered translation, as best he could. "She says now she will do the talking. She says she's here in town."

"*Ne!*" Mila said, and spat out another round of guttural venom.

"She says 'No!'" Sasha gave Bill an apologetic look. "She says she's not here with you, that you turned out to be a bigger asshole than ever. She's here on her own."

Now Mila listened for a bit. "Yah! Yah!" she said, and then: "*Ne!*"

I heard Sasha's name several times.

"She says she's made me stop what I'm doing, because she found something that might endanger all of us. Bring shame to our name. That she wants to turn it over to Zarko. She says I got in too deep, that she's afraid, and only Zarko can fix it."

Smart, I thought. Appeal to his ego.

"Yah! Yah!" She mimed writing something down, her gesture urgent, and Bill passed her his notebook and pen.

We'd underlined how critical it was that Mila insist the meet take place at the Agvan Supply site. I just hoped she remembered. The air around her rippled with tension, and her cheeks were ablaze. She might have gone completely off the rails.

She ended the call. Her chest heaved from the exertion of the exchange, like an Olympic sprinter at the end of a close race. Once again, I found myself admiring the ferocity of her commitment.

"So?" Bill's eyebrows migrated to midforehead. "What's his answer?"

"He will do it," she said. "We meet at Agvan Supply, in about one hour. I tell him I am by the airport, so he gave me directions for taking a taxi from there."

I went into my bedroom and retrieved what I needed from my safe.

"Here," I said, and passed over a men's button-down shirt.

She inspected it, curious.

"Third button down," I said. "And Bill, you're not seeing this."

Way before my time, if you wanted to record something in secret, it took a portable, reel-to-reel tape recorder the size of a shoe box and weighing at least ten pounds, plus a wired microphone head taped to the chest—sure to leave a raw strip of hairless skin upon removal. The rig was very dangerous and way too easy to find with a pat down.

And before that, in Sherlock's day, your only chance to eavesdrop was an ear to a door, or an eye to a peephole. Come to think of it, someone, somewhere must have started it all by hiding under the house's eaves, as if to find shelter from the raindrops.

But like so much else, spying had gone wireless, micro, and much, much harder to detect. A tiny, covert wireless camera and recorder, small enough to hide in a pen cap, or, in this case, a shirt button, was not only available, it was legal. The tricky part, legally speaking, lay with streaming the event in question to another site.

Thanks to a wealthy former client—a real estate scion determined to catch his business partner making commissions on the side—I'd been able to purchase, on his dime, a nano-size, high-resolution, wireless video and audio kit.

And thanks to Mike, my laptop computer was set up to receive the stream.

Mila returned from my bedroom with the shirt knotted around her waist. It looked good on her—even better, it looked normal. I showed her how to activate the camera, and we checked the feed on my laptop. A fairly clear image of Bill from the waist down appeared. We'd be seeing a lot of midriffs.

"Somebody say something."

"Old MacDonald had a farm," Bill said, and his voice crackled from my laptop.

"One last thing," I said. Bill and I had discussed this on the deck. We'd both decided it might best come from me. "Mila, if this is about revenge, about killing your brother, we can't go ahead with it. Finding out the truth is one thing. Continuing the cycle of violence is another thing entirely. It's up to you."

She looked between Bill and me, scowling. But then her eyes found Sasha, and she softened.

"Truth only," she said. "I promise."

"Then we promise to help you, whatever it takes."

The four of us crammed into the Neon. I'd been tempted to take the Shelby, in case we had a need for speed, but I didn't have the seats—or, more to the point, the seat belts—to accommodate more than one other passenger.

We arrived at Van Nuys Airport in less than half an hour, and I pulled into the passenger loading and unloading zone in front of Terminal B. I waited, hazard lights flashing, as Bill, Mila, and Sasha walked past the terminal to the taxi stand. They looked like any other normal family, and I had a brief moment of wondering what might have been. Bill and Sasha put Mila into a taxi, a brand-new, bright-yellow Prius, almost the exact same shade as my Shelby. Yellow Cab had gone green.

They returned to my car, Bill up front, Sasha in back with the laptop. The taxi wove around the airport, eventually turning left onto Sherman Way. It beetled its fuel-efficient way toward the thicket of warehouses where Zarko had his headquarters.

"Body check, my friends," I said. "Everybody remembering to breathe?"

Bill and Sasha grunted.

"Okay, then. Off we go."

I fell in behind, and soon reached my previous surveillance spot in the alley close by. By now, the streets were largely deserted. I cut the engine. I'd given Bill my newer Barska Gladiators. Now I dug out my older, smaller binoculars and adjusted the lenses. High-tech surveillance was great, but sometimes you just wanted to see things with your own eyes.

"There they are," Bill said.

I focused, and found the taxi pulling into the lot.

"That's Zarko's car," I said after spotting the BMW.

We watched.

Sasha said, "What's happening?"

"She's ringing the bell," Bill said. "Okay, now the door's opening and she's in. I can't see who opened the door."

"You getting anything?" I asked Sasha.

"Not yet. Okay, wait, now I am."

I heard Mila's low, muffled voice, and another lower response. "Can you increase the volume?"

Now they were audible enough to understand, if I understood Bosnian. Sasha gamely translated, struggling a little to keep up.

"Zarko says it's good to see her. She says the same. Now he's taking her into his office. He's offering her tea. She says no."

"Let me see," I said. Sasha tipped the laptop my way. Mila's button camera had picked up a murky figure, but only one.

"There's not much light in there," Sasha said.

Zarko says: "Do you have it?"

"*Da. U torbi,*" I heard.

"She says, 'Yes, in my bag,'" Sasha translated. "He's asking her to give it to him. Now she's saying she needs his word. Needs him to promise that once she's given him the disc, nothing will happen to her or to Sasha, I mean, me."

Mila's voice rose, and Zarko responded with a burst of angry words.

"*Sranje!*" Sasha said. "I mean, shit! She just said, 'like happened to my father!'"

The voices calmed. "Okay," Sasha said. "She's pulled back from that."

I watched the screen. Mila's arm floated across, handing something to the blocky arm and body of Zarko.

"She just gave him the disc," Sasha confirmed.

More discussion. "He wants to know if this is the only copy."

"*Da! Naravno!*" I heard. Then something that sounded like "*Glup!*"

Sasha translated: "'Yes, of course! I'm not stupid!'"

Zarko's next words seemed conciliatory. "He said, 'You should understand something. I'm not the one you need to fear, sister.' Now he's offering to drive her to the airport. She says the taxi's nearby. That she already booked it to take her back."

Strange thing to say, I thought. *I'm not the one you need to fear.*

Zarko switched to English, the words curt. "Then call taxi. Good-bye." Chairs scraped. A door opened and closed. But nobody said another word.

I raised my binoculars again.

Mila walked outside, cell phone to her ear. Her tense whisper filled the car. "I am calling the taxi driver. He is not answering."

The repetitive buzz of her unanswered call, transmitted through the laptop, rasped my already jangled nerves. Mila snapped the phone shut. "What should I do?"

"Shit!" Bill twisted in his seat. "God damn it!"

An SUV skidded to a stop and two men jumped out. Two men I knew. Ponytail pinned Mila's arms from behind as Bozo sprinted into the building.

"Stop! What are you doing!?" She sounded more enraged than afraid.

"Ten, start the car!" Bill yelled, but I was way ahead of him. I pulled nose first out of the alley.

"What's happening?"

"Uncle Zarko's outside again!"

Another burst of Bosnian over the wire. "He says, 'Mila, what game are you playing? Do you want to die?'"

"She says, 'What do you mean?'"

"He says his guys talked to the cab driver, and he told them two men put you into the cab. That one of them sounded like Sasha, and the other one, your boyfriend." I heard *policija*, which needed no translation. Sasha's head whipped around to me, his eyes wide.

"Go!" Bill said. "GO!"

I floored the Dodge and we shot out of the alley. We took the corner hard, tires squealing, and swerved onto Sherman Way.

My Wilson was in the right pocket of my windbreaker. I steered with one hand as I dug it out. Bill already had a firm grip on his Beretta. I could no longer hear any sound from the laptop. Either the connection was broken, or the hiss of adrenaline had hindered my ability to hear.

We were close. If I kept going, we'd be fully visible. I threw a look at Bill.

"Full frontal," he said. "There's no other choice."

"Glove compartment," I said to Bill. "Airlite." Bill punched it open, grabbed the gun, and passed it over the seat to Sasha.

"Don't shoot at anything that's not right in front of you and trying to kill you," Bill told Sasha, who was staring at his hand as if it held a dead spider.

"You'll be fine, Son," Bill said. For once, Sasha didn't flinch at the term.

I floored the Dodge. It was small, but fearless. Zarko and his two men were waiting for us. Ponytail dropped to one knee, aiming a Smith & Wesson much like mine. Bozo's wide-legged stance and bulky arms supported a very familiar assault rifle. He raised the sight to his right eye.

"Duck!" I screamed.

My front and back windshields exploded, showering us with kernels of glass.

"Hold on!"

I slammed on the brakes, tossing us hard against our seat belts. I flung open my door and took immediate cover behind its opened flank. Zarko was dragging Mila into the SUV and twisting her arm high behind her back.

"Fuckers!" Bill yelled from the other side of the car.

Another shot, a single one. The door kicked. My body compressed into a single, hot ball of rage. I'd just started to bond with this car.

I heard the slap of a fresh clip going into a magazine. More shots, this time from Bill's Beretta, to my right.

Roll and shoot, roll and shoot. I rolled, academy-style, and came up on one knee, just as Bozo prepared to unleash a deadly rainstorm. I beat him to it, with a single, steady Wilson Combat Supergrade shot in the lower right shoulder, where bone and muscle meet. His rifle dropped as he grabbed at the blast site, howling with pain.

A second howl echoed, but from my right. Bill spun around, clutching his right arm. Before I could reciprocate, Ponytail jumped inside the SUV. It roared away.

Bill and I had run negative scenarios, but this degree of fuck-up surpassed even our ability to anticipate problems.

Sasha was helping Bill to his feet. Bill's shirt was torn, blood dripping from the wound in a steady stream. I ripped open the sleeve. Not a mortal wound, but I could see muscle laid bare.

"We've got to get you to the ER," I said.

"No. We have to find Mila! It's not that bad!"

"Yes," I said. "It is."

Sasha stood, pale and still. The Airlite dangled from one hand. I removed the weapon, cool to the touch and scentless. He hadn't taken a single shot. I was glad for that.

"Sasha, help your father into the car! We have to get him to the hospital!"

Bozo lay moaning, his blood spreading beneath him on the asphalt. I called over to Bill, as he lowered into the car.

"Bill, cuffs!"

"Left back pocket," he told Sasha. Sasha fished them out and tossed them to me.

I raced to my gunshot victim. His face was chalk-white, his pupils dilated and unseeing. He'd gone into shock. I kicked his assault rifle several yards away, and cuffed his wrists together, across his front. As much as I disliked the guy, I couldn't see wrenching his arms behind him. Not with that jagged, ripped shoulder.

I pulled out my phone and scrolled quickly until I found Deputy Sergeant Gaines's number. I got his voice mail.

"Deputy Sergeant Gaines," I said. "I have something for you, regarding the Moorpark shooting!" I recited the address for Agvan Supply. "I'm pretty sure you'll find your murder weapon, as well as Bozo, the clown who pulled the trigger."

I got Bill to the ER at Providence Saint Joseph Medical Center in under 15 minutes, even with a wounded door that wouldn't close properly and only the jagged outline of a front and back windshield.

I helped my friend inside, where the hospital's police liaison awaited. I'd made Bill contact his bosses en route. He was on temporary leave, but still, he'd get the royal treatment, which would do less than nothing for his foul mood.

Nothing worse than being sidelined by a bullet wound when your girlfriend's been kidnapped.

Ex-girlfriend.

I shuddered to think about the protocol and paperwork Bill now faced, as well as the irate chief on his way.

"Go!" Bill said, just inside the emergency room entrance. "Find those fuckers before it's too late. And please, Ten, make sure Mila and Sasha come back alive. I couldn't bear for something to happen to my son, or his mother. Go on! Get out of here."

Yeah, but driving what?

Thank goodness for Enterprise Rent-A-Car. Sasha and I limped north on Buena Vista Drive at 15 miles an hour, jigged across San Fernando, and parked just up the road from their small Burbank office on Winona.

Twenty minutes later, we were buckled into a Chevy Tahoe, the closest thing to an armored truck they had in their lot.

I'd deal with the wounded Neon later.

Sasha was without words. My computer lay open on his lap, as silent and blank as his face. We'd completely lost the stream from Mila. I didn't want to guess why.

"You okay?"

"What are we going to do?" he asked, his voice very young.

"We're going to find your mother," I said, with more firmness than I felt.

"Can I ask you something?"

"Of course."

"That was the first time I've been in a gunfight. And, I feel different. Like something changed, deep down. Do you know what I'm talking about?"

"Maybe."

I dropped into the arena of spacious listening. I needed to know, with absolute certainty, whether or not Sasha could continue. If he'd lost his center, his further involvement could torpedo any hope for a positive outcome.

"There's this knot, down in my gut. I got really scared." He shot me a quick look.

I nodded.

"But also, something else, a kind of, of stillness. My ears are ringing, but I've never felt more, like, clear inside."

I exhaled with sharp relief. Work that requires deadly risk is not for most people. Those special few share an odd sense of quiet when under stress or attack. They also feel fear, of course—that wiring got installed in our bodies millions of years ago—but their primary response is stillness. Clarity: you need it to be able to face down, as well as survive, certain dangers. And Sasha had it.

I said, "Nothing I know clears the mind like getting shot at."

"Yes," Sasha said. "I feel that way. I feel right."

You feel like your father.

I made up a quick blessing, on the spot: *Long may this boy avoid bullets, and taste only the sweetness of survival.*

I was glad to have an extra gun-hand, however inexperienced. The deck was heavily stacked against us.

We'd arrived back at Agvan. Apparently Gaines hadn't gotten my message yet, which was a good thing. I pulled into the lot. Bozo was still down, but his pulse was nice and steady, and the tourniquet had stopped the bleeding. I grabbed a tire iron from the Tahoe. The office door didn't budge, not even with a swift kick, so I used the edged part of the iron as a crowbar and snapped off the hinges, one by one.

With Sasha's help, I shoved the door aside and stepped into a dark reception area, empty as a tomb. Sasha slipped in behind me.

I tried the switch, and fluorescent tube lights blinked on. They buzzed and spat, as if to scold us for breaking and entering. I did a quick scan. No filing cabinets. No laptops. No nothing. The place had been emptied, picked as clean as a carcass after the vultures finished their feasting.

Not good.

The distant siren sent us scampering back to the Tahoe.

I raced to the Taco Bell parking lot, and pulled over to call Mike. Seven P.M. He'd probably just woken up.

"Good morning," he said, his voice all bright and shiny.

"Mike, we're in trouble over here. Any luck with the Agvan website?"

He sobered up fast. "No. And, boss? It's gotten even weirder. Now the entire NDRSNT directory is coming up as error pages, too. I ran some automated crawlers last night, to check if the blackout was web-wide, but the shutdown seems to be localized, thank God. In other words, just their users, and just with each other. I'd hate to think someone turned my fellow geek-entrepreneurs into involuntary spying machines. But either way, there's no way to access anything having to do with NDRSNT right now, Agvan Supply included."

"Well, keep trying anyway," I said. I disconnected. I glanced over at the laptop screen. Also completely silent. The feed was dead. I just hoped Mila wasn't dead, too.

I closed my eyes.

"What are you doing?" Panic was shredding the borders of Sasha's voice.

I opened my eyes and turned to him. "I know this seems counterintuitive, but I need to switch gears here. Move from planning to receptive mind. I need to let go of expectations. To listen for a moment. It won't take long, I promise."

I closed my eyes again.

Inhale. Exhale. Allow.

Our technology has failed.

Inhale. Exhale. Allow.

When has this happened in the past?

Inhale. Exhale. Allow.

A totally weird and seemingly random memory rose, shimmering and whole like a bubble, in my brain: *the last time I'd been to Providence Saint Joseph with Bill.* It was maybe three hours after Lola and Maude were born. I'd tiptoed into the room with two pink balloons and a bottle of champagne. Bill and I had only been partners for a few years, but he was already family. Martha was sound asleep, flat-out exhausted from the ordeal of twelve hours of giving birth to two six-pound babies. They were next to her bed, bundled side by side in a raised container with clear, Plexiglas sides, like a pair of cabbages in a crisper drawer.

Bill stood guard, marveling at the swaddled mounds. He was still in hospital scrubs.

"How'd it go?" I'd whispered.

"Fine," he'd said, keeping his voice low. "Martha was amazing. A total trooper. Only one real scare. They had her hooked up to this high-tech monitor during the labor, you know, to make sure the babies weren't in any distress. All of a sudden, all the nurses started to run around in a panic. I thought they were going to boot me out, you know, for emergency surgery. Never been so freaked out in my entire life."

"So what happened?"

"They'd paged Martha's doctor. He strolls in a minute later. Chinese guy, looks kinda like you, actually. Anyway, he checks the monitor, then, cool as you please, pulls a stethoscope out of his coat pocket. He listened all over her belly— front, back, top, and bottom. Then he folded up his stethoscope and put it away. 'The babies are fine,' he said. 'It's the machine that's broken.'"

It's the machine that's broken.

I opened my eyes, sent a reassuring smile to Sasha, and pulled out my phone. Our machine might be broken, but I still had a good old-fashioned stethoscope up my sleeve.

Petar answered as if he'd been waiting for my call, although it was four in the morning over there.

"Monkevic! You read my mind!"

"Petar, we have a situation here." I explained as succinctly as I could. "Our surveillance is down," I concluded, "and my usual means of hacking into systems won't work either. We have a kidnapping victim, and a trail that's gone completely cold."

"Maybe not completely," Petar said.

"What do you mean?"

"I mean I find Josip Tomic. I stubborn, like you, Monkevic. I don't like leaving things alone."

My heart executed a handspring of hope.

CHAPTER 30

"I reach Tomic, finally, last night. Good man. I first meet Josip—"

"Petar, please!" I broke in.

"Sorry, sorry, I like too much to talk. Tomic have big file on Stasics, like you think. And the Radovic boy, Sasha. Also grandmother, and mother. He say they are about to make raid, when Stasics leave country."

"Interesting."

"He know about Agvan, too. He say when your partner, your Bill come by, he leave out address of company, on purpose. He have children, too, feel sorry for parents when boy is missing."

That cleared up one mystery.

"And he have more of them," Petar said.

"More of what?"

"Addresses. Three more, in your Los Angeles. He think maybe they are houses, for putting the girls and boys, maybe."

"I need them," I said. "Right now, Petar!"

"Easy, Monkevic, easy. You check your phone, okay?" Petar said, and my cell phone simultaneously blurted a heads-up of an incoming text.

"Petar, you are the best," I said.

"Maybe not best, but still pretty good. Okay. *Idi s Bogom.* Go with God, Monkevic."

There were three addresses listed in the text: the first was in South Central, the 3600 block of Venice Boulevard and 6th Avenue, between Crenshaw and Arlington. I knew the area because I'd visited a Zen center very close by about six years ago, and the experience had made an indelible impression on me. My then-girlfriend Charlotte had dragged me to an excruciating dharma talk on "Never Leaving the Now." I couldn't wait to leave the talk.

The second address was also near Venice Boulevard, but much farther west, in the no-man's-land of shitty apartments and clustered, run-down cottages that hunkered like bums along the outskirts of Venice proper.

The third address was far more upscale, an address in Malibu, although it might be a million-dollar trailer on an empty acre of land, for all I knew.

I'd called upon Petar, my Sarajevo stethoscope. Now I needed muscle. I hoped Tory was as good as his word.

Sasha and I got to the Crenshaw location first, a squat, one-story brick-and-wood bungalow with a slanted overhang of a roof. The front carport was empty, the windows dark. A rusted, white wrought-iron fence enclosed the residence, low enough to vault easily.

"What's that smell?" Sasha said.

The sickly sweet odor of deep-fried dough hung in the evening air like a wet, sugary towel. A Winchell's Donut House, shaped like a cardboard box, occupied the corner of Venice and 6th. It must have just closed for the night—the building still emitted pungent evidence of its wares.

"S'up," I heard from behind me.

My heart sank. I had asked for muscle, I hadn't asked for G-Force. Now I was faced with a whole new dilemma.

G-Force had swapped his Pacer for Tory's tricked out Escalade. He waved us into the backseat. The driver sat face-forward, as G-Force climbed in the passenger seat next to him. The interior smelled strongly of leather. Also, donuts. G-Force must have snagged some before the shop closed. A Winchell's donut box balanced on the armrest between the two men, the fragrance irresistible. It was all I could do not to pounce.

"So. What's the plan?" G-Force said.

"G-Force, I really don't think you being here is . . ."

G lifted up a serious-looking MAC-10 automatic machine pistol, complete with suppressor.

"Check it," he said.

Oh, boy.

Next, the driver, a compact fireplug of a guy, twisted to face us, cradling a Norinco 9 millimeter Uzi like it was a baby. Or maybe a baby hippo, with a 16-inch barrel snout.

"This here's Chain-Link," G-Force said.

"Chain-Link?"

"Used to do a little fencin' on the side."

Chain-Link smiled, flashing a gold-grilled fence of his own.

His upper lip was suspiciously powdered, and for a minute I thought I was dealing with a cokehead, until I remembered the donuts.

As Julie liked to say, *alrighty then.*

That reminded me. I opened my phone and wrote Julie a quick text: I'M SURE YOU'VE HEARD FROM BILL. DON'T WORRY. SASHA AND I ARE

What were we, exactly? I deleted the last four words.

DON'T WORRY. I AM OKAY. SEE YOU AT HOME LATER?

I found my fingers typing three more words, so innocent on the screen, so potent to the heart. I wanted her to know, in case I wasn't okay. In case I never made it home.

"You ready to rumble," G-Force said, "or you just plannin' on shootin' the shit with whoever?"

Chain-Link chuckled. His eyes were bloodshot, and even with the old-donut and new-leather smells, a faint whiff of something else, something grassy, reached my nostrils.

"Chain-Link, are you high?"

Chain-Link shrugged. "Nah. Bowl of weed, 'fore G picked me up. No big thing."

"Chain love his weed," G-Force said. "Take his edge off, people like him better."

"I know what it's for," I said, my own voice edgy enough for all of us.

"Don't worry," G-Force said. "Chain ain't gonna go off on anyone doesn't deserve it."

This was supposed to reassure me?

At least our arsenal, and with it our odds of survival, seemed much improved. I gave Sasha a quick lesson in how to handle the Airlite, thankful there wasn't an extra assault rifle for him to get his novice hands on. Giving a 19-year-old a gun is like giving him a Harley and a bowl of cocaine. Begging for trouble, in other words. One of the lesser-known facts about shooting a weapon is that the sound itself resonates with a specific place in the male genitalia, that indeterminate area bridging sex and fear. Teenagers have an especially big zone of this in their developing bodies, so gunfire has a large drumhead to vibrate against. It feels good—so good the urge to repeat the sensation easily overpowers any other response, such as patience, or self-preservation.

I looked at my three cohorts. We were going into battle. Our outsides were armed. I wasn't so sure about our insides.

"I want to say something out loud," I said. "Something important. Chain-Link, try not to laugh."

I'd learned this petition for insight from one of my elder lamas, who'd learned it from one of his elder lamas, during a time of terrible upheaval, violence, and revolt in his Tibetan monastery in Lhasa.

A Buddhist survival cry, in a way.

"May we learn essential lessons about injury or death through insight, rather than personal pain," I said.

"A-men," G-Force added, with enthusiasm.

We climbed out of the Escalade and stood on the sidewalk, looking at the bungalow, a squat shadow in the evening gloom. Still no sign of life.

"What's your feeling?" I said.

"Look deserted," G-Force said. "Look like nobody home."

I decided to case it on foot anyway.

"Anybody have a flashlight?"

G-Force found a black Maglite, about as big as a cigar, in the glove compartment.

"Stay here. Watch my back." I slid the Maglite into my pants pocket. Using both hands, I hurdled the wrought-iron fence and marched to the front door, as if I belonged there. I found a small round button of a doorbell, and pushed. A tinny buzz echoed inside. After that, silence. There was a narrow walkway along the right side of the house. I moved along it until I reached a window. The curtains were pulled, but not completely. I pressed my face close to the glass and flashed the cone of light over the interior.

A living room. Orange shag rug, a couple of plastic chairs, a moldy-looking sleeping bag in the corner. An upholstered velvet sofa, its arms shiny from wear, with a few tufts of cotton ticking protruding from the frayed material. A camera-less tripod. A card table, upon which were stacked several laptops. Next to them, two more desktop computers, a digital video recorder, and a shoebox-size carton filled with flash drives.

I had seen enough.

I would send this address and information to Federal Agent Gus Gustafson, as soon as we found Mila.

I leapt the fence a second time, and shook my head. G-Force could see by my face that whatever was back there didn't warrant further discussion.

I fed the next address into my iPhone. Sasha and I led in the Tahoe, G-Force and Chain-Link followed. We took the 10 West toward the ocean and exited on Lincoln Boulevard. We drove into the flats of Venice. By now, night had dropped a curtain of dark over the entire city.

G-Force and Chain-Link joined Sasha and me on the sidewalk.

"Stay here," I said again.

This stucco cottage was close to derelict, walls peeling, roof tiles cracked and buckled. No doorbell, and my sharp knocks went unanswered. It, too, looked deserted, but when I aimed the Maglite inside a side window, I could see it was very much occupied. There was furniture in the living room, and evidence of food in the kitchen. A light was on somewhere.

"Hello? Anybody there?"

The light went out.

I heard a sound, a door slamming, and ran to the back of the house. A slight figure was running full speed down the narrow back alley that paralleled homes, toward Venice Boulevard. I was about to give chase, when I heard something else—a child's soft cries, from inside.

I ran into the wide-open back door.

"I'm here. I'm here," I called out in the dark. "You're safe now!"

My Maglite illuminated the source of the sound, a bedroom with several small cots crammed into tight rows, like a crowded, hellish dormitory. The floor was littered with potato chip fragments. A child-size set of pajamas lay crumpled on the floor.

My flashlight caught a glint of reflected glass. Empty syringes.

Please, please.

And the light found them: a cluster of small bodies huddled together in the corner, like a litter of kittens trying to survive a storm. There were four little boys—two fair-skinned, two dark.

Their eyes. Their eyes were pools of terror.

"Hey, little men," I heard behind me.

G-Force hunkered down, his voice as gentle as silk. "Hey, there. Everything gonna be okay now. I bet you hungry. You hungry?" He held out the opened Winchell's donut box, still half-full.

One by one, they crept from the corner, drawn by the sweet smell of donuts and sweet sound of kindness. They each took a donut from the box and nibbled, terrified, as if expecting a blow to fall at any moment. G-Force didn't push it. He placed the box on the floor and sat quietly nearby, his hands clasped. He was a natural with these children, and they slowly seemed to realize he meant no harm.

The universe had resolved my dilemma, and in a perfect way.

I crouched on the other side of G-Force.

"I need you to do something for me," I said, handing him Gus's name and scribbled phone number. "Call this number; it's an FBI agent, and a friend. She'll know what to do next. G, can you stay with these boys? Make sure no one else comes for them."

G-Force started to shake his head.

"Listen. You just got free of trouble. I am not landing you in more of it. This other thing, it isn't your fight, okay? You need to move ahead with your dreams. I'm taking the gun, for the same reason. Are we clear?"

"You the boss," G-Force said, after a moment. I'd love to think it was my forceful argument, but I suspect the reason he capitulated had more to do with the boys. Two of them had crept to G-Force's side and, just like Belma had, curled up next to him, as if for shelter.

I ran outside, and explained the change in plan.

"You guys okay with this?" They both nodded. "Okay. Let's head for the Malibu address. Chain-Link, you follow Sasha and me in the Escalade."

"S'cool," Chain-Link said.

We backtracked to the 10, which quickly merged onto Pacific Coast Highway. The traffic was fairly light by now, and we sped toward the far end of Malibu, the Escalade maybe two car lengths behind our Tahoe. A patrol car raced by in the opposite direction, its lights flashing, a good reminder to slow down.

Sasha kept fiddling with my laptop, trying to reengage the feed with his mother, but the connection remained severed.

"She'll be okay," I said. "She's strong and she's smart."

Our destination was on the northernmost boundary of Malibu, past Leo Carrillo State Beach. If I recalled correctly, this part of the coastline held a scattering of beach houses, some so small they'd be called shacks if they didn't cost so much.

"Your destination is ahead, on your left," my GPS announced in a voice much calmer than I felt.

I put on my left-hand indicator light. The Escalade did the same. I peered at the row of little houses, their brightly lit windows signaling inhabitants. The problem was, the homes all looked alike, and not one of them had a visible number.

I guess you paid for anonymity, as well as the ocean view.

During the day, the Pacific side of this highway was jammed with parked cars and eager surfers, but almost all of them had packed up their boards and gone home.

I pulled the Tahoe onto the soft shoulder. Chain-Link parked right behind me.

Sasha and I joined him by the Escalade. "You two wait here," I said. "I'll do my thing, and call you if it looks like Mila's inside."

I heard a few muttered grumbles from Chain-Link, but no outright argument. My fingers touched the warm wooden grip of the Wilson, buried deep in my pocket. Just making sure. For a moment I considered also taking G-Force's confiscated MAC-10, but in truth I felt safer without it.

I tugged the hood of my windbreaker over my head and approached the cozy column of houses, moving at a slight diagonal toward the water.

And then I saw him. A man, standing at the corner of the second cottage, just under the jutting roof. His body, while still, seemed coiled with tension.

Lookout man, or eavesdropper—I knew which I'd place my money on.

That probably meant one more lookout, on the beachfront side. I stuck my hands in the pockets of my windbreaker and trudged across the sand until I was skirting the shoreline, pretending I was a lone and lonely beachcomber, contemplating some troubled aspect of his existence. It wasn't that hard.

Sure enough, a second shadowed figure lurked at the front corner. This guy I knew: the stringy ponytail gave him away. His eyes swept in my direction. I lowered my head and tromped along the hard-packed sand, resisting the temptation to look. It was dark. Maybe he wouldn't recognize me. I kept walking.

The lifeguard tower, a white wooden shed perched on a metal stand of raised, triangular stilts, was as much cover as I'd get out here. I crawled between the legs and finally looked back. The beach was deserted. The dank, salty smell of the sea filled my nostrils. The air felt damp and gritty, almost alive.

I called Sasha.

"Yes?"

"Put me on speaker, so Chain can hear."

"Okay."

"I think they're at house number two. Guard in back, and one in front."

"You thinking drive-by? Take 'em both out?" Chain-Link's voice was eager.

"Slow down," I said. "I need a lot more evidence before you decide to cancel some guy's ticket."

"Just saying," Chain muttered.

My nostrils filled with an acrid imitation of lavender and musk.

"HANDS UP!"

Ponytail had somehow circled the lifeguard station without a sound. How could someone so intellectually challenged be so good at sneaking up on me? Maybe because he was built like a whippet, and just as fast and light on his feet.

"Do it," I said, and snapped the phone shut.

"What you say?" Ponytail snapped.

"I said, I'll do it. Just let me climb out from under here."

I squeezed between the metal legs and pushed upright slowly, my hands in the air. Ponytail was working on a sparse goatee. Not a good look for him. At least he'd been downgraded from a Heckler assault rifle to an Airlite just like mine.

The muzzle aimed directly at my chest. He looked me up and down.

"You again."

I said nothing.

He waved the Airlite. "Take gun from pocket."

I did.

"Drop it on ground."

"No," I said.

He blinked.

"I'll hand it over, but I won't dump it in the sand. It's a Wilson Combat Supergrade, okay? Made to order."

He thought this over. Held out his hand.

"Give. Handle first."

It killed me to do so, but I gave.

He hefted the burled wooden grip. "Nice gun. I like."

A thought flicked through in my mind: *Don't get too attached.*

"Okay. Move," he said. I trudged through the sand, vainly attempting to center my breath.

"Faster." A gun barrel prodded my spine.

Up on the road, squealing brakes pierced the air, followed by the roar of an SUV engine.

I must have flinched.

"What?"

"Nothing. I'm nervous," I said.

"You should be," he said. "Stop here."

He had a push-to-talk function on his phone. I saw him thumb the button a couple of times. "Bosko?" He paused and repeated: "Bosko?"

First Bozo. Now Bosko? Were these guys for real? They seriously needed a lesson in re-branding from G-Force.

We'd reached the cottage.

"Bosko?" he again called out. His eyes narrowed, and with a quick jerk he trained my own Wilson at my forehead, "Get on your knees!"

I did, but not before spotting the other lookout man, sprawled facedown. The back of his head was a splintered, bloody mess.

Ponytail's breath was rapid and hoarse behind me. His voice was a snarl: "You did this?"

"No. How could I? I was with you."

"Your negroes?"

Issues of political correctness aside, how did he know about Chain and G-Force?

Before I could ask him, help arrived.

"Hands up your-self, mofo!" Chain-Link was planted like a double-barreled redwood trunk, MAC-10 and Uzi up. Then Sasha stepped around the corner, popgun at the ready.

"Fuck," Ponytail said, reaching two hands and two handguns in the air.

"Weapons on the sand," Chain-Link said.

"Not the Wilson!" I said, for the second time tonight. Maybe I was the one with the unhealthy attachment.

Ponytail had a better idea, at least in his mind, but before he got off a shot, three *pfttt-pfttt-pfttts* from Chain's Uzi, center mass, flung him backwards. It was like watching a truck hit a rag doll. He collapsed in a heap, let out a single wet rattle, and bled out in a matter of moments.

I was too disturbed by this violent display of overkill to summon a single chant of ease. Sasha, too, was dumbfounded. His eyes were open, but his brain had vacated the premises.

I extracted my Wilson, gritty after all from the dead man's final fall. I closed Ponytail's eyes. His skin was growing cool and clammy to the touch.

And now, the words came: *Om mani padme hum,* I mentally chanted. I included his dead colleague, Bosco. *Om mani padme hum.* And I improvised a personal addendum, to address the violence of their passing: *As painful as your dying was, may the lessons learned someday bring an equal portion of bliss.*

Someone inside pulled up the blinds, barely ten feet from us, throwing a bright square of light onto the sand. As one, we launched ourselves close against the wall.

A door on the other side of the house opened. If anyone came around the corner, we were perfect targets, all in a row. "The lock!" I gestured. "Shoot the lock!"

Pfttt. With a splinter of wood and metal, the lock exploded, along with half of the street-side door. Chain-Link hurled his battering-ram body against the rest, knocking the planked wood inward, onto the entryway floor.

I heard a muffled sound, like an animal in distress. Then I found the source.

Just beyond the foyer was a small living room. In the center, Mila was gagged and trussed and sitting on a wooden chair. Her shirt was ripped, and her forehead bulged with a bruise the size and color of a plum.

Mila's black eyes flashed above the gag. She rocked and struggled, strapped to the chair with duct tape, her hands bound somehow behind her.

Sasha squeezed past me and dropped to his knees by her side. He clawed and ripped at the tape.

The door to the beach stood ajar. As I ran toward it, Zarko, all in black, rose from the sand like a desert demon. He jerked his rifle up, then down again, and disappeared to my left without shooting. I realized why when I saw who was directly behind me.

He doesn't want to hit Sasha or Mila. Why not?

My next thought carried with it no words, only an instinctive warning a millisecond after I glimpsed movement at the window.

"Hit the floor!" I screamed while diving as an explosive barrage shattered the glass to the left of the back door, away from Mila and Sasha. The wall erupted, showering great clots of plaster and dust.

I elbow-crawled toward the open gash that used to be the other door. Once through, I half-stood, zigzagging outside and diving off the porch. I rolled to one side, as another round of deadly sound and earth danced around me.

I pushed up and aimed my Wilson, but Zarko ducked and ran off again.

I shouted to Chain-Link, "Go around! Other side!"

I heard the *crack-crack-crack* of Zarko's assault rifle, deafening in the still evening air. Where were the neighbors? Where were the cops?

A fourth volley of bullets, as spitfire-sharp as firecrackers.

Firecrackers. We were only a week past the Fourth of July. There was my answer.

Someone howled, an "I've-been-shot" howl.

Please. Not Sasha.

Chain's voice rang out. "We clear back here. Dude is down."

Zarko gasped for air as he writhed, clutching his left thigh. Chain-Link's barrel rested about an inch above his left ear. Beneath him, spilled blood was staining the area pinkish-brown.

A part of me wanted to fill Zarko's mouth and nose with sand. Watch the life ebb from him. The thought of those little boys . . . that camera.

I called into the house. "Mila! Sasha! Out here!"

Zarko Stasic was their family, his immediate fate was theirs to decide.

Mila knelt beside him. She examined the seeping wound. The sand was soaked by now. He wouldn't survive without help.

"I should let you bleed to death," she said, even as she took the cloth that had recently gagged her own mouth. She cinched it just above the wound, stanching the flow.

Zarko spoke through gritted teeth: "If I die here, I say same thing. Whatever else I do, I did not kill your father."

She sat back on her heels and raked him with her eyes, that internal frisking I'd also experienced once upon a time.

"I believe you," she said. "Now take me to the one who did."

"Mila, leave alone." Zarko was almost begging. "You are not bad person. Leave this be."

"No." Mila said. "No. I owe it to him."

Zarko groaned. "All right. I will take you, but do not expect to find satisfaction."

"Sasha," Mila ordered. "Get me clean cloth, sheet, anything, and tape."

Sasha ran inside, and soon reappeared with a pillowcase and duct tape, as well as a small bottle of hydrogen peroxide he must have found in the bathroom. Mila cleaned the wound, tore the case into strips, and field-dressed the injury, not gently, but as best she could. Her medical school experience was finally serving a purpose.

I sent Chain up the road to fetch the Escalade, but not before confiscating his coat and weapons, and making him and Sasha use the peroxide to clean off any residue on their hands and faces. I wiped down both assault rifles and tossed them into the beach house, along with the silencer. Some forensic team was going to have a challenging time of it, once this crime scene became official.

I still had my Wilson and Airlite, not to mention Zarko's assault rifle.

A young man finally poked his head out of the neighboring cottage. Tanned skin; bleached, spiky hair; terrified eyes.

"Can you call 911?"

"I j-j-just d-d-did," he stuttered.

"Call again, and ask for an ambulance as well. There are two men down back there."

I was coated with fine white dust and speaking from the shadows. I wasn't too worried about being identified. Anyway, this kid was too scared to swallow, much less focus on my face.

The Escalade pulled up. Sasha and I helped Zarko to his feet and half-dragged, half-carried him to the backseat. Mila climbed inside first, Zarko next, and finally Sasha. I handed Sasha the Airlite, and his eyes thanked me.

"Wait here," I said to Chain-Link. "I'll follow you in the Tahoe. Where are we headed, Zarko?"

"Latigo Canyon." His voice was bleak and devoid of hope.

I sprinted the hundred yards to my rental with the other two guns, using the physical exertion to process some of the adrenaline back into my bloodstream. For a panicked moment, I'd thought I'd lost my keys, but they were in a different pocket.

Faint sirens. Not much time. I wrenched the Tahoe onto the road, my tires spitting soft sand. I pulled up behind the Escalade and flicked the high beams. The Cadillac took off, and I fell in behind.

Flashing LED lights and blaring sirens screamed past us, followed by a wailing ambulance. Emergency responders answered the call for help, and not for the first time tonight. We'd left a veritable gold mine of fallen villains around the city.

Too bad no one would ever know it was us.

CHAPTER 31

For a brief moment, I was tempted to turn the Tahoe around and head back to Topanga, to the peace of the canyon and the warmth of my home. The violence had left me drained, scooped out from the inside until I was more husk than man. Even my skin, with its dusting of plaster, was ghostly.

Anyway, what was left? Agvan Supply could not possibly survive this, not with its sites and its leader exposed. Zarko Stasic, if he survived his wound, would soon be behind bars. And if I knew him, he'd take his brother down as well.

They were finished.

"*Ne,*" I heard from the seat behind me, followed by a crackle of static. For a moment, I thought my car was possessed, until I remembered Mila's button-camera, and the wireless connection between my laptop and her. Then all was silent again.

I stayed two car lengths behind the Escalade. The ocean was a vast expanse of liquid blackness.

If Zarko was telling the truth, if he hadn't killed Mila's father, that left only one other candidate, the far more elusive Stojan. I'd only caught the one or two glimpses of him, younger and a little slighter than his brother, with that odd bent arm and fingers that plucked at nothing. His nerves had suffered damage at some point, either literally or from some kind of emotional trauma. And damage breeds more damage.

Maybe it happened during the war.

When the Buddha talked about suffering, how it followed wrong actions as inevitably as the wheels of a cart follow the oxen, he could have just as easily been talking about nations that have lost their way. The Bosnian War was still causing so much harm, perpetuating so much pain. Cycles of hurt, spinning around and around and around.

A car zipped between the Cadillac and me, a Toyota Highlander with an attitude. Automatically, I glanced at its plate: MKNG LV, it said. My brain filled in the vowels: "MAKING LOVE."

I wish.

I speed-dialed Julie and put the call on speaker just as an idea nipped at my brain. It darted off before I could grab hold.

"Ten?"

"Julie. It's so good to hear your voice."

"Are you okay? You sound a little weird."

"I'm exhausted, that's all. How's Bill?"

"A little doped up on painkillers. He's tucked under the covers back at the house."

"Can you tell him Mila's okay? Sasha, too?"

"Will do. The minute I get off. Hang on a minute."

I heard her talking softly.

"I'm back. Tank and Homer want to know when you're coming home. The boys and I miss you."

The sensation spreading through my chest was shocking, so warm and bittersweet it almost pained me. Like that first swallow of *chocolat chaud,* with my mother beaming at me from across the table.

Like I could do no wrong.

My breath caught in my throat, and for a moment I couldn't speak.

I love her.

"I'll be home as soon as I can," I said. "I'm really glad you're there."

"Me, too, Ten. Me, too." Her voice was already so dear to me. I wanted to kiss her again.

MKNG LV darted into the passing lane, and I saw that the Escalade was taking the next exit, up toward the canyons.

"I have to go," I said. *My love,* I thought.

Between Westlake Village and Woodland Hills, a parallel series of twisting arteries link the 101 to the coastline, roads with intriguing names like Kanan Dume, and Trancas, and, of course, Topanga. I had traversed much of the city using one or the other of these byways, but I was unfamiliar with Latigo Canyon.

The road proved to be a steep, somewhat treacherous climb, slithering between rocky shoulders and canyon drop-offs like an asphalt snake. There were no streetlights, and the looming darkness added to my sense of peril.

I called upon Palden Lhamo once again for extra protection.

About seven miles up, the Escalade turned left at a "For Sale" sign that was stuck in the ground by a green metal mailbox and was at the foot of a gravel driveway much like my own. I flashed my lights, and the Escalade stopped.

Chain-Link lowered his window, silent and smooth.

"I can take it from here," I said. Chain stared at me as if I'd suggested he put on a tutu and twirl onstage. "I mean it. You did your part. This is a family matter now. Thank you."

He chewed on this, but only for a moment. "S'cool," he said, and flashed a final metallic smile. The smoked glass rose between us, snuffing out the gleaming grille of gold.

I waited until the rear lights of the Escalade had disappeared into the canyon. Sasha now sat next to me, with Mila and Zarko in the back. My tires crunched as we slowly rolled up the driveway. Maybe 20 yards in, a man waved us to a halt, a black silhouette in the headlights. His bent left arm strummed and fingerpicked the air.

"Stojan," I heard Mila murmur behind me, but I already knew it was him. Stojan stuck his head inside my window. I smelled stale garlic, and something faintly fruity, like incense, which was odd. His eyes darted and jumped, until they landed on Zarko. They exchanged maybe three Serbian words before he waved us on up the driveway.

We continued in strained silence.

"Okay," I finally said. "As far as I can tell, we've disabled most of the soldiers in this little army. So unless I'm missing something, I expect this won't take long."

Zarko snorted. "You miss!" he said. "Miss everything."

"Shut up!" Mila was a coiled spring of tension.

I thought about Zarko's words. They changed nothing. Either way, I'd given Bill my word that I'd protect Sasha and Mila. I'd see this thing through to the end.

"Mila, you have to promise me. Promise me this isn't a mission of revenge."

"I already tell you. Not revenge," she said. "The truth."

"Okay. The moment you have it, I'm calling the police."

I'd locked my Wilson in the glove compartment, and I kept it there. No way would I be allowed to walk anywhere with a hand cannon. But I made sure to retrieve the Airlite from Sasha.

The driveway ended at a huge, boxy, modernistic house, still under construction. Scaffolding and ladders crisscrossed the outside walls, metal bracings supporting a hollow frame.

I was wrong. There was at least one more soldier, if you could call him that—he was from a different tribe entirely. White and lanky, his skin was pale and smooth, like a baby's. He wore a kind of tunic, and his neck was so thin you could see the ridged cartilage and the small knob bobbing up and down in his throat.

He opened the back door of the Tahoe. He leaned inside and took Zarko's arm, pulling him through the opening with one long tug. Zarko bit back a yelp, and fresh blood bloomed on the bandage wrapping his thigh.

For the most part, the man in the tunic seemed almost deferential, treating the rest of us more like guests than a carload of trouble. He didn't even frisk me, and I regretted leaving the Wilson behind, though the feel of the Airlite in my jeans pocket gave some comfort. The air smelled of smoke.

He ushered the four of us inside, to an unfinished space of exposed beams and sawdust. Two floor lamps were plugged into exposed sockets.

The finished fireplace against the wall was full of ashes and soot, and empty filing boxes lay scattered on their sides nearby. Two laptops were askew, their screens smashed into spidery shards.

"Wait here."

He left us to stare at a small television set in the corner, and a soccer game underway, with the sound off. Moments later, Stojan walked inside. He opened two folding metal chairs and set them in the middle of the room, facing right.

"Sit," he said to Zarko. He lowered into the other chair, left-hand fingers twitching and plucking.

Zarko and Stojan exchanged a long look before turning to look straight ahead. They looked like a couple of kids awaiting punishment.

The blue flickering light of the television was distracting. I wished I could turn it off.

Mila had had enough.

"Stojan! You tell me," Mila said. "Now."

He answered in Bosnian.

"No," Sasha said. "Speak English, Uncle Stojan."

Stojan started, as if realizing who the boy was for the first time. He seemed a little zoned out to me, high maybe, although I hadn't smelled anything worse than mild garlic on him when he leaned into the car. "Okay. I speak English. Tell you what, Mila?"

"Zarko is injured. He needs a hospital. Stop playing, Stojan."

"I ask you again. Tell you what? Why you come here?"

"Because it had to be you," Mila said, almost in tears. "And I want to know why."

Stojan's fingers curled and plucked.

"You do not understand," he said.

"But Zarko says that he did not kill my father."

"And so?"

Mila's eyes filled. "Why, Stojan? He was a good man. Why did you have to kill him?"

Stojan turned his head away. Plucking, plucking.

Mila said, "Please, look me in the eye!"

"You look in wrong place," a female voice said from the shadows, and Irena stepped into the room. "Always."

"Mother?" Mila turned toward her mother. "Here? But . . ."

Irena's eyes were black obsidians. She wore another caftan-like tunic, this one ice blue, down to the floor, with the same combination of one short and one long sleeve. Her headscarf was gauzy and gray and framed her face like fog.

"I am the one. I kill your father."

Mila howled, lunging toward Irena before buckling, just at her feet. She clutched at Irena's hem. "Why? Why?"

A movement from Stojan. I wheeled, my hand on my Airlite, but he'd only pulled a necklace from beneath his shirt. He was rocking back and forth, his lips moving. I stared at the strand of carved prayer beads.

What is going on?

"Your father could have lived. But he refuse to understand. The world is broken, Mila. I try to tell you. Only evil can save us now."

Mila shrank from her mother's gaze. Irena's eyes had lost their center—they were like spinning platters of dead light. It occurred to me she had actually slipped off the bindings of sanity.

"Your father think he can stop us. But nothing stop us. You will see."

She reached into a fold of robe. As if in slow motion, I saw the hand come out, the cold blue steel of a gun barrel at the other end of it.

"Mila, move!"

Everything happened at once. Me tackling Sasha, pinning him under my body. Mila scrambling away on her hands and knees. Irena blasting a hole in Stojan's chest, then two more in Zarko, one in the throat, one in the heart.

She pointed the barrel of death at me.

Palden Lhamo, protect me.

Irena smiled, a strange, demonic mixture of ecstasy and hate.

"On kaže da ti kažem da on dolazi," she said.

She pressed the muzzle under her chin, pulled the trigger, and sent herself to another space and time, or maybe to nowhere at all.

Three bodies: a mother, and her two sons. Three reprehensible acts of violence.

And still, more questions. Why had she spared Mila and Sasha? Why had she spared me?

A thought crashed me into action. "The other guy! Where is he?"

I ran outside. He lay by the front door, his throat gashed, the knife still in his hand.

I called 911.

My mind spun crazily, tipping first in one direction, then another. Sasha walked outside and stood next to me. I placed my palm against his back.

The action steadied us both.

Sasha spoke, his voice cracking. "I can't . . . I just didn't expect . . ."

"I know," I said. "No one could have."

Mila's soft sobs drifted to where we stood outside.

"But what do I do with this?" Sasha said.

I thought about his question. The answer came easily.

"You've already done it, Sasha, by being who you are. You've already stopped the cycle. Now let the rest go."

He nodded. Once again, distant sirens approached. This time, I would stay put and try to help explain this madness as best I could.

"Ten?"

"Yes."

"Do you want to know what she said to you? It doesn't really make sense."

I thought about it. I could let the rest go, too. But Irena's message, however meaningless, had been meant for me.

"Yes," I said. "What did she say?"

"On kaže da ti kažem—da on dolazi."

"And what does it mean?"

"He says to tell you—he's coming."

CHAPTER 32

"Where are we going?" Julie was jumping up and down in her seat like a little kid, like Maude on her way to the pony rides in Griffith Park.

"You'll see." I reached over and patted her knee. The throaty growl of the Shelby provided the perfect background *thrum* to my singing heart.

I'd decided to take the back route, which meant we exited onto Stadium Way.

"Is it Dodger Stadium? Are we meeting Bill and Sasha at the game?"

"Good guess, but no."

Back in June, before everything went upside down and inside out, Bill's biggest problem had been the absolutely abysmal start of his beloved Dodgers' baseball season. Expectations had been through the roof, but as he kept moaning to me, they'd skidded right to the cellar in April, and stayed there ever since.

But now it was late September, and the team had gone on a crazy winning streak that defied all logic and went against all odds.

Proving to me, at least, that baseball, like life, required the same letting go of expectations to really allow enjoyment.

Bill had quickly roped Sasha in. As long as game days didn't interfere with Sasha's training program—he'd been accepted, with a little departmental strong-arming by Bill, as a police cadet, the first step to becoming a rookie in the force—they were either glued to the television or, on mini-plan days, yelling and whooping in Bill's upper reserve seats.

Martha and I had agreed this was a good thing, as it took the pressure off those of us who maybe didn't share Bill's fanaticism.

Mila, meanwhile, had returned to Sarajevo, along with the ashes of her family. She'd buried them next to her stepfather, and planned on returning to medical school, to finally become a doctor. Her hope was to join Doctors Without Borders as soon as she could.

I turned off Stadium Way onto Academy Road, and we drove by a children's park in a grassy area to our left. The climbing structure was full of toddlers and kids sliding, climbing, and running around. I had a moment of happy fantasy, imagining that the little boys we had rescued from that squalid Venice dormitory might someday play with the same freedom and joy. Gus had traced them back to the ring of Bosnian traffickers Sasha had first followed, and Sasha had confirmed that two of the boys were the ones on the plane. Stephanie assured me they would at the very least receive shelter and care, and whenever possible and appropriate, be returned to their families.

Not everyone had been rescued: the workers from the bus had vanished into thin air, and countless other victims of trafficking were still out there. But Agvan Supply was shut down, along with the Oceanview Vista Motel, and the ripples were still spreading as the FBI pulled what it could from the smashed computers.

Gus had called me again two weeks later with another piece of news.

"We may have found your Yolanda Wiggins."

"Tell me."

"Remember that Crip raid I never mentioned?"

"I do."

"Well, after eighteen months of multiagency investigating, we completed the operation, with flying colors I might add. Forty-five gang members from six different gangs, Los Angeles all the way to Riverside: we got them on racketeering, prostitution charges, trafficking across state lines, kidnapping, you name it, we caught them doing it."

"That is incredible news. Congratulations."

"Well, it's only one raid, but it was a doozy. Sends a pretty strong message."

"What about Yolanda?"

"She was with a pimp called Bone, right?"

"Right."

"Well, the bad news is, she's under arrest. She was part of his recruiting team, you know, they had her bringing in other girls. But I'm pretty sure a good lawyer can get most of the charges thrown out. You did not hear this from me either, Tenzing, but it shouldn't be too hard to prove she was acting under duress."

So I'd finally been able to make a full report to Tory, who wept like a baby at the news. He'd been visiting Yolanda at the women's correctional facility almost every day. He'd also insisted on doubling my fee. I'd donated the money to various organizations in Los Angeles that addressed the trafficking epidemic, from safe houses and free counseling to groups that were bringing yoga and meditation into juvenile halls. All I could hope was that their good works, like scattered seeds of goodness, would grow and flourish, balancing out the bad.

"You've gone very quiet," Julie said.

I reached for her hand. "Thinking about stuff," I said.

We passed a woman and her dog jogging along the road. The dog leapt and barked joyfully. So far, the Tank and Homer experiment was going splendidly. My theory was that Tank actually thought Homer was *his* pet. He certainly acted as if Homer belonged to him, and if it was a ruse, Homer went right along with it. They also required the same enormous amount of sleep, which helped.

Academy Way had become Academy Drive. I parked in the visitor's lot. We climbed out of the Shelby, and I took Julie's hand.

"You ready?"

Had I even been back here since the graduation ceremonies? I couldn't remember. I did remember that I was
sworn in by a newly elected mayor and his newly appointed
police chief, a controversial appointment in reaction to the
Rampart scandal that had rocked the force and the city. It
was an August day, scalding hot, and we were all dripping
with sweat in our uniforms.

Hand in hand, Julie and I strolled to the entrance, a gray
stone turret on the left, a stone and tile information booth
on the right.

"Los Angeles Police Academy," Julie said, reading the
sign, her voice amused.

"It's not what you think," I said.

The security guard waved us through. He gave me a
wink and a thumbs-up—I'd called ahead.

The year of my graduation ceremony, 42 of us had successfully completed our 900-plus hours of training: 36 males
and 6 females. For some reason, I could even recall the cultural mix: 22 Caucasians, 16 Hispanics, 3 African Americans,
and 1 half-Tibetan ex-monk. For reasons of its own, the
Police Commission had decided for the first time that year
to replace the traditional public prayer with a moment of
silence. That suited one of us just fine. I took the opportunity to express gratitude to all who had gotten me to this
point: my teachers, my fellow cadets, Lama Yeshe and Lama
Lobsang, even Arthur Conan Doyle.

I gave Julie the quick tour: "Pool." "Gymnasium."
"Shooting range, up there to our left."

Julie nodded, pretending all this made sense.

"Oh, and there's a café that makes unbelievably good
pea soup."

"Good, I'm starving."

"Nope, not here for the soup," I said.

That night in July, the night of so much violence and
confusion, I'd crawled into bed an exhausted, un-centered
wreck. Julie had woken up, listened until I could talk no
more, and then held me in her arms. I finally slept, but my

mind must have kept on working, sorting and moving the pieces, because the next morning I had solved another puzzle question.

"It's Indra's Net!" I'd shaken Julie awake. "The site is Indra's Net. Not an acronym. A bunch of consonants, in search of vowels. *N D R S*. Indra's. *N T*. Net. Like the vanity plate! Like making love!"

Julie, to her credit, hung in there with me, and after I'd explained and explained, finally agreed that my interpretation made sense.

"But what *is* Indra's Net?" she'd asked.

"It's like a web, a vast web of interconnection. Indra is an ancient Vedic god, and it was believed a giant net hung over his palace on Mount Meru, the center of the Vedic universe. Every gap in the net held a jewel, supposedly, and every jewel held within it a reflection of every other jewel. Infinite reflections, infinite connections. It's a Hindu concept originally, but Buddhists adopted it as well, only they called it *dependent origination*."

"Everything connected to everything else," Julie had mused.

"Exactly. So if you touch one jewel in the net, it affects all the others." For a moment, I'd felt a rush of respect at the ingenious choice of name. Then another realization hit. "So maybe DNA-coins stand for dana. The practice of generosity! For Buddhists, the giving of and receiving of dana is part of our eightfold path."

Julie had kissed me then, a deep, long kiss that filled my body with light.

"What was that for?"

"For being you," she'd said. "For the way your mind works."

Much later, I'd called Mike with my theory, and he'd been momentarily excited before he reminded me that Indra's Net had vanished from the dark web.

"Maybe when we destroyed Agvan Supply, we took down the whole thing," I'd said.

"I highly doubt it," Mike had answered. "Web directories like Silk Road and Indra's Net? You can call them jeweled cosmological networks all you want, but really they're more like intestines, huge coils capable of moving all sorts of shit around. And Agvan Supply? That's just a polyp, you know? If it starts to go bad, develops cancerous cells, say, the dudes behind the directories just cut it out. Excise the problem. The rest of the organism keeps on keeping on. Even the Internet lives by Darwinian laws."

Despite Mike's pessimistic outlook, I'd been pleased at my aha experience. As for Irena's dire last words, I could only hope it was her madness talking. Whoever the "he" was, the one she thought was coming, he hadn't bothered showing up.

Julie and I passed a final building on our right, an attractive Spanish structure housing offices and display cases of ceremonies and heroes from the past. My heart was beginning to race. I covered her eyes, and guided her the final ten feet.

"Okay. You can look."

It was every bit as unexpected—both stunning and incongruous—as my memory-based expectations. And maybe even better.

"Oh," Julie said. "Oh my."

Water cascaded down the layered rock configurations—fountains and falls created by carefully placed confections of stone. Back in the 1930s, the parks department had commissioned a famous landscape artist to design and build a rock garden that would do their city proud, and he had responded by creating a hidden treasure. There were cascades and pools and recessed stone seats. Pine trees and an amphitheater. Steps and stairs leading up to more fountains and scalloped falls, and carved stone benches amid the splashing water.

"This is amazing," Julie said.

"Come on, it gets better." I pulled her by the hand up the stone steps to a second level of garden, a more intimate setting, where the rock overhangs created a kind of private grotto with a deep pool water nymphs might visit at night to dive and splash in secret. I led her past these, too, up yet another, steeper set of stone steps, and onto a footpath that doubled back on itself, climbing steeply.

"There."

Behind and below us, the waterfalls splashed and played. To our right, the green carpet of Elysian Park, and the stadium, where so many gathered to cheer and hope. Beyond us, the Los Angeles skyline shimmered in the afternoon sun, the city that had taken me in, and that I had vowed to keep safe. While I no longer wore the badge, I was every bit as committed to protecting this city's peace and serving its higher good.

A city of angels, and demons, too. My time here had not always been easy, but it had exceeded all expectations, especially when I remembered to let go.

Now I needed to do so one more time.

Whatever she says, everything is as it should be.

I surrendered the outcome. I breathed in the silence, and I felt Julie, beside me, somehow doing the same. Spacious listening. Spacious loving.

So this is what it feels like, when two people are as one.

Waves of love met, danced together, amplified each other. I had never felt this close to another human being.

"Julie?"

"Yes."

"Will you marry me?"

She kissed the underside of my wrist, the sweet spot just below the palm. It turns out I have more than one sweet spot. Many, in fact.

"Yes," Julie said.

ACKNOWLEDGMENTS

GRATITUDE FROM
GAY HENDRICKS

With each book we write, my appreciation for Tinker Lindsay, which started out as lavish, grows even more so. Tinker, you're brilliant, wise, funny, big of heart, and impeccably responsible; Katie and I treasure your loving presence in our family.

A deep bow of gratitude to Reid Tracy, Patty Gift, and the Hay House team—your support has been invaluable. I'm so grateful to have a publisher who has no upper limit on their vision.

My mate of the past 35 years, Kathlyn "Katie" Hendricks, hears every word of every Ten book first. The gift of her generous listening and thoughtful feedback is a highlight of the creative process for me.

Many thanks to two masters of the crime-writing field, Robert Ferrigno and Diane Mott Davidson, for their enthusiastic support for our Ten books. It felt deeply satisfying to be welcomed into a community I've admired since I picked up my first Hardy Boys mystery in the second grade.

Thanks also to Jack Kornfield, teacher of Buddhist meditation for 40 years. It meant a great deal to us to have a Buddhist teacher we admire so much read our book and say he loved it.

I send love and gratitude across eternity to the memory of my writer mother, Norma Hendricks. She turned out a newspaper column every day throughout my growing-up years. The clack of her old Underwood typewriter was part of the soundtrack of my childhood. I learned so much from her about the value of meeting deadlines and other important aspects of being a professional writer, but the one absolutely indispensable thing she taught me was to take time and pleasure looking for just the right word. I'd see Mom sitting at her typewriter, always accompanied by a cup of coffee and a Camel cigarette, staring out the window for minutes at a time. When I'd ask her what she was doing, she'd say, "Waiting for the right word to come." Although I didn't really understand the full meaning of it at the time, now I surely do. Now that I've spent many hours of my own writing life waiting for the right word to come (thankfully minus the cigarettes!), I know what Mom was talking about. It's really the sacred space of writing, the honoring of the craft enough to wait for the magic to happen. To honor the craft and meet your deadlines at the same time; it's a gift from Mom I use every day of my life.

I would also like to honor the memory of my first writing teacher, Dr. Stephen Sanderlin, who taught English composition at Rollins College back in the '60s. He was the most mild-mannered of men, but he taught composition like he was the only one standing between Western Civilization and the barbarians. He was passionate about how to write a topic sentence and construct a cogent paragraph, tireless in his willingness to give you feedback until you got it right. It paid off; I wrote and rewrote the first paragraph of *Conscious Loving* more than a hundred times, even before I sent it out for anybody else to look at, but I was rewarded for all that benign obsession in ways I could never have imagined at the time. Thank you, Dr. Sanderlin.

I've been blessed to have Sandy Dijkstra as an agent in these new fictional endeavors of mine. Her experience in the area has been most useful in the new field. May our collaboration, spanning back 25 years now, continue long and fruitfully!

GRATITUDE FROM
TINKER LINDSAY

First, last, and always, I am grateful for Gay Hendricks, my co-author in crime. The longer we work together, the more I appreciate him. His wicked humor, easy flexibility, and immense creativity inspire me, and his generosity of spirit makes our collaboration pure pleasure, not to mention a boatload of fun. And speaking of fun, his wife and partner, Katie, only makes the dance more delightful.

Big thanks to my intrepid writer's group: Monique de Varennes, Kathryn Hagen, Emilie Small, Barbara Sweeney, and Pat Stiles. Accomplished writers all, they once again read and critiqued our latest work promptly, and responded with the perfect balance of enthusiasm and careful criticism, making sure every plot point, tonal shift, and character arc fully satisfied. Friends, knowing you are there gives me the confidence to stretch my writing wings.

I am so grateful for our Hay House family—Reid Tracy, Patty Gift, Sally Mason, Laura Gray, Charles McStravick, and so many others—for taking such care with our books. We couldn't be in better hands. And thanks to all at Sandra Dijkstra Agency for helping shepherd our books out into the world.

I could not write with confidence without the help of those who are willing to share their expertise with me. Thanks to Susan Kinsley, and to Laurinda Keys, each of whom imparted invaluable "boots on the ground" reporting from their time in Bosnia-Herzegovina. A big "e-wallet" of thanks to Rick Amore for his insight and patience as he spent hours explaining the mysterious worlds of Tor and bitcoins to this Internet Luddite, and to Cesia at Spytech Support for introducing me to the latest spyware nano-technology. Special thanks to Nan Narboe for sending me a small stone talisman from Bosnia precisely when I needed it.

I am not so much standing on the shoulders of certain authors as riding piggyback into the unknown, carried by their works of immense courage. I relied heavily on the following writers, who bravely reported from the trenches of both the Bosnian conflict of the past—Peter Maass, Roy Gutman, and Noel Malcolm—and the heartbreaking present tragedy of human trafficking—Carissa Phelps, Kathryn Bolkovac with Cari Lynn, and Rachel Lloyd. I learned so much from your hard-earned wisdom. Thank you.

And finally, a big shout-out to my husband, Cameron Keys, who tells me every morning to "write like the wind," and then, guess what? I do. You never waver in your support—not just of my writing but every other aspect of my life. Your humor buoys me, and your love steadies me, whatever rapids I may face. Lucky me.

ABOUT THE AUTHORS

ABOUT
GAY HENDRICKS

Gay Hendricks, Ph.D., has served for more than 35 years as one of the major contributors to the fields of relationship transformation and body-mind therapies. He is the author of 36 books, including *The Corporate Mystic, Conscious Living,* and *The Big Leap,* and with his wife, Dr. Kathlyn Hendricks, has written many bestsellers, including *Conscious Loving* and *Five Wishes.* Dr. Hendricks received his Ph.D. in counseling psychology from Stanford in 1974. After a 21-year career as a professor of counseling psychology at the University of Colorado, he and Kathlyn founded The Hendricks Institute, based in Ojai, California, which offers seminars worldwide.

In recent years Dr. Hendricks has also been active in creating new forms of conscious entertainment. In 2003, along with movie producer Stephen Simon, Dr. Hendricks founded the Spiritual Cinema Circle, which distributes inspirational movies to subscribers in 70-plus countries around the world (www.spiritualcinemacircle.com). He has appeared on more than 500 radio and television shows, including *The Oprah Winfrey Show* and *48 Hours,* and on networks including CNN and CNBC.

Cameron Keys

ABOUT
TINKER LINDSAY

Tinker Lindsay is an accomplished screenwriter, author, and conceptual editor. A member of the Writers Guild of America (WGA), the Independent Writers of Southern California (IWOSC), and Women in Film (WIF), she has worked in the Hollywood entertainment industry for over three decades. Lindsay has written screenplays for major studios such as Disney and Warner Bros., collaborating with award-winning film director Peter Chelsom. Lindsay and Chelsom wrote *Hector and the Search for Happiness,* which stars Simon Pegg, Rosamund Pike, and Christopher Plummer (among others) and was released by Relativity Media in September 2014. Lindsay and Chelsom recently completed a screenplay about Charles Dickens and a spin-off of the Hector franchise, for Egoli Tossell Film. She also co-wrote the spiritual epic *Buddha: The Inner Warrior* with acclaimed Indian director Pan Nalin, which is in preproduction, as well as the sci-fi remake of *The Crawling Eye,* and *Hoar Frost,* with Cameron Keys, the latter currently in preproduction.

In addition to the Tenzing Norbu detective series, Lindsay has written two books—*The Last Great Place* and a memoir, *The Sound of One Heart Breaking*—and worked with several noted transformational authors, including Peter Russell, Arjuna Ardagh, Dr. John C. Robinson, and Dara Marks.

Lindsay graduated with high honors from Harvard University in English and American Literature and Language, and was an editor for *The Harvard Crimson.* She studied and taught meditation for several years before moving to Los Angeles to live and work. She can usually be found writing in her home office, situated directly under the Hollywood sign.

READING GROUP GUIDE

A NOTE FROM THE AUTHORS: We are delighted that you have chosen *The Fourth Rule of Ten* for your reading group. While we hope our book engaged both your heart and mind, most especially we hope that it entertained you! We love writing these books, and find that with each one, we, along with Tenzing, forge new paths of discovery, both inner and outer. As an ex-Buddhist monk living and working in Los Angeles, Ten is uniquely challenged to balance his commitment to Buddhist principles with his deep desire to live in the world and "right wrongs." While we may not be Tibetan Buddhist monks ourselves, we face similar challenges when it comes to living balanced, mindful, passionate, and creative lives. We are constantly discovering new insights as authors of this series of books, which is why we love to write them! We hope that you like the result, and find yourselves at times inspired to incorporate Ten's hard-earned wisdom into your own personal journeys. Think of these questions as signposts along the way. Have fun with them, and above all, enjoy!

Questions for Discussion

1. In the opening chapters of *The Fourth Rule of Ten*, Tenzing has formulated a new life-rule: let go of expectations, for expectations lead to suffering. What were Ten's expectations of his Fourth of July celebration with his friends Bill and Martha Bohannon, and how did they lead to suffering? Have you ever been a part of a special event or celebration that went drastically awry? What did you learn from the experience?

2. Ten is shocked and confused by an unexpected rev-
    elation concerning Bill and Martha's marriage. Have
    you ever had a relationship change drastically as a
    result of something you suddenly learned? How did
    the discovery affect your relationship? If you could
    go back and do anything differently, what would
    that be?

3. Ten's motives for going to Sarajevo are very mixed,
    and he finds himself struggling to make a final deci-
    sion. Ultimately, he draws on a technique from his
    past for help, turning inward to have a dialogue
    with his heart. Do you think he made the right
    decision, and for the right reasons? What tools do
    you draw upon when faced with a complicated
    choice?

4. In writing this book, we discovered that human
    trafficking is an international epidemic with a
    global reach, yet is also widespread in our own
    communities. As one of our readers from around
    the world, you, too, may be affected by this press-
    ing issue. What do you know about the presence of
    human trafficking in the area where you live?

5. Thousands of years ago, the Buddha taught that to
    be human means to struggle. Today, we still experi-
    ence that eternal push and pull between past regrets
    and future longings, seldom finding the ease that
    comes with staying in the present. For Tenzing,
    breathing, allowing, exercising, and meditating
    are some of the ways he brings himself back to the
    present moment. Do you experience difficulty stay-
    ing present in your life? What are some of your
    solutions?

6. Ten's troubled relationship with his mother figures

prominently in *The Fourth Rule.* As a child, he often functioned more as a caregiver to his parent. How did this past experience affect his current perceptions and relationships with the women in this story, including Martha, Mila, Julie, and Stephanie? As a child, did you ever experience this child-as-caregiver phenomenon with an adult in your life?

7. Ten learns a few life lessons of his own from Kim, his new assistant. What are they? Do you relate to her odd but astute perceptions? Do you have any "teachers" like Kim in your world?

8. Did you relate more to Bill, Martha, or Mila in the awkward and unexpected triangle this book explores? Why?

9. Irena's behavior throughout *The Fourth Rule of Ten* is puzzling and inconsistent, and only at the very end do we find a clue as to her motivations. Tenzing brushes aside her final mysterious warning, but what do you think she is trying to tell him? (Note: there may be hints and warnings from Tenzing's past at play here!) Do you find the ambiguity intriguing or frustrating?

10. At the end of the book, Tenzing poses a scary (for him) question to Julie. What do you think was the key learning moment in *The Fourth Rule of Ten* that allowed him to make this leap? Have you had any similar moments of clarity that enabled you to change a behavior, or do something life-changing?

We hope you enjoyed this Hay House Visions book. If you'd like to receive our online catalog featuring additional information on Hay House books and products, or if you'd like to find out more about the Hay Foundation, please contact:

VISIONS

Hay House, Inc., P.O. Box 5100, Carlsbad, CA 92018-5100
(760) 431-7695 or (800) 654-5126
(760) 431-6948 (fax) or (800) 650-5115 (fax)
www.hayhouse.com® • www.hayfoundation.org

***

Published and distributed in Australia by: Hay House Australia Pty. Ltd.,
18/36 Ralph St., Alexandria NSW 2015
Phone: 612-9669-4299 • *Fax:* 612-9669-4144 • www.hayhouse.com.au

Published and distributed in the United Kingdom by:
Hay House UK, Ltd., Astley House, 33 Notting Hill Gate, London W11 3JQ
Phone: 44-20-3675-2450 • *Fax:* 44-20-3675-2451 • www.hayhouse.co.uk

Published and distributed in the Republic of South Africa by:
Hay House SA (Pty), Ltd., P.O. Box 990, Witkoppen 2068
Phone/Fax: 27-11-467-8904 • www.hayhouse.co.za

Published in India by: Hay House Publishers India,
Muskaan Complex, Plot No. 3, B-2, Vasant Kunj, New Delhi 110 070
Phone: 91-11-4176-1620 • *Fax:* 91-11-4176-1630 • www.hayhouse.co.in

Distributed in Canada by: Raincoast Books,
2440 Viking Way, Richmond, B.C. V6V 1N2
Phone: 1-800-663-5714 • *Fax:* 1-800-565-3770 • www.raincoast.com

***

Take Your Soul on a Vacation

Visit www.HealYourLife.com® to regroup, recharge,
and reconnect with your own magnificence.
Featuring blogs, mind-body-spirit news, and
life-changing wisdom from Louise Hay and friends.

Visit www.HealYourLife.com today!

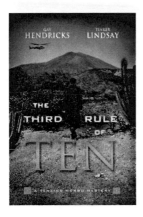

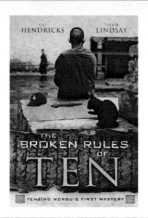

Look for the next installment
of the Dharma Detective series:

THE FIFTH RULE OF TEN

CPSIA information can be obtained at www.ICGtesting.com
Printed in the USA
BVOW07s1618091114

373705BV00002B/2/P